A MEANS OF GRACE

A MEANS OF GRACE

Edith Pargeter 1913-

Thorndike Press
Thorndike, Maine USA

This Large Print edition is published by Thorndike Press, USA.

Published in 1996 in the U.S. by arrangement with Deborah Owen Literary Agency.

U.S. Softcover ISBN 0–7862–0684–5 (General Series Edition)

The text of this Large Print edition is unabridged.
Other aspects of the book may vary from the original edition.

Set in 16 pt. New Times Roman.

Printed in Great Britain on acid-free paper.

Library of Congress Cataloging-in-Publication Data

Pargeter, Edith, 1913–
  A means of grace / Edith Pargeter.
    p. cm.
  ISBN 0–7862–0684–5 (lg. print : sc)
  1. Large type books. I. Title.
[PR6031.A49M43 1996]
823'.912—dc20

96–3375
CIP

PART ONE

THERE

Theme:

'"Be careful! There are human
beings over there!"'

The Good Soldier Schweik:
Hašek.

Above the city they came down through thick layers of cloud, lurching lamely. Cold air breathed gustily across the outside of the window beside her face, leaving a tenuous whiteness like rime, and heat in unsteady waves rose within her body, mounting towards her throat, as though their slow curving descent were bearing them down into the steamy emanations of a jungle. She recognised wearily the familiar qualms of airsickness, convulsions with no terror left but that of boredom; but this time she knew them from an indifferent distance, her anxiety too little involved with the physical to respond even to these stimuli. The whorls of cloud undulating past her eyes troubled her mind with suggestions of impermanence, made her feel for the first time that she might indeed be returning in search of something which no longer existed, revisiting something which would no longer even remind her of what it once had been.

The neat, upright little Polish business-man, across the gangway from her, completed the fastening of his safety-belt, and resettled his brief-case tenderly in the hollow of his side, as though, in the event of a crash, he could not contemplate allowing even death to part him from it. The warning notice was not yet lit, but he knew this airfield too well to need any nudging. The thickset dark woman in front, drawn back deeply into the privacy of her seat, held her breath hard at every lurch, and gulped air in difficult, moist gulps at every recovery. Her one visible hand, clutched tensely upon the arm of her seat, was a broad, blunt, housewife's hand, touchingly incongruous against the glossy grandeur of her mink coat. The thick, over-upholstered body displeased, but the hand had a pathetic and reconciling humanity, timorous, stoical, infinitely solitary. In the deep, enclosed seat of an airliner with only three passengers, hanging momentarily almost motionless over a still invisible port of arrival, you can be as alone as anywhere on earth.

Emmy pressed her knuckles against the freezing coldness of the glass, to shock her senses out of the contemplation of nausea, and looked for land below; but there was nothing but the weaving, flying whiteness, coiling past at a terrifying speed, continually rolling away, but never revealing anything except more layers of cloud beneath. It was then that she panicked for a moment. They had said she was crazy to go back, after what had happened, crazy to take such risks, crazy to expect to find the same country, the same city, the same people. A piece had been broken from the world for them; to attempt to go back there was a cosmic folly, like believing one could go back to birth and innocence. The land she had known was simply gone, eaten by the wolf, overrun by the enemy; its people were swallowed up. When Emmy had protested that she was still receiving letters from these ghosts, her friends had ridden over her protests without even hearing them. It was only an illusion of hers, of course, a superstitious fallacy, like table-turning.

'You're going back *there*?' they had cried incredulously, unable to conceive how one set about such an interplanetary adventure, even if one had the foolhardiness to wish to attempt it. She had seen behind their eyes the struggle to understand. 'Don't be a fool! You'll never get a visa.' And when she had received what they could not credit she would ever achieve, they looked at her with wonder and suspicion, and asked how she had contrived it. And all she had done was to ask for it. It was a formula they had never considered. How can you ask for a visa, for a country that has been devoured by the dragon?

Then they had said that she was wrong to go, though they had urged a dozen different reasons for the amorality of her action. Was it responsible to rush head-down into a chaotic situation in which every Westerner would be an enemy, and suspect? Her friends would worry about her, her country might be put to endless trouble and expense extricating her

5

from her follies, her talent might be lost to the world, or her willingness to go in there through the impassable barrier misinterpreted and misused, to her own damage and England's. She had listened with impatience, with amusement, with derision, and finally with anger. She was going where her friends were; it was as simple as that. Where they could breathe, she could breathe, too; and if they could no longer find air enough in their own country, all the more reason why she should go to them, and at least share their painful compressions. It seemed to her sufficiently easy to understand, but no one understood it. She began to wonder if none of them had any friends of their own, that they found it so incomprehensible that she should adhere to hers.

Even Malcolm, seeing her off at London Airport, had asked at the last moment, almost in spite of himself: 'Emmy, aren't you afraid?'

Her stare of incomprehension had perhaps seemed to him as stupid and impervious as their lack of understanding had seemed to her, as she had said: 'Afraid? Of what? I never have been afraid there, why should I begin now?'

He had protested quietly but warmly that she was insisting on closing her eyes to the change that had taken place over there. It was a Communist country now, and she still refused to realise it.

'It's the same country it always was,' she had

6

said, 'and contains the same people it always did.' But she knew that he thought she was merely denying, still with closed eyes, the possibility of change, while in reality she was saying literally what her words meant, that the same fields and streets and stones, the same individuals, were all the material change had to work upon, and that its power was limited by their ties and memories. That distant upheaval of heart had worked also upon her, impeding her tongue so that she could no longer communicate satisfactorily even with Malcolm. Only Lubov's restrained letters, suddenly thin and clear in texture like colours in a cold dawn, continued mysteriously eloquent, communicating distress and tenderness while they withheld information. It was the tone of those letters which had drawn her across Europe to experience for herself the quality of change. Hoping was not enough, believing was not enough, it was necessary to partake, to be one in the communion of events with her own people.

For of course they were her own people. Everyone you have ever loved without reserve or suspicion is your own flesh and blood.

Malcolm had said, with a sudden impulse of despairing jealousy: 'I believe if you knew it was hell, you'd still go!'

She had replied, with only half her attention upon him, and therefore with no instinct to deprecate foolhardiness or forswear heroism:

7

'Of course I would!' But he did not recognise an unguarded acknowledgement of truth, and thought only that she was a little overwrought.

The billowing floor of cloud thinned and darkened, and fragmentary glimpses of the earth came through. So it was still there! She saw the long dun streaks of fields, the ink-blots which were acres of conifers, the undulating green-brown patches of mixed woods, all turning slowly, slowly as the aircraft turned; then the sudden dazzle of crumpled red roofs, mottled corrugations of ridge-tiles, reeling towers, the revolving margins of the city. She saw the deep scar of the ravine splitting the border hills like lightning, the russet of its rocks wet and bright after the soft autumnal rains, between the darkness of its crowded trees. She saw the Citadel spinning gravely, grandly upon the axis of the cathedral spire, court beyond court spread whirling down the terraces of the hill, clinging to the earth with flattened hands of stone; and thrown down beneath it in the valley, the river like a cord of silver spilled intricate coil within coil, and put on bridges like bracelets. Before she had swallowed the first pang of gratitude and delight all the last, lowest, trailing gossamer of clouds had ascended above her, and the pattern of the city was clear, in a soft and silvery air without sun, its shifting centre steadily enlarging, its edges falling away in every direction until her horizon shrank into the familiar shape of the airport.

She had never seen it in autumn before, but apart from the decline of its colours into this subdued minor key it did not seem to have changed at all. The rigid ribbons of runway gleamed moistly, reflecting the white movement of wings above them, the splayed arm of buildings, pale and austere as the superstructure of a warship, thrust upward its remembered tower, dwindled to a flagstaff, flowered into a flag, the limp little bud upon that petrified stem. On the apron of terrace before the restaurant, leaning upon the white rails, a cluster of tiny people watched the strangers come in. Nothing had changed.

With her cheek against the fierce cold of the glass, she strained to keep her eyes upon those minute human creatures, until the wheeling curve of the aircraft's approach to the runway took them from her sight. She hardly noticed the touchdown, but in a moment was aware, acutely and mysteriously, of the earth bearing their weight. Through the fabric and the frame of the under-carriage, through the revolving wheels, she felt the contact with earth as dear to her as England. The running grass edges, the insecure white walls, tightened and grew still. The ground of the city stood as firm as she remembered it.

The stewardess moved languidly down the gangway, stretching, and smiling at her three passengers as they gathered their belongings together and rose from their three separate upholstered worlds to enter this enlarged phase of being. The girl was sleepy because she had not enough to do on these flights. So few people came now. How could three people receive the whole of her beneficent energy? It had grown heavy and stale in her, unused.

The passenger door was opened upon the blank blonde air peculiar to airfields. The Polish business-man stood back with a punctilious little smile and bow to let Emmy go first down the steps. His face, which was sensitive and preoccupied, wore all the time a faintly anxious friendliness, as though his own nature had imposed upon him a correctness he was afraid he might not always be able to sustain. When he had descended he turned to offer a hand to the woman in the mink coat, who felt her way down carefully to the tarmac upon stilt-like heels, clutching her enormous handbag in one nervous plebeian hand. She looked ill, but happy. Her eyes turned at once to the distant figures along the railing, where a hand and arm, young, male, wildly excited, waved insistently. She found him, and joy came out of the air like a shaft of sunlight upon her plain face. All the way to the enclosure and the swing doors of the reception hall she waved back to him, the wide fur sleeve spilled to her plump elbow. Emmy thought: her son. It was not even a guess, simply an act of interpretation.

10

The little figures followed them distantly along the rail. Emmy, craning to see above the heads of the foremost, looked for her own people. She did not know which of the Ivanescu would be there, but she knew there would be someone. Probably Wanda, she thought, searching eagerly. Or Miloslav, if he could evade one of his classes for once. Ilonna would certainly be cooking a fantasy of cakes and biscuits in the minute kitchen of the Lucerna flat, rosily fair over her hot stove, with a new ribbon in her ash-blonde hair, waiting for her children to bring home the strayed child with them. The city was still there, the people would still be in it, erect, intact, no way changed.

It was not Wanda, it was not Miloslav. Suddenly she saw, drawn back to the upper step of the terrace because he could not get to the rail, the figure of Lubov standing flourishing his hat at her, and struggling to draw her questing eyes with the urgency of his smile. Milo would have yelled, but Lubov was thirty, and the weight of his years and his doctorate kept him from yelling in public, he could only wave, and strain after her attention in exasperation and delight, until he drew her to him by the force of his desire to be recognised. Her face flamed into the mirrored joy for which he had waited. She raised her hand, in a classic gesture of salute rather than a wave, and still luminous, still looking back, she passed into the hall. Neither of them had uttered a sound; the distance was too great for speech, and they had their own strange, composed shyness. But for each of them the silence afterwards lingered aching in the throat, a constriction of pain.

All the family had been present, life-sized and unsubdued, in Lubov's smile; she had only to wait a little, there was no more wondering to be done. She surrendered her passport with the rest, gazing down the ramp through the open door into the Customs Hall. This reception-room seemed to her smaller than she remembered it; the big production posters masking the plain cream walls had caused it to contract, and one corner was draped with long red streamers and flags, alternately native and Russian. She thought it a pity that so small a wall-space should be expected to carry so heavy a burden of decoration.

'Miss Marryat?' called the clerk, looking up at her obliquely through the grid. He had her passport open before him; the photograph in it was five years old, and showed her with long hair, and the bored young frontier policeman at his elbow kept thoughtfully switching his blue glance from the image to the reality, and back, as though he found the change of style faintly suspect.

She rose from the bench with alacrity, already turning towards the ramp. 'Yes?'

'You can go down to the Customs Hall, please.'

He had seen that she knew her way there, and that pleased him, and he smiled. Her openness expressed an eagerness and pleasure which made the room seem momentarily lighter and larger.

He luggage was already set out upon the long bench in the Customs Hall, and a porter was idly trundling away, one-handed, the empty trolley. It was very quiet there, only a handful of people moving outward behind the opposite barrier, and here no one but the mink-coated matron, hobbling down the ramp on Emmy's heels. There were no flags here, and no signs of change; even the Customs officer who came strolling down from the office, leafing through her passport at leisure as he walked, was the very man who had seen her through on her way out, the previous summer. She thought that he remembered her, by the readiness of his smile, and the way he visibly abandoned the struggle for English phrases and addressed her in his own language. She did not speak it at all well, but almost all the vocabulary she had was concerned with this very business of arrival and departure and she was adept in the necessary sentences.

'Have you any currency, in addition to cheques? And perhaps a camera?' The camera was entered with the money on her currency certificate. He held the pad steady for her on top of her cases while she signed. It was almost

13

as if he knew that the invisible cord between her and Lubov was contracting unbearably and dragging her away, for he looked down briefly at the cases, pleaded once with a quick, prompting smile for her assurance that they contained only personal things, and motioned to the porter to take them to the bus. 'Yes, all right—that is all. I wish you a pleasant stay in our country.'

She would need money, but she could not bear to waste time on the bank now. She thrust back the swing door and went through into the entrance hall, and, stopping on the threshold, looked round for Lubov.

He was standing with his back to her, looking at the draped silks in a glass showcase, and watching from time to time, with a meditative smile of sympathy, the feverish antics of the very young man who was waiting for his mother to emerge. Lubov himself had all the patience and self-control in the world, of course, except when dealing with his own family. He was tall; all the Ivanescu ran to length, taking after Matyas rather than Ilonna. She had one moment in which to study him, and feel her heart melt at the very sight of him, at the un-English cut of his loose brown overcoat, with its wide shoulders and ample waist upon his slenderness, at the long, grave line of a hollow cheek, and the young and almost fragile look of the back of his neck, so severely barbered beneath the thick brown waves of his crown. All the tensions of her being relaxed in a warmth of joy. She released the door, and at the small, dull sound it made as it swung back into place he spun round, already alight with expectation, and sprang to meet her.

She remembered everything, not only with her mind but with her body, the long, decided stride that brought him across the width of the room in three paces, the way his left hand flashed up and snatched off his hat, and the lunge of his head to meet the hand, so that his rather long hair should not be too much disarranged. She wanted to laugh, and for a moment also she wanted to weep, for joy and relief. He took her hand. She remembered, this time with her flesh only, for her mind had closed its senses upon a small, perfect instant of delight, the family procedure which never varied, and lifted her mouth to his to receive the meeting kiss above their gravely clasped hands. It was in the midst of this changeless greeting that she felt, through the hard, fresh coolness of his lips, through the faint, newly-shaven scent of his cheek, her first awareness of change.

Lubov said: 'Emmy, darling!' and put both arms round her, and hugged her, laying that smooth, cold cheek against hers. She encircled him with the same grave candour, her arms about his neck, and then held him off once more to look into his face.

'It's wonderful to see you! Is everybody all right?'

'Yes, of course! Wanda couldn't come, they have some special meeting at the works; but she'll be home as early as she can. She was almost crying at having to trust me to meet you. And Milo had to be at the Faculty this afternoon. But everyone's very well and wild to see you again. Mother's baking. Aren't you hungry now? Wouldn't you like something before we leave?' He remembered that she was a bad traveller, with some dismay at not having asked already. 'Did you have a rather rough flight? I do hope not!'

'A little bumpy dropping through the cloud, but it was nothing. I was quite all right. But I'm not a bit hungry, thanks; we had a meal on the plane. Yes, really, I ate it. Let's get home! I can't wait to see everyone.'

'And your cases have gone out to the bus already? You've nothing at all to carry?' He took her arm. This more sober contact was a new earnest of the unchanged reality of all of them, and she received it with a calmer, more measured joy. They went out together to the airport bus, and two long streamers of dark red swung above their heads as they stepped through the doorway. Somewhere away to the right, from the direction of the restaurant, a loudspeaker was pouring out the music of a Russian song.

16

There were half a dozen passengers in the bus already, all of them gathered in seats near the front, and two or three of the airline staff going off duty sat nursing shabby, over-full brief-cases, their uniform caps pushed back from seamed foreheads. Emmy found herself selecting a place with a care which testified startlingly to her own state of mind. At first she had thought of going right to the back of the bus, to remove herself and Lubov as far as possible from the ears of their fellow-travellers; but within the few seconds it took her to pass by the seats already occupied she had discarded that unwise precaution, and sat down in the first vacant place. With equal decision she put away from her all the momentary ideas she had next entertained of limiting their conversation to what could be said in his language. There could be no one in this country who would not know her for English on sight. She sat with the others, she turned upon Lubov at once with a flood of clear English enquiries; and she knew upon the instant that the significance of everything she had thought, of every course she had considered and rejected in those few seconds, was as plain to Lubov as if the metamorphosis had taken place in his own spirit rather than hers.

Meeting his eyes, which were wide-set and

had the brackeny brightness of well-water in the sun, she recognised there the real significance of her own selective behaviour. 'Everything here looks much as usual,' she had admitted without a word said, 'but I can't feel sure that it is. I don't believe in the reign of terror people can see here from England; but I'm already walking delicately in case the crust of normality is thinner than it looks.' And this Lubov perfectly understood. His smile at once accepted her care for him and his, and deprecated it.

He drew her arm through his, and held it closely against his side. 'I can't tell you how fine this is! How long can you stay? Are you giving any concerts here? You didn't tell us your plans.'

'I'm booked for two recitals, and then in ten days I have to go to Vienna.' Her eyes added: 'I had to make the tour look convincing, I couldn't just run to you.' This, also, she was aware that he understood. 'I must go and see Ferdis tomorrow, and get to know my accompanist. Everything's been done in rather a hurry. I thought I could stay at some quiet hotel in the town. It would make things easier.'

Lubov's eyes opened wide in astonishment. 'You'll stay with us, of course! Do you think we'd let you get away from us? Do we see so much of you—once a year, perhaps, for a few weeks? A hotel, indeed! Wait till Mother hears that!'

18

'I only thought—' she said mildly, and let the sentence slip away into silence because it was unnecessary to finish it. He knew what she had thought, and what she was thinking still.

'We've been looking forward ever since your letter came. The flat's been cleaned and polished out of recognition, and the pantry's bursting. Don't talk about deserting us. We'll get you into town on time for rehearsals, don't worry.' His affectionate voice, the solid pressure of his arm, brought the lost half of her world closing warmly about her, as if she had never left it. This was the reality; London was on some other planet. Even the dizziness of the too rapid transition was already subsiding. 'What are you going to sing?' asked Lubov.

'Mozart, Beethoven, Dvorák—and some folk-songs.'

'Ours?' said Lubov, clairvoyant as before. She had never realised until now what a creature of crystal she was to him.

'Yes—if you'll lend them to me?'

He made no reply, but she felt through the pressure of his fingers, through the contact of his side, the pure, fierce heat of his gratitude and pleasure. She thought: this is love of country, and it was through them I discovered it: not a noisy patriotism, as closed and limited as a frontier between enemies, but this passion of receptive happiness whenever the stranger responds, as naturally as a flower to the sun, to the ungrudging warmth of your country's

19

music, and art, and virtue. And this is not limiting, but enlarging, for with all your doors and windows open to shed your native light over other men, you let in to yourself other men's light.

Two air hostesses in uniform climbed into the bus, and after them the driver mounted, and slammed the door. The bus heeled away slowly from the pillared porch and rolled down the concrete roadway.

Lubov said: 'As soon as you come back, Emmy, it's as if you'd never been away.'

'So it is to me,' she said.

And it was almost as if she need never go away again, at least on this first day, when she had discharged in advance all her debts to the people who leaned upon her in England. Only later, grown uneasy with her absence, would her brother, and Malcolm, and all the rest of them who peopled the English half of her life, come plucking at her sleeve and asking anxiously when they would see her again. For the moment they seemed so distant and so far removed in time that she could hardly recall their faces. They could be forgotten for a while, safe on their island.

'I wonder,' she thought, 'how I lived in England? What did I use to fill up the empty places Matyas and the family left in my days? But of course, there were no empty places,' she answered herself, enlightened; 'they never left me, they never do leave me. We are never really apart.'

On either side of the wide concrete road, blonde and featureless as yet, like the approaches to airports everywhere, the dun fields rolled away to the skyline, stippled with new ploughing and punctuated with the white buildings of farms. Then the first undulations of the city's hundreds of hills began, heaving out of the level land head after head of stiff black hair, the mysterious leafless woods of late autumn. The comfortable hollows began to be full of villas, pale, elegant, with flat roofs and ample windows. The lamp standards of the city already flowered austerely beside the road. Then there rose gradually upon the right the long, dark, tragic outline of the hill where the battle had been fought, the battle three centuries old and still an aching wound in the memories of the people of this land. Out of all the millions of fields contested in the history of the earth, a handful only keep this poignant, unhealing grief fresh in their very names, because from them civilisation lurched away, disoriented, on a changed, a disastrous course. More was lost at Mohacs field! This was not Mohacs field, but it had the same sense of doom about it. Even in sunshine a shadow fell here.

On the left, beyond a narrow belt of fields, the ground dropped away into the first narrow cleft of the ravine, and the russet-shining rocks gleamed for an instant through the black gauze of trees. Emmy thought: why am I always more alive here to the poignancy of history, to the sense that these opportunities did arise once, and were missed, and the world has spent centuries paying for the mistakes it made here?

New buildings closed in suddenly upon the road, blocks of flats, shops, small factories; and the final curve of the twenty-one tram route cast its looped lines about a concrete island. The first tentacle of the city touched them and drew them inward. From this point on she knew the way so well that the few new details caught and troubled her eyes like changes in a beloved face. The eruption of a newly-built house on the hillside, already occupied, but with walls still raw in rough unpointed brick because they would some day be plastered over; the long red banners streaming down the walls of a local party office, like dark venous blood; an enormous heroic statue of a Red Army soldier and an embracing peasant woman, in plaster, standing over some old, inoffensive building now emblazoned with posters; a piece of half-developed land cleared and levelled for grassing over: all these caused her contractions of the heart compounded equally of shock and jealousy, as if some human creature in whose stability she lived had begun to grow away from her.

Since she had known it the city had been expanding vigorously, had swallowed and assimilated changes, and digested all into a miracle of reconciliation. The new office blocks, the modern shops and flats, had settled down cheek to cheek with the pink-and-blue-washed cottages, and the green bleaching-grounds, and the little duck-ponds of the villages the city had devoured alive, and within a year they had produced between them a new and comprehensive harmony. Colour had mellowed into colour, marbled pallor into ripe, ridge-tile red, pastel colour-washes into the sparkle of neon signs, without anger or discomposure. The small baroque of monasteries, cream and honey and russet among their lime trees, smiled over the roofs of angular white cinemas. Every sharpness smoothed into the scene, weathered into serenity. The red of the frequent flags was the only red which had ever assaulted her eyes here as a separate, an indigestible thing; the opaque white of the plaster group, as impersonal as the faces they had shaped in it, was the one white she could not imagine even time warming into ivory.

'You see, we've been doing a lot of building,' said Lubov, nodding towards the colonies of new four-storey dwellings outspread up the hill-slope on their right. 'You'll find the tempo has accelerated a lot since last year,' he said seriously.

With the new sensitivity she had brought with her from England she felt this to be a warning, yet she could find nothing in his voice to indicate a double meaning. With all other subtleties she let this go until they should be home; there would be no evasions or reserves there, not between her family and her.

Already the city enfolded them, they were driving along a spear-straight highway into its heart, past the old stadium, past the summer palace, past the square where the vegetable market sprang up mushroom-like before dawn, three days a week. From their high plain they could look upward at the Citadel, its circling towers rooted in the rock, its cathedral spires soaring, celestial Gothic out of terrestrial Gothic, from the coronal of stone, as a cross grows out of a crown and binds all its golden ribs together into a unity. Or they could look down, between the tall buildings on the other side, towards glimpses of the coiled and gleaming river, beyond a wild profusion of ridge-tiled roofs, their earthy, corrugated red filmed over with grey in the silvery, moist air. Everywhere in between the colours of tile and stone the trees gushed upward like dark foam, a few still bearing their dead and rose-red leaves.

The steep, plunging roads which she remembered so well brought them down into the first busy shopping area of the town, and presently to the embankment and the bridge. The river was running peacefully high, quiet and rapid between its many hills, its waters

24

lambent with a pewter sheen. Beyond, the full remembered fever and roar of traffic received them, as they entered the great square in which the air terminal building stood. Trams, trailing second and third cars behind them, threaded the wide space from six different routes, in intricate dancing patterns, clattering and jolting over the points between long, low islands of stone, and a wild ballet of cars swirled round them along the edges of the pavements. There were other sounds, too, spectral between the clanging of the trams, skirls of music, strands of the same frayed Russian song, flung from at least three directions. The streamers were there, too, draped from upper windows at every corner, notes of violent excitement in the muted palette of the autumnal town.

'Give me your baggage check,' said Lubov, 'and I'll collect your cases. How many are there? Two?'

'Yes. The big one is just concert dresses, it isn't heavy. You haven't got a car here, have you? Let's take a tram!'

She could really feel that she was home again when she had boarded the right tram without having to wait for him to prompt her, and tendered the right coins for her anywhere-in-town fare, silently, casually, like a native. Better still if she could flourish a small, bedraggled note under the conductor's nose before Lubov could deposit her cases and get a hand into his pocket for his wallet, and best of all if she could utter the brief, necessary: 'Two, and two pieces of luggage!' in the right mild monotone, as though she did this every day, so that the conductor would clip her tickets and flick out her change without giving her a second glance. This she managed perfectly, and could not understand for a moment why Lubov, wallet in hand a few seconds too late, began to laugh even through his quick, reproachful frown.

'Now what did I do that was silly?' she asked, reaching upward to share a strap with him, and swaying against his shoulder, for the tram, like most of its kind from morning to night, was full.

He turned back the outer fold of his wallet to show his season ticket, with the photograph which was already ten years old, and as wide-eyed and wary as a child. 'You wasted twopence-ha'penny. Had you forgotten I've got this?'

Several heads turned to hear them break thus into English after her few accomplished words in the city's own intonation. Those who looked round smiled. Their eyes seemed to her as frank and direct as ever, their voices were certainly as loud and uninhibited. She tried to follow their rapid exchanges, and realised that for the most part they were talking football. There was evidently an important match to be played next day. Two girls, already wrapped in

26

the dark brown frieze which was almost as much a uniform here as the *loden* in Austria, were talking anxiously but happily about the expenses of the coming winter, and lamenting that they needed new ski-ing boots, which would cost the earth. Two elderly women were discussing their daughters' pregnancies and their grandchildren's prowess. Two middle-aged men were comparing notes on the beet crops of the two country regions with which they had the closest ties. There was nothing surprising in that. Every family of sophisticates in this most elect of capital cities had a foot still in the soil somewhere, and had lost no skill in the language.

They rattled their slow way through the streets already growing filmy with autumn dusk, between the lit shop-windows, over the river again by another bridge, and round the abrupt bend below the Lucerna hill. Steadied within the arc of Lubov's arm, she moved sideways between gently swaying bodies to the doorway, and picked up the smaller of her two cases. Lubov's hand slid down beside hers, and with apologetic gentleness took the burden from her. The touch of his fingers affected her with the same profound and still unease she had felt at the touch of his cheek. Through all the sameness of people and streets and speech, the tremors of change passed sourceless but palpable, and no one spoke of them. Out of fear? It did not feel like that to her. Rather, she

27

thought, out of bewilderment: they don't speak of it because they simply do not know what to say, how to define it, what it means, what will come of it.

The tram turned uphill by a quiet street, dark between high stone walls, and swayed to a standstill at a street island. They descended, and from the edge of the pavement watched the three cars rock radiantly away into sudden deep twilight.

'My season ticket was the only thing you forget,' said Lubov. 'You really knew the stop!'

'Do you expect me to forget where I live?'

They walked to the next lighted corner, and turned into the hallway of a large block of flats. The stony vestibule was cold and dark. She reached for the minute-switch, and the resultant flood of light found her smiling because this, too, she had remembered without even a conscious effort.

'Oh, you are too good!' said Lubov. 'Now, for that, you must work the lift, or I shall refuse to do it and make you walk up.'

The lift was an open metal cage, elderly and temperamental. It lurched upward with a heavy, dogged slowness, but she got it to continue its grudging progress to the fourth floor, and halted it there quivering. The Ivanescu flat was at the back of the block; its windows looked down over roofs and gardens and the tall heads of trees to the river, and the lights of the city centre beyond. To ears which knew the sounds of the house accurately, the double click of the lift halting at this landing was a sufficient report on arrivals. Emmy walked into Ilonna's arms in the doorway of Flat Seventeen, and was drawn into the warmth within.

'Emmy, darling! Come in! I've been cooking for you, all the things you like, come and see!' The family kiss, the soft, warm pressure of Ilonna's round, fair cheek against her cold one, the cushioned resilience of Ilonna's round, fair body, confirmed that she had come home. Plump and quick of movement, with a skin like plum-blossom and a coil of honey-coloured hair, and eyes of the pale but profound blue of summer skies under honeyed lashes, Lubov's mother was fifty years old, and still looked thirty-five. Matyas, her husband, who was two years older than she, sometimes appeared to be of another generation. He was tall, the pattern for his children, dark and sallow of colouring, his face as deeply engraved with the lines of experience and care and humour as hers was smooth and untouched. He came into the small vestibule of the flat now from the kitchen, his shirt-sleeves rolled up, his glasses pushed up on to his forehead, and Ilonna brought Emmy to him in her arm like an inspired gift.

'Matyas, here is our Emmy! She is really here! Kiss our girl, she is like Christmas, she comes only once a year.'

Emmy went into his arms, and was engulfed.

29

He was a house in himself. Her own father, who had acted as a father also to this man's chance-met daughter during the long years of war, had died soon after the war ended. 'If I had not gone to that particular girls' hostel when Father left London,' thought Emmy, 'I might never have met Wanda and, through her, Lubov. I might never have known any of the Ivanescu.' Matyas had sent his two elder children to England in 1939, when war had already become inevitable, and the fate of his own country only too predictable. Lubov had worn out two tedious years in the Pioneer Corps, along with large numbers of his countrymen, before the RAF had taken him and made a pilot of him; and the fifteen-year-old Wanda had worked in a factory by day and the Fire Service by night, until in her eighteenth year Emmy's father had got her into broadcasting, where she had done good work for both her own and her adoptive countries. From the time that Emmy had taken brother and sister home with her, they had never wanted a father in England; and while Matyas lived Emmy would never want for one here.

This was the real moment of arrival, when they brought her into the living-room, the heart of the household, when she felt the Ivanescu walls all round her and the door of the flat was closed upon the outer world. It always seemed to her that they shut in with them all that was vital and generous and responsive, that nothing of the beauty and honesty of the world could be excluded from the place they made their own, and nothing of its brittleness and anxiety could get in. She drew deep breaths of content, looking round the familiar room, at the white tiled triangular stove built from floor to ceiling in one corner, the elaborate four-bowled light over the table, the heavy net curtains, the two wide couches with their box bases and sprung cushions, one of which was Lubov's bed by night, the other Miloslav's. They stood round her, smiling gently and in silence, while her eyes reassured themselves of the sameness of all here. Lubov slipped the coat from her shoulders with a touch so light that she hardly felt it, and went and hung it carefully upon a hanger in the hall wardrobe. Matyas turned towards her the largest chair. Ilonna began to spread her best embroidered linen cloth over the table, moving with ardent quietness as though to avoid disturbing a sleeper.

'You look at everything,' said Lubov, without surprise, 'as though you'd never really expected to see it again.'

'That's how you're all looking at me,' she said, her eyes returning instantly to his face.

'Oh, we believed we should see you again. We were almost sure of it. Only there was always that last possibility—'

Ilonna, trotting back and forth with dishes and cutlery, brought in savoury smells from the kitchen in her movements.

'Sit! Rest! You are tired and hungry, you left home early and travelled a long way. I will make the supper very soon, and Wanda will come. Matyas, bring Emmy some beer! Lubov, there are cigarettes in the box there. The plane was late?'

'Not more than a quarter of an hour—it was a very good flight, considering the time of year.'

'And smooth? You were not ill? It is wonderful, to think you can get into a plane in London this morning, and now already be here! Even with the difference in time, it seems so very short a journey, to bring you so far from home.'

Matyas, pouring beer, asked: 'Did you have much trouble in getting a visa?'

'No. I filled in the forms, and the answer came through just as usual. It may have taken a week or two longer than last year, but not more than that. Did you think they might refuse me?'

'Didn't you?' He looked up at her with a smile under his thick, straight eyebrows, handing her the glass. 'There was no particular reason why they should, it's simply that we no longer know what considerations determine these cases. We no longer know what constitutes a *reason* for action. We see the effects of undoubted causes, but we no longer know how to deduce the causes from them.'

Emmy drank coolness, and felt suddenly

relaxed and tired in this stillness of achievement. She had set out in what she saw now to have been a state of extreme tension, simply to recover this room and these people, in whom the whole of their country was implicit for her. She had them again, and the time had come when she could ask all the questions she had kept to herself in the airport bus and the city tram. And in fact, now that she examined that torrent of penned-up, anxious enquiries at leisure, they had all cooled and hardened into one question, and she was already aware that there could be no exact answer to it. All the same, she asked it, looking up into Matyas' face.

'What really happened?'

She saw father and son exchange quick glances, and knew that they were debating how to answer her honestly, rather than how to avoid answering her. Their faces appeared amazingly alike at that moment, with a faintly satirical gleam in the eyes, and a heavy, perplexed gravity upon the brows. She thought the look went far to achieving a true reply to what she had asked, but after a few seconds of thoughtful silence they attempted more articulate answers.

'The bridge broke,' said Lubov, proffering the cigarettes.

'More accurately,' said Matyas, 'we were trying to be a colossus, and the strait grew too wide for us to keep our balance. So we had to

33

draw back one foot or the other, and, to be truthful, there was never any question of choice in the matter. We stood on the foot that had the solider ground under it, and drew back the one that felt more insecure.'

'Yes, I can see that well enough—that was the cause. But the *occasion*—What went on here at the time? I'm discounting much of the comment they made in England, but there did seem to be a good deal of agitation among the various parties—'

'Ah, I'm not in the confidence of any party. No doubt a certain amount of churning up of muddy ground did take place as one foot took the weight and the other one thrust off to rejoin it, but since the flood-water's already covered part of that abandoned ground, I don't see much chance of tracing the exact movements now, much less working out the sequence in which they took place. Nor does it seem to me very important which grains of sand budged first, or which clods gave way. As a matter of history it would have had its interest, but an academic one for us. It's a good deal more urgent to find out the true geography of the place where we're standing now, and see if it will serve, or if it could be bettered. What did your people say had happened?'

'You know! They said this whole transformation was a Communist coup. All the left wing were villains, and all the right wing victims. Except for the handful of

34

people—a very small handful—who said the Communists had acted quickly to avert what was meant to be a right-wing coup, in which case, of course, the left were the heroes, and the right the villains.'

'And you thought these two versions about equally probable?'

She smiled. 'You must remember that ninety-nine per cent of the voices in England were shouting the first version, and apart from a distant whisper now and then one couldn't hear the other. It didn't compel belief, but it commanded anxiety. It wasn't that I accepted either version without reservations—but I had to come, I had to be here.'

'Did you know,' said Lubov, 'that you began to write as if you expected your letters to be opened?'

'Did *you* know that I caught that tone from you? With nothing in the world to hide, we immediately began to hide it. We didn't really believe that any responsible power in your country or mine could misinterpret or mistrust us. Only, *as* you said, there was always that last possibility—' She smiled, because in spite of the gravity of his face she had justified her careful optimism in this first march of the campaign. He was there within touch of her; no one had felt the need to keep her out.

'We are talking now,' said Matyas, 'about the modern human predicament. It's bigger than a national affair.'

35

'Yes, but we have to live in countries. They may be as helpless as we are, but they also enjoy the means of destroying us. We may be big enough not to blame them for feeling, in certain circumstances, that they have to obliterate us, but there's no need to point out to them in advance how wise such a course might be.'

It was good to hear Lubov take up her tone with that quick, delighted spurt of laughter. She could afford to laugh, too, now, whatever the truth, however good or bad the situation in which they were all caught, simply because she was there with them. She began to understand the emancipation of comradeship.

'And what's happening now? How has it affected you—you in particular? Are you happy?' she asked, watching his face in an abrupt stillness of concentration.

A shadowed smile deepened in his cheek. 'Ah—happy!' he said thoughtfully. 'What is that—happiness?'

*　　*　　*

Wanda, in too great a hurry to wait for the ponderously descending lift, ran all the way up the stone stairs and erupted, panting, in the doorway of the flat, one hand still tugging at her latch-key. The blaze of her dark eyes, excited and intense, lit up the hall with a brittle radiance. She cried: 'Emmy!' in a high, child's scream of joy, and flew with outstretched arms, dangling handbag and scarf from her wrists, to embrace her friend.

'Emmy, darling, darling! I couldn't come to the airport, forgive me, but I really couldn't. It was so important I couldn't put it off. I'll tell you all about it, we've been doing such tremendous things ... Oh, my darling, how are you? How long can you stay? Will you come to an evening meeting at our works, and sing for us? They'd love it if you'd sing one of their own songs—I didn't tell them you could, I wanted it to come as a complete surprise. Oh, my dear!' she laughed and sobbed against Emmy's cheek, 'I'm doing so much talking you can't get in one word, and really I want so much to hear all about you. Can't you stop some of your countrymen from saying such stupid things about us? I've almost hated them! I should quite have hated them, if you hadn't been English, too!'

She held Emmy off from her, scrutinising her face passionately with those enormous, lambent eyes. She was tall, and very slender, straight as a poplar, her flesh so worn and wasted with the pressure of the spirit that even in stillness she seemed to give off an uneasy and quivering light. From this vehemence of her bearing and her being, the simple clothes she wore with so little regard acquired an electrifying elegance. The thin, ivory face, hollow-cheeked within the shadow of short, cloudy black hair, was very beautiful, but within Emmy's memory of her it had never been happy. She had been sent away from her country and her home at fifteen, to grow up abruptly in the forcing-house of war, and her own intense spirit had amputated her childhood once for all before the proper time for parting with it. All the same, she had grudged its loss, and carried somewhere in her an unfocused ache of resentment against the circumstances of her initiation, against the factory and the Fire Service switchboard which had filled up her student years, and left her unable to go back afterwards and pick up what she had missed. Hers was not a nature which could turn back, even to draw breath for a fresh spurt. Even the two years she had spent broadcasting to her own country had given her no outlet for her wild originality, nor any training which could launch her on a creative path when she returned home; and yet Wanda, efficient and self-contained in a factory office, had always been an offence against nature. She had never complained, but they had all felt it, Emmy most grievously of all from the time that she herself began seriously to sing. Those first years of her career, spent in such close and loving proximity with Wanda's silent, self-wasting frustration, had darkened every satisfaction with a reverse of pain.

'I'll sing wherever you ask me to,' said Emmy, 'in the stadium, in the street, anywhere you like, provided the Ministry of Culture doesn't mind. Wanda, you look much too tired and thin; what have you been doing to yourself?'

'Oh, that's nothing, it's only that we've been overdoing things a bit lately, perhaps—too much overtime, with taking over the factory, you see, after the muddle it was in. But that will soon change now, because we've been re-organising. That's what today's meeting was about. I wish it hadn't been today, but I'm secretary to the Interim Committee, and I simply had to be there. Did Lubov look after you properly?'

'As well as anyone could but you, darling. Take your coat off, and come and eat. If you've been hard at this meeting all afternoon you must be famished, and now I'm getting hungry myself.'

Wanda shrugged the coat from her shoulders and gathered it carelessly into one arm. Her long, emaciated fingers folded for an instant, with a touch curiously firm and cool in so highly-strung a creature, about Emmy's forearm, and the resolute contact and decisive release conveyed a new sense of inward calm in her. Overworking she might well be, but at least it was with purpose.

'I'll tell you all about it over supper. There are such changes beginning, and everything's moving so quickly, it's difficult to keep up. I dare say you've felt it yourself—if you haven't yet, you will before you've been here many days.'

She flew to hang up her coat, and came back with her black hair smoothed and glistening from the comb. Ilonna had brought in the soup and was placidly serving it.

'Sit here, Emmy, and Wanda will be here beside you. So sit now, and begin. You are hungry, we shall not wait for Miloslav.'

'Where is he?' asked Emmy.

'At the Faculty. There is a meeting of the Students' Committee, they have some cases to discuss. But he will tell you everything himself when he comes.' Ilonna's manner never conveyed either approval or disapproval of her family's vagaries, but only acquiesced in the adjustments they demanded in her own time-table. The circumstances of the day could not be so rearranged that Ilonna would not be a match for them. 'There, now tell us, Emmy, how is everyone in England, and what you will do here in this so short visit.'

Ilonna had never seen London, it was for her children she desired to launch the inevitable reminiscences. In a few minutes they were saying 'Do you remember?' all together, laughing and glowing with the pleasure of recalling days once merely endured and survived. The women's hostel in Ealing had acquired a patina of fond recollection. Lubov's rare week-end leaves, harassed by bombing and curtailed by the times of trains, shone now in remembrance with an improbable gaiety.

'Come back with me!' said Emmy, suddenly laying down her spoon and turning upon Wanda. 'You know you'd love to see England again. Come back with me when I leave, just for a few weeks. I have two concerts in Austria, and then we can go home.'

The impartiality with which they all three applied that term 'home' to both their countries was not a deliberate thing, and had never struck her as significant until now, but in this moment it went into her heart like a knife, a knife of such keenness that the sensation it produced in piercing was only one of intense and astonishing coldness, undisfigured as yet by any pain. She sat islanded in a moment of utter silence. They had all stopped eating, and were looking at her with wide, quiet, intent eyes, and their faces had stilled into delicate awareness of one another and of her, as if every one of them hesitated to make an untested movement or an unrehearsed sound, for fear of scarifying unprecedented sensitivities in the others.

'I can't,' said Wanda then, shaking back her hair with a rueful but decided gesture. 'I should like to, you know I should, but I can't come now. There's so much to be done here.'

'Only for a fortnight! Things couldn't get too far ahead of you in a fortnight, and surely they could spare you for that long.'

But the black head shook again, vehemently.

'No, really it isn't possible!'

'No,' said Matyas, watching them both across the table, with a faint, saturnine smile, 'it really isn't possible. She is telling you the truth, Emmy. If she asked for a passport now, it would be refused.'

Emmy looked from him to Lubov, who met her eyes with a look of neutral gravity, and said nothing. He was surprised, she thought, to see her so little surprised; he should have known that in a situation as unprecedented as this, surprise became an inadequacy and an irrelevance. But perhaps he was allowing, too generously, for the difficulties of adjustment between country and country; the thought displeased her, seeing she had deep roots here in this soil, too.

'People do still come,' she said reasonably. 'Apart, I mean, from the ones who come for good, and without passports. I know of several who have paid visits in the last few months.'

'In parties, I think. Trade Union delegations, student delegations, all manner of delegations—yes. But a friend to a friend, without official blessing or approved sponsors, or any public affiliation whatsoever—no, Emmy, this no longer happens.'

Wanda's long lashes rolled back fiercely from the wounded black eyes. 'Father, you are giving Emmy a false impression. You make it sound as if we have slammed the door and shut all our own people in, and all the rest of the

42

world out—'

'Half the rest of the world,' said Lubov; but he said it gently, almost lightly, and he smiled at his sister as he spoke.

'All right, I give you that. And what Father says is very nearly true, Emmy, only he takes it out of its context. Look, you know how your country has behaved to us over this crisis here, and you know, you have said that you know, about the ones who came running without passports, because they have found their privileges shrinking, because they failed to get their own way, out of spite, out of pique. At first they did not have to go without passports. Everything was as it had been before, they could ask for the papers they wanted and get them, and go, and then in England they could declare themselves refugees, and be received with open arms—you know it! You know the mischief they have made, and the stories they have told against us. Did you believe them, too?'

Emmy, picking her way among doubts and reservations which had perplexed her for months, said meticulously: 'Some, the most moderate of them, I could believe. But I was always inclined to be very sceptical of the more sensational ones, partly because I find it advisable to treat with reserve the evidence of people who may be trying to ingratiate themselves with one government by blackening another, but even more because I knew a great deal more than the average English person does about your people here, and what was credible of them, and what was not. But that there were some genuine grievances seemed to me inevitable, at a time like that. With the whole world making such large and messy omelettes, broken eggs are not very surprising anywhere.'

'In your situation, that was fair enough,' agreed Wanda with a brief and blazing smile. 'But some of these people, it was infamous what they did. There was a girl in our factory, I knew her well—I believed I did! She had been writing to a family in Scotland, the father was very enthusiastic about work for UNA, and that is how this correspondence began. After the change here, she had an invitation to go and visit these friends, and she asked for a passport and some money for the trip, and they gave her a student grant, and all she needed. She did not come back, and, more than that, she even dishonoured her Scottish friends, for when she landed she did not go to them, she went to some refugee organisation and asked for asylum. We know it, because the poor man was expecting her at the docks, and she gave him the slip, and he was worried about her, and wrote to us at the factory, to know if she had set out as arranged. He had promised to look after her, and put her on the boat again to come home at the end of the visit, and the first he saw of her was headlines and a press photograph, with a tall story about her escape from tyranny. The tyranny of a travel permit and a student grant! And this girl is not the only one of her kind, as we have found out by bitter experience.'

'Yes,' said Emmy, 'I can understand that a few cases like that began to make it seem rather tempting to shut the gate. It's happening to some extent in other countries, too. But I still think it's a terrible pity.'

'So do I. And a terrible mistake. But when I think of it, I consider it in its context, not as a wilful compression without any cause, which is what Father is making it out to be.'

'Well, you have restored the picture,' said Matyas, smiling at her, 'if I pushed it out of balance. Remember the context, too, when you think of the disapproved persons in America who are not allowed to have passports. Perhaps even in England a few!'

'Do they do us so much justice?' asked Wanda fiercely.

'No. But the business of the just in a world like this is to remain just, not to expect justice.' Matyas said these things with the half-teasing, half-grave, wholly affectionate smile which cast over every argument Emmy had ever heard in this room the same unshaken warmth of reassurance.

Ilonna, collecting soup-plates, her round arms smooth and glossy under the direct light, said comfortably: 'You have begun a very

45

indigestible conversation, and it is quite the wrong time for it. Emmy has ten days to hear us put the world straight, and there is no great hurry. Wanda, you did not tell us yet about your meeting. Wanda was chosen as secretary to the temporary management committee when the tool factory was taken over,' she explained with simple pride, for trust was trust to her, and achievement was achievement, and no narrow party considerations dimmed her pleasure in seeing her children singled out for promotion. 'She has worked very hard, and now today they had this final meeting to elect a permanent committee. It was sad that it should happen just the day when you were coming, but it could not be avoided.'

Wanda began to glow again, twin points of excited colour rising into her ivory cheeks.

'You heard, I expect, that all businesses employing large numbers of people were taken over by the State? The factory where I work had been very badly run, and we have had to fight like tigers to get everything straightened out there, but now it's going steadily. We have over four hundred people working for us. They all came to the meeting, and every department brought its own proposals, but the whole meeting voted.' She blinked suddenly, as if her own new and blazing brightness, reflected from her friend's face, had dazzled her for a moment; and she flushed and laughed at the sound of her own voice, growing happy over

46

the reorganisation of a business she had disliked, and disliked yet. 'It's funny, isn't it, to grow excited about machine tools! Funny, at any rate, for me! But I like things to be done *well*!'

'And now they are being?' said Emmy.

'Oh, not in every case—it wouldn't be human. We do make mistakes, we do cause muddles, we do waste time and energy. But there, at our works, now—yes, truly, Emmy, we have made it run, and run well. And to see the names they sent up to us, and the way the voting went! To see people put into management who never would have had this chance the old way, never, never! I tell you, Emmy, I believe in people! They do know worth, they do choose it, when they are free to choose it.' She stretched a hand suddenly across the table to her father, laying her fingers confidingly upon his wrist. 'Do you know who will be the new assistant manager? Petr Kasel! Yes, Petr!'

They were moved to interest and enthusiasm, too, they gleamed back at her across Ilonna's outstretched arms as she set down the steaming bowl of dumplings.

'Good!' said Matyas heartily. 'So he has his opportunity, after all. He is a very good young man, I'm glad they knew enough to value him.'

'He left school at fourteen,' explained Wanda, turning upon Emmy a face like a rose. 'He has worked so hard, and had no help at all,

47

and now at last he will have his real place. If you knew how capable he is, and how good, and how much one must respect him!'

Lubov, nodding thoughtful agreement, regarded his sister with a warm and private smile. Emmy perceived it, and might have wondered if Wanda's judgment of the unknown Petr's abilities did not owe its warmth entirely to a more personal interest in the man himself, but for Matyas' undoubted concurrence in it.

'It is so fine,' said Wanda, with a quiet and child-like solemnity, 'to see someone's life open and grow like that—like a flower.'

'Yes,' said Lubov, and looked at Emmy. There was no irony in his assent at all, the bracken-brown eyes were cool and clear. The word and the look meant: 'Everything she says is true. She likes the boy Petr, but what she says is not coloured by that. These things are happening.'

Ilonna looked from her plate to the clock, and said: 'Miloslav is very late. Surely they cannot be discussing class business until now! But he would come straight home, he knew Emmy was coming. He was hoping for a short meeting.'

'It was something he couldn't cut?' asked Emmy.

'One does not cut classes now,' said Lubov dryly, 'or Faculty Meetings, either. It is no longer done.'

48

'Not even by Milo?'

'Not by anyone who wants to remain a student. Things have tightened up with a jolt. If you miss too many classes you risk being removed from the rolls. If you fail to make the regular examinations, all of them, you're out at once.'

'You know that the schools have been overcrowded ever since they re-opened after the war,' said Wanda, with the same restrained gentleness he had used towards her preoccupations, 'and students were taking everything much too easily. It wasn't fair for part-timers to keep out other students who wanted to work hard. And there were always so many poorer boys and girls who couldn't get in. It was getting to be just a nice exclusive club. Now it's very much a university. You work or get out.'

'Or both,' said Lubov. 'That's the worst of this kind of tidying-up, it offers so much scope to people with private grudges.' He looked up at Emmy with an apologetic smile. 'This isn't much help to you, is it? You wanted to come and find the facts, and here we are turning over layer after layer of change for you, and all we manage to reveal is that the complexity and confusion we've created has us baffled. We don't even know, half the time, which way we're facing.'

'Yes, we do,' said Wanda with absolute decision. 'We always know that.' Her face

49

calmed upon the words into angelic conviction, fixed and fierce. She had no doubts at all; she was done with doubts.

*   *   *

It was nine o'clock when Miloslav came home.

In the living-room a tired and rather sad silence had descended upon them all, as though the evening had already eaten its share of words and sensations and thoughts, and could absorb no more. Looking back, Emmy could hardly believe that she herself had said so little. Most of the direct questions she had brought with her, aching for answers, had already faded unspoken into irrelevance.

'I'd forgotten,' she thought, studying them, face after Ivanescu face, familiar and self-possessed and proud, 'how very honest they are, and how fair. Balanced and just minds are a deadly handicap to action. Only the vehement have jumped. Only Wanda has made up her mind, once for all. She knows she is accepting, for the sake of what she believes to be the big thing, a great many little things which she regrets, and will change if she can. But she's made her choice. But Lubov—'

A key grated in the outer door of the flat. Matyas heard it, and pushed back his chair to look round at the clock, with a sigh of obvious relief.

'That's Miloslav! And more than time! I

began to think they were going to keep it up all night.'

The door of the living-room burst open, Miloslav's shoulder hurling it back until it jarred against the corner of Ilonna's glass-fronted cabinet, so sharply that the glassware and ceramic pieces within quivered and stirred upon their lace mats. He made a half-hearted clutch to save the crash, but abandoned it savagely as though, after all, so trivial a disaster as breakages among his mother's domestic treasures could hardly be worth averting. A gust of frosty air came through the doorway with him in the folds of his greatcoat and the ends of his scarf, and the touch of frost was in the hectic red-and-white colouring of his cheeks, the curling crispness of his hair, and the pinched look of his mouth and nostrils. He looked cold with more than an October coldness.

'Milo!' protested Matyas mildly, frowning at the crash of the door and the momentary rocking of glass.

Miloslav said nothing at all. He stood just within the doorway, looking at them all beneath drawn brows, and through the frosty tightness of his face his blue eyes stared with indignant heat. He was twenty, the youngest and the slightest of the Ivanescu children, because he had passed his adolescent years here at home under the German Occupation, when not even the most devoted of parents

51

could always ensure for their growing sons an adequate diet. He had none of Wanda's beauty, and little of Lubov's calm, but a certain irregular attractiveness of his own, ebullient and responsive, unrecognisable now in these fixed and outraged features.

Lubov asked with quick alarm: 'What's the matter?'

'Do you know what they've done? Lubov, you've got to do something! They—' He had begun in English, the presence of the guest oppressing his meticulous young mind, but he could not keep it up. He cast an anguished glance of apology in her direction, and to compensate her for being shut out for a while, stretched out his hand and caught hers in a cold, convulsive grasp. He began to pour out a flood of words in his own language, far too fast for her to follow. Moved by the passionate grip he kept upon her hand, Emmy leaned and kissed his cheek; it had the smoothness and the sting of ice under her lips, but already, in the warmth of the room, tiny beads of sweat stood on his upper lip. In a moment Ilonna crossed the room to his side, and quietly unwound the scarf from his neck and completed the unbuttoning of his coat. Miloslav, intent as a single-minded child, tilted his head to see beyond her, while he continued to stammer furious sentences past her listening and comprehending ears. He let her detach him from his overcoat, with Emmy's help, and hardly noticed the deprivation. Others might have to solve the problem which was agitating his mind, but Ilonna took steps to preserve her youngest from getting overheated.

When she had the coat in her arm, she straightened his tie, smoothed back the hair from his forehead with a quick sweep of her finger-tips, and went to hang up coat and scarf. She smiled at Emmy as she went. 'His manners are very bad, but he is a little upset. Don't be angry with him!'

But Miloslav had unburdened his indignant heart by now, and more of his mind was aware of the visitor. He bit off his outpourings into a breathless silence, and, turning with a dazed and miserable smile, struggled into English.

'Oh, please, Emmy, excuse me! I am sorry! I am so late, and I wanted so much to come to you. But I couldn't help it!' He threw his arms round her and hugged her vehemently, and then turned his lips, still tremulous with rage, into the curve of her cheek, and bestowed on her the briefest, most furious and touching of kisses. She hugged him back with goodwill, her eyes anxiously questioning Lubov over his shoulder. 'What is it? Is he in trouble over this check-up at the university?' But she did not speak, except with her eyes. What Miloslav wanted her to understand he would explain to her when he had words enough.

'I am a wretch,' said Miloslav, emerging, 'I haven't even said I'm glad to see you, but, darling Emmy, I am, so very glad! You know that. It's this horrible business about our class! I didn't know what was going to come up, I never thought there could be anything like this. And so of course we couldn't get away. I felt terrible, but I had to stay, because it was Yuri they were threatening, you see—'

'Not you?' she said, in a sharp breath of relief; and yet Yuri's name had made her heart contract, too, for she knew him almost as well as if he had been an Ivanescu, and indeed it was as almost another son that Matyas and Ilonna regarded him.

'Oh, no, it isn't me! Not yet!' he added disdainfully. 'Not that I haven't done for myself, too, I expect, after the things I've said! But Yuri—they've dismissed him. I was the only one who voted against it. I dare say I only made things worse,' he owned feverishly, 'losing my temper and letting fly like that. But what could I do? Somebody had to speak up for him. But it was no use, they've thrown him out just the same. Some of them must have known it was coming up,' said Miloslav, raging still at the thought, 'and they never said a word to either of us. We just walked into it, head-on.'

'I don't suppose anything you said made any difference,' said Lubov, frowning, 'if that's any comfort to you. Except to your own prospects,' he added sombrely.

'Oh, that!' Miloslav shrugged off his own future troubles almost with contempt. He could accommodate only one anger of this quality at a time. 'But, Lubov, you've got to do something about it, we can't just let it go. You don't know how terribly he's taking it.'

'He went out of his way to ask for it,' said Wanda, but she said it with the exasperation of an anxious friend rather than the satisfaction of an opponent. 'And it sounds as if you've been doing your best to land yourself in the same mess.'

Matyas asked practically: 'Where is Yuri? Why didn't you bring him back with you? You shouldn't have left him on his own.'

'I wanted him to come back with me, but he wouldn't. He doesn't want anybody. He didn't want me. I told him Emmy would be here, but he wouldn't come. I went back to his room with him before I came home,' said Miloslav unhappily, 'I didn't like to leave him too soon.'

'Then you've done all you or any of us can do for him tonight, so come and sit down, and have your supper. We'll have to think what's to be done.'

Miloslav approached the table and sat down to his soup obediently, though without any great show of appetite. He would have regarded being put off his food by trouble as something of an affectation. Ilonna waited on him unobtrusively, and then sat down with Emmy and Wanda on one of the couches, and gravely watched him eat.

'Was the Dean there?' asked Lubov, after

long and troubled thought.

'No, just Kovar. It's always like that at meetings. I don't believe the Dean dare veto anything they've decided on. Besides, it was all arranged beforehand.'

'You've no right to say that,' said Wanda, sharply but not unkindly. 'And you've no right to make statements like that about the Dean unless he's been given the chance to put the thing right.'

Miloslav shot her a dark look, and said with the remnant of the vindictiveness he felt against his classmates: 'I expect *you* think it *is* right, in any case. You've said enough about him yourself!'

'I said he was a fool, and so he was, and I said those diatribes he wrote in that paper of his were practically actionable, and so they were. He got no more than he asked for then. But that doesn't mean I think it should be brought up against him a second time. When a thing's over it ought to *be* over.' Wanda chose and measured her words carefully, Emmy could feel her arduously controlling them. Perhaps one would have to do that with Miloslav, who if you said 'White!' to him would certainly say 'Black!', but if you asked him his honest opinion was very likely to consider carefully and reply 'Grey!' All the same, for Wanda in her passion of conviction such exercises in restraint couldn't be easy.

'But what's Yuri done?' asked Emmy. 'I

thought it was a matter of class attendances and examinations. He hasn't written to me for months, but I thought there was an understanding about missing a certain number of classes if you were working through, as he is. And he always used to take the examinations in his stride. What have they got against him?'

'There was an understanding just as long as they wanted to understand it,' said Miloslav, crumbling bread viciously, 'but as soon as they wanted to get rid of him, the handle was there to be used. And he has taken all his exams, easily. So they couldn't say his work's been neglected. But he's just short of a few class attendances, so technically they can kick him out and quote that as the reason. But everybody knows what the real reason is,' he said fiercely, his eyes flashing in Wanda's direction. '*You* knew it, didn't you? It was you who said it, not me.'

'But what was it he'd done? You haven't told me.'

'He wrote and published three highly critical articles at the time of the crisis,' said Lubov, seeing that it was on him she had fixed her urgent eyes. 'They were extremely outspoken, and made some serious charges about party leaders mismanaging the voting at party meetings.'

'Charges that were quite unjustified,' said Wanda warmly.

'He gave plenty of evidence for them,' said

Miloslav, flaring up instantly in defence of his friend.

Emmy, watching Lubov's face, waited.

'I shouldn't like to say all the evidence was very good,' said Lubov, after some thought. 'Yuri was making a case with anything that came to hand. It may have been true—the trouble is that he can't really have *known* whether it was true or not.' He added, not without a sly flicker of a smile through his dark anxiety: 'Any more than Wanda does!'

From him they let it pass, only with long, withdrawn looks reserving their own judgment and acknowledging his right to his.

'The police raided the office and closed the press,' said Lubov. 'Yuri and his leader-writer were fetched away to police headquarters, but as soon as Yuri told them he was the author as well as the editor they turned the other fellow out again. Yuri was there twelve hours, and didn't have a very comfortable time of it. Oh, he wasn't knocked about, apart from the usual amount of hustling one expects from the police anywhere, but they seem to have made things as humiliating for him as they could. You know the sort of thing—being made to stand about in corridors for hours, and then again for twenty minutes in front of somebody's desk before he notices your existence. And combing over his articles sentence by sentence, looking for sedition—'

'Were they seditious?' asked Emmy.

58

'About as near it as the utterances that have been the ruin of some dons in America. No, maybe a little nearer to it than the bulk of those. But if you're asking me, do I find them seditious by my standards—no, I don't think so. But then, I'm not in a position of responsibility to government—not as the police are. And after about twelve hours of pushing him around and trying to make him feel small, frightened and ashamed of himself, they did let him go, you know.'

'So he was never charged! Then there can't be any mark against him.'

'He was never charged, but there is a mark against him. In theory it works your way, but in practice this way. Just like anywhere else.'

'He has only to breathe rather loudly now,' said Miloslav bitterly. 'He's being watched all the time, wherever he goes. And now, just because of a few classes missed, they've got an easy way of dismissing him from the university. And it's so unfair! Lubov, do please talk to the Dean about it, and get him to do something! He *knows* Yuri's brilliant, he *knows* he hasn't been wasting his time! They all know it! They just want to get rid of him. His degree means so much to him. What on earth is to become of him if he can't study? It's his *life*!'

'Drink your coffee,' said Lubov. 'I'll talk to the Dean, and the Rector too, if I don't get any satisfaction from the Dean. God knows whether I can do any good, but I'll try.' He

59

added, in tones sharp with protest and warning by reason of the instant lighting-up of Miloslav's face: 'Don't expect anything! You know these things are happening, and you know he'll survive it if he has to. I only said I'll try.'

Miloslav's eagerness to disclaim optimism was instant and pathetic. 'I know! We can't build on it too much, I know that. And, my God, you can't be less effective than I was! No, of course it isn't really his life, that was a silly thing to say.'

'I'll go and have a talk with him in the morning,' said Lubov. 'He'll be in his room? His classes are all stopped at once?' Miloslav nodded speechlessly over his coffee. 'Then I'll see him before I go in to the Faculty and get him to be on hand in case a circumspect appearance may help with the Dean. All right!' he said with a wry smile, seeing Miloslav's lips open upon a needless warning, 'I know he won't be feeling in the least circumspect, I won't ask him to go on his knees to anyone. But even keeping his mouth shut and listening to other people without smouldering might be something. I'll do what I can.'

Wanda, who had been watching Lubov with a look of dubious anxiety in her eyes, now said in tones schooled to quietness, but retaining something of severity, too: 'On top of all your own lame dogs, Lubov, must you carry Yuri as well? I know it isn't just pigheadedness, I know

60

you feel you have to do it—but I think you ought to consider your own position a little, too.'

'Lubov must do as he sees fit,' said Matyas; and, 'But they're all such nice boys!' said Ilonna in the same breath, with marvellous simplicity, and no anxiety or reproach at all.

'I do consider my own position,' said Lubov. 'All day, every day! These days, I seldom consider anything else. Before I move a foot or a hand, I consider it all over again.' He got up to fetch the cigarette-box, and brought it to where Emmy sat. She yawned over his lighter, and looked up into his face with an apologetic smile. 'You're terribly tired. This is the last for tonight, then Wanda'll help you unpack, and you must get your beauty-sleep, ready for tomorrow. I'm so sorry! We'd much rather have had a party for you than a wake for Yuri.'

'But I'm concerned for him, too. I know him almost as well as I know you, naturally I'm anxious about him. I must go and see him—I should like to see him again, very much.' She turned to look at Miloslav, and was in time to see his lips shut tightly and his throat contract upon a gulp of dismay. He sat looking at her in miserable embarrassment, feeling for the kindest words in which to express, without wounding her, Yuri's violent objections to having an Englishwoman ask for him at the desk of his hostel. She saw him entirely transparent, like crystal, agonised sensitivity

61

glittering through a prism; and she wondered if she had not contracted this clairvoyance from Lubov, who knew well how to answer all her own unspoken thoughts.

'Who would think adjustments could be made so quickly?' she said to herself. 'I'm becoming an adept already.' And she made haste to rescue the boy, a little astonished at her own dexterity: 'Not at his rooms, of course, I know I'm bad medicine to him now, being English. I wouldn't let him walk in the town with me, either, where we might both be too recognisable. But if you could fix a time with him, Milo, perhaps we could meet at one of the little cafés by the river, or somewhere in the New Park. Ask him, tomorrow, if he would like to do that.'

'Oh, yes!' said Miloslav, weak with relief. 'Yes, I know he would! He *does* want to see you, only, you see, the least little thing now could do him so much harm. Oh, you do understand!' he said, breaking into a smile as bright as it was sad. 'I *knew* you would!'

* * *

Long after they had put out the light in the second bedroom, and opened the window upon the coruscations of stars above the river, they heard the voices in the living-room still in soft, insistent conversation. They lay side by side in Wanda's big bed, watching the crackle of stars in a frosty depth of sky, and listening to the subsiding murmurs of Miloslav's generous indignation.

'He's very upset,' said Wanda, whispering. 'You know he thinks the world of Yuri. They've been together so much, and then they have all the excitement from the time of the Occupation between them.'

'I know! After all they went through together for that underground paper, they know how to value each other.'

'Oh, that paper!' Wanda remembered it with a small, dry chuckle in the darkness. 'With Yuri as editor and Milo as errand-boy—yes! Though I think the errand-boy took a good many more risks than the editor, if the truth be told.'

'Wanda! You don't mean that!'

'Oh, well—perhaps it wasn't a thing I should have said. Milo was fifteen when he began carrying messages for them—it's something I've always had against Yuri, you know, since I found out about it. Just because the kid adored him, I used to think, how selfish to make use of him in a dangerous business like that! But fifteen-year-old boys can be extremely strong-willed people, too, and I dare say Yuri didn't have much say in the matter. Only I don't like to see situations like that repeating themselves.'

'You think Yuri's got to be a persecuted hero now to live?' asked Emmy, hearing through her own murmuring words the fretful sound of Miloslav still celebrating Yuri Dushek's wrongs. 'Don't you believe he's sincere in his attitude, then?'

'I think he is entirely sincere. I think he is living in accordance with the needs of his nature, what could be more sincere than that? But I don't like his dragging Milo into his forlorn stand a second time.'

Emmy turned her head upon the pillow, and saw faintly in the glimmer of starlight the pallor of Wanda's oval face islanded in its lake of black hair, and the wide, lambent shining of the wonderful eyes. 'You're very fond of Miloslav, aren't you?'

'Milo is a spoiled little boy,' said Wanda, but she smiled. 'He is unreasonable, and brave, and very obstinate, and we fight a great deal. But I love him, and I want him to be able to live happily in this new world we're making, and I think he has difficulties enough without having to break his heart over Yuri Dushek, and his head against Yuri Dushek's self-induced troubles. Whichever of them is the force that holds the two together, I should be glad to see them separated. I hope they will send Yuri a long way off, where he can find someone else to admire him and fight back-to-back with him against the movement of the clock.' She turned her head, still smiling, and looked into Emmy's eyes. 'Don't think me too hard! I don't speak like this to anyone else, and with you I speak first and think afterwards, so I am very vulnerable. Dear Emmy, I am so glad, so very glad you are here!'

'So am I to be here. Just to see you all again, with my own eyes—that was what I needed.'

'You've been worrying about us.' Wanda folded her long, cool hand about Emmy's fingers. 'I can understand it. And there is enough cause for worry, in a way, for, you know, this business of changing course is not easy. Not easy at all for people like us, who have been privileged all our lives. One can feel goodwill for those who have had no such privileges, and wish to help them, and even be glad when there are changes which ease their position; but it is not easy to understand the real differences there have been between us, and to feel what it means when they are levelled out. Father always had the factory. It was his, and it kept us all in comfort, even if we were not rich. We never had to worry about money, we always had enough to eat, and plenty of decent clothes, and everything we really wanted and needed. It might be easier to feel the justice of change if we had been very rich indeed, so that the contrast could have been more marked. But now, for us, everything tightens, and it is natural to feel and say: "We were not rich people, we only employed a dozen men at the factory, and they lived very much as we did. We have never oppressed anybody: why should we suddenly be made so much poorer?"

65

And that is all true. But still, Emmy, we had more than our share. That's what it's so hard to grasp. Father didn't tell you about the factory?'

'No, he didn't say anything about it. It's so small,' said Emmy, wondering, 'they can't be thinking of nationalising that?'

'Not directly, all those small firms are going on as usual. But Father has seen already that it will come to that. He's feeling the pinch now in all kinds of small ways, chiefly because some of the colours and materials they use are in short supply, and he finds himself at the end of the queue for them. The big national concerns have precedence. And you can see that it has to be like that, it's quite inevitable, but still it seems to him a wrong. So he has seen already that everything is pushing him towards nationalisation, and he has begun to negotiate about handing the business over voluntarily.'

'Will he get compensation for it, then?' Emmy was dismayed, not by the thought of Matyas in straitened circumstances, but by the memory of his delight in the small, sprawling factory out on the southern road, where he had manufactured paints and lacquers for twenty years. He had made the place, and a piece of his heart and a long succession of his warmest memories were built and glazed into it. But still she asked the obvious question, because no price could ever be put upon Matyas' years of joyful industry.

'Yes, of course! Not, perhaps, as much as he thinks he should, but they have not settled a figure yet, and he will hold his own very well, I think. But just because I see that this has to be, and that it is not a terrible tyranny and a sin, but only a rather hard necessity, you must not think, Emmy, that I don't know about the other part of it, the love he has for it, and the hold it has on his life. You must not think I don't understand how much he will be hurt, not in his pocket or his pride, but in his spirit. Even though he will certainly be able to go on there as manager under the State—that is something, but not the same, because it will no longer be his.'

'But he *can* do that?' In pleased surprise she had raised her voice for an instant, and the sudden sound startled her. She subsided into a careful whisper: 'They will really take him on as manager? And the same staff under him?'

'Oh yes, of course, why not? It's human and practical, it helps everyone. It's how it's usually done where people volunteer to give up their works—unless there's some very strong argument against it. Father will be all right there—only, as I said, he will feel it very much that it will no longer be his.'

'And Lubov—do you really think he is laying up trouble for himself? I could see you're uneasy about him.'

'Ah, Lubov!' Wanda stirred and sighed, and uttered a sound like an infinitely distant and

67

rueful laugh. 'Lubov wants to be fair to the devil! And he is in quite the wrong place to be able to indulge it with safety. In universities there is always subversive activity, because the very act of thought is subversive. And so of all the troubled places in our country he stands in the most exposed. Poor Lubov, he has need to be a doctor of philosophy!'

'You think he's calling too much attention to himself by his efforts for people like Yuri? Can a man really become an object of suspicion just because he doesn't join in the stone-throwing?'

'I would not describe it in that way,' said Wanda sternly. 'I, too, would like to be fair to the devil, if it could be done without cost to the others. But we have not time for it. And a man who is seen to be giving too much of his time to salvaging the minor casualties is soon going to have it pointed out to him that he could be contributing all that energy to the main drive of events. Don't think I don't see the casualties—I do, and I know that some of them are quite innocent, but I have not time to run back and pick them up and bathe their broken knees. Don't think, either, that Lubov makes the mistake of thinking them all innocent, just because they get hurt, and seeing people hurt offends him. No, he does after his kind because it *is* his kind. He has no protective mutabilities, my brother.'

'They don't always protect, in any case,' said

68

Emmy. 'Honest consistency sometimes pays better in the end. To be permanently visible and recognisable is at any rate a way of avoiding being shot in mistake for something you're *not*.'

Wanda lay silent for a moment, staring up into the gently swinging folds of the net curtains; then she said very seriously: 'You see, it's easier for me than for the others. Lubov had his degree before he ever left here. He was past that formative phase, and his position among the privileged had never been shaken. Milo, in spite of the deprivations everyone suffered during the Occupation, remained among the luckier ones—everyone's standard went down, but he was still living better than most, and his life had no real dislocation, only the added stimulus of getting drawn into the Resistance. By the time he was ready for the university, it was re-opened and ready for him.

'But *I* began to earn my living at fifteen and a half, in a strange country, and there was neither high school nor university for me. Lubov was parents and family and all to me when we were together, but most of the time we could not be together. And you and your father were angels to me. But still I had this experience of living without privileges, and making my own way with my own hands. When we speak of the workers, and their hours, and their standard of living, and all the insecurity they suffer, in this house, every one

69

among us makes an imaginative effort, and makes it with goodwill. But *I know*. Lubov was formed here, before he ever went to England. But I was formed in England, Emmy, and England made me a socialist, and taught me where I belonged.'

'You could have had the other experience, too,' said Emmy thoughtfully. 'Since the university had been closed for five years, most of the entries when it re-opened were as mature as you. You could have added a degree to the qualifications you already had. I'm not decrying the school of experience—far from it. But I think you could have added something more to your powers.'

'I know it, and sometimes I wish I had done it. It would have made me more valuable than I am now. Yuri is three months older than I, and he found no difficulty in turning back. But I could not do it. I have no machinery for turning back. There had been a time for studying, and I had been made to use it in another way, and it was gone. There was no help for it. I don't regret the exchange,' she said, laughter bubbling suddenly through her whispering voice, 'but I am human, and I wish I could have had both.'

'At least,' said Emmy, 'you seem quite sure where you're going. God knows that's rare enough.'

'I am quite sure. If it were only for myself I would like to run, I would like to fly, I would

70

like to hurry through this phase of trying to reconcile people, of explaining to them, of reasoning with them, of making allowances for them. But we all have different speeds, and I have to learn to go slowly and be content. It gives me, at any rate, time to watch people like Petr expand and grow. And that is something, Emmy, that is very much!'

'What I find so strange,' said Emmy, growing relaxed and drowsy now in the warmth of the bed, 'is that someone like you, as convinced as that, in as big a hurry as that, should be able to see the other fellow's point of view at all.'

The murmurs in the other room had ceased. Miloslav was probably asleep, exhausted with emotion. Lubov, as surely, lay awake in the darkness, pondering the fate of Yuri Dushek.

'Ah,' said Wanda, yawning and sighing, 'there's nothing like loving someone who is not of your opinion, to teach you tolerance.'

*   *   *

Ferdis Marvan had worked at the Ministry of Culture for three years, and in that time had received and looked after hundreds of visiting artists. He liked Emily Marryat because she came alone, instead of surrounded by accompanists, agents and relatives, and did not require to be squired about the city, nor even to be provided with an interpreter. Nor did he

71

have to book rooms for her at a hotel, for it seemed she had friends in the suburbs somewhere. All he had to do for her was introduce her accompanist, give them both coffee and cigarettes, and run through the arrangements for the two concerts, one to be given in the intimate atmosphere of the concert room at the Musicians' Club, the second in the formidable baroque splendours of the Mozarteum. He had done as much for her once before, in the summer of the previous year; the only particular in which this occasion differed from that was the identity of the pianist. Last year's accompanist had been an elderly man, the leader of a distinguished piano trio; at the time of the crisis he had been on a tour in America with the trio, and he had declined to come back. The end of a good trio, for the violinist and the 'cellist had left him there and headed indignantly for home.

This year's accompanist was a young and attractive girl, as vivid as a newly budded shoot, and with something of the same air of wonder and achievement. It seemed she had just won a national scholarship, and was still dizzy with the abruptness of her rise. She looked, Emmy thought, as Wanda's voice had sounded when she proclaimed the advancement of Petr. Her name was Helena. They could use one of the rehearsal rooms at the club any afternoon they liked, and Helena was so quiveringly eager to prove her mettle that Emmy made an appointment to meet her there that same afternoon at three. It was not likely that Miloslav would bring her a message from Yuri so soon, she thought, for he seldom came home to lunch between classes. However, in case his impetuosity had swept Yuri into agreeing to a meeting that very day, she had better go back to the flat.

The early ground-frost was gone, and the sun had come out and dried the streets. At noon it was still and warm, and the chestnut trees along the avenues of the New Town shone with an incandescent radiance, chandeliers of thin, clear leaves. The din of the shopping streets had a note of hopeful gaiety; she had always found this a high-spirited town, a merry town. The crimson-and-gold slogans decorating newspaper offices and party clubs, the long, heavy red streamers, made new and disturbing exclamation points of excitement for the eye, the frequent street-corner loudspeakers were pouring out turbulent music unheeded in the cheerful daily hubbub. The girls, wide-faced, with generously spaced, wild, aloof eyes, walked purposefully, with high-poised heads and striding steps, swinging net bags in their hands. Young men, the distinct tall type, long-boned and fair and of a striking physical elegance, with lean flanks and flat stomachs and large, suave shoulders, swung along under the trees, their hats tilted and their brief-cases bulging importantly. The

73

others, the sturdy square ones, were less noticeable but more frequent, and walked with a bull-terrier's muscular, rolling gait. Most of the small children had already gone into their characteristic winter knitteds, stockings and pants in one garment. Two tiny girls, packed up by a loving mother before the frost melted, clung to their father's hands in the arcade, globular in fluffy white fur, like puffs of thistledown. Emmy smiled at them, reminded that here it was the children who must have fur coats to be in the fashion.

The display-windows in the tall modern shops were full of goods, but the range did not seem to Emmy so rich as a year previously, and the textiles, especially wool, were very dear. Along the embankment the few small, elegant windows showed pictures, delicate linens and laces, glittering glass, and antiques, and across the road from them young couples leaned on the stone balustrade to watch the rapid slate-grey water filling and stilling above the weir. Beyond, the Citadel soared, and tier upon tier the trees, green and gold-sprinkled and skeletal black, climbed to the long sweep of wall, and the turmoil of roofs huddled, old houses braced temple to temple like the formidable ancestral battle-line.

She walked back to the Lucerna, climbing from the bridge by the hidden flights of steps instead of the streets, to see if she could still find the way. The wide, shallow stairs, their cobbles

74

laid in patterns of diamonds and stars, dazzled her eyes in the sunshine. Dead leaves, drifted into the corners, silenced her footsteps as she climbed. When she reached the level of the street where the Ivanescu lived, she turned to look down over the maze of roofs, Indian red and black, corrugated by sunlight, and outward to the distant hills between the aspiring towers. In the Old Quarter churches jostled, elbowing one another, squat romanesque lantern roofs craning under the shadows of tapering Gothic spires, the bright light glinting from their vertical tiles as from the scales of dragons, and the shell-crested façades of baroque buildings shone suave and pale under their green copper domes. Regained and reassessed, the city appeared to her more beautiful than it had ever been before, even in the foam of spring blossom, even in the quivering wheat-gold air of summer. She stood gazing out over it, her breast full and aching with delight and desire. Places, like people, can be loved placidly and pleasurably until one awakes to the fearful realisation that they can be lost.

When she reached the flat, she found Ilonna alone. It was seldom that Lubov and Miloslav came home to lunch, and the factory where Wanda worked, like Matyas' small property, was too far out of town for them to undertake the journey twice a day.

'I hoped you would come back and eat with

me,' said Ilonna, laying the small table in the kitchen. 'It is so expensive to take meals in the town, and you will want all your money to buy things to take back with you. Lubov telephoned—he is sorry he can't get back to be with us, he meant to, but it is impossible, because only now can he get a word with the Dean. But he says he has tickets for the Chamber Theatre for tonight, if you would like to go. For the children, too. I don't know how he managed it,' she said admiringly, 'it is one of the labours of Hercules to get them now. Except for some propaganda piece, perhaps!'

Ilonna had no discretion, in the ordinary sense of the word, at all. Her idea of taking care what she said was to avoid any utterance which she might, on second thoughts, regret as untrue or unkind, but it would never have occurred to her to impose a censorship on herself on the grounds of unwisdom. All through lunch, and all through the washing-up afterwards, she talked with unsubdued candour about her husband and her children. She saw the stresses of the times only through them; not the turmoil of the world, but its small private effects, exercised her energy and inventiveness, and for her the crisis, it seemed, had been summed up in her husband's longer-than-usual absences at the factory, in Lubov's frequent nervous headaches, and the bruises Miloslav had brought home from certain turbulent but relatively bloodless disturbances

76

among the students.

'He is so hasty,' she said resignedly, polishing glasses to the rhythm of her own sentences. 'Of course who would be in the front of the column when they tried to force their way where they were not allowed to go? Naturally Milo! And of course who is more indignant when he gets his toes trampled on as a result? Still, they made their demonstration and it was a relief to them, even if it didn't really do any good. He was a little damaged, but not so badly as once when he boxed five rounds with some boy at the gymnasium who was too far above his weight. The poor child, when he came home he made an entrance so forbiddingly dignified, and then his nose began to bleed, and it was all spoiled.'

This particular reminiscence seemed to belong to the disastrous bout at the university gymnasium rather than the students' demonstration. Emmy, her hands immersed to the wrist in hot suds, fished out forks and spoons on to the draining-board, and smiled, and waited, as you wait for a particular little boat, launched well upstream, to pass under the bridge of a steadily flowing river.

'He had a bruise here in the shoulder,' pursued Ilonna cheerfully, 'quite black, and very large—shaped so! He said it was from the butt of a rifle when they were forced to turn back. It hurt him, but he was a little proud of it. After I had bathed the place and massaged his shoulder, and Matyas and Lubov had told him how silly he was, and I had told him how wonderful—but he knew I meant the same thing!—and we made him go to bed, he got up again as soon as we were out of the room, to look at his bruise in the mirror, and see if it had a good colour.' She laughed, remembering. 'It was all quite a mistake, it turned out afterwards. They were trying to get to the Rector's house, because they had heard that the Ministry were threatening to dismiss him, and all the time it was quite without foundation. And the soldiers thought they were demonstrating against him, instead of trying to defend him. It was the day of the big march, and everything was very confused. But no one was really hurt, and, you know, in a way they enjoyed it. The same Rector is still there,' she added inconsequently, perhaps as a comment upon the futility of most human activity. Her own limited but effective actions achieved with remarkable consistency the antithesis of futility.

'Was Yuri involved in that skirmish, too?' asked Emmy, wiping her hands and carefully hanging up the wet cloth.

'No, he was with the police just then. Milo did not know, or he would have wanted the students to march there instead of to the Rector's house. But we knew nothing about it until they let him out late in the evening, and he came back here. He was very sick all night, but

I think it was from chargin, because he felt he had not cut a very wonderful figure. He would have been more satisfied if they had beaten him.' There was no irony in this analysis; Ilonna did not deal in irony. She was entirely sympathetic and utterly serious about the pretensions of the young. 'He stayed with us for a week,' she said. 'We did not want him to be alone when he was so depressed. But he wouldn't stay any longer. He thought he was dangerous to us. He dramatises himself a little, of course,' she said tolerantly, 'but he is a very nice boy.'

Emmy was putting on her hat again to go down to the Musicians' Club and her appointment with Helena. Encountering Ilonna's light and direct blue eyes in the mirror, she said seriously: 'Wanda thinks he's a bad influence on Milo.'

'It all depends on the point of view,' said Ilonna, unimpressed. 'You might as well say that Milo is a good influence on him. It is only the reverse of the same crown piece.'

'And which side do *you* think is on top?'

'Well, of course Yuri is older, and calls a great many of the tunes. But Milo does not always dance to them, or join in the choruses, either. Wanda cannot help pushing people, you know, they never go fast enough for her. But I have found it more practical not to push Milo. He pushes back. I have noticed,' she said, with a gleam of laughter in her eyes, 'that he

79

can push quite as hard as Yuri when it is necessary.'

'Maybe, but if Yuri's example doesn't get him into trouble, still his affection for Yuri may. That's what Wanda's afraid of.'

'Oh, it is of no use to be afraid of *that*. About affections,' said Ilonna with serenity, 'there is nothing to be done. No one can dictate to us whom we shall love.'

*   *   *

By the pond at the woodland end of the New Park there was just one seat, lonely in the autumnal sunlight with no trees or bushes about it, looking at the green water. The place was well chosen, Emmy thought, approaching it, for its openness and innocence. She had half expected Yuri to appoint some meeting-place so furtive as to be far more conspicuous than the common-room of his own college. Perhaps she had let her memories of him become too lavishly coloured by Wanda's prejudices. She tried to recall what she knew of the boy himself, but it was difficult to separate recollections of a bold, bronzed face and imperious eyes from Wanda's: 'I think the errand-boy took a great many more risks than the editor,' or Ilonna's: 'He dramatises himself a little, of course!' And now that she came to examine what she knew of Yuri Dushek, it seemed that she had always seen him through the prismatic brightness of the Ivanescu family.

She sat down at one end of the wooden seat, and waited, for she had arrived a little before the hour. Miloslav, delivering the message the previous evening, had implored her not to be late. 'He doesn't like to hang about anywhere for too long. Once you're a marked man, everything you do is suspicious.' She was not sure how seriously he himself treated these hypersensitivities of Yuri's, for he was conducting an embassy on behalf of another person, and Miloslav was punctilious in these matters. What was of importance was that Yuri's fears should be respected, not that they should be shown to be justified.

Behind her, among the flower-beds at the edge of the formal garden, a few strollers passed, their voices clear and small in the still air. There was going to be a frost again tonight, she could feel and hear it already through the cool gold sunshine of early afternoon. An occasional solitary figure hurried along the gravel path on her left, passed the pond with all its iris-spears and lily-pads and furtively moving fish, and disappeared into the copse beyond, where the tall, strange trees, each labelled with its exotic name and far-distant country, stood spaced among the native oaks and elms and beeches, beautiful, aloof exiles withdrawn into unending dreams of home.

She had expected Yuri to approach, as she

had done, from the gardens, and she was startled when he came out of the woods beyond the water, and walked towards her without haste or hesitation along the green rim of the pool.

She knew him at once. As soon as he appeared, even while he was no more than a distant young man coming towards her at a lofty and decisive walk, it seemed incredible to her that she had not been able to recall him as being exactly thus, in every detail. Such a creature should not be easily forgotten, nor soon grow shadowy in the mind. He was as tall as Lubov, and more nobly built, long of limb, large of breast and shoulder, and since he wore no hat she could see, long before he was near to her, the high carriage of the small Greek head with its curling light-brown hair, poised well back on a columnar neck and wide shoulders. Because of the resplendent gait, she remembered now his athletic record, the disdainful way he swept off tennis honours in summer and ski trophies in winter. It was difficult to diminish him again into the embittered and rather frightened boy the family had made of him, or to imagine him needing or encouraging Miloslav's fiery championship.

She watched him come, and when he was near enough for her to see the expression of his eyes, she saw that they were fixed upon her. It seemed that she was equally unmistakable, and without the revelation of movement to make recognition easy. He came to her directly, swinging in across the grass. His hands were in his pockets, his overcoat open, and his college scarf trailed an end over one shoulder. She had never seen anyone who presented an appearance less furtive or subdued than this, though he did, upon examination, carry the marks of strain upon him, and perhaps even the haughtiness of his bearing and attitude were sustained as a means of self-protection.

She did not get up to meet him, nor turn directly towards him, nor give him her hand, preserving her casual examination of the landscape, and of him as a feature of it, until he came up and seated himself beside her. No one in the gardens, no one between the pond and the wood, seemed to be taking any interest in them. She dropped her hand casually upon the seat between them, and he shut his over it instantly, and held it hard. His grip, like his person, was large and positive; and like his temper, passionate.

'Emmy, this is very good of you. I'm sorry to be behaving so abnormally, and ashamed to be asking you to do the same.'

His voice was quiet and grave, and she thought its calm was not achieved without an effort.

'I understood, Yuri. I'm glad to see you again, even like this.'

They sat smiling at each other, with pleasure

83

but without gaiety. His features, like the set of his head upon his shoulders, were pure Greek, the line of brow and nose straight and clear, the nostrils full and curling, the mouth short, passionate and resolute. His summer bronze had faded to a mellow gold, or he might have looked still more like an antique half-god. None the less, his eyes, which were full and brown, had an expression of tired but unrelenting anger.

'They told you,' he said, 'what happened to me?'

'Yes. I'm very sorry!'

'Better now than later! At least I know where I stand now. It would have come to the same in the end. As other people will discover,' he said, his voice burning.

'Lubov is trying to get the decision reversed,' she reminded him eagerly, folding her fingers more closely and comfortably about his. 'You know he'll do everything he can.'

'He's wasting his time, and if he expects me to come and put ashes on my head, he's wasting more than that. I told him so, but that won't stop him. Oh, don't think me utterly ungrateful,' he burst out, meeting her unreproachful but perplexed eyes, 'I know I owe him more than I can ever pay back, and you must know how much difference it makes, just to know there's someone who has the guts to stand up and speak for you. But I don't want to damn anyone else. I'm finished, I don't want to drag anyone else down with me.'

'But, Yuri, you're not being fair to them! You're like the people in England who've just written off this country, the people who go round saying no one can get a visa now, when they've never asked for one. You can't say the Dean and the Rector will do nothing for you, unless you give them the chance.'

'You even talk like Lubov,' said Yuri, marvelling, and his fine eyes lingered upon her for an instant with something very near to dislike. Then he shook his head, and frowned the illusion away impatiently. 'You don't understand, Emmy! How could you? You're English, and in England this simply couldn't happen, how can you possibly appreciate what it is? Look, don't expect reason, or justice, or human values to hold good any more! That's over! This isn't just a change of government, it's the end of democracy for us—it's Communism! It's no use thinking the quality of the arguments is going to change anything any more. You mustn't criticise! I did. That's all about it. I criticised, and I'm damned, Emmy! It was only a matter of how long they were going to take to get around to my case— everybody has his turn, nobody need think he's forgotten. I'm a wicked reactionary, Emmy, a traitor to the State. You know what happens to them!'

Here was another, it seemed, who had no doubts at all, who was done with doubts. His voice was level and fierce. He had been horribly hurt, but it was not through any faltering in utterance, or eye, or hand that she sensed it. If you are so utterly devoid of any respect for your opponent's integrity, she wondered, why should you be so bitterly wounded by his abuse?

Very carefully she said: 'I know I've no right to air any views on this business, Yuri, I'm a foreigner, and I've no knowledge of what's happened here, except what one can glean from the news reports—and you know how suspect they must be now. But since you're in this mess, what on earth can you have to lose by trying at least to make the best of what's left to you? No one expects you to humble yourself and ask for favours. Lubov won't do that, either, not for himself, not for you. If he can gain anything for you by the only means he'll use, honourable means, don't you see that it will be something gained for reason, and for all the others who're threatened like you? You'd do what you could to help him, wouldn't you?'

Yuri rocked her hand in his, and shook his beautiful head hopelessly, and sighed: 'You just don't understand! It doesn't arise. There's no possibility of his achieving anything.'

She wanted to press him further, but she could not bring herself to do so. Whether he was right or wrong, it needed more impudence than she possessed to urge her own views against his. She watched his clear profile with disquiet, and asked instead: 'What do you intend to do now?'

'I intend to get out,' said Yuri.

He heard the quick intake of her breath, and turned with a wild smile, his full lips curling. 'Why should that surprise you? What is there for me here? Do you know what it's been like for me all these weeks? Watched everywhere, in the college, in class, in the streets, everywhere eyes on me sliding away when I caught them. All my theses combed through, everything I said copied down for the security people to study—no freedom of movement, no freedom of speech, no soul to call my own, and now that they've decided to move, no more freedom even to read and study. That's what's going to happen to everybody who doesn't hand himself over entirely. Do you wonder what people do when they're thrown out of the university, like me? They do two years in the army first, because they're no longer deferred, and then they go into jobs they're directed into—labourers' jobs in road gangs or on building sites, or, if they're lucky, in the mines. *And*, of course, they're still marked men there, too. They're marked for life. Once a reactionary, always a reactionary! You want me to make the best of *that*?'

She looked across the pond towards the woodland, remembering the almost violent directness and decision of his walk towards her. She asked: 'Do you think, then, that we are

87

being watched now?' Her voice was carefully empty of all suggestion of irony; she found his situation, whether it was as grim as he made it or not, too near to tragedy to wish to make any kind of capital out of his exaggerations. But that he could exaggerate was somehow a shattering shock, as though Achilles had signalised his imperfection by an ugly limp.

'I think it very likely,' he said with conviction.

'You don't mind involving me, then?'

He got up instantly. The movement was outraged, but she was not sure that his anger was not complicated by satisfaction at having in hand so easy and infallible a way of calling her to heel. 'I was given to understand that you were aware of the position before you sent Milo with your message. I'm sorry! If I'd realised you were in the dark about the danger of being seen with me, of course I wouldn't have come. I did arrange matters so that we could hardly be overhead, do me so much justice. I'll leave you now, before I do more damage.' He turned to plunge away from her, and for a moment she felt that he was sincere in his desire to withdraw now, with all the honours; but he checked so abruptly at the touch of her hand detaining him that she knew he had been relying on it.

'No, Yuri, don't go like that! I didn't mean to hurt you. You said yourself I couldn't be expected to understand. Help me to try, at least. Sit down again.'

He let her draw him down beside her. He was trembling a little now, so moved with his own passion that there were tears in his eyes. 'I am sorry! But you have to experience it before you can imagine how futile it is to ask all the usual questions: "What evidence have you that anyone's following you? How do you know the security police are watching you? How do you know everything you say is reported to them?" You can't understand, Emmy, how stupid it seems to us now to be asked all these things, as though the usual standards still applied.'

'I won't ask them,' she said very gently. 'I won't ask any of them, Yuri.'

She did not know why she found him suddenly so moving, now that he had dwindled a little from his singleness and maturity into an image Ilonna would have recognised readily. And, after all, he was right in this, that one can know, absolutely and irrevocably, truths for which little or no evidence exists. If he sweetened his desolation with occasional attitudes, that did not make his wrongs any the less.

'You see I have to go,' he said. 'There's no future for me here now, there never can be. I've got to get out of the country, Emmy, there's nothing for me here.'

She did not know how it had come about that she was suddenly so much the stronger of the two, but she acted as if she had no doubts about it, and was not aware of any

89

presumption. She shut her hand upon his, and drew him nearer to her, compelling him to look at her earnestly.

'Yuri, *don't do it*! It isn't that I don't think you'd be justified in looking elsewhere for a life, it's simply that I don't think you would find it. You haven't seen what happens to the uprooted, Yuri—I have. You think you could cross the frontier, and after, no doubt, some delay and some hardships find a place somewhere else, a place where you can make a life simply on your merits, doing the work you wanted to do here, using your own judgment, saying what you see to be true, not being owned by anyone. You want to be yourself, an individual. But do you think that's easy anywhere, with the world broken in two, and both halves putting pressures on people to conform? And do you think it's even possible once you've committed yourself by abandoning your own country? The act of crossing the frontier seems in itself to identify you with the other half. It's even harder then to resist the pressure to conform. Yuri, don't go! Stay and put up your fight here—this is the place for it.'

He set his handsome and stubborn mouth solemnly, and sat looking at her for a moment in silence; then he said: 'But in your half of the world it is at any rate still possible to state an unpopular view, and stay free.'

'Yes, it is, I know it is. I haven't said it isn't.

90

But there is a terrible temptation to earn your keep by behaving as your city of refuge wants you to behave. Yes, it *is* possible to keep your balance, even in those circumstances—but, Yuri, it doesn't happen. One man in a thousand has so much courage and honesty that he can still say: "No, you are wrong!" there as he said it here. He has to be a hero, Yuri.'

'And you are sure I am not a hero!' he said, with a sad but brilliant smile.

'No, but I am sure it is too much to demand of any man, that he should guarantee to be one.'

'I am going,' said Yuri inflexibly. 'Forgive me, and try to believe that I shall not lose my balance, nor sell myself body and soul to the other side, any more than I have here.'

He stood up, and with a hand beneath her arm drew her to her feet. 'It's getting cold here, you're shivering. Let's walk slowly through the woods this way, and I will put you on the tram at the gates. This is the quietest part of the park, and a man and a girl walking arm-in-arm along these paths will be something very ordinary, not worth looking at twice. If I am compromised, you know, you are English, we are well matched.'

She went with him silently, her arm in his. He had recovered his composure, but not his challenging assurance. He walked slowly, as though reluctant to reach the streets and part from her. Under the trees he looked down at her with shadowed eyes and tragic brows, and said again: 'I *am* going!' She thought he need not have made his assertion again if he had been really resolved, and from that moment she ceased to believe that he would ever accomplish his flight. In the deepest gloom of the trees, secure from observation, he stooped his head suddenly and kissed her cheek. She felt his long lashes flutter and blink against her temple, leaving upon the smooth, cold skin a colder dew.

*　　　*　　　*

When she took up Helena's muted chord, and began to sing a sad little folk-song from the eastern provinces, she felt what had been a friendly, attentive quietness turn into something strange and moving. A hush, positive and profound, settled upon the three hundred people in the room. Their bodies became still with a new stillness; they no longer avoided movement out of consideration for her and one another, they forgot they had the machinery of movement. Watching their faces as she sang, she saw all the conscious alertness relax out of them, saw every line soften, and all the eyes dilate as though in the dark. She saw the lips part and quiver, and the eyes grow vague and luminous with tears. Something single, intense and unbearably moving distilled moving distilled from their motionless faces, and filled the air.

She recognised, released here from its critical restraints, the same emotion she had felt two days previously, in the Musicians' Club. There her audience had been forewarned by a printed programme and armed with professional sensibilities, able and willing to criticise her pronunciation and performance, to distinguish between what was true folk-song and what was secondary Mozart, airs carried off from his city concerts, transmitted from singer to singer into country districts where not even his name was known, fitted out with spontaneous words, and assimilated into the music of the countryside. They had not been taken by surprise by a pretty compliment to their native airs from a visiting singer. And yet even there she had felt the mere civilised absence of sound become the intense, the translated silence, the positive gift offered and received.

The tool-makers of Wanda's factory had had no warning, nor did they wish to make any resistance. The hush which had laid a finger so secretly upon her senses at the concert now folded a hand closely about her heart, and held her as it held her audience, rapt into an anguish of joy. But her mind, recoiling, questioned and doubted in disquiet; the power to move people like this was something to which she knew she had no right; it belonged to great art, and she was most competently aware that her art was

93

limited, pure and minor, something to be happy about but not to mistake for the transcendent gift. No, what they were giving to her had not been earned by her voice.

There was a moment of absolute silence when she ended the song, and then they stirred and broke into movement again, and the applause came immoderately. The fixed faces flashed into animation, she saw them alight and glittering with pleasure. When she looked towards the corner where Wanda sat, with the young man Petr beside her, she found in their faces the same released and proprietary joy. Behind Wanda's shoulders Ilonna and Matyas smiled with a fond parental pride, sharing the credit for this prodigy who came from the West, now, when the West had turned its back on them, and who knew their songs, and cared enough for them to sing them. Emmy thought, as she had thought before in moments of revelation: these must be the most responsive people in the world; it is out of the question that anyone should make the least gesture of generosity towards them, and not be repaid for it ten times over.

The folded red drapings on either side of the dais of the recreation hall wavered slightly in the draught from a window; the gilt slogans along the white walls exclaimed complacently. The glassed-in shelves of the brand-new library, climbing from floor to ceiling at the other end of the room, paraded their glossy

94

virgin books proudly, and reflected the cluster of lights. Emmy had been shown round on arrival by a young man who had left his game of chess to display his treasures; he was the librarian, and he had led her joyfully from the solid unbound volumes of Marxist writing, through classic poetry, and drama, and criticism, to fiction, with meticulous explanations of the lending system and the rules of the centre. She saw him now, leaning against the pillar at the back of the hall, his long arms folded, his brown face eagerly smiling, waiting for her to go on singing.

She sang a song from this very district, a gay one, with a dry country joke in it, perfectly translatable into rural English. It made her laugh as she sang, and she felt their gratitude rising like a warm wave for even so trivial a thing as her appreciation of the point. And then a pastoral song from the foothills of the mountains, and a love-song about the eternally dividing river, Danube, Kysuca, Tyne, Yarrow, what difference did the name make? The themes of folk-songs, as universal as the changelings, and time-lapses, and talking animals of fairyland, crossed Europe without passport, and made their way through the width of the world, modulated only by the slight adaptations of later culture. And yet, she thought, they try to persuade us that there are fundamental differences between us, and we let them get away with it!

At the end of it she took Helena by the hand, and drew her to her feet to share in the ovation. By the dazed smile and the swimming eyes, here was one more creature who thought far too well of her. She was repelled by her own success; it could not be sustained like this, she had either to withdraw from under the weight of it or produce some prodigy to justify it. She felt her own inadequacy. She felt, too, the urgency of their need, since her very modest gift could be received with so much passionate gratitude.

Wanda embraced her as she came down from the dais. 'You see, I told you how it would be! Come and talk to everyone; look, they all want to speak to you!'

The young men and women of the factory came round her thick as bees, shaking her hand, patting her shoulders, asking eager questions: where had she learned to use the language so well, who had taught her the songs, how had she acquired so wide a collection of them, why had she fallen in love with the country in the first place, out of all the countries she might have chosen? This they asked most often and most ardently of all. Their excitement had communicated itself to her, she found her knees trembling now, and her heart racing, and was glad to sit down at one of the low tables, with Wanda and Petr like attendant angels on either side, and fence herself in with coffee and cakes. The rest of the

96

family had abandoned, for the moment, their rights in her. Beyond a circle of vociferous young people she caught an occasional glimpse of Lubov across the room, and once he caught her eye and gave her a small, understanding grimace and a quick flicker of his eyelids. Whenever she was in need of the reassurance of one other creature who understood fully all the implications of what was happening to her, she looked for Lubov; and his eyes were always quick to meet and comfort hers, as though he had reached out to take her hand in the darkness of the world's perplexity.

'It was so good of you to come,' Petr was saying, 'we are all so grateful.' It was not for her singing he was thanking her, it was just for existing and being present, for knowing and caring that this land had songs of its own, and people, and a history. For being involved in them, for being caught by the heart.

She understood the attraction this man might have for Wanda. He was perhaps twenty-six, her own age, burly and solid and serious, with the slight diffidence and the unwary modesty which would call forth all the protective fire of Wanda's nature. He had an artisan's hands, large, confident and kind, and the eyes of a surprised and elated boy, dazzled by his new luck, but sure of his ability to keep pace with it.

'I'm only sorry about the lack of transport,' he said anxiously. 'We have only a two-seater car here at the factory, but I thought that perhaps Dr Ivanescu could drive you back to town, and the rest of us will come along by tram. Then I can collect the car when I bring Wanda and her parents home.'

It was a matter of habit to protest that she could very well go by tram with the others, but she checked herself in time. Probably it would suit Petr admirably to be left to make a leisurely way back to town in company with Matyas and Ilonna, whom he seldom saw, and whom, if her guesses were near to the truth, he might very well wish to cultivate at every opportunity. So she said, smiling: 'That would be very kind, if it doesn't inconvenience you. I *am* a little tired.'

Leave-taking after so sudden and passionate an adoption was something of an ordeal. Every hand that intercepted her on her way to the door laid another small, perceptible weight of responsibility upon the load she was carrying away with her. Every valedictory smile pressed home the question of how this burden was to be borne without dishonesty and without weakening. She was glad that the hand at her arm as she walked was Lubov's. There was something about him so deflationary, she reflected with an inward smile, so destructive of all exaggerated attitudes, that the thought of having him beside her in the closed world of a two-seater car for the next twenty minutes was wonderfully calming. If he could be like that and continue to exist, in a world intent on forcing one into this posture or that, both equally deforming, then she could retain her natural shape, too; and a close study of his methods might be helpful.

They went out into the factory yard, a rectangle of concrete brightened by narrow flower-beds, contained by matt white walls pierced regularly with tall windows. Petr brought the car round for her, and a score or more of the young people from the recreation hall streamed out to see her off, linked in twos and threes, chattering and singing. When Lubov got in beside her and started the engine, they closed in about the car, smiling in upon her, and as the car drew slowly away they followed it for a little way, waving and calling their good-byes. The factory buildings withdrew, gathering themselves into their austere grouping, white, angular and sharply outlined in the starlight. She waved until they had disappeared, and then relaxed with a long sigh against Lubov's shoulder.

'I hope you don't mind,' said Lubov, watching the curving drive unwind before them, 'this was my idea. Petr would have brought you home himself, but I thought if he constituted himself escort to the parents it would give him time to break whatever ice there is.'

'You're sure,' said Emmy, 'that there's something serious brewing there?'

'Not sure, but I think it likely. Do you think he'll do for her?' he asked with an affectionate smile.

'I liked him. I should think he very well might.'

They were clear of the gates, and turning into the concrete road. The quietness and stillness seemed to Emmy extreme for ten o'clock in the evening. Even the city kept early hours, and this remote, bleached white suburb, modern and spacious, its front windows all chromium and plate glass, its back windows looking across fresh plough-land into farm-yards, was already dauntingly asleep, even its breathing hushed. The starlight, softer and stranger than the heavy pallor of the moon, unrolled before them in dim silver along the roadway.

She let her cheek rest against Lubov's shoulder, watching through the smudged windscreen the unpeopled pavements sliding by. 'That was an incredible experience,' she said in a low voice.

Lubov looked down at her briefly, and she was aware of the solemn gentleness of his regard, though she did not raise her eyes to return the look.

'Yes, it must have been. You understood what happened?'

'Yes, I understood.' She did not elaborate; he must take her word for it. She pressed her cheek more closely into the rough cloth of his

100

coat, and lay trembling in reaction, weary with perplexity rather than physical fatigue. 'I suppose it's liable to go on happening?'

'Wherever you sing a local song, or try to say a few words of acknowledgement in our language. You'd better get used to it, Emmy.'

'I don't know how to set about getting used to it. I don't know that I can stand it. It might be better to stick to Mozart and English. Or go back to England,' she said, her voice sharp with protest.

'Why, did you find something morbid in it? Something bogus? I'm sure you didn't; there was nothing like that to find.'

'Nothing in them, no. But you know as well as I do that I had no right to a reception like that. I got it on false pretences.'

'You think so? Then, tell me, from which side do you think that outburst came—from the enthusiastic Communists, or the disgruntled reactionaries? Oh yes, you can be sure they've got both among their staff—who hasn't?'

'I think it probably came from both,' she said, marvelling at the extent of her knowledge.

'Then do you think both sides were laying claim to you? Do you think the enthusiasts loved you because they thought you were heart and soul on their side? And do you suppose the discontented understood you to be bringing them a message of encouragement from the West—a promise of liberation?'

101

'No, nothing of the sort ever occurred to any of them. It might,' she owned, 'later on when they think it over, but it certainly didn't while I was singing. I don't believe a soul in the room had a political thought in his head.'

'Of course not!' said Lubov gently. 'What they saw in you was a woman who has come here from the West, at a time when the West has drawn away even its skirts from touching us. A woman who has listened to our songs and felt warmly enough towards them to want to learn and sing them, who has found us attractive enough to want to make friends and stay friends with us. One who, if she has noticed that her own countrymen have written us off as damned, has not therefore assumed that she's bound to do the same.'

'But, good God!' she protested, 'you can't be worshipped for something as small and simple as that—just for sticking to your friends!'

'Sometimes it takes a lot of guts to claim friendship, and a lot of tenacity to sustain it. If you'd just come, and sung, they'd have liked you, because even that takes courage when it's become the thing not to do. But that might have been political perversity, or benevolent curiosity, or just plain cussedness. But when you begin to sing their own traditional songs, Emmy, and then go on to show that you haven't just learned one for a show-piece, but know half a dozen of them, and know what they mean, too, and have a feeling for the

102

language—no, that couldn't be curiosity, that could only be love. Emmy, you can't love my people without being loved back. It's the way they're made.'

'But they love back too intensely,' she said, her voice almost inaudibly low.

'Ah, that's only because they're a little hungrier than usual for what you brought them. If you think they overrated it, look round and see how little of it there is about— love from the West. Political affection, yes, heaps of it, facing this way, facing that way. But not much ordinary, straightforward love, Emmy, my darling!' He inclined his head to hers for a moment, caressing her with cheek and chin, and as suddenly drew back from touching. She was used to the hearty embraces of meeting and separating, in which her part was that of a sister, entirely accepted, entirely trusted, but this was something so different that it filled her with charmed astonishment. Motionless against his shoulder, she recovered within her senses the swift, smooth warmth of his chin upon her forehead, the swoop of his cheek against her hair, experiences so tiny and ephemeral that it seemed foolish to suppose they had changed anything, however persuasive was the sensation of change.

'There could have been more if your people had wanted it. There are other people,' she said, listening to her own voice as to the arguments, just but distant, of a stranger, 'plenty of other people in England who have wanted to come, and haven't been so fortunate as I was. I proved it wasn't impossible to get a visa, but others have proved it isn't easy.'

'Yes, I know, and we won't forget them. But when they've been added in, is the number who care about us really very high?'

She looked up at his profile, which was fixed and mild against the faint light of the window, flickering with passing shapes of brightness and shadow.

'No—I suppose there aren't many of us. I might well have looked to Wanda's friends like the only survivor.'

Lubov said, staring straight ahead along the white ribbon of road: 'You're not going to refuse what they offered you, are you?'

'You know I can't. All I want to know is how to carry it and have my honesty, too.'

They were coming into the city already, she saw the lights rippling along the river, and the coronal of lamps climbing the Citadel hill. They turned left to cross the Sentinel's Bridge, and began to thread the leafy traverses of the Lucerna.

'I am not afraid,' said Lubov, 'that you'll fail to find a way.'

She felt the subject being folded and put away, in his heart, in hers, not to be shown to anyone else, not even the family.

'Poor old Milo!' said Lubov, as they turned into their own street. 'I suppose he's still sweating at those political economy papers. I told you he's taking his classes dead seriously now. Nothing less than a life-and-death matter would have kept him from coming with us tonight to show you off. Milo is a classic example of the national genius for loving people back. Hating people back, too, for that matter, if that's what they offer. Every emotion is a little large, a little fiercer than life-size for us. It makes it even more difficult to keep one's balance—and even more essential.' He pulled up in front of the open door of the house, and turned and gave her a teasing smile, as though he wanted to make it easy for her to believe he had all along been speaking lightly. But his eyes remained grave, and it seemed to her that his cheeks had a higher colour than was usual with him. 'I'm going to put the car in the court, to give the boy an excuse for lingering, and Wanda an excuse for asking him in. Go on up to Milo, won't you? I'll follow you in a few minutes.'

'We're early,' said Emmy, 'he won't be expecting us for half an hour yet.' She got out of the car, gathering up handbag and gloves, and looked along the street towards the enormous double doors which led to the interior court. The house was old, late eighteenth century, with some of the monumental features of the palace period still upon it. 'Shall I open the doors for you? Then you can drive straight in.'

Lubov laughed. 'You couldn't—I shouldn't like to tell you how much they weigh. But it's all right, they'll be open. The housekeeper closes them and locks up at eleven. I'll do the job for him tonight if the others are late—he won't mind. You go on up, and I'll come in by the back way from the court.'

He drove on, accelerating briskly, as she climbed the steps to the open doorway of the house. The vestibule was in darkness, and its marble chill made her shiver as she entered, her hand reaching out for the minute-light she had located so accurately five nights ago. Just as her finger rested on the button she heard Lubov slow down for the turn into the cobbled alley to the courtyard, and then the sound of his engine was muffled by the bulk of stonework between them.

The light sprang up. In the cold, pale nakedness of the polished stone hall she saw Miloslav and Yuri Dushek staring at her from the staircase.

They were a few steps below the last turn of the stairs, and by the way they were braced back and half turned away from her she thought that they had intended to retreat, but given up the idea because there was manifestly no time for them to get out of sight. Their eyes, which had flared wide and wild in the first instant, narrowed and blinked in the sudden brightness, but remained fixed on her; and when they had recovered themselves they

106

relaxed their tense grip upon the iron rail of the staircase, and came down to her, Miloslav in the lead. He was wearing a light raincoat over his overcoat, which seemed to her a curious thing to do on a fine, dry night. Moreover, this raincoat was large for him, even with this extra bulk to fill its shoulders; it was nearer Yuri's size than Miloslav's. And she could not remember ever seeing him in a hat before. It was curious how she was seeing more detail in this one dazzling instant than she had noticed in three years of knowing him. The brief-case, for instance, which he clutched under his arm was not his brief-case; she could not remember ever having paid much attention to his, but she knew that this shabby black one, coming unstitched at one corner, was not the one he habitually carried.

'I didn't expect you back yet, Emmy. Yuri came in to see me,' said Miloslav, in a tone faintly challenging but extremely determined. 'I'm just going to walk back to the college with him. Tell the others, please, and say I shan't be long.'

She stood looking at him searchingly, and he stared back at her with his head up and the light full on his face. His blue eyes were large and anxious, but as steady as stone. She looked from him to Yuri, who was gazing at her warily over his friend's shoulder. That was certainly a brand-new coat Yuri was wearing, he had never affected the dark-brown frieze before.

107

He had a soft felt hat with a drooping brim
which shadowed his forehead and obscured the
pure line of his brow and nose; and a brown
scarf wound high round his neck, blurring its
haughty carriage. The brief-case he carried was
cheap and not new, but she thought it was new
to him by the way he grasped it. It was not, like
Miloslav's, thin; it bulged to the limit of its
straps. 'The new Yuri!' she thought, admiring
its anonymity.

'Lubov brought me back by car,' she said
deliberately. 'He's just driven round into the
court. The others are following by tram.'

It was said without emphasis, and noted
without alarm, but Miloslav understood all its
implications. 'I didn't expect you back yet,' he
repeated.

'I know you didn't.' She looked significantly
into the shadows beyond the staircase, where
the courtyard door lay. 'You'd better hurry.
They lock up the hostel at eleven, don't they?'

'Yes, we must go. Tell Lubov where I am—
and the others if they're back before me; but I
shall only be about twenty minutes, I expect.'

No one said anything about the dark
vestibule, and the two young men feeling their
rapid and quiet way downstairs without lights.
They offered each other, with reserved but
unquestioning eyes, the civilised fiction that
everything was normal.

'I'll tell them,' she said. 'Good-night, Yuri!'

They were already in the doorway when the

minute-light, reaching the end of its fixed and niggardly life, went out. From the darkness, as he slipped away into the street, Yuri said: 'Good-bye!'

* * *

All the way up the four flights of stairs she was advising herself insistently: 'I must tell Lubov!' But she did not tell him. When he rejoined her at the door of the flat, astonished to find her waiting there to be let in, she gave him Miloslav's message word for word, and explained that she had quite forgotten that there would now be no one to open the door to her, and evidently Miloslav had forgotten it, too, in his haste. She did not mention the hat and coat and briefcase which were not Miloslav's, for she was quite sure he would come home without them, nor the new and nondescript clothing within which Yuri had chosen to conceal his brightness, nor the furtive manner of their exit. She would have put her own life into Lubov's hands cheerfully, but this plan, whatever it might be, was none of hers to give or share. There was also, perhaps, another motive for silence and abstention. The less Lubov knew, the less the weight upon him. He was carrying, Wanda had said, enough lame dogs already.

Miloslav came in with the rest of the family, when they brought Petr home with them half

109

an hour later. Either he had been lucky enough to fall in with them by chance, or else he had lain in wait for them, to make his own return inconspicuous, and close questioning impossible. He was as she had known he would be, his dark overcoat open, his hands empty, his head uncovered. He came in flushed and laughing, and his gaiety was understandable and genuine. Some people glittered like that when they had successfully evaded action, but Miloslav when he had acted; or laughed like that when they had kept a threatened line of retreat open, but Miloslav when he had burned his boats. He did not avoid her eyes, but met them with blazing candour; and the moments when he was utterly serious were the moments when they were looking at each other. And yet he encountered the casual questions which did come his way with round and large-eyed lies.

'Why didn't you get Yuri to stay a little longer?' Ilonna asked him reproachfully. 'We'd have loved to see him again, he knows that.'

'Yes, of course, but he hadn't got a pass. And, you know, he doesn't want to pile up any more black marks, even if he has got to leave his room in any case. So he had to be in by eleven.'

'Did you walk all the way back with him?'

'Well, nearly. I left him at the corner of the park. He had to run, it was nearly time.'

'Oh well, I expect he's all right. But, darling,

do get him to come and spend an evening with us again. I do think he needs to be taken out of himself a little, poor boy. Ask him tomorrow, if you see him.'

'I don't think I shall,' said Miloslav. He did not flinch from this misleading truth, but Emmy thought that he looked at it, as soon as he had said it, with some distaste and even distress. He added firmly: 'I might the next day, though; I'll have a go at him then if I do.'

He had become wary of his mother, and until Petr left them he attached himself to the newcomer and was particularly charming to him, for what could be more helpful to him just now than a stranger in the house? Assiduous in good works, he went down to the courtyard with Petr when he departed, switched on the gateway light for him, and locked up after the car had gone. Returning, he met Emmy in the tiny hall of the flat, in her dressing-gown, and hunting along the rods of the family wardrobe for a spare hanger. Tired from the triumph of the evening, they were already drifting towards their beds.

Emmy turned when the boy came in. He was not laughing now, the lids were heavy over his blue eyes, and his mouth was anxious, and for a moment almost irresolute. He came and threw his arms round her, pressing his face, all cold from the outer air, into the warm hollow of her neck. The vehemence of his embrace was the only sign of strain he gave. She thought for a

111

moment that he was going to pour out thankfully into her lap the confidences she had earned by keeping his secrets; she was sure he would have liked to do so. But he only loosened his clinging arms from her at last with a sigh, and kissed her, softening his silence by a special and dutiful tenderness. 'Not bribing me,' she thought ruefully, 'just paying his debts!'

'Emmy—'

'Yes, Milo?'

'Oh—nothing! Good-night, Emmy!'

His arms, and the pressure of his hard, impulsive young body, had been more articulate. She watched him go from her into the living-room, his head drooping a little now, not with the weight of what he had done, but with the foretaste of loneliness. From the big bedroom where Wanda talked happily of Petr Kasel, she heard Miloslav moving desultorily about the making of his bed. She knew that he was thinking of Yuri; and after a while, when the strain of following his movements no longer distracted her attention, and all was quiet, she could feel in her heart the aching lack which was beginning to gnaw at his, the pain of the place in his life where Yuri Dushek had been.

*   *   *

Emmy spent the next afternoon at the

Musicians' Club, going through her programme for the Mozarteum concert with Helena, and listening to a piano recital in the concert-room there. The pianist was the holder of one of the new State scholarships in music, a young man from a mining district, whose thick brown hands, blue-stained with several little coal scars, drew from his instrument without apparent effort the most molten and delicate of sounds, distilling into the charged air all the fire and fantasy and nervous, stylish arrogance of Chopin. When Marvan carried her off to drink wine with him in a cellar near the embankment, she went with her mind full of music, and her heart full of a pleased speculation; for if they had performed many beneficent miracles like this one, she could not believe that they could be on a wrong course.

Mist was coming up from the river when they emerged into the early evening air once again. The soft and constant roar of the weirs, so close to them, caused the riverside wall of stone to vibrate, for one side of the wine-house was built out on piers above the dark water. They looked over the wall towards the bridge above them, and the furry green of the island opposite, growing near to black in the dusk. Lights came out along the embankment, and their images quivered in the olive-green surface of the water until the glow from the tenth light shattered in splinters of gold at the edge of the fall. The streets were full of office-workers

113

rushing homeward, and the tram she boarded at the bridge was already bulging with people. Like an old hand she squeezed herself into the corner behind the unused driving gear in the second car, so that the struggle to get out at the top of the Lucerna hill should be only a short one. To go right inside one of the cars at this hour was to spend five minutes and miss one stop in fighting one's way out.

She was a little afraid of the rickety old lift at Number Seventeen; after all, she decided, she used it without hesitation only when one of the family was present to put her on her mettle. This time she walked up, and let herself into the flat with the latch-key Wanda had insisted on giving to her last night, when she had heard how Miloslav had gone off with Yuri and left Emmy to wait on the mat. Milo, scolded for his thoughtlessness, had been as wildly penitent as even Wanda could desire. Small defections agonised them. Large and painful compressions, like the loss of the lacquer works, they took in their stride with a shrug and a sigh, and went on.

Coming into the welcoming warmth of the living-room, she found the table already laid for supper, and Ilonna trotting backwards and forwards from the kitchen with the final touches. 'Am I the last?' she said, and looked round to count them. Wanda was bringing in the soup, Matyas was reading, without much respect, the headlines of the evening paper,

114

Miloslav was sitting over an array of Spanish books at his desk in a corner of the room, and bending his head into his hands with an unusual desperation of concentration, which she thought might have more than one motive behind it. 'Isn't Lubov home yet?'

At that they all looked up, even Miloslav turning a sidelong glance upon her in the shadow of his sheltering hand; and as though they were disconcerted by the unanimity of their response, as resolutely went back to what they were doing. Ilonna said: 'No, he's a little later than he said he'd be, but he'll be along just now. We won't keep supper waiting for him.'

People should not, it seemed, be later than they have said they'll be, Emmy thought, watching them gather composedly to the table. Last year Lubov or any of the others could run into an unexpected friend and stay out until all hours, and no one began to imagine disaster. Now they sigh with relief when Miloslav at last comes in from the Faculty, and begin to watch the clock when Lubov is an hour behind his time. The crack in the surface of normality is not very wide, hardly noticeable unless someone points it out, but it seems it's wide enough for uneasiness to get in. Not fear, nothing so large could negotiate it; just uneasiness, the feeling that there may be something wrong somewhere, for someone.

They did not wonder aloud, even when they had finished supper and cleared the table but

115

for Lubov's still-vacant place; to wonder aloud was to begin something which might lead them too far for comfort. But when Lubov's key clashed in the lock at last, just after nine o'clock, they all subsided into instant stillness, seized and verified the sound, and perceptibly relaxed, taking up their interrupted movements with an eased certainty. Ilonna went out into the hall to take his coat from him, and kissed him briskly. Through the open door they heard her voice saying roundly:

'About time, too! We've eaten all the supper. Whatever kept you until now? You haven't been at the Faculty all this time?'

'Yes, I have. I'm sorry to be so late, but I couldn't come away before, really.'

He sounded much as usual, perhaps rather over-tired, but not otherwise changed; yet Miloslav, watching the doorway through his fingers, charged the air with such fevered anxiety that Emmy wondered none of them turned to stare at him rather than at Lubov. None of them, however, had her reasons for divining his uneasiness; for them, Lubov's lateness had, as yet, no connection with Miloslav, and perhaps it really had none, and her foreboding spirit had merely caught the infection of the time, and begun to knot coincidences together with unjustified neatness. She watched the boy gnawing his knuckles, and wondered if the sickness of the world had not begun to seep through even these inviolable walls.

Lubov came in and dropped his brief-case into the cushions of the couch. Ilonna, close at his shoulder, closed the door and stood looking at him with a carefully neutral face, not going to meet trouble, not pretending that it held no warrant to come in with her sons as freely as with any other woman's.

Matyas took in the weary calm of Lubov's face in a long, shrewd look, and asked: 'What kept you?'

'The police,' said Lubov simply. 'They've been at the university for the last three hours, and none of us could leave until they'd seen us.'

They were all looking at him now, their eyes quickening into wariness but not yet into alarm. Once the position was stated, and its implications for him understood, they would all step back into the proven processes of their day as though nothing had happened, but for this moment they consented to halt and wait, acknowledging the assault of new realities which would have to be accommodated. Even Miloslav uncovered his face, looking round incautiously from his desk, and flinching from too direct encounter with Lubov's inconveniently perceptive glance.

'Yuri's disappeared,' said Lubov. He dropped the words, she thought, as lightly as he could into the expectant silence, but they fell like stones. 'They think he's heading for the frontier into Austria—if he hasn't crossed

117

it already.'

Matyas said: 'No! Not Yuri! My God, what possessed him to do a thing like that?'

'It must be a mistake,' protested Ilonna. 'He was here with Milo last night. Why, Milo saw him back to his college just before we came home!'

'Well, he can't be found today. It seems the porter at the hostel saw him come dashing in at the last minute last night, but no one's seen him today. He said yesterday that he was going out this morning to look at a room he'd been offered, somewhere in Ledva. Everybody took it for granted that was what he'd done— no one's been noticing his movements particularly, why should they? But he's nowhere to be found now; everybody's been looking for him since three o'clock this afternoon.'

Miloslav asked from his corner, in a precariously sensible tone, as though he felt himself to be walking on very thin ice: 'But just because he hasn't been back to his college today, why on earth should they conclude he's run away? He can stay out until eleven if he likes, without a late pass. Why the panic in the afternoon? He hasn't got any classes any longer, how could he possibly know people would be looking for him?'

He did not look at Emmy, but she knew what he was thinking as clearly as if he had turned and taken her into his confidence with one anxious flash of his eyes. He had been relying on the conditions he had mentioned to give Yuri a longer start than this. With moderate luck he should not even have been missed until eleven o'clock, and the porter might well have given him another night's grace before his absence was actually reported. Instead, it seemed they had been looking for him for several hours already.

Lubov agreed sombrely: 'He may easily walk in as they lock up for the night, and ask what on earth all the fuss is about. But that isn't what the police think. You're right, of course: no one would have thought of looking for him if we hadn't telephoned the college to ask for him.' He was looking steadily at Miloslav across the room, and, under the weight of those searching eyes, a distressing red began to mount in Miloslav's cheeks. 'The Dean sent for him,' said Lubov. 'I've been trying to get them to take him back into his class. They wouldn't do that, but they did promise to try and get him into a job where he wouldn't be wasted. I didn't say anything to him about it, because I didn't want to raise his hopes until I was sure something was going to come of it. His languages are something they couldn't afford to throw away. They were going to offer him a job under the Ministry of Overseas Trade.'

Miloslav had nothing to say. The red had ebbed again from his cheeks, leaving him paler than normal. He was twisting a pencil nervously in his fingers, and as the shock of this last irony went deeply into his mind his hands tightened abruptly and the wood snapped, splintering with a small, cruel sound. They had made kindly haste to send Yuri good news, and started the hunt after him. Miloslav frowned down at the broken pencil in his hands, and saw whole complications of breakages, all equally pointless. And yet even if Yuri had known that they'd successfully moved earth for him, if not heaven, would he have changed his mind?

'That's why the call went out for him,' said Lubov. 'He wasn't in his room. His key was in the door on the inside, as though he'd gone out and forgotten, or simply not bothered, to lock up. So they rang up the woman who was supposed to be going to let him a room, and he hadn't been there. They tried all the places they could think of, and nobody'd seen him. After they'd been trying for a couple of hours to locate him for us, it began to look to them as if he'd vanished rather too completely for it to be any accident. So they had a more thorough look round his room. All his things were there, as far as they could see, even his hat and overcoat. His letters were still in his pigeon-hole in the hall. I think that's what they liked least. If he left before the post came, he left much too early to be going room-hunting. So they told the police all about it. And after that, it wasn't for us they were trying to find him.'

Matyas looked from his elder to his younger son, and observed with exact impartiality the quality of the fixed look which was passing between them. He asked quietly: 'They don't think any of you people at the university could have known anything about his going, do they? It was through you they began to look for him.'

'That helps,' agreed Lubov with a faint smile. 'But of course it doesn't write us off altogether. Though naturally they must see that if we'd smuggled him out and were trying to cover up our part in the job by raising the hue and cry ourselves, we should hardly have started it quite so early. No, they're simply making all the routine enquiries. It's hardly begun yet.'

That direct warning was for Miloslav, thought Emmy. And now they were all looking at him; he turned away to his desk again, but even with his back turned he could feel the long, speculative, unquiet glances scalding him, causing his very forehead to burn. He flattened his Spanish grammar open with a hand which was trembling slightly, and lowered his eyes obstinately to a page which he surely could not see.

Wanda said, in a tone arduously level and reasonable: 'You *did* see him back to the college last night, didn't you, Milo?'

'You've got better evidence than mine,' said Miloslav, with surprising firmness, but without

121

looking up. 'The porter saw him come in according to Lubov.'

'Miloslav,' said Matyas, 'are you sure you don't know anything about this?'

The tone demanded some show of attention from him. He turned upon them all a face now under complete control, closed and resolute and resignedly gentle. 'How can I possibly know anything about it? I can tell you where I've been every moment of today, and there must be dozens of witnesses who can bear me out. I had two lectures this morning, and I came straight home after them, and Mummy can tell you I've been working ever since, apart from running a couple of errands for her just down the street here. I haven't been near the college, and I haven't set eyes on Yuri. The first I'd heard of this hunt was just now, when Lubov came in and told us.'

The closing circle of eyes, mildly measuring him, asserted disbelief, but only Wanda gave words to it.

'I don't believe you,' she said abruptly, advancing upon him a few steps in concern and exasperation. 'You were always in all his secrets, he wouldn't leave you out of this. If he didn't need you to help him, he'd have to have you to admire him and worry about him. I believe you know all about it, you damned little idiot!'

'I tell you,' said Miloslav, raising to her a face already hardening into conscious

122

resistance, 'I haven't set eyes on Yuri today, I haven't had any message from him, I haven't done or said anything I couldn't go and tell to the entire police department. Are you calling me a liar?'

She brushed this provocation aside with an impatient toss of her black hair. 'You're trying to start a fight that will give you an excuse to march out of here, but it won't do. If you're telling the truth, it's a carefully selected truth. You'd better tell the rest of it. If you've been fool enough to get yourself involved in Yuri's mess we'd much better know the facts.' She stood before him, her beautiful mouth set, her outraged eyes fiercely intent, ready to rearrange his life for him, ready to salvage him from Yuri's wreck at the cost of her own reputation, if need be, and already despairingly aware that he would never let her have the satisfaction of translating her love into action.

'So that you can go and do your duty by the State?' said Miloslav unkindly. 'You're dying to shepherd me through penitence into reformation, aren't you? A sharp lesson now, and I might make a nice, tame little comrade yet!'

She drew in her breath as if he had hit her, and then, flaming into indignation, raised her hand as if she felt, but could not quite indulge, a passionate desire to hit him. Not so long ago she would have done it, and suffered no obscure agonies over the lapse, but nothing so

123

obvious could meet this case. She stood staring at him silently, her eyes dilated with angry sadness; and it was Lubov who said sharply: 'Don't be a fool, Milo! You know you don't believe that.'

'How do I know what to believe about her? She seems to care a lot more for her precious party than she does for anything else; why shouldn't she want to acquire merit? It's her *duty* to go and tell the police she's convinced her misguided little brother helped Yuri Dushek to make an illegal exit from the country. It's her duty to *me* as well as to the party. People who're on the wrong road, like me, have to be saved from themselves.'

Matyas said peremptorily: 'That's more than enough, Milo! Now be quiet!' And to Wanda, more gently: 'Let him alone, girl! If he says he hasn't seen Yuri, take his word for it. I don't know that he's ever given you reason not to.'

She hesitated for a moment, looking down at her brother through the mist of her painful anger, while he gazed back at her unhappily but defiantly, fending her off from any further hostilities as effectively as from reconciliation. After wavering for a long minute she shrugged suddenly, and turned and swung away into the kitchen, where they heard her moving about violently among the pots, to emerge at length with Lubov's soup. The incident was over, not because it had been resolved, but because in

124

some secret agreement the family had compounded to carry it no further. Wanda was perhaps quickest of all to sense when they were approaching the point of danger; she would have withdrawn from the too damaging contact even if Matyas had not so clearly warned her back to safer ground. Now she came to the table as though nothing had happened at all, and served Lubov's soup. There was a strong strain of Ilonna in her daughter; it would always come out in a crisis.

Lubov was a well-trained Ivanescu, too; he moved obediently to take his place, but then, visibly refusing to turn back from the cold, final ground which the others had relinquished, he suddenly walked across the room to Miloslav and, looking down into the shadowed blue eyes which were lifted to him so reluctantly, he asked with a severe and deliberate mildness: '*Did* you have a hand in Yuri's going, Milo?'

Miloslav began patiently and obliquely: 'Look, I told you, I haven't seen him or heard from him since—'

Lubov took hold of his brother's blond forelock, not at all gently, and tilted his head back. 'Yes or no, Milo—*did* you?'

The face and the eyes came out of shadow thus, held to the light, and looked squarely back at him at last. Emmy saw Miloslav emerge from his defensive stiffness, and relax into serenity. He gazed up at Lubov with

125

affectionate impudence, and smiled, and uttered a fine, round, confident 'No!' as magnanimously as though he were giving them all a splendid present.

There was no more to be said after that finality. Lubov paid him for the smile in kind, and for the lie with a twist and a tug at the thick locks he was grasping, and abandoned him, sitting down resignedly to his supper.

But it could not end there; they were too much disturbed at the implications of the news to let it rest so easily. Questions and surmises came from them at intervals, without their will, and Miloslav, bent over his books again with long eyelashes sweeping his cheeks, listened and contributed not a word more. Ilonna was the worst, because she did not ask directly, but only wondered distressfully where Yuri was tonight, and if he had somewhere to sleep, and if his clothes were warm enough, and whether he had any money. Miloslav was sick with wondering the same things. And it might go on for days before he could feel reasonably sure that the escape had succeeded, for even if Yuri got caught at the frontier the news would not be allowed to leak out until it suited the authorities to release it. Not until Yuri found some way of smuggling a message back to him would his mind really be at rest. He found it fantastic and distasteful that such a melodrama should somehow have evolved out of the substantial and continuing normality of their lives. His sense of fitness was outraged; the situation had not justified this. But Yuri would go!

He wanted very much to talk to Emmy, and there was no chance until she cleared away Lubov's dishes and went off into the kitchen with them. Then he got up and followed her, closing the door carefully behind him. She looked round from the sink, and smiled at him, and then, as he stood frowning down into the suds and hesitated for the right words, put a tea-cloth into his hands. She had a daughter's privileges here, and a sister's too. He gave her one brief, troubled smile, and began meekly to dry cutlery.

'You're not angry with me? About last night?'

'No, why should I be? It's up to you what you do. But somebody should really have boxed your ears tonight for all those off-lies. Do you really think you've got the kind of family that can't be let into the secret when you feel you have to break a few laws?'

'They do know,' said Miloslav, raising his clear eyes from the spoons he was drying. 'Surely you could tell that! And they know I know they know. But if I admitted anything, then what they know would be evidence, and as it is, they haven't got any evidence. I'm not going to unload my responsibilities on to them. But it isn't that I don't trust them, you know it isn't.'

'And that holds good for Wanda, as well as the others?'

Miloslav flushed a little, and said almost stiffly: 'Yes, of course.'

'All right, don't scowl at me! If you like to tell *me*,' she said simply, 'it can't do any harm. I've already got the evidence, so in any case I've got to lie. A few more lies, if the occasion arises, won't make much difference.'

'You're so *sensible*!' said Miloslav, heaving a great sigh of relief and appreciation. 'I knew you would be! Yuri said you'd tell Lubov exactly what you'd seen the minute we were off the premises. Oh, we knew you hadn't missed anything, you may be sure! I *told* him you wouldn't. He said you didn't feel as he does about things here, so we couldn't blame you if you felt you had to try and stop us. But I knew that whether you approved or disapproved of him was beside the point.'

She took her hands out of the hot water, and stood looking at him closely for a moment, her fair head on one side, her grey eyes thoughtful. 'What made you so sure of that? Was it because approval or disapproval had no bearing on your own attitude?'

'Well, of course I could hardly have helped him if I'd thought it actually wrong, could I? I tried to make him change his mind,' owned Miloslav, feeling his way painfully along his own personal tight-rope. 'I thought there was no sense of proportion about it. He *has* been

128

badly treated, and it does make me angry to think of it. But to dig oneself up by the roots—! But he wouldn't be turned. And it was his life. I think he has a right to go to another country if he likes, and if a government seals people up inside its boundaries when they've done nothing bad enough to forfeit their rights, then I think they're free to use other methods to get where they want to be. It seems to me the contract's already been broken. So when he wouldn't change his mind I had to help him. He's my friend.'

'I tried to get him to change his mind, too,' she said, turning back to fish at the bottom of the sink for one more fork. 'Oh, yes, he told me he was going. I didn't really take him seriously, or I might have made a better job of it. But I don't think anyone could have persuaded him. It was you who checked in at the hostel for him, wasn't it?'

'Yes. He went straight from here to the station yard. Someone—I don't know who, I didn't ask—was going to take him nearly to the frontier on a night lorry. He should have been able to try the crossing this morning, before it was light, but if there was any hold-up he'd have to lie up until tonight, and try again. And now, if he did have to put it off until tonight, he won't have much chance. They'll be looking for him all along the line.'

She had a momentary vision of Yuri in custody, beautiful, persecuted, exalted, so wrapped in the detail of his own drama that the very fervour of his silence about this partner of his might speak only too eloquently. She knew that it was not of this possibility that Miloslav was thinking.

'It's too early to dwell on that,' she said firmly, 'or too late. He may be clear of the frontier and miles away. How did you manage the porter at the hostel?'

'I waited until the last minute, and then made a wild dash in and across the hall to the key-board, as anyone naturally would if he'd only just beaten the rounds. The porter was in his office, he looked through the window, and saw me just grabbing the key, so all he got was a back view, and he knew the clothes. I muttered good-night, and rushed on and into Yuri's room, and put away everything, brief-case and books and clothes, in a devil of a hurry, because I had to get out again at once.'

'How did you manage that part? I should have thought getting downstairs again might have been far too risky. He'd just be locking up and making the rounds.'

'Oh, but, you see, Yuri's room is on the ground floor. If it hadn't been, we'd have had to work it some other way, and maybe we couldn't have got a night's grace. No, I just went out through the back door into the court as he was locking up at the front. The doors on the court he always locks up last. We had it all worked out. All I was afraid of was that someone else might dash in just at the last minute, too, and run full tilt into me, but nobody did. So it was easy.' He added, slanting a bright blue glance at her from under his lashes: 'I was sorry it made me miss your evening at the tool factory; that was what I really regretted.'

'You don't have to sweeten me,' said Emmy. 'I've known you too long to be fooled.' But she smiled at him. 'You don't regret the rest of it?'

He thought it over honestly as he hung up the coffee-cups, and said at length: 'No. It may not turn out well, but they broke the rules first. I'm sorry he went—but I think that's for my own sake, really, not his. At least, it's so much for my own sake that I daren't take too much notice of it.'

They had finished, and no one had interrupted them to take the job away from Emmy. She realised that it was by the family's silent consent that she had enjoyed this interlude; solitude was rare enough in a family flat to make an agreeable gift. She sat down on the edge of the table, and he came and stood before her, his eyes very serious but remarkably tranquil. She took him by the wrists and drew him closer.

'What happens now, Milo? What happens if they question you too?'

'We could hardly blame them, could we?' said Miloslav reasonably. 'After all, I suppose I must have connived at breaking two or three

131

laws. Fair's fair! But of course I shall lie like a fiend. I don't feel guilty about anything. Wanda thinks Yuri is a great reactionary, and will go straight and join up with our most violent enemies in the West, and do us as much damage as he can. But I don't. I think he just wants to be somewhere where he can study and write as he thinks fit, and he feels that he can't do that here any longer. I'm not even sure if he's right to feel that way about it, but I know he does, and that's a hard enough fact for anyone.' He shut his fingers round her arms, gripping her firmly, and said with intense gravity: 'I don't know how to make you understand, Emmy. It's so different for you, coming from England, even though you know us so well, and care so much. You can't imagine how difficult it is to know what to do.'

He had come to this admission quite simply, because she had not prompted him, and her respectful silence helped him to explore, more dispassionately than had been possible for him while Yuri was burning at his elbow, the ethics of self-exile. He was quiet for a while, considering with sceptical calm the motives which lead people to forswear their own countries, and the mutilation of personality which they risk in doffing thus a part of their own identity. She could feel him looking round, in some wonder but very shrewdly, upon the circumstances of his own life, testing its stresses cautiously, and casting a critical eye

132

about its changed orientation, to see if all this could justify a man in uprooting himself.

'But you know,' he said then, making his judgment with conviction, 'I could never go like that.'

* * *

It rained, and the city wept through the day in a grey haze, under a cobweb sky. In the parks and on the hills the leafless trees, heavy with moisture, shook off great drowning drops at every languid stirring of the air, and the towers withdrew into cloud, and drew up the grey ladders that kept them accessible to the world. By dusk, buildings had only one storey, streets only one building. The opposite pavement was a traveller's tale.

No message, bad or good, came for Miloslav. Watching him go about the business of his ordinary day, and observing the minute signs which set it apart from the ordinary, the unwonted quietness, the inward-gazing eye, the occasional heavy sigh, Emmy thought of her own first acquaintance with the physical phenomena of anxiety. When the crisis had broken here in the city, and the confused news-reports had shouted their chaotic interpretations of it across the world, she had grown used to carrying that burden in her body. Now she saw Miloslav disputing the ground of his own heart against the same parasitic guest, and could do nothing to help him.

'If this were fiction,' she thought, 'something positive would happen to resolve it, one way or the other. Either he'd get word that Yuri was safely out of the country, or else that he was arrested, or dead. But this is reality, and nothing will actually happen at all. A great part of reality consists of waiting and worrying, until the waiting gradually loses its tension, and the worrying wears off from sheer daily attrition.' But she knew that it was going to take Miloslav a long time to get over Yuri. Every day that passed without alarm would strengthen the probability that Yuri had got away, but it would be months before he could feel that probability had become certainty. And he had to adjust himself, at the same time, to the immediate and intimate loss; for safe Yuri might or might not be, but lost to Miloslav he was, beyond any reasonable expectation of recovery.

The day passed, with all its amorphous greyness, and in the night the temperature dropped and the sky cleared. On the next morning they rose to a world of rime, glittering in pale, fierce sunlight. The trees along the slopes of the Lucerna had grown inch-long blossoms of hoar-frost, and tinkled like thin glass when the reverberations of traffic shook them. All the tiles of all the city roofs were sparkling with encrusted whiteness. The spires pierced a sky like a dome of turquoise with an amber rim. The streets clanged, calling up iron echoes after every footfall, and the horns of cars at the busy crossings in town became angelic trumpets in the ringing air. Lubov and Miloslav went off to their lectures together in the cold early sunshine, slithering precariously down the worn steps to the embankment. Wanda snatched up her bulging brief-case and ran for the suburban bus which passed the corner of the street; and Matyas, trampling the blue hoar-frost still crisp in shadow, went off in the opposite direction, to the tram-stop. Every morning the family flew apart, every evening it drew strongly together again into a formidable cohesion. But every particle contained its own individual crises, unrelieved by that unity. In the last resort every man is alone.

Emmy spent the morning at home with Ilonna, pressing the dress she had chosen to wear that evening, and washing her hair. For the white-and-gold splendours of the Mozarteum, Wanda, rustling through the four concert dresses on their hangers, had decreed the stiff, beetle-green silk, with dull embroidery at the shoulders. Draping the full skirt into its many folds, Emmy thought of the curious shaping this career of hers had imposed upon her life. The approach to every major concert was like the long climb up a hill, over which she could not see. Until she came over the crest, nothing beyond existed; and she never knew what lions might be waiting for her in the valley on the other side. The heart cannot prepare itself for more than one climax at a time.

She had extracted from Marvan tickets for all the family, and the early evening in the flat was a wild and crowded flurry of dressing. Miloslav arrayed himself in the good black suit which had been made for the celebrations when his class passed its High School finals, two years ago, and which came out of the wardrobe now only for parties and official occasions. He looked oddly subdued and forlorn in it, like a well-behaved young relative at a funeral. When the Ministry car came to take her to the hall, he was the only member of the family who had yet emerged, and he jumped at the chance of accompanying her.

'May I, really?' He ran to bring her coat and hold it for her, and the meeting of their eyes in the mirror raised slowly through his dark preoccupation a dazzled, admiring smile. 'You look lovely, Emmy!'

'Do I, Milo? Thank you!' She was genuinely surprised; compliments from a younger brother came so rarely. 'Be sensible, and wear a scarf. It's very cold out. I'll tell them you're coming ahead with me.'

She rustled out to the lift on his arm, and down to the long, glossy car, which, like the sumptuous dress, and the careful make-up, and the black lamb coat, would be a little crumb of comfort and flattery in the tedious

136

desert of his loneliness. She could feel, when he settled himself in the car beside her, the slow pulse of his anxiety shaking the air between them with its distressful beat. She drew his arm through hers, and retained his hand between both her own. He would enjoy arriving in style and handing out Emily Marryat at a private door, but as a companion in this brief isolation no doubt he would prefer Emmy.

'Nothing happened today, Milo?'

'No, nothing happened.'

He responded gratefully to her touch, relaxing against her side.

'Every day is something gained,' she said.

'Yes, I know. Only I can't help being anxious.' And in a moment he said, in a voice carefully schooled into casualness: 'I didn't tell you, Emmy, that my position's under fire, too. I'm not sure that I shall be allowed to re-enter next term.'

She jerked round on him in consternation, gripping his hand. 'At the university? But why? You haven't done anything!'

How much English, she wondered, did the driver know? And how much interest had he, in any case, in the troubles of a passing boy? Miloslav seemed to pay very little respect to such considerations, but someone had to think of them. She frowned him down to a whisper as soft as her own.

'Yes, I have. I've laughed in the wrong places, and looked at various people in a

137

derisive manner, instead of with the reverence that's due to them.' He kept his voice obediently low, murmuring the words into her ear in the shelter of the upturned collar of her fur coat; but she thought that this show of reasonable caution was a concession to her scruples rather than a genuine thing. There was even a note of derisive enjoyment in his tone now; she could well imagine how scathing could be the comment of his silence in a chorale of enthusiasts.

'And you've cultivated the company of somebody who was known to be irreconcilable—is that it?'

'I think it would have been the same in any case, even without him. Nothing new has happened now—I just thought I ought to tell you. And I don't even know yet if it will happen. I think it will, but I don't know.'

'But even at this late hour, if you began to be serious in the right places—?'

'And cultivate the right people? I couldn't,' he confessed with the ghost of an unmistakable giggle; 'they just make me laugh. If I tried it I should only make matters worse.' He turned quickly, in the darkness delicate with the perfume she usually forgot to use, and planted a brief, unsteady kiss upon her temple. 'Don't worry about me; it won't be the end of the world, even if they do kick me out.'

She said untruthfully, lifting a hand to hold him against her cheek for an instant: 'I'm not worrying about you, I'm just thinking of all the opportunities such a serious world is going to offer you of laughing in the wrong places. You'll really have to be fitted with a suppressor, Milo.'

'Oh, I shall get that fitted in the army, of course.' In the passing lights along the embankment he made a wry face at her. 'It's part of the official issue in any army, isn't it?'

'I doubt,' she said smiling, 'if they have a model that will be effective on you.'

She had understood, as much by the close pressure of his shoulder and the tone of his voice as by any words he had used, that he was repeating for her, vehemently, that he could never go Yuri's way. His road, once his status as a student ended, led him not to the frontier but into the army for two years, and after that into some job as yet unplanned and unguessed-at, but here, but in his own proper identity. He intended no criticism of Yuri; and yet he offered her this repeated promise to remain in his country as a reassurance. Every man must make his own decisions; he, it seemed, had divined with conviction that this decision would also be pleasing to her.

In the bright, frosty night the façade of the Mozarteum glowed with lights, and a flurry of cars was already busy about its great pillared doors. The baroque shells and whorls of the tympanum high above revolved in light against a dark-blue sky. They drove round into a quiet side street, to a deep doorway whose lintel was propped by Titans of stone; and Miloslav, pleased with the passers by who halted to watch, leaped out with alacrity, and handed her ceremoniously out of the car and through the open door. Upon the pavement he stood and smiled at her, exaggerating for the benefit of the curious his attitude of deference, but with eyes bright with irreverent laughter.

'I don't think I dare call you Emmy again, after tonight! You know where to look for us? You must look, Mother will be waiting for it.'

'I shall be looking, all the time, whether you know it or not.'

She went in to the retiring-room, where Helena waited for her, a small, charming figure in a dull-gold dress and a brand-new coiffure, against a background of late baroque grandeur, pale-blue, white and gilt, as large as a private salon in any of the city's palaces. She took off her coat and tidied the strands of hair which had become involved in Miloslav's impulsive kiss. The mirror showed her a beauty she did not truly possess, the splendour of her heart's excitement mantling in her cheeks with the fiery delicacy of a rose, and kindling in the depths of her grey eyes a purple fire. She was almost at the crest of the hill, she could feel the horizon preparing to unfold before her upon the farther side. When the climax was reached, it had already begun to pass; and in a little while now, before the evening ended, she would have to look down, and see what waited for her on the next stretch of the road. But not yet, not until she began to sing.

Helena was nervous, for, though she had often played accompaniments at the Musicians' Club, this was her first full-dress concert. It was as well that they had three-quarters of an hour to spare before their appearance, and could sit and make civilised conversation like duchesses in the aristocratic fantasy of this two-hundred-year-old elegance. Marvan came in while the string quartet were playing Beethoven, and brought two or three of his colleagues to be presented to her. The setting, as well as the distractions, had its influence upon Helena's nerves. No one should come in here who was not mistress of her situation, and a large impervious calm, the complementary gift of baroque's violence and agitation, descended upon her spirit. When the time came for her to lead the way out to the piano upon the vast dais, and all the tiers of faces sprang into being suddenly, concentrated upon her, she blazed into masterful excitement. It was Emmy who felt herself drooping for a moment under the burden of the eyes, and the assault of the applause.

She looked for the family as she took her stand near the piano, and gathered her stiff skirts into silence about her, their burning green intensely dark against so much gilded whiteness. As Miloslav had said, she knew

141

where to look. They were in the third row of the small segment of circle not built up into boxes, right at the back of the hall, distant, small, but so much her own that her eyes fastened upon them without any search. She saw Lubov lean to the left in his seat, to have a better view of her, and for a moment saw herself as he saw her, a small figure, very erect under the glittering chandeliers, her head tilted back, the fairness of her hair quivering light as thistledown in the electric air. She could not see the expression of his face, but to look towards him was always to have his image vivid and kind before her inward eye. Did he carry her within himself in the same way? She did not think so perfect a conviction of communion could exist in her unless he did.

Her group of songs was all Mozart: 'Evening Reverie', 'To Chloe', 'Children's Game', 'Contentment', 'Louise Burning the Letters of her Faithless Lover'—such strange companions, if Mozart had not reconciled them. She did not know if she sang them well; all that mattered to her was that she sang them to Lubov, and with no sense of failure. When she had finished the group, and the generous applause came, it was as if she saw and heard no one but him, and this whole beautiful and elaborate setting had been designed for nothing else but to restore to him the remoteness and urgency he had mislaid for a little while by being too close and too familiar.

Thus in the distance, among unknown thousands, his smile too far away to be seen, his voice too remote to be fully understood, she saw him as he would be to her when the aeroplane taxied along the steely ribbon of runway and left him behind at the railing, straining his sight after her. In two days' time that would be the relationship between them. And after that, no more Lubov, until miracles repeat themselves; as perhaps they do, but who dare expect such favours?

She was over the brow of the hill now, she saw the descent before her, open, void and cold. She had always known that in two days more she must go on to Vienna; she had known it when she planned the venture, she had known it every moment of the time she had been in their beloved society, but in spite of the necessity of leaving them again she had felt them to be recovered for ever. Now, standing under the blaze of the chandeliers, bowing again and again with the blood high in her cheeks, and the white, smooth points of her shoulders holding the light like ivory, she saw that she had only passed through the precious days of this visit as through a dream, and that the onward journey might be as final as an awakening. It was all to do again from the beginning; so many days of precarious happiness gained, certainly, but none of them carrying any promise for the future. When you know you can return at will, departure has no weight. When you can advance to meet each other freely at the first impulse of need, separation is without terrors. But when you have to pull the broken halves of the world together in your arms in order to reach the creatures you love, then indeed you have discovered what separation is. And what love is, she thought, bending her head yet once more towards the place where Lubov was, before she swept from the dais and was hidden by the gold-fringed curtains.

In the interval, Marvan brought in some musical celebrities to talk to her, and the ten minutes passed in mutual politenesses which left her no time for gazing into her own mind. But when the pause was over, and the quartet were again playing, she sat before the mirror in silence, listening with the surface of her attention to Helena's voice chattering excitedly at her shoulder, and thinking how her world was now to be reassembled for the next assault. 'I have come this time,' she thought fiercely, staring into her own grey eyes, whose calm was something too large to be recognisable as an emanation of her unremarkable being; 'I shall come again. I asked for what I wanted, and they gave it to me; and I shall ask again, and if one door closes against me I shall look for another. I will never take no for an answer.' She could determine on that, and still know that the world's no might outlast her lifetime, if not her persistence. She knew, too, more clearly than ever before, that the great denial belonged indeed to the world, that some part of the guilt of it was everywhere, that casting accusations back and forth over the gulf was a game for lunatics, playing ball with apples from the atomic tree.

Helena said, with a child's reverent gravity: 'I shall never forget tonight! Imagine it, only a few months ago I was serving in a grocer's shop, and only playing a little sometimes for my friends, in the café where we used to meet. I thought it would be like that all my life, at least until I married. And instead, I am here at the Mozarteum, playing accompaniments for you! It is as though the world had suddenly been changed, as in a fairy-tale. I can hardly believe in such marvellous luck.'

'It isn't luck,' said Emmy, smiling at the radiant face in the mirror. 'You're a very good accompanist, and you will be a very good solo pianist, too. They haven't made any mistake.'

She was touched and delighted, she flushed with pure pleasure. 'I am trying very hard to justify what the State has done for me. But the opportunity—that was the wonderful thing! I owe it to my country now to become as fine an artiste as I can, to go as far as I have it in me to go. And I shan't fail the people who trusted me!'

'I'm sure you won't. And will you play accompaniments for me again, if I come here to sing next year, Helena?'

145

'If you would really like me to, you know I will. I have been so happy, working with you. When you sing our songs, and I have a share in the beautiful, kind way you sing them, don't you know how happy it makes me, and how proud?'

'But you have a share in the achievement, if that is really what it is. Your feeling for what we are doing helps me to do it well.'

'Then I am *very* proud,' said Helena, 'for you do it very well.'

It was as though the ceremonial leave-takings were already beginning. They blessed each other as they turned back to the last act of their partnership. This is a world in which everything that comes to an end may be ending for ever, it is well to complete every encounter with all the motions of grace, to give expression to every kindness, every gratitude, to make the clearest declaration of love. Better to give too readily than to keep back gifts for another meeting, when there is nothing certain even about tomorrow, and what is withheld now may wither away unused, divorced for ever from the creature whose due it was, and who had need of it.

The respite was almost over, and the two remaining days would dissolve at her touch no less confoundingly. She turned the sheets of music upon the table before her, the songs she had chosen for her chief assault upon the heart of the city. She remembered the joy she had in

146

collecting words and music from Wanda's lips during those years in London, and the delicate bridge she had seemed to herself to be building then, outward towards the submerged country from which the flood-waters would one day subside, and give those green woods and black forests and goose-whitened pastures back to the sun. All woods were green in this tongue, all forests black, almost all horses black, too, only here and there in the borders of fairyland a mysterious white horse, with the luster of the supernatural still upon him, and a human voice. And always the waters of separation, flowing between divided lovers.

The applause which marked the end of the Haydn quartet called them from their retirement. From behind the gold brocade curtains they watched the repeated acknowledgments, watched the four players bow themselves out at last with their laurels. It was time. Helena gripped her portfolio with the last almost blissful convulsion of nervousness, and led the way across to the piano.

The gilded cavern of the auditorium, tier on tier of gold cord and white caryatids, soared into an oval of blue ceiling encrusted with constellations; and all the roused, expectant faces within it glimmered like stars, shedding upon them a benevolent but confounding light. Emmy lifted her head, intent for silence, and her eyes found their way to where the Ivanescu

147

were. Almost hidden from her, craning over the heads of strangers, Lubov was only a lofty forehead, a generous span of brows, and a crest of brown hair, but she found him, and was satisfied. Her folded hands relaxed in the stiff paniers of the green skirt, lying eased and quiet there.

If there ever was a moment when she began, fully and consciously, to love him, it was then; but it could scarcely be held that any such instant of revelation existed, for as soon as she had let in the exquisite, untimely conviction of love, it was as though it had always been there, and had wanted only the sharp light of separation falling bleakly upon it to be recognised and revalued. Later there would be time, all too much time, for lamenting the wasted years of his accessibility. Now she could do nothing but look up at him, dazzled and astonished, and let the recognition become song, the only voice she had here, before so many witnesses.

She sang a song from the south-east, about young lovers at pasture, she with the geese, he with the horses, and of the disastrous results of their encounter upon the standing rye. And after it a sad song about a girl whose lover had been forced into the imperial army, and left her waiting all night for him at the trysting place. The dedicated silence grew out of the small clinging shadow of the skirts she hushed with her hands, and filled the hall, and the starry glimmer of faces swam into a softly glowing unity of emotion, still, intent and complete, embracing every creature who had native blood in him and racial memories of these pleasures and these griefs. She no longer looked at Lubov, except inward into her heart, where he most perfectly was and would always be. She saw nothing more definite than a vague and shining cave into which she poured forth like a pure spring the discovery of her love; and from the limits of her singing, out of space filled to overflowing with her unmeasured tenderness, love flowed back to her. It came back as she spent it, without moderation. Love to this people could never waste without its harvest, love to Lubov was no sooner cast into the ready soil than she felt the bursting growth rise, the bud fill full, the flower open.

She was no longer troubled with the littleness of what she had to offer, and the inadequacy of the gesture with which she offered it. All you have is enough. Nothing less would suffice, but whether you yourself are much or little, all you have is enough. The flood which had frightened her before flowed back now into her heart with passion and power, and somehow it was accommodated, somehow with great joy and greater pain she contained it, and was enlarged with it.

The songs, chosen in innocence, took to themselves all the significance of foreknowledge. She sang, impressing the

delicate, solemn tune upon the air like a vow
taken before so great a cloud of witnesses:

'From the forest riding
Comes a young man hither.
They watch and stand between,
Lest we come together.

'Do your worst to part us,
Vainly you assay it!
Our sacred word we gave—
You cannot unsay it.'

Who could pledge more, to a man or a
country? And the declaration was for both. All
the words took to themselves meanings she
had not known they carried, they were
communications between her and her audience
in an immediate and direct way she had not
even ventured to intend. But they were dual,
they had still one more voice for Lubov, the
heart of the heart of the matter.

When the group of songs ended, the silence
hung for a long moment before anyone stirred,
and in the hush she felt her enormous elation
assaulted by all the enmity of the outer world.
Then, stirring out of their spellbound quiet,
they broke into applause that rang and echoed
in waves round the blue vault where the
constellations drifted, and filled the hall with a
deep pulse of excitement. It went on for a long

time. She tried to bow herself away from them, shining and trembling with the weight and brightness of her own achievement, raising to them time after time her dazed and marvelling smile, which perhaps they mistook for the signature of modesty. There was no room for modesty in her now. What she had recognised and accepted, with no reservations this time, was no burden for a diffident woman. But even when her arms were full of flowers they would not let her go. On their side, too, there had been an acceptance. She might never win her way back to them again, if the madness of the world continued, but they would never be altogether bereft of her. What she had left here tonight would companion them still in thought and feeling, until no memory remained. 'I am one of the imponderables of the cold war,' she thought, and was glad to have trespassed into the affairs of the world. 'I am a cinder which refuses to grow cold. I am a chemical particle upsetting the calculations of history.'

She chose, since they were not yet satisfied, one of the songs of the severing river, the most beautiful she knew; it needed a harp to do justice to the accompaniment, or a cymbalo, perhaps, with its limpid rolling notes round as tears, but Helena was charged full with the self-forgetfulness of happiness, and played it with angelic simplicity, so that even the piano escaped its sophistication for a few minutes under her hands. The silence expanded again instantly, and filled every box, every fold of the curtains, every cranny of the gilded carvings and plasterwork of the ceiling.

'O quiet stream, flowing down to Danube's shore,
Lost is my love, my love returns no more.
Yet grant, my God, he may share my grief and pain,
And this heart that loves him he may love again.

'This night I dreamed a dream that he was near,
That he, my dear, my dearest, entered here.
He laid his cheek against my cheek as I slept,
And with gentle chiding asked me why I wept.'

The rippling of the little tributary, ecstatic and assured under Helena's touch, plucked at her heart as at a secret instrument. It was well that she should be reminded now, in her moment of committal, how high the cost might come. There were wider rivers than this, and wider than the Danube, separating lovers now.

'Barren, O God, O my love, this life must be!
Still my head aches with longing after thee,

And my lost heart with its sorrow sure must
    break
    Ere it can forget thee, darling, or forsake.'

The piano repeated, regretfully rippling, the
last limpid fall, the soft chords lengthening out
along the current of the river, borne away
eastward into silence. They held their breath,
charmed into silence, too, their senses drawn
out after the notes, far from the city, and
farther still from the foreign singer, floating
with the quiet waters which had grown into the
cosmic flood of Oceanus, circling and
recircling the world.

*   *   *

They sat in the most retired box of a little
wine-cellar under an arcade in the New Town.
The room was L-shaped, and the tail of the L
was a dance-floor about four yards square, a
tiny dais for a trio of musicians, and three
discreet booths, in the last of which they sat.
The field of their vision was limited to the end
of the floor, the curtains of their booth, and an
occasional glimpse of the trombone slide when
it was fully extended. Now and again a pair of
dancers, or a wandering waiter, drifted past the
opening of the curtains, and cast a vague,
impersonal glance at them for an instant before
disappearing again without a word. The
unrelenting reverberations of the trio covered

their voices. Mozart was not two hours past yet, and the quiet waters flowing down to the Danube, almost as pure and clear as Mozart, had hardly withdrawn their hill-coolness out of her lips. Now the hot piano and the caricaturing brass extracted a raucous sadness from hack American tunes, and offered the cloak of inaudibility for true lovers, as simply as the gifts come in fairy-tales, and as incongruously.

How had they come there? She hardly knew. All she clearly remembered was Lubov's hand gripping her arm suddenly among the dozens of people who had come to congratulate her, and Lubov's voice, violently quiet, saying in her ear: 'Come away with me! Come now!' as though he owned her, and her own voice replying as wildly: 'Yes, I'll come—only give me ten minutes to get away!' as though she perfectly concurred in being owned by him. They had extricated themselves somehow without damage, he from the family, she from her well-wishers; they were here, sitting on a spindly cane-and-gilt settee in a wooden box curtained closely enough for amorous encounters, their shoulders touching, their hands clasped in one complex, quiet knot upon the glass table, their eyes contemplating the tangle of hands. The half-bottle of Bulgarian wine stood neglected, their glasses untouched. The bored blonde girl who danced silently by and away again, her eyes languid over the

154

shoulder of an elderly man, must think them the most ordinary of sights in this place.

The trio moaned of a white Christmas, without much sense of anticipation. Emmy said, a slow smile curving her lips: 'I'm surprised you still borrow this stuff from the West.'

'Give us time,' said Lubov. 'In a year or so we'll have abolished all that, and be producing stuff of our own.'

'About on the same artistic level?'

'About! But with a healthier moral tone.' He smiled, too; she felt the warmth of it caressing her lowered eyelids, and looked up. His brown eyes, widely set above the fine, urgent cheekbones, received her gaze as the summer earth receives rain, and were refreshed. 'This is a fine time,' said Lubov, without bitterness, 'to begin to love each other!'

'Do you think I haven't been telling myself the same thing? All those years in London, when there was nothing on earth to stand between us, and every reason in the world for cementing the alliance! And then 1945, and everyone coming back here with foreign wives and young families, and still we hadn't the sense to see that it might not always be as simple as that!'

'It wasn't as simple as that then,' said Lubov warningly. 'It only looked simple. Alliances made then are coming to pieces now. Only the very durable are going to survive.'

155

'Don't talk as if you believed in national differences, like the rest,' she said protestingly. 'You know we feel alike, think alike, value the same things. Our marriage would have been more than durable.' She did not say 'it will be'; only 'it would have been'. She observed the careful phrasing, and knew that in honesty she could not change it; and she translated the spasm of pain it gave her into a long, sudden pass of her finger-tips along Lubov's hand from knuckles to wrist.

'I know it would,' said Lubov. 'Much more!'

'But we missed our chance. Why, Lubov? Why didn't we realise in time? I know it began with Wanda and me, and you were just Wanda's big brother. I know we practically finished growing up together. But surely it should have dawned on us what we had and what we wanted—if you feel as I feel now?'

Very quickly and softly he said, as though he too had just realised how little time was left for giving voice to the things which should have been said long ago: 'I love you more than any creature on earth, and I shall as long as I live. But when we knew each other first, the war was everything that was left in the world to me, my eyes were always on it, and my feet were always itching to go home. And afterwards, with the excitement of coming back here, and having you here—and for you, your singing career beginning—and with everything, as we thought, growing open and friendly and free, so that we could go back and forth just as we liked—what sense of urgency was there, and what did we lack? We were both living happy lives, full of satisfactions, why should we realise yet that we needed something more? But now we—now all of us—have lost that sense of openness and freedom. There's room for us to need satisfactions now. And when something is threatened, one looks at it again.'

She said with furious sadness: 'What chance did we have? Everything changed in a moment. We looked again, but it was already too late. Lubov, what are we to do?'

'Do?' he said, suddenly laying his cheek against her hand with a deep, quiet sigh. 'Are you asking me? What have I found to do about anything, Emmy, except to stand dead still in the middle of events, afraid to stir a hand this way or a foot that for fear of doing an injustice to somebody? All I do for anyone is pick up a few people who get knocked down, and brush their coats for them. When everyone else has taken sides for or against, I'm still there trying to reconcile Petr with Yuri, and Father with old Grosz, who worked for him for twenty years and is soon going to be his regional director for the industry, and my new ex-miner students, all big, jubilant eyes and carnivorous memories, with some of the old ones who got pushed out to make room for them—There's no end to it, Emmy. Every time I begin to feel that I've collected enough evidence to justify me in voting for, something like Yuri happens. Every time I've almost been driven, because of one more Yuri, to vote against, I see my new students again, and feel the release of energy and hope they bring with them. In fact, every time I contemplate positive action at all, I see only too well that it's going to hurt somebody unfairly, as well as giving away ammunition to one faction or the other. The good and the bad are so chequered together, I curse both sides a hundred times a day—but I don't move against either. It isn't just a verdict I want—it's justice!'

'You want to be fair to the devil,' said Emmy.

He raised his eyes, and in the shadow of the curtains the pupils looked almost black. He did not recognise the quotation, but he considered it seriously, and had no quarrel with it. 'Do I? Well, if you believe in justice at all, surely it's due to the devil as much as to anyone else? And who needs it more? But what good am I, Emmy? All the result of all my weighing and measuring is paralysis. Whatever I might do would be unjust to someone, so I just do nothing. The only thing I can do is try to keep my own personal field of action as pure as I can, and deal as gently as possible with everyone who moves in it. What use is that to anyone?'

'A great deal of use,' said Emmy, 'to the people you pick up and salvage. And it makes other people stop and think about their own position, surely.' It seemed to her that the course he had tried to expound to her, with angry derogation because it was his own, and had cost him constant difficulty and pain, was the attempted solution of all the best of his nation, and that it was doomed from the start to misunderstanding and misinterpretation by the partisans of both sides, inside and outside his own country. It seemed to her, too, that this was the almost inevitable fate of integrity, and that many even of the best would be forced into enlistment very soon, on this side or that, in order to continue somehow the business of living. If it is hard for a country to be a bridge, how much harder is it for a man? And how many Lubovs would you need in order to reduce the individual strain to something which could be borne?

'Who, for instance?' asked Lubov with a sceptical smile.

'Me—for instance.'

'Ah, *you!*' He turned his lips suddenly into her warm palm, which opened tenderly to receive his touch. She thought for a moment that he was going to remind her that she was English, and her problem something apart from his, but he did not. 'You do not prove anything,' he said, 'except that God got tired of reproducing the second-rate.'

She shut her eyes for an instant upon starting tears of inexcusable joy, frivolous surely in this extremity, and pressed her fingers over his lips.

'Miloslav, too,' she said. 'And others, more than you can possibly know. You mustn't think that we're alone.'

'We may be, Emmy. We may be, before the pressure eases.'

'Then we'll go on alone.' It was a strange way of describing the state of suspended animation he had outlined, the loss of the possibility of speech or action, the motionless silence. Yet it did not seem to her to call for any alteration. She let it stand, closing her lips decisively when it was said.

'Oh, Emmy, Emmy, my dear!' he said, shaken with a tremor of affectionate laughter. 'And *you* ask *me* what we're to do!'

The waiter, skating to the end of the dance-floor with a tray poised on one hand, darted a look in at their untouched glasses, and raised his eyebrows resignedly as he scurried away again. The band began to play the tearful waltz the continent of Europe had made of 'Auld Lang Syne', and the blonde girl, revolving indifferently in her partner's arms, surveyed with large blank eyes the two people holding hands so desperately in the last box. She displayed no interest in them at all; only the eyes, distantly plaintive, marked and recorded the gown, the lamb coat, the locked glances, the neglected wine, the arms pressed together, the tranquilly despairing faces. They were ordinary enough. The muted trombone, breathing orgies of farewell, barely covered

160

their voices, which no doubt she supposed to be working out, without haste, the usual approaches to love.

'Tell me,' Lubov was saying, watching her across their clasped hands with an agonised smile, so faint that it barely hollowed his cheek, or inflected the tired gravity of his mouth, 'if I were to ask you to marry me, Emmy, what would you answer?'

She leaned forward, and kissed the mouth she had so often kissed before, but never like this. She said in a whisper: 'No, Lubov!'

He had closed his eyes instinctively to contain and keep the nearness of her face and the moment of the kiss; now they opened again wide and dark, unfocused as though he had just come out of a deep sleep. 'Because you feel that if you came to me now, you might be enough of a handicap to tip the scales against me? In my delicate situation, and with the amount of suspicion there is everywhere now between one man and another, an English wife might be my ruin. Unless, of course, she came on certain terms which you would never be likely to consider, and which I certainly wouldn't ask of you. Is that why it would be no, Emmy?'

'Something like that. And you, Lubov, are you going to ask me to marry you?' She knew the answer already; her smile drew forth his answering smile, comforting though comfortless.

161

'No. I believe if I could have you by cutting off my hand, I'd do it happily. But there are parts of my identity I won't cut off, Emmy, and if I did, I should no longer be worth offering to you, and you would no longer want me. If you came to me now, you would be welcomed—as an important propaganda specimen. I am not judging my country, I am only saying what is true of every person who crosses from one half of the world to the other now of his own will, and without a return ticket. You know that it happens upon your side, you must know that it happens here. Naturally! They believe there is only one reason for making that crossing, they expect you to act in accordance with it. If you came, and if you embraced the régime here utterly and vocally, and allowed yourself to be paraded as a woman who has repudiated England and the West, it would be possible to live. But if you refused to live up to their ideas of you and earn your citizenship, would it still be supportable? And I know you would never repudiate England, any more than I would repudiate my country.'

She heard again her own voice arguing and pleading with Yuri in much the same terms, but without the absolute trust in him which Lubov claimed in her. It seemed that whenever she desired to know what Lubov would think, and say, and do in any situation, she had only to look deeply and honestly enough into her own mind.

'It's all right, my darling,' she said very softly. 'As soon as I realised how things went with us, I knew that marriage was out of the question.'

'And yet I love you so much,' he said in anguish, 'that I would do almost anything in the world to have you—except that if I got you by surrendering whatever makes me myself, you could not love me.'

'And I,' she replied, 'should love you however you belied yourself. But I should hate myself for having been the cause of your deformity. I would rather love you as you are, and keep my own respect.'

The room had grown suddenly darker as the waiter switched off one of the lights, over a corner where no one now sat. Only the blonde girl and her partner, untiring in their languor, revolved slowly upon the polished black floor.

'It must be nearly midnight,' said Lubov, stirring like a man coming out of sleep. 'I suppose we'd really better drink this wine.' And when she took up her glass at last, and lifted it to him silently, he reached and touched the rim of it with his. 'To Emily Marryat's voice!'

She smiled, and drank willingly. 'Yes, we need a lifeline. And after all, we're lucky! I might just have been a shorthand-typist, I had no other talents.'

Another lamp went out. The waiter appeared suggestively outside the booth. The trio had ended their last number, and were shuffling their music together wearily.

'We'll get a taxi in the square,' said Lubov, opening his wallet.

'Couldn't we walk? If we cross by the Captain Evian bridge it isn't very far.'

'But in that dress—? And your shoes aren't for walking.'

'They're quite comfortable, really.'

'But much too thin for a late autumn evening. No, we'll take a car.'

'Lubov, I beg you!' she said, suddenly trembling. 'There's only one more day, Lubov!'

They walked. Did it matter, after all, if she risked a cold? Whatever she wanted of him, whatever she demanded of the time, if it was in his power to give he would give her. But what she wanted was to hold time still, in the night, in the day, so that the last hours might never pass; and this he did not know how to give her.

They went down to the embankment, and crossed the bridge of dead Captain Evian, who had fought back the German garrison from the escape route northward at the end of the Occupation. At the crest of the slight rise, by the plaque in the stone parapet where his unfailing flowers withered in the frosty air, they stood together looking down the river, between the terraced darkness of its banks, where the late house-lights, steadily burning, cast quivering reflections in the ebony water, and the beautiful royal cliff of the Citadel soared, its spires blotting out whole galaxies of stars. The air was absolutely still. Their breath sent forth fragile clouds of mist, ephemeral as may-flies. Beneath them in the water, when they turned to look up-stream, the regular steelbacked wedges of the ice-breakers caught glimmers of light, and severed the steadily rushing waters with the hiss of a scythe in grass.

They wound their arms about each other, and matched their steps, and once, if never again, they walked like lovers, for only a few people remained about the embankment to see them, and on the narrow stone stairways of the Lucerna there would be no one at this hour, except perhaps other pairs of lovers, lingering in the shelter of the dark.

Lubov said, his voice aching: 'If you should run into Yuri, somewhere over there, be good to him. What he did was a mistake, but it was not all his fault.'

'So Miloslav thinks, too,' she said. 'He feels he should have stayed, but that going was an error he had a right to make.' And she added simply: 'If he ever needs anything of me that I can give, of course I'll give it.'

He walked beside her for a moment in silence, the hollow of his shoulder cupping hers, his long arm folding her closely. She knew that his mind was torn by the cruelty of this paradox, that Yuri, who had in his estimation falsified the facts of his situation, should be

165

able to make his way by this emotional fraud into Emmy's presence, while he, who had refused to be satisfied with less than truth, should be thereby barred from her. But there was no need for him to explain that in his case the possibility of a solution by flight did not exist. That was one way out she had never for a moment considered. All the same, he felt for the words in which to state, not his own determination, but the mysterious compulsion which left him no choice, and therefore set him free of all consciousness of virtue or superiority.

'I think when you've lived in two countries, and loved both, you begin to understand nationality better, and how little it has to do with nationalism, or patriotic feeling, or any of the distortions of itself. You can't feel the claims of any other country, much less of the world, until you've realised your full relationship with your own. And it seems to me that adhering to your own, even when you must refuse yourself to its policies, even when it doesn't offer much except trouble and persecution, is a part of the acceptance of your own identity. The less nationality in the ordinary sense means to you, the less logically can you discard one to take up another. The man who belongs consciously to the human race can never escape his citizenship.'

They came to the end of the bridge, and walked along the Island which was not an island, to cross by another tiny bridge the stream which was not a stream, but a rapid backwater drawn off from the weir to turn five mill-wheels, all now motionless.

'The name has always been a vital part of the magic of identity,' said Lubov, smiling with melancholy gentleness at the sparks of starlight diffused along the rapid, humming water. 'So is the country where your roots are. If you cut off your roots you have given away more than your name, for you can never grow new ones to any depth worth striking. But the ones you have from birth will extend, if you let them grow, a long way beyond any frontier.'

'There are cases,' said Emmy sombrely, remembering vividly the Jewish family, gay, civilised and indestructible after terrible experiences, who had once lived in the flat above hers in Kensington, 'when a man doesn't uproot himself, but is thrown out by his own earth.'

'Ah, that's quite another matter! God knows he has a right to go where he can to find some soil willing to accept him. As we had a right, I think, during the Occupation to take our own earth to England with us, or to Russia, or wherever there was sanctuary for it, to make sure of keeping it sweet and ours until we could take it home again for everyone. We were hiding our birthright from an alien invader, not from our own people. But none of these is Yuri's case now.' He did not add: 'Or mine!'

but she heard it clearly, and did not even wish to deny it. She desired him to be as he was, never to retract by one particle the amplitude of his being.

'So I must go,' she said, 'and you must stay here.' She felt that he struggled to defend what needed no defence, as though she had accused him of not loving her enough to follow her to England, and she lifted her hand and hushed him with passionate fingertips. 'No, you have nothing to excuse! I won't sell out my country here, and you won't sell yours in England. We'll deal fairly with both of them. What else can we do? What else could we want to do?'

'To most people,' said Lubov wryly, 'it will look much more like simple fence-sitting. Both sides hate the uncommitted. They'll want to implicate us, or destroy us.'

'It sounds,' she said ruefully, 'as though we shall be the most committed people in the world. Committed to being uncommitted— uncommitted to any cause in the world smaller than the truth.'

They had reached the first steps of the stairway; the high stone walls with their chipped sgraffito, mottled with stonecrop and lichens, folded closely round them, comforting them with a darkness in which they seemed more intimately drawn together, more nearly one.

'You almost make me believe,' said Lubov, 'that we are going to save the world by sitting

168

down obstinately and folding our hands.'

'You know that won't be what we shall be doing.'

'No,' he agreed with a sudden spurt of genuine laughter, such as he could achieve sometimes out of his most urgent solemnity, 'it won't be at all like that. Our inaction is likely to be about as peaceful and easy as the stillness of unarmed men caught between two barrages. People who camp between opposing armies must expect to get hurt.'

'Only lunatics,' she admitted, 'wander about in No-Man's-Land.' But she could not echo the laughter, she was too deeply aware of the justice of his metaphor. Every blow launched in the world draws blood from the man who has transcended nationality and taken a foreigner into his being. For to outgrow one frontier is to outgrow all.

They had reached the top of the staircase; the lamps of the city, thinning out now in the dead hours of the night, lay outspread far below them, the coils of the river outlined in lights, the water achieving here and there a lambent radiance of its own. They looked back only once. The distance drew them, and they felt towards each other, breast to breast, for a moment of intolerable longing; and then, as inevitably, bore it and drew back from kissing, because this day would pass like any other, and to make too much of it would be to destroy a compact they had made without words. Unless

169

she left him intact in mind, how could she expect to find him undamaged and uncompromised when she returned? Unless he refrained from troubling her too deeply, how could she sustain the journey without him?

They went on, hands and arms linked, and the closed door of Number Seventeen loomed before them. Lubov opened it with a key ludicrously small for such a ponderous portal, and groped for the minute-light. They went very quietly up the stairs, for the lift was far too noisy to be used at one o'clock in the morning. When they were in the middle of the second flight the light went out, and they climbed in the dark, slowly, trembling now, their cold hands clinging.

In the living-room the curtains were drawn back, and starlight showed them Miloslav fast asleep, flushed under his billowing feather quilt. He had made Lubov's bed, too, the virgin pillows had been smoothed punctiliously, the fat cover turned back to receive him. They moved softly across the room, careful of the boy's slumber, and moved by the vigorous and mature calm of his unconscious face. He also, contained and alone, pursued his own way. Above his sleep they kissed briefly, with cold lips that touched and parted, and hands and bodies and cheeks that refrained, with terrible, careful tenderness, from the destroying embrace they desired. Then she went away from him softly, and let herself into Wanda's room, and into Wanda's bed.

*　　*　　*

They were all three sitting with her on the blue leather benches of the air terminal, with hardly a word left to say between them, and ears strained unhappily for the flight number which would call her to the airport bus. Her luggage was already weighed and whisked away, to reappear only in the Customs hall, and the slack, frightened, run-down feeling of departure had closed on them all, inhibiting their tongues though their minds pursued in panic all the things which ought to be said, which should have been said earlier while there was time to say them gracefully. Many, the dearest and most urgent, would inevitably be forgotten until it was too late.

It was half-past two in the afternoon, still full daylight but without lustre. Wanda had stolen an extra hour at lunchtime in order to come with Emmy this far, and could not accompany her to the airport, even if there should be room for friends as well as passengers in the bus. The other two intended to go with her every step of the way to the Customs barrier, and then to watch her plane take off for Vienna, but no tickets were issued for friends until all the travellers were aboard, and it was by no means certain that there would be places to spare for them. They sat braced neatly, listening, side by side, looking more alike than Emmy had ever seen them before. Their faces, animated now and then as they spoke to her, became pale and grave in repose. Miloslav hugged Emmy's lamb coat dutifully in his arm.

The last day was gone like a gleam of stormy sunshine, fevered and beautiful. The air was still, the cloud light, a day good for flying. Within an hour and a half she should be in the air. Lubov would go back to the lecture he was preparing, Miloslav to his cramming for examinations which would probably never be allowed to count in his favour against the burden of his political unreliability. And she would sing Mozart and Beethoven and Brahms in Vienna, not yet far from them in space, but already out of reach. She watched Lubov's calm face, and marvelled that no one else could see its motionless desperation.

The loudspeaker crackled, and the flattened voice of the girl announcer called the Vienna flight to bus number three. They rose, gathering themselves as if to an expected ordeal, their faces growing instantly sharp and intent. Numbers of other people were snatching up their hand luggage and making for the doorway; there would be few, if any, seats to spare.

Miloslav was already out upon the pavement, buttonholing the driver and making

172

a plea for whatever places there might be. He counted the passengers jealously as they mounted, his eyes anxious. Wanda, near to tears, embraced Emmy fiercely.

'Darling, come again! Come next spring, if you can—don't let your agent fix you a full programme at home, please keep a corner for us. Oh, Emmy, it was beautiful—but so short! Give my love to your brother, and all the others who remember me.'

'You know I'll come again as soon as I can. And, Wanda, if—if it's at all possible for *you*—'

Wanda let the inarticulate hope pass by her, and made no direct reply. They kissed, and Emmy, last to enter the bus, hovered upon the lowest step, unwilling to go in until she knew if her farewells to Lubov and Miloslav must be made here. The driver looked along the loaded seats, and counted rapidly.

'I can take one extra. Sorry, but I'm not allowed to carry standing passengers, you know.'

They hesitated for a second only, staring at each other. Then Miloslav, thrusting the lamb coat unceremoniously upon Lubov, threw his arms about Emmy and hugged her vehemently, kissing her hard upon the mouth. It was the family kiss become self-conscious because of its own possible finality; it was Ilonna's kiss on the landing, Matyas' kiss on the doorstep of Number Seventeen. He did not say a word, but on releasing her stepped back to the pavement, and gave Lubov a push towards the bus. Then Emmy was groping her way to a seat, the last seat, with Lubov close behind her, and the bus was already beginning to move, wheeling slowly away from the pavement, and Wanda and Miloslav were walking alongside it, waving and smiling with that worn and arduous smile that troubles all departures. In a few moments they fell behind, and the first curve of the way swept them from sight.

They were alone now among so many people, they were private under so many eyes. They linked arms, and under the folds of the coat they held hands tightly, palm pressed to palm, trembling at the embrace, which was as truly an act of passion as though they had lain together. She had never imagined such happiness or such agony.

She said in a startled whisper of gratitude: 'He knows! Milo knows! After all, he can't have been asleep!'

'Yes, he was asleep. He doesn't *know*—it's simply that he's always quick to feel things about people. Without even troubling to go so far as to know.'

His finger-tips caressed with all the longing of his body the tensed muscles of the back of her hand. The bus, unbelievably rapid, had already whirled out of the square, and was crossing the bridge. The river, tumbling its slate-grey water along at a rolling pace, ran higher than when she had arrived; and along the embankment on the other side the trees had lost most of their leaves now, and stood sinuous and black against the sky. They began to climb from the waterside to the plateau, passed through the high square where the market stalls were just folding themselves away into bales of canvas and naked steel frames, and cleaners were sweeping up the refuse of straw packing and cabbage leaves.

'Milo told me,' said Emmy, 'that he may not be allowed to enrol next term. He said he had nothing definite to go on yet, but he seemed to feel very sure of it, all the same.'

'Milo doesn't imagine things—unless someone else denies them.'

'You think he'll really be dismissed?'

'I think he will. He has accepted that position. You mustn't be afraid,' he said, 'that he will let it change the shape of his life. Miloslav is a very practical person.'

'I know! He told me himself, it won't be the end of the world. But he has nothing to look forward to now but military service. And he's going to miss Yuri so badly.'

'Yes—I know it. He's very unhappy. But he has not lost his sense of proportion. He will find plenty of reasons for being happy again.'

'And you,' she said, her fingers contracting jealously upon his, 'I worry about you.'

Lubov said with gentle protest: 'Surely we've

175

gone beyond that. I have as much reason to trust in getting fair treatment here as most men have anywhere. Wherever you are, thought is subversive—even living at all is a risky business. I am not worrying about anything—except whether the world can bear the strain. And whether you will come back again.'

'You know I shall,' she said.

'I almost know it. There's only that last possibility—'

Against the dull grey sky the spires of the cathedral raised their august shapes of blue-grey Gothic lace. The bus overhauled a Number Twenty-one tram climbing towards its looped terminus, and the three cars roared hollowly at them as they went by.

'I love you,' said Lubov, 'I shall always love you. I don't know how to tell you how much. I would rather have had this—just this—from you, and never anything more as long as I live, than years and years of an ordinary happy marriage with anyone else. I would even rather love you like this, and not be loved in return, than enjoy a mutual love with someone else. I want you to know it, and to remember that I said it.'

'Things ought to be said,' she agreed, with a faint but luminous smile. 'But you don't leave me anything to say. I should have liked to say all those things to you, but my language isn't good enough. Simply, I love you, Lubov. Do you suppose we are talking about happiness?

This ought to be happiness.'

'It is happiness,' he said with conviction. 'We can't complain if that isn't all it is.'

Beyond the colony of new white apartment houses the first village slid by them silently, its round green pond half encircled with snowy resting geese, like a string of pearls, its pink and blue cottages clustered about the scroll-topped stucco gateway of a farmyard, perfect small baroque. The svelte modern shop-windows closed in again brightly after its passing. The tram-route curled about its oval island and vanished. The stretched finger-tips of the city touched green fields and new ploughing, rich and dark, and on their right, as they rolled along the high, straight road, the plunging cleft of the ravine was torn open for a moment to let them see into its rocky heart, growing dimmer now with mist. Then the earth closed again upon the secret place, and the long wooded ridge of the battlefield drew near them upon the other hand.

'You'll have to listen to a great many slanders against us,' said Lubov. 'Some people in England will think they're doing us a favour by throwing stones at our country—things like this are never understood, always over-simplified. Do you think you could convince a few of the more perceptive people that, whatever our reservations, we haven't divorced her yet?—that we, the ones who have been in England, too, the ones they know, are the first people to be hit by the brickbats they throw? We have to blush for the English as well as for our own people, you see, it's rather an exposed position.' He was smiling, the smile was even in his voice; she knew with the deepest sensitivities in her that gift he had of being solemn and merry in the same breath, and both so gently and modestly that neither his distress nor his gallantry in muting it should be so obtrusive as to distress another.

'Every word I say and everything I do will be as an advocate for you,' she said simply. 'It isn't that I shall make any conscious adjustments—just a natural response to my pole. Thought won't be necessary.'

'I think you're over-simplifying the position in England, now,' said Lubov, his smile deepening into silent laughter.

'My mechanism is simple. If anything more subtle is needed I shall have to grow it. But what I have is accurate.'

'I know it,' said Lubov. 'I am only afraid that you have no sense of self-preservation. Your position is as vulnerable as mine now.'

'You told me we have gone beyond being afraid,' she reminded him, raising her grey eyes with a sudden shining smile.

The hill of the battle stretched darkly along the sky upon the left hand, lengthening out like a cry the shadow of its ancient and still unredeemed tragedy. The high, rolling fields opened beyond, the upland country proper to

178

airfields. They were drawing near to the end of the road.

'Take care of them all,' said Emmy. 'I love them all so much in their own right, and so much more because they belong to you.'

'They will be all right, and so shall I. But it's my mother, not I, who will look after everyone,' said Lubov. 'Do you know, Emmy, there are people who think my mother is preoccupied with trivialities to such an extent that she can't see the essentials? Whereas she has clarified everything to the one essential. In every situation, after every change, in every individual crisis, my mother sets about recreating the conditions in which living will be possible for the people around her—all the people round her, as far as she can reach. She doesn't do it because it makes her feel good, or because she thinks it her duty, she does it because it's the function for which she was constructed, and she can no more divert herself from it than you could desert a friend in trouble.'

'Or you,' said Emmy, 'any creature, friend or foe, who needed someone to stand by him.' She felt him shrink from being praised, and in the shelter of the coat she drew his hand close to her body, holding it tightly against the warmth and thunder of her heart. 'We're hurrying to say everything, while there's time, and really there's no need. As far away as I shall be, Lubov, I can be quiet in you.'

'And I shall rest in you.'

'Until I come back,' she said. 'Lubov, I've been thinking—it might not be wise to be too greedy. I shan't ask for a visa in the spring, unless things get better—or much worse. The autumn again would be reasonable, wouldn't it? I don't want to be too insistent. But within a year I shall try to come.'

'I think it might be wise,' he agreed, 'to wait a year.'

They had turned in from the main road, along the wide white drive to the airport. The angular low buildings rose into sight, a plane sailed up lazily into the grey sky, and circled, and made off purposefully westward. The bus drew in before the concrete steps and discharged its passengers indifferently into the 'Departures' hall. Emmy handed over her passport, and sat down under a showcase of expensive leather goods with Lubov beside her. They watched, with eyes as remote and incurious as stars, the restless perambulations of her fellow-travellers about the room. Their hands, which had disengaged reluctantly, remained bereaved now. It was too late to repeat that pain of separation.

'I hope you'll have a smooth flight,' said Lubov. 'I think you will, everything seems to be going out on time, and it's beautifully still.'

'I shall be all right. It has to be quite bumpy to upset me.'

'Write to us from Vienna. Or send a card, if

180

you don't have time for a letter. Wanda's always terribly down when you go.'

She liked the 'always', it made everything sound so regular and permanent. She smiled at him, and said she would write, of course. Then her name was called from the desk, and she had to rummage in her bag for her ticket. He attended at her shoulder, resolute not to lose these last fleeting minutes. When she had put away her baggage tags and was ready to go through Customs Control, several passengers were still waiting to have their tickets cleared. They would have liked to fill the time with all the purpose and eloquence love deserved, but neither of them had anything to say now, their mouths were dry, and their eyes clung despairingly, though they had disclaimed despair.

A glass door opened. A Customs official looked through it and motioned her forward.

'Miss Marryat? You may come through, please!'

They could go no farther together, for Lubov this was the barrier. They kissed, mouth to mouth in the old family kiss, released by the sudden familiarity of the moment from all pain in the encounter. Their hands parted with a reluctance and tenderness which could at least be borne.

'Good-bye, Emmy, darling!' His cheek was pressed to hers for a moment; he had forgotten to be careful. 'Have a good flight! And write very soon!'

'Good-bye, Lubov! Yes, of course I will! Good-bye, darling!'

She went through the door, and he was left behind in the fitful noise and bustle of the hall, looking after her. Still the delayed anguish did not come. She was too much hemmed about as yet with the small business of passport and currency and Customs, there was no leisure to feel pain.

When her flight number was called, half an hour later, and she followed the rest of the passengers out under the blue light on to the tarmac, she looked towards the terrace in front of the restaurant, where a dozen little figures stood to watch them embark. He was still there, she found him and waved her hand, once as she came to the foot of the ladder, once from the door of the plane, before she went in and took her seat. Now she could still see him, but he could not see her, the plane itself that held her must become the focus of his regard. He had become infinitely small and solitary, and had about him a kind of unpretentious symbolism, standing there obstinate and apart as though he signified man's inescapable singleness, the final state of Everyman, not so much deserted by his fellows as disencumbered of them. She felt his loneliness, and his ability to sustain it, without despair or resentment, because she alone was not banished by it but identified with it. She fixed her eyes upon him,

182

turning as the aircraft turned, until they had outrun all possibility of seeing him still, and the whole superstructure of terraces and offices and towers had fallen away out of her field of vision as they taxied into position for the take-off.

The engines raced, thundering in her ears. They began to roll forward into the wind, lumbering into that lunging run she knew so well, that quietened suddenly into a sigh of achievement. She saw the ground heel away from under them, the flat grey-and-green map of the airfield, most artificial of the works of man, spinning slowly and diminishing with wild rapidity as it span, until on every verge of it the mottle of red roofs and whirling towers rushed in, and the whole city sprang together for a few magical moments beneath her. But in a short time they began to climb through low cloud, and the blown and tattered convolutions of mist rushed between, and, gathering greyly fold upon fold, hid from her sight the man, the city and the land.

PART II

HERE

Development:
'Lístky si psáváme malé,
Ježnedojdou,
"Myslím na tebe stále,
Bratře za vodou.
Nemyslím na mosty stržené,
Neklesám. Rostu.
A my se spolu sejdeme
Uprostřed mostu."'

Snad Kdesi za Piavou:
Fráňa Šrámek.

'The letters we write each other
None can deliver.
"I think of you always, my brother
Beyond the river.
No broken bridge be our token.
No dwindling. Growing.
We'll meet on a bridge unbroken,
Above the waters flowing."'

Somewhere Across the Piave:
Fráňa Šrámek.

Malcolm Innes met her at London Airport, and drove her home to the flat in Chelsea through the mid-evening dazzle and the pre-Christmas glitter of London lights. The flight had been smooth, and admirably on time, and immeasurably boring, a long, monotonous cruise over a floor of uniform grey cloud, in an air as clear and still as crystal. The first experience can be wonderful, but after that it dismays with its immovable sameness. She had felt grateful for the feverish dash through the controls at Zürich, and the change of aircraft; and she herself was amazed at the eagerness and longing with which she strained after the winking green lights drawing them in at the end of the journey, and the rigid pattern of the lit runways which meant home to her. One home—this home. Home here. The other seemed already lost to some other continent, a floating land-island towed away into unattainable distance. Yet in reality it was not unattainable; she had been there. To that she clung, against every instinct of irrecoverable loss.

Malcolm asked, as they passed the Ace of Spades, and the lights began to thicken and glow round them, familiar and friendly: 'Well, how was it?'

'Oh, quite good! They're splendid audiences, I think they made it easy to do well. Everything went smoothly, and everyone seemed pleased.'

'I meant the other thing,' said Malcolm. 'You're not going to pretend you went first and foremost for the concert engagements, are you?' His voice was warm, but she felt unmistakably the smart of his jealousy. 'How did you find things with your friends?'

He would never use their names; that was another thing she had never really understood until now. He affected to forget the Slav syllables, or to be unable to pronounce them; she had not realised until now that it was a ritual gesture of exclusion, tribally English.

'Very little changed,' she said. 'Everybody's well, and things are going on there almost exactly as they were last year. There are changes, of course, but on the face of it they take some seeing. Yes, it was successful—I've seen everyone, and I know they're all right.'

'Good, then you're satisfied? The trip was worth it?'

'Well worth it!' Worth anything, she thought, anything on earth, even though the treasure I found I possessed there turned out to be a blocked account, non-transferable.

'What, everything normal? Is it all lies we've been told up to now?'

'Everything's considerably more normal than we admit it is, anyhow. Of course there must be changes. I don't know about lies—

there must have been plenty, certainly, but probably even more exaggerations. On a small foundation of comparatively mild fact you can raise quite an erection of tall stories when you're excited.'

'I hope you won't be too tired,' said Malcolm rather hesitantly, 'but Pryor has arranged a little press conference for you at the flat. He thought that as it was fairly early you'd rather get it over tonight than have it called for tomorrow. And, you know, it's a first-rate opportunity, from his point of view.'

'A press conference?' She turned her head and stared at him disbelievingly, breaking into irresistible laughter. 'For *me*? For a completely unimportant singer coming back from a little winter tour in Europe? But why on earth do they want to get anything out of me? And what do they expect to get?'

'You're *not* unimportant, your reputation's going up steadily. And at this moment you're news as well. Don't you realise you're the first singer to crash through the iron curtain into those parts since the coup?'

The stupidity and lack of feeling in the cliché lacerated her nerves; she could not let it pass. 'Don't use that silly phrase, Malcolm! Not to me, at any rate! I don't like to think of the damage it's done to people's thinking already.'

'We use it to be understood readily,' he said, annoyed. 'It doesn't mean anything.'

'That's what I complain of. I asked for a

visa, I got one, I went there and was received with exactly the same courtesy they've always shown me. They've behaved with integrity to me, and so will I to them.'

Malcolm lifted his bulky shoulders with a resigned sigh. 'All the more reason why you should talk to the press, then. You can't blame your agent for seeing the possibilities, at any rate, can you? It's his job to make your name known.'

She said, with a sudden, sharp premonition: 'I doubt if he'll get much out of this. I doubt if they'll want to print what I have to say.' And already she was wondering what she would say, what she could bear to say. Yuri had his rights, his voice ought to be heard. But so ought Wanda's, and so, above all, ought Lubov's, that perplexed voice scrupulously balancing Grosz against his father, justice to one against the grievance of another, one freedom achieved against another curtailed, liberation against compression. She could not imagine any newspaper-man voluntarily concentrating upon so unsensational a story. It was so much simpler to give it a slant one way or the other, and be done with it. And, at the moment, so much more popular.

There could be other reasons, besides love of truth, for answering with extreme care. It must be well known who had been her hosts over there; her reported opinions here might well be attributed largely to their influence, and have repercussions for them. On the other hand, Pryor would undoubtedly be horrified if she expressed too uncritical an enthusiasm. Pryor knew what disastrous effects too much candour can have upon a reputation. She began to smile secretly to herself, pondering the thin ice over which she was expected to cut arabesques. She thought Lubov would have been pleased to know that she could still find the prospect a comic one.

'What are they going to expect of me? I didn't go there to study the political situation.'

'Whatever you say,' said Malcolm ingenuously, 'will be political enough for them.'

She laughed, but he was not conscious of having made a joke. She often had the disappointment, with him, of finding no echo to her laughter.

Her flat was in a house on a quiet street going down to the Embankment, where the noise of traffic fell away distantly on either side, and even the street lamps stood back discreetly from the door. The lights from the first-floor windows greeted them as the car drew up. Ralph or his wife must be here, a party to the plan, for they kept her keys while she was away, and came over to open the flat whenever she was due to return. Naturally they would be eager to aid and abet Pryor in his schemes to make capital out of her eastern connections. Her career afforded them a disinterested satisfaction, they would have done anything to advance it.

She went up the stairs slowly, trying to anticipate something of which she had no experience. But when she entered the lounge of the flat, and encountered so many strange, expectant and alert glances, it seemed to her more of a stage entrance than a home-coming. The familiar room was full of people and hazy with the smoke of their cigarettes. There were even a couple of cameras; she had thought no one but film stars or generals rated those. When Grace rose from a settee with a little shout of welcome and ran across to kiss her, a flashlight bulb hissed and flashed a salute to the scene. The kiss also, though she knew it to be genuine, managed to acquire from its setting a dismaying bogusness.

Pryor came forward out of the little group of strangers and took her hand.

'So you got back safely, after all! All her friends prophesied she'd disappear behind that curtain and never emerge again.' He was at the top of his form, he looked as he looked only when he felt himself to be on the crest of a wave, radiant, handsome, almost young again. He was fifty-five, and getting fat, and baldness was stealing upon him gradually, elongating by a little more every year his monumental temples, between which the dwindling widow's-peak of straight brown hair clung obstinately to the centre of his forehead. He had melting dark eyes which would have been an adornment to the fine musician he had never quite succeeded in being, and a lean square jaw obviously designed for the same too ambitious picture. 'Did Malcolm warn you of this reception?' he asked, aware already that she was resigned to it. 'I hope you're not too tired to give these gentlemen just a quarter of an hour—we won't ask for longer than that, after the journey you've had.'

'I'm not at all tired, thank you, Alan. Of course I'll give them as long as they like. Be an angel, and get me a long drink, while I take off my coat, then I'll be with you.'

She settled herself in a chair drawn back against the wall, where she could see them all, and sat back with the glass Pryor brought to her. There were not so many of them as she had at first supposed, for the room was not designed for numbers, and made seven look a multitude; but seven was more newspaper-men than she had ever before had hanging on her lips. Most of them were young, and there was one girl, sharp-eyed and quick of movement, her thin fingers spread over her notebook as if braced in the starting pose for a race. As soon as Emmy was seated their questions began, at first with decorous slowness, then more ardently.

'You've been over there before, I believe, Miss Marryat. Could you tell us how the situation there is changed on this visit?'

'Remarkably little, as far as one can see,' she said. 'The most noticeable thing is the number of flags draped about the streets—native and Russian, yes, both. Apart from that the place looks essentially the same as it did last year, except that an enormous amount of building and rebuilding has been done. Mostly houses and flats. They have a housing problem on about the same scale as ours since the war.'

'Are the police very much in evidence?'

'The only ones I saw were on the usual traffic duties. I can't say they were more frequent than usual.'

'But there are two kinds of police, aren't there?' It was the girl, burning with knowledge.

'If you count the Customs and frontier police, yes. They wear blue tabs instead of green,' said Emmy, not without malice.

'Oh, yes, I see—I was thinking more of the secret police.'

'If they're secret, you wouldn't expect them to be much in evidence, would you? I don't know anything about any police except the ordinary force and the Customs men. So far I haven't talked to anyone who claims to have had dealings with any others.'

'Did you see much of the Russians?'

'I didn't see anything of them. I suppose there must be a fairly large embassy staff somewhere there, but I haven't heard of any other Russians being seen about the town.'

'But surely,' two or three of them began

briskly, 'it's beyond dispute that the Communist coup there was brought about by the Russians?'

'I don't feel competent to pronounce upon that. I never had it suggested to me that there were any Russians actually involved—even by people who resent and regret the change of alignment. I certainly didn't see anything of any Russians myself.'

'How do people act in the streets, Miss Marryat? Do they look happy? Talk freely?'

'They look as happy as most people in a world as worried as this. They certainly talked as freely as last year, from my observations in trams. There's a certain feeling of over-excitement about the streets, I would say. But really, it's hard to think of any substantial change in the people or the atmosphere.'

'I suppose a reign of terror doesn't really show in the streets,' said one of the men, his pencil lagging.

'I saw no signs of terror. I think occasionally one does feel a sense of uneasiness, but I wouldn't put it more strongly than that.' There was no need to, she saw; they had brightened, and were gazing at her expectantly over their scribbling fingers. They would make the most of that uneasiness. She put away carefully the words she had just been weighing, and added nothing more. She had felt obliged to detail the curious sensations which visited a family when one of its members was late in coming home,

195

but after all she let it rest. The thing itself was so subtle that almost any description of it would do it violence.

'You speak the language, don't you, Miss Marryat? Enough to talk to people?'

'My conversation is very limited. But, yes, I can get along.'

'Did you find people willing to talk to you?'

'Oh yes, even anxious. They like to be visited.'

'They weren't afraid to be seen talking to an English person?'

Thinking of Yuri, she said meticulously: 'I met only one person who claimed he was afraid to be seen with me. He's a young man I already knew fairly well. He didn't want me to come to his university hostel to ask for him, but he consented to meet me in the park, and I can't say that he seemed to me to be taking much pains to conceal his movements, or to avoid being seen in my company.'

Now they were all alight, they wrote industriously, and hurriedly fastened their shining eyes again upon her face. Yuri was what they wanted. Yuri was the right line. She saw Pryor smiling contentedly.

'And what did he tell you? Did he talk about the régime? He must have told you how it was affecting him personally?'

'He was wholeheartedly opposed to it. He had to terminate his university studies, because they're tightening up the regulations on attendance, and he hasn't made all the lectures he should have done.' She enlarged upon the exchange of students which was going on, thoughtfully watching them seize upon her careful phrases. So now she knew what they wanted, and knew that it was all they wanted. When she reached the credit side, and began to talk about Lubov's eager new students from the mines and the factories, their pencils rested. One of the young men yawned.

Would she, in any case, have told them about Yuri's seditious articles and his brief experience of police persecution? She could never now be sure. It was a part of the whole truth, but they were not interested in the whole truth; their reading of truth was conditioned by the tendencies of the time, and it was partial in every sense. The result of telling them the whole truth would still be so partial as to be no longer truth at all.

From that moment she began to censor her own answers. The mild, the innocuous praises and criticisms they could have, but they were not to be trusted with stones which could be used to throw and relied upon to hurt. Silent and motionless still, she must go softly and contain what she knew, refraining from word or act which could provide either side with ammunition to use against the other. She was no longer editing to evade the possibility of any stricture of hers being a threat to Lubov and his family; she was quite simply standing between his country—her country—and the ferocity of its enemies.

'Did you meet any other people who're against the regime?'

'No one else who declared himself definitely against it. A good many who expressed reservations about it. And some who were emphatically in favour.' She described the transformation of Wanda's factory, the promotion of Petr, the young pianist with the coal-scarred hands, the ardent devotion of Helena. They edged her back, fidgeting, towards the debit side.

'All this was through official contacts? I mean, they'd naturally bring you into touch with the enthusiasts. It would be practically an official hand-out.'

'Oh no, not at all. The musicians I certainly met through the Musicians' Club, but apart from that I had no official contacts.'

'But weren't you a guest of the Ministry of Culture?'

'On the contrary, I went there entirely independently. I stayed with my friends, a family I've known since two of them were here in England during the war. In their country I am a private person.'

'Your friends are Communists, I take it, Miss Marryat?' That was the girl again, growing angry because the material she was getting would not keep the form she meant it to have.

Emmy laughed. 'Do you know, I've never asked them. They certainly never used to be. I should think it very unlikely that they are now. But I don't know. It never occurred to me to wonder.'

'Would it even be safe for someone who was in England during the war to stay out of the Party now?'

'Of course it would! With your attitude,' she said frankly, 'you might just as well ask if it would be possible for such a person to get *into* the Party. It's just as logical. And just as silly.'

'How about the standard of living, Miss Marryat? Is there any change there?'

'Not very much. On the whole I'd expected it to go down a shade, because they had a very bad drought last year, and have had to import a lot of grain, where they'd have been practically self-supporting with any luck. It meant they had to export finished goods to pay for the grain, and it's kept the shops rather empty and prices rather up. On the whole the effect was less than I'd expected.'

'Would that be the official account, too?' asked one of the young men, candidly hostile.

'No, it's personal observation, if you mean the drought. I was there last August and saw the disaster for myself. It hadn't rained since April.'

'We've heard that even small factories are being taken over by the State now. Can you tell us anything about that?'

'I don't know of a small one which has been confiscated. I do know of one which is in process of being handed over voluntarily, though it hasn't changed hands, yet. Small proprietors are having a struggle to get materials, in competition with the big nationalised concerns. This owner has found it better to hand over, and become manager of his own business under the State. I imagine the same thing might be happening to many others.'

'He's handing over without compensation?' said the young man, with a knowing smile.

'On the contrary—with compensation. I didn't ask him how much; I don't think it had been agreed yet, they were still in negotiation.'

'And will he ever get it?'

'If he's perfectly confident of getting it,' she said, 'I don't think you need worry.'

'And this owner—would he be a model case produced by the State to impress visitors?'

The idea of Matyas in this rôle was so funny that she laughed aloud. 'He would not! He was my host. I've known him since 1945, and there was nothing in the least official about our introduction.'

They hovered, dissatisfied, probing for a more effective approach.

'It all sounds very normal and pleasant, Miss Marryat, but surely the background is always palpable. The one-party government, the elections where voters can only say yes or waste their vote—'

'That may be true,' she said, 'though I haven't the knowledge to make such a statement with authority, and I very much doubt whether you have, either. It would be necessary first to examine a lot of other aspects of the matter, such as the part communities other than parties play there in the actual selection of prospective candidates, before they ever get into the list. But I'd prefer not to make any assertion on that subject at all, since I wasn't there during an election and I've no first-hand knowledge of what happens. I can tell you only what I know from my own observations. I went there to sing, and to visit my friends. I've done both without hindrance, and certainly without supervision.'

'Isn't it a fact that all the airmen who fought with the RAF are in prison now?'

'The son of the house where I stayed was a pilot with the RAF. I'm glad to assure you that he's still at large.'

'Aren't the police armed? And aren't the people terrified of them?'

'Armed police begin on the other side of the Channel, not in Central Europe. We're the exceptions, not the rule.'

'What about the riots in the summer—'

It was really a pity to disappoint them, and a worse pity to let them go away in such good conceit with themselves, even though it was not their fault, even though they were only pursuing what they were expected to produce in order to earn their bread and butter. She was growing angry, with a cool, contained anger which moved softly and lay smilingly behind her equable face. If she set forth for these people Lubov's plea at her departure, would they even understand it?

'I should like to tell you, gentlemen—' she said.

The gravity of her tone produced its own silence.

'I should like to tell you that I did witness one incident—'

She let her imagination run, conjuring up out of her own anger the whole scene as they would love to have it, the unknown young man who had followed her out of a café to tell her of his father's arrest, his own dispossession, the sad fate of his country. It ended with the inevitable police emerging from the shadows to haul him away. They accepted every word this time without reserve, taking it down avidly; they had lost the faculty of doubting anything which fitted so well into the pattern of their culture.

'Yes,' she said, vengefully contemplating their moment of fulfillment, 'I should like to tell you that, gentlemen—I should like it very much, because I feel it would give you so much pleasure. But nothing in the least like that happened, so I'm afraid I can't satisfy you.'

She rose and, putting down her glass upon

the table, faced them with so bitter a smile that none of them could find anything to say. Stupefied, clutching their frustrated pencils, they stared back at her with dropped jaws and flaming faces, outraged and hurt by a snub they felt they had done nothing to earn.

'Things are not so simple as that,' she said, more quietly. 'If you want something really urgent to say to the British people, say to them what was said to me the day I left for Vienna. My friend the ex-pilot asked me if I thought I could convince some of the more perceptive people in England that he and the others like him, the ones who have lived here and worked alongside us, have not divorced their country yet. He asked me to tell you that the stones you throw in that direction hit them first and hardest. He said: "Ours is a very exposed position: we have to blush for the British as well as for our own people." Could you, do you think, persuade your readers to give a little thought to that view?'

They looked back at her with the impervious arrogance of prejudice, so incandescent with offence that they could not even try to understand her. None of them bothered to make a note of the words, and she knew that, as far as the press was concerned, she would never hear of Lubov's plea again. It was not the kind of thing to catch the eye or the ear; it was too original to be news.

'If you have anything else to ask me,' she

said, 'I'll answer it if I can.' No one spoke; they considered themselves, perhaps justly, to have received their dismissal, and began to gather together their belongings with reddened cheeks and pursed lips. She said with a contemptuous but composed smile: 'You won't forget to cut out my fairy story, will you? Your editors probably wouldn't recognise it as a flight of fancy, either.'

She was not being conciliatory, and she knew that they had some right to grow angry in their turn, but she regretted nothing; not even Pryor's helpless stare of reproach and quick, emollient efforts to undo what she had done. As they rose with restrained murmurs of offended thanks to her for the interview, he moved in among them with his masterly smile and reassuring voice, tackling them individually, and persuading each one, she was sure, that the cut had been aimed at all the rest, but not at this one intelligent and honest journalist. Divide and reconquer was Pryor's rule. She watched him at work, the savage smile curling her normally tranquil and contemplative mouth. Grace, sitting back awed and quiet, exchanged a worried glance with Malcolm, but said not a word until the last of the reporters was out of the flat and Pryor's calming tones had receded with them in the direction of the stairs. Then she ventured, in a distressed tone:

'Need you have been so unkind to them?

They were only doing their job.'

'You think I was the one who was rude? You didn't notice the implications of the things they had to say to me? That I was either a liar or a dupe, that my friends were also liars for partisan reasons, or boot-lickers for reasons of self-interest? What did you expect me to do, thank them for putting me right about what I'd seen with my own eyes, and feed them the stuff they wanted?'

Grace bit her soft, full underlip, and turned the empty glass round and round in her plump, child's hands. 'No, of course not, Emmy! I know they were a bit brash. But to hit them like that—'

'You yourself,' pointed out Malcolm placatingly, 'admitted that several things were wrong there. Why shouldn't they report that side of the bargain?'

'Why not, if they reported the other side, too? But did you really fail to see the complete lack of interest they showed in anything good that came out of the set-up? They wanted just one thing, they'd been sent to collect just one thing—stones to throw. Well, I'm not providing stones for anyone to throw at anyone.'

The sounds of departure had ceased, dying away down the well of the stairs. Pryor came back into the room, and slowly and resignedly closed the door.

'Well, you went to a lot of trouble to throw

that away. It could have been useful, but now we may as well forget it. If you intend to mishandle every legitimate opportunity for publicity in the same way,' he said exasperatedly, 'I might as well not be working for you.'

She raised her grey eyes and looked at him for a long moment in thoughtful silence, before she said deliberately: 'That's just what I was thinking myself, Alan. I'm a singer. I prefer my publicity to be limited to my musical capabilities, if you don't mind. I'm not a professional politician, to think all the rest of humanity outside these islands expendable in the interests of my career. In particular, my friends are not expendable. If those are the only headlines you can guarantee me, I'll gladly manage without them. But I suppose,' she said, sighing, 'you could hardly know quite how biased they were going to be.'

All the same, she thought, it would not have mattered to him if he had known. Headlines were headlines to him, to be acquired by any reasonable means, and for him reasonable means included selling down the river any remote little group of unfortunates in a far-off land of which we take good care to know nothing. Perhaps no longer nothing, but never too much; never enough to disturb us in contemplating their re-sale. In any case their country's gone Communist, he would reason, and we're all agreed that's as good as going to the devil; so why look for the grains of virtue that only vex the situation? Pryor's devils were not entitled to any measure of justice whatsoever.

'If you see more of that interview,' he said, in a prophetic burst of candour, 'than a couple of paragraphs in perhaps three papers, I shall be very much surprised.'

It did not occur to her, until she turned over the daily papers next morning, that what seemed to him a tragic waste of good material might be matter for profound gratitude to her. His estimate had been sound; four papers in all mentioned her return, all using the catch-phrases she resented so much. Two of the items were so small that they hardly mattered at all; the remaining two had naturally selected Yuri as the only crumb of news worth inflating in her report. 'Friend was Afraid to be Seen with Me,' proclaimed the first: 'Singer reports from behind Iron Curtain.' The other said: 'Purge of University Students in Iron Curtain Country': 'Singer's friend a victim.' There was no mention of Petr, none of old Grosz and his late-flowering honours, none of Helena's scholarship, nothing that could be seen as good and honest and a motion of justice. Even the sparing truth she had felt able to tell, it seemed, could be vetted and turned to account.

'Well, I did no good, Lubov,' she said to her own heart. 'But at least I've learned! There's nothing to be achieved that way. Individuals might be able to listen—evidently professional ears can't.'

She looked into a future in which she must deny herself all motion but the ceaseless, shadowy motion needed to maintain her position between the levelled guns and their targets, all speech but the constant interventions in defence of the wounded.

* * *

One of the wounded sent a message on Christmas Day. She had gone to stay with Ralph and Grace for the festival, as usual, in the cottage the family had kept together, after her father's death, to shelter them all in their occasional flights from town, and her letters followed her from London, the last thin and sad diminuendo of the season, the stragglers of the army of goodwill. Among the half-dozen unsealed cards there was an unexpected letter, a large envelope of unmistakable continental origin; the stamps on it were German, the postmark somewhere in Bavaria, though she could not read the name of the town. She could think of no one belonging to her who was in Germany. The address was typed, but when she slit open the envelope she unfolded a thick foolscap sheet covered closely and precisely with a handwriting she knew to be familiar, though she could not at once identify it. It was a headlong hand, and yet achieved in the completed page an effect of curious primness, a self-consciousness which made its vigour look rather petulant than formidable. She regarded it for a moment with foreboding, because the unknown and unexpected was always to be feared in a schizophrenic age like the present; then she braced her mind, and turned to the signature.

Yuri! So he had made a success of it! Miloslav need not have devoured his heart daily, the fugitive was safe, and over the frontier into his promised land. She felt her mind eased of one tension, at least, and was glad for all of them, not least for the authorities, caught in their own not all unreasonable fears, who might have been faced with a captive whose disposal could cause them nothing but trouble and distress and injury, and who now were spared that encumbrance. Yuri recaptured would have burned a lot of other fingers beside his own. Yuri in Bavaria might have dangerous properties, too, but he was a preferable problem.

*　　*　　*

'Dear Emmy,' Yuri had written from a displaced persons' camp in the border regions of the province, 'I hope you will not object to my writing to you, however much we may differ in our views on the events which have brought me here. I know that you guessed, on

209

the last occasion when we met like that for only a moment, what I was going to do, and I am afraid that you do not approve of it, but I believe that it is possible for us to be friends even while we think differently, and I hope you can welcome me as a friend on those terms. I have no one now within reach who knows me, except you. I have never been out of my own country before, and now it is a very sad and a final journey I have undertaken, and I must admit to you that I feel very lonely for the company of someone whose acquaintance with me has not just begun here, without any yesterdays at all. If you feel that you can write to me, you will help me very much.

'I have been here now for over a month, but was not at first allowed to write letters, for the distrust, naturally, is not all on one side, and I have been kept segregated, and questioned and re-questioned, for some time before I was allowed to come into the camp, and join the many others like myself—not only from my country, but at least half a dozen others—who are living here until they can find a permanent home. I do not complain of this screening at all, and you can see that now I am trusted I am allowed to tell you about it freely. About my flight from home I will only say that it was a success, and not very eventful. I am chiefly anxious about Miloslav, because I have no way of sending a message to him, and if you can let him know in some way that I am safe and well,

I shall be most grateful. I know that you would not consider smuggling any other kind of message, and I would not ask it, but I think you will feel yourself free to inform friends of their friends' survival and welfare at any time, and through any barrier. If I am wrong, I beg you to excuse it that I ask.

'Since I feel that you have doubts still about my stamina, and expect me to go over entirely to the most extreme Western view now that I have crossed the frontier, I must tell you once again that I am determined to avoid that surrender. I shall act, here and wherever I may ultimately find myself, in accordance with my principles, and shall make my judgment in every case according to the relevant evidence. In case you should imagine that because I made the judgment that what I have left is evil, therefore I am obliged to find everything here good, let me say that it is not so. I am not deceived in that way. Here in this camp, among the people who have abandoned their countries as I have abandoned mine, one can see every kind of meanness and intolerance. They fight over food, and over beds, and over a few coins, and I have seen them more often cheat one another than make any generous gesture to help one another. They are not all people who have come across the border because of principles. Some were wanted by the police for civil crimes, and you can easily imagine that this provides for them an easy way of escape. Some have come simply because they think it will be easy to make a living as a refugee, and that full co-operation with the Americans for propaganda purposes is easier than working for wages at home.

'There are, of course, also the genuine ones, who are truly to be pitied, but they are the least noticeable of all, because they do not know so well how to get what they want, and how to attract attention to themselves. I have been working now for one week, because of my knowledge of several languages, in the camp office which deals with all their domestic affairs, and I have seen many things to shock me. These are certainly not an élite. They steal even from one another. Do not be afraid, therefore, that I shall accept these as an army of saviours!

'The conditions here are not good, and do not help people to be unselfish. We have not enough bedding or fuel, and it is very difficult to keep warm now that the snow has come. The new coat which you saw is not thick enough, but I am very fortunate by comparison with some of the others, who have none. If one has extra coats or blankets it is possible to sell them for quite a lot of money, with which one can buy extra food. It is quite necessary to have a little money to buy food apart from our rations, because they are not sufficient for health. I do not mean to remain here long, but it is more difficult than I had thought to make application to go to another country, and I think it would be best for me to work here for some time, because I am useful in the office, and so to make some reputation for reliability which could help me to be acceptable somewhere else. Naturally no one has any reputation at all on coming here, we have only each man's word for what he is, and his reason for being here. I cannot say that one ever takes that word without more evidence.

'It is not a good life, but it must lead to one, because I cannot and will not waste the sacrifice I have felt obliged to make. I am glad I had no family to leave behind—I think I could not otherwise have left as I did—but I must confess I miss my friends sometimes very badly.

'Please write to me if you are not absolutely estranged from me now. It would be so fine to hear from you. And if there is an opportunity, do send my best regards to Miloslav and all his family. I think of them very often, and of you, too, my dear Emmy.

Yuri Dushek.'

*   *   *

She read it through, and felt her heart melting in her for the careful phrasing, the literal translations from his own language, all the revealing touches which brought back to her not only the vivid presence of Yuri Dushek

213

himself, but all the Ivanescu, the flat on the Lucerna, the wintry beauty of the city and the land. She ached with the stress of containing her gratitude. It was a revealing letter, touchy, correct, stiff and pathetic, like Yuri himself, and it moved her because in the effort to set forth his strength it most treacherously revealed his weakness. His sense of the indignity of appearing to go straight from one camp to the other, his consciousness of the virtue of his balancing feat in avoiding the fall, his scandalised acknowledgement of the disintegration of others, and his unawareness that any such decline could affect him, drew her to him rather than repelling her. The thought of him suffering doubt, cold, hunger and loneliness was as unbearable as if these deprivations had threatened a child.

What was really so irresistible about him, she thought honestly, was that he was someone she could reach, and something she could do. That, and the remembrance of Lubov commending him to her if ever they should meet again. 'Be good to him. What he did was a mistake, but it wasn't all his fault.'

She wrote first to Miloslav. The sense of release in anticipating his joy at receiving this late Christmas present warmed her to the heart, and the form of communication was as simple as truth itself. 'I had a letter from George today. He's fit and well, and I hope to see him sometime, but I can't hope for a visit

214

just yet. He'll turn up eventually, probably when I least expect him, but he couldn't get leave from Germany in time for Christmas.' The letter grew long and talkative with small family news, to contain and conceal George. It did not matter how inconspicuous he became, Miloslav would not miss his significance.

Then she wrote to Yuri, with all the warmth she felt for the family, since almost he was one of the family. In a few days when the shops were open again, and she went back to London, she would send him some of the things he needed, blankets, a duffle coat, thick underwear and socks, some tinned foods if the regulations allowed it. In the meantime she wrote that of course she had always looked on him as a friend, and always intended to, that he was to let her know what help he needed, and if he thought of coming to England she would try to take up his case with whoever was the appropriate official at her end, so that the delays could be cut to a minimum. By the time he received her letter, the Ivanescu would already know that he was all right, and he could make his mind easy about them.

When it was done she read it through, an act so unprecedented with her that it had its own disturbing implications. In dealing with Yuri it would always be necessary to consider every word twice, to look carefully for any unsuspected shades of meaning which could lacerate his already damaged sensibilities. If a

215

sentence lacked warmth and tenderness, it must be softened before it reached him, or his shrinking flesh would recoil from it as from ice. On the other hand, if a possessive word encroached on his fastidious dignity, he would spring away no less fiercely. One must offer everything, and demand nothing. Could so much of him, unconsidered until now, be learned from one letter? Or was she drawing now upon knowledge she had gathered gradually throughout the three years she had known him, and never needed until this moment? Or was it rather that the new illumination of her love for Lubov shone upon all other creatures who had ever so much as been in his presence, and rendered them both clear and dear to her for his sake?

Ralph saw her come down the stairs with the letters in her hand, and laughed. 'Only conscience letters get posted on Christmas Day—acknowledgments that should have gone a week ago, or New Year cards to the people you forgot.'

'Only peace-of-mind letters,' she agreed, smiling. 'Just like these!'

As soon as he saw that she was going out, Christopher, the older child, dropped even his new toys to walk to the village with her. He was four years old, sturdy, sweet-tempered and handsome, and to be with him, as they went hand-in-hand across the fields, was joy, because everything amazed and charmed him

216

so much that its newness and wonder became visible also to her. He carried the letters carefully in his free hand, dancing and chattering incessantly beside her, and sometimes tugging her to an unexpected stop to investigate a coloured stone, the broken stars in a sheet of thin ice over a puddle in the wheel-rut, a lingering fringe of frost on a blade of grass. Looking down at him in his erratic flight among wonders, she thought with indignant longing:

'If only we'd realised that there was any hurry! If we'd known there could be other separations besides just dying we might have had a boy of Christopher's age at this moment. I might have been walking to the village—what does it matter what village?—with my own son. We might have been going home again to Lubov.'

But the unthinkable acceleration of uncertainty had caught them unawares, and they had no child, and probably never would have any, except, in a sense, Yuri Dushek, that difficult and perilous child reborn in a displaced persons' camp in Germany. He was the only being Lubov had committed to her kindness, and on him alone could she pour out some part of the enormous tenderness which belonged to Lubov.

The village in its fold of leafless woodland and rusty black ploughland was a dream of winter, still and deserted in the mysterious

Christmas hush of afternoon. The border hills of Wales, ominous under a low iron sky, withdrew into leaden distance, bearing upon their shoulders the level dark layers of cloud. The only human creatures remaining were a woman and a child, moving through a world of loneliness and silence.

*　　*　　*

The coat and the blankets, arriving without warning, caught Yuri off-balance, and caused him to write her a letter for which he afterwards apologised, though it had done more to endear him to her than any of his more careful compositions could have achieved. He did not like to remember the smudged signature, or the reckless unrehearsed utterances of gratitude, not so much for the gifts as for the existence of someone who had wished to give them. He said severely that he had had no right to inflict his mood of depression upon her, or distress her by sending a hysterical letter post-haste on the receipt of the parcel. He was ashamed that he had not read it through, and realised what a babyish outburst it was.

In fact it was a boy's warm scrawl, an unguarded shout of joy on seeing a friend after being too long alone. If it hurt his self-esteem to recall its terms, she thought, he must be recalling them through some distorting sensitivity within his mind, and what he regretted was something he had never written. Warmth is not a self-betrayal, but something due to other people; to withhold it is a betrayal of your neighbour. But in Yuri's situation he might be forgiven for some degree of over-anxiety about his own equilibrium. She had not, she realised on reading this third letter, given him enough credit for maintaining his balance as he had. He might be urging his impartiality rather pompously, but that ought not to detract from the magnitude of his achievement. To keep an equal eye open for the pitfalls of freedom was something worth boasting about. And if he called her attention to his stand, it was because she had questioned the possibility of the feat for anyone but a hero. He was not crying: 'Look what an incorruptible critic I am!' to be heard by anyone else.

She paid him the due acknowledgements faithfully in her letters, which, once launched, continued steadily through the decline of the winter and into the flush of the spring. She was profoundly grateful to him because he was one person at least to whom she could talk about the Ivanescu, and be understood. To say 'Lubov' to the rest of the world, and start no echo, was a daily deprivation, so that in time she must have contained him utterly within her own silence but for Yuri.

*   *   *

'In case you should be afraid that I have accepted everything here without question,' wrote Yuri, on his mettle and his dignity again now that he was sure of her, 'I must tell you, from time to time, how we live here. You would not find it a very inspiring place, and I am sure that you know already how it must look, for army camps are the same everywhere. We have only large huts in our part of the enclosure, so that many families must share together, and we who are alone must fit in wherever there is a spare bunk, or room for a mattress. They try to get a little privacy by hanging up blankets, or they did so until it became so cold, for now it is impossible to spare any cloth, even the few old curtains we have, merely for preserving decency, one needs them to preserve life. So we sleep rather indiscriminately in company, and there is some immorality. The people here have not very much hope or belief in the future to keep them upright, therefore it is understandable that they should seize on whatever pleasure and satisfaction the present can offer them. There are girls here who are absolutely promiscuous, and wives, too, and even husbands who encourage their wives to cultivate those few people who have a little money when the rest have none. Constant hunger and cold, without hope of early change, without the respect of other people, and ultimately without self-respect, makes such things inevitable.

'Other things, also, are done for money, besides the procuring of wives, daughters and sweethearts. A middle-aged man here, the father of a family, got some money from a relative in America last week, and was found in the darkest corner of the camp the next night, with a fractured skull. The money was, of course, gone. Fortunately it is probable that, when he recovers, his relations in the United States may be able to get him an entry there. I am sorry to say that I am almost sure that the man who robbed and injured him was a countryman of mine. These things happen here, there is no pretending they are unusual. Morale, if by that we ought to understand the stiffening that keeps men erect, rots away very quickly in this atmosphere.

'That there are exceptions I need not tell you, since you believe in humanity as I do; but that they *are* exceptions I must tell you, in honesty. Some at least of what you tried to tell me about the self-exiled is only too true. I wish it was not, but I came away from my own country solely in order to be able to say fearlessly whatever I saw, to report my observations and record my deductions without having to falsify or suppress anything. Therefore I owe it to myself, as I do to you, to use the freedom I now have, and to use it with a sense of responsibility.'

*　　*　　*

This was Yuri on his fellow-exiles. On their hosts he reported no less scrupulously, and with the same proud, embittered eye upon his own incorruptibility.

*　　*　　*

'I have now been working for a month in this office, where I am directly responsible to the US Army authorities, as it is they who maintain the camp. At first, when they asked me to remain here, I was not sure that I could feel justified in doing so, because this work carries some privileges. I can go in and out much more freely than other people, and there is a bed for me in a small room which I share with only three other men. The work is also fairly well paid, at least for this place. So I hesitated for some time, but some of the people in the common huts asked me to take it, because they said I could help them very much if I would. And I am here, in such quiet and privacy as I have not seen since I left home. You would not credit how wonderful it can feel to have only three room-mates, after having something like fifty. I still feel guilty because they cannot all share my good luck, but I think I am useful sometimes in smoothing out some difficulties for them, and even some injustices.

'I can well understand that when new

refugees arrive they must be rather severely screened, because it would be easy to send over a few spies to mix among us and make trouble; but I have sometimes been very alarmed at the cynicism which marks the attitude of the authorities towards these poor people, even after they have been cleared of any suspicion of being agents. One cannot say that any form of democracy is in force here, or that justice has any part in the way they are treated. If one is important, perhaps having been a minister in some previous government, one arrives here to be met with press conferences and a warm reception, and very soon one is moved to some much more comfortable spot, and can get entry to the United States with very little delay. But if one happens to be a poor, obscure person, a small factory hand of no skill, or a peasant farmer, who cannot tell a very sensational story, and is not fluent in broadcasting propaganda talks, then one is thrown in here and forgotten. To the humble and unimportant, who do not make very good capital, they are not even polite. Please do not misunderstand me, they have been both civil and kind to me, but I cannot help seeing the contrast in their behaviour to others. They say that they are hampered by lack of funds, lack of time, shortages of all kinds, and confess that they are often irritated by conditions here, and by the shortcomings of their enforced guests. This I find easy to understand, but if they stand for justice they ought to observe justice in their dealings, so that one would recognise their sincerity. But when I make this point to them they find me unreasonable. They say that they are in a state of undeclared war, and it is inevitable that human rights have to give way to the urgency of the time. Therefore they must make the greatest possible use of any important people who come over the frontier, and cannot possibly do all they would like to do for the others. It is perhaps true, but it does not satisfy.

'And all the other countries behave in the same way. They take in only the immediately useful: craftsmen, engineers, technicians and their families. It is a strictly realistic approach. That is the approved word. If one is old, or unskilled, or ill, or a child with no useful father to offset the liability, one can stay here and die here. What can I say when they claim in surprise that it is perfectly natural, that it would be idiotic to expect any country to invite in the old and the maimed, creatures who could never be anything but a non-productive burden? It is natural. It *would* be idiotic, seen in that way. But there is supposed to be a principle of humanity involved, and if we cannot find it in action here, where are we to look?'

*   *   *

By the time March came in with deceptively mild airs and a rush of tulips, and sent her north to sing in Liverpool, he was a trusted person about the camp, on terms of personal friendship with at least two of the US Army officers to whom he was responsible, and was going back and forth on official business into the near-by town. What he found there did not afford him any comfort. The more relaxed note which had crept into his letters since he had found a measure of privacy and usefulness faltered indignantly as he wrote to her:

'The situation in this town, as I hope, is not at all typical of the general conditions in Germany, but I have found it very disquieting that it could exist even here in the frontier areas. I would not have believed it could be so bad, if I had not by now seen so much of it for myself, and talked to so many people here who are also concerned about it. Of the officers of the local authority and the town council, all but three or four people are known to have Nazi records, some of them in a very minor way, it is true, but the working people here are in no doubt about their being seriously implicated. One was challenged lately by a man who had been some years in a concentration camp, and since there was little evidence to be found at this stage, it was one man's word against another's, but it was the known democrat and victim of Nazism who was disregarded by the Americans, and the suspected Nazi still holds his office. Only when such a direct accusation is brought do they seem to me to go to any trouble to suppress their records. In ordinary dealings they still show exactly the same attitude which was theirs under Hitler.

'The reason for this is still more frightening, because the truth is that the town on the whole approves such an attitude. They have their citizens behind them, so they have no fear of showing their hand. In particular their contempt for us is terrible, they still look upon us as inferior races, and I believe have not given up the idea that in time they will once again make slaves of us.

'It is all the worse because there is in the town a greatly inflated population, owing to the fact that Germans expelled from the border regions of our countries are concentrated here, thus adding to the difficulties with regard to labour and supplies and living accommodation. I cannot understand why the Americans allow them to remain here on the borders, instead of dispersing them to new homes throughout Germany, as I am sure they could have done with the organisation they have at their disposal. But no move is made. These people fester here, doing casual work where they can, and never attempting to go on to a permanent settlement somewhere else, and it is really as though they are only sitting here waiting until the Americans shall take back their forfeited lands and re-settle them there. I have talked to many of them, and I know that they really believe this, they are quite confident of it. It is something taken for granted. They approach the American authorities almost aggressively, as though they had an understanding with them.

'What is still worse is that they are allowed to function as a separate political party. The party has only one aim: to recapture by any means the lands from which they have been expelled; and this aim is preached quite openly at all their meetings. Yet the authorities apparently see nothing wrong with this, and will not interfere. When I have spoken about it to the Colonel, he says that he deplores it, and is trying to discourage it by all fair means, but that until re-education has produced some results we must bear the stresses of our belief in free speech, and remember that it would be a greater disaster to surrender a principle in order to rid ourselves of a nuisance. But I tell him that he has never been under a German occupation, or he would know better where freedom becomes licence.

'There are people here among us who are very bitter about this state of affairs, and I must tell you that some would like to go back if they could. They say that if they had known the

West could openly sponsor this hope of reconquest they would never have left home, for whatever is wrong there, it is still home, and they would still fight for it against the Nazis and all their allies. I need not tell you that I do not go so far as that, simply because I do not agree with them that the West is aware of this danger, much less deliberately exploiting it. But I do think they are criminally blind that they do not see it, and I wish someone with more influence than I have could show them and convince them how much goodwill they are losing by letting this state of things go on. We want to believe in their honourable intentions, we want to believe in their desire to treat all countries with equal justice, but they go out of their way to make it hard for us.'

*   *   *

This theme, though he developed it with many details in later letters, nevertheless faded into an assuaged diminuendo by the end of May. She had never argued with him about anything, never attempted to take up any of the points he made, but only received his reports with grave respect, and probably he no longer felt that he had to treat her as an opponent to be convinced. Or was it merely that time and custom had begun to make the necessary adjustments in his nature? You can get used to anything. Yuri was getting used to exile. In the tense and acrid months of the summer, while Europe tore at its own flesh, he got used to having no roots, used to working with the Americans, used to their methods, in which they would certainly persist in spite of any arguments of his, and therefore, with time, used to not arguing, used to not even wanting to argue. She followed the change until the note of criticism ceased to sound, and marked the increasingly bitter fervour with which he compensated himself for the loss. The same weight of guilt settled now upon one tragic head, since he could not dissolve it away and be done with it.

* * *

'I blame my country,' he wrote in June, 'for this whole disaster which has overtaken Europe. I know the tendencies and the distrusts were there, explosives waiting for a detonator, but it was my country which set off the explosion. We fail, too, we make grave mistakes, we have much to reproach ourselves for, but that crime at least is not ours. We have no option but to bear our own failures, and oppose the absolute evil with every weapon we have. There is no other way of saving the world.'

* * *

He had used that noble plural, acknowledging
229

his membership of other men, many times before; it took more than one reading to distinguish this 'we' from all its predecessors, and open her eyes to the significance of his new identification.

*   *   *

Yuri came to England towards the end of October, by the night boat from the Hook of Holland. She went to Liverpool Street early in the morning to meet him, and stood at the end of the platform, scanning the hurrying travellers as they boiled out of the boat-train among a scurry of porters and a thumping of luggage. Yuri would come clutching the second-hand brief-case he had bought for his flight, and perhaps one cardboard suitcase or a kitbag with his few effects; she was moved by the contemplation of his nakedness. Possessions are nothing until you have left them. But Yuri had never had many to leave, he travelled light through the world even in his own country.

She saw him first, unmistakable even in the distance, between a slow-moving elderly woman in a fur coat and a large and deliberate business-man, his fine, striding gait cramped into short, uneven steps as he tried to disentangle himself from the crowd. There was much changed in him, but she knew him at once by the set of the head, with its uplifted

230

forehead like a tower, and its lofty brows outspread like wings. Nothing but age would ever change these beyond recognition. She raised her hand to capture his attention, but he came onward at the same nervous and irritable pace, so preoccupied with avoiding luggage trolleys and dogs and children that he hardly lifted his gaze until he was approaching the end of the platform.

Then quite suddenly he looked up and saw her, and for an instant halted abruptly, as though he could not feel ready to meet her, as though he had need of a moment of retreat into the closed world of his own senses before he could translate the long written communion with her into speech. The crowding travellers jostled him, and he plucked himself away from their touch with a start and came towards her, his wide eyes fixed upon her face in what seemed to her a stare of fear, though he was smiling with a tremulous pleasure.

What did he fear? That she would want to claim too much of him in payment for her few gifts and her stubborn pestering of officials on his behalf? That he had let her in too intimately to his jealously guarded spirit, and was no longer virgin? Or that what she had given of herself had been less than he in his loneliness had thought it, and that she felt for him in reality nothing but the cool kindness of pity? It was hard for her to know how to reassure a dread she could not yet identify; and greetings are dangerous gestures, setting their mark upon the future like a fingerprint.

All the same, she kissed him. Better fear of a surfeit than fear of hunger, and she could make it clear to him, whenever he showed signs of restlessness, that he was free as a swallow, to go or remain as he pleased. She drew him aside out of the flow of people, and he dropped the shabby imitation leather bag he carried, and accepted with vehemence the invitation of her uplifted mouth. She felt his arms trembling as he held her for a moment, and his body against hers felt at once thinner and less hard and resolute than she had expected. She disengaged herself gently, and held him off from her, considering attentively the evidences of his ten months' banishment.

He wore the duffle coat she had sent him, because it was too bulky to go into his travelling bag; and he looked borne down by its weight, a little stooped and insubstantial within the thick, shapeless fawn fabric. The hood, bunched behind his neck, made his small, classic head look smaller than ever, meanly small for a body so bulky; and the effect was accentuated by the close crop of his hair. Camp cutting had straightened and dulled the russet curls, and poor diet and sedentary living had muddied the clear gold of his skin to a sallow, soiled brown. He had lost, it seemed to her, the sense of his own grandeur. The spare beauty of his bones burned through his diminished flesh as a pure flame shines through a dusty lantern, and his eyes, grown large and fierce with fretting, stared from hollowed settings upon a world he felt to be peopled largely with enemies.

'Yuri, I'm so glad to be saying it at last: Welcome to England!'

He said, with what seemed almost a physical effort, and yet with passion: 'Emmy, dear Emmy, I'm so glad to be really here with you. I don't think it would ever have succeeded without your help.'

'Oh yes, it would! It might have taken a little longer, but they would have accepted you. Did you have a quiet crossing? Are you awfully tired?'

'Oh no, not tired at all. I had a cabin, and slept all night. It was extravagant,' he said guiltily, 'but I felt that I was coming to a new life, and I wanted to make a gesture to celebrate it.'

'I'm glad you did. There's no need to worry, because there's a job waiting for you, if you care to take it, and just for the present, until you get your bearings, I have a room for you in a flat in the same house as mine. As soon as you're acclimatised,' she reassured him gently, marking the involuntary stiffening of his head in recoil from too much indebtedness, 'you shall make whatever arrangements suit you best, but there'll be plenty of time to think about that. Have you had any breakfast yet? I expect they served it on the train?'

'Yes, they did, but I could not eat, I wanted to be here,' he said, flushing. 'I was too excited to swallow anything.'

'Then shall we go and eat somewhere here, or would you rather go home and eat there? It won't take us long, I borrowed my brother's car for the morning. And then you can rest and talk before you need think of anything else.'

'I have to report to the police on arrival,' he said.

'Oh yes, but there's no need to worry about that. We'll go together. Is it to be home, or eat here?'

'Please, home!'

He picked up the shabby bag and followed her out to the car. She drove slowly through the vibrating morning traffic, letting him stare at London and keep silence until he wished to speak. Words came to him hardly now, he thrust them arduously into sentences, and brought them out self-consciously, aware of his disability.

'Please excuse it if I am not very fluent. I have been speaking mainly German for so long, I forget my English. And it is you, too! It is being here beside you! I am used only to conversing with you by letter, one has time and leisure for forming sentences then. And also, because you are here, I cannot even say what I would like to say—'

His hands, like his cheeks, had grown both

234

thinner and softer, their lines less sharply defined. They lay tightly clasped together in his lap, and their clenched fingers had a look of hysteria.

'Emmy, you have been so kind to me!'

There was a note of such questioning pain in his voice that she made her reply with extreme care. 'Friends have obligations to one another. You would have done as much and more for me, if I had needed it from you.' And then they had turned on to the Embankment, and she nodded him eagerly to the contemplation of the shining water, broad in a brief autumnal sunshine. 'Look, the Thames! I always wanted to show this to Miloslav. We used to talk about London in front of him, and he sat and made his own pictures, and never complained. But I always meant him to have the reality, some day.'

'It won't be possible now,' said Yuri bitterly. 'There'll be no exit visa for any friend of mine, even if they begin to issue them again. Milo will never see London unless he comes here by the same route that brought me.'

'Unless things change again,' said Emmy, forbearing to mention Miloslav's aversion to that route.

'Ah!—if things change again—!'

He saw only one possible change now, and it did not involve, like the one for which she hoped, the gradual relaxation of the tensions of the world; it could be achieved only by an explosion. Its beginning and its end were violence, and he contemplated it with ardour, with vindictive eagerness, with longing.

'I told Milo you were coming over today,' she said, deflecting him from an appetite which horrified her.

He was concerned. 'But you must be very careful what you say in letters. They could be opened.'

'They could be opened in any country. But of course I'm careful. Milo understands everything; and what I have to tell him is, after all, not very terrible.'

'I would like to write to him myself,' said Yuri in a low voice, 'but I have made that impossible.' He looked down at his painfully knotted hands, and the long, curling lashes lay on his cheeks darkly. 'He is well? And all of them? Has his father still the factory?'

'He is the manager now. They are thinking of enlarging the works, and they've surfaced the little dirt road up to it. I think he's finding a certain amount of compensation in watching the alterations. He never had the capital to expand as he'd have liked.'

'But he has been robbed of his life-work,' said Yuri.

'I doubt if he'd agree to that. He has been squeezed into a position where he saw that he would ultimately have to go out of business. So have a lot of small shopkeepers here in England, pre-war, in hopeless competition

236

with the big stores. Matyas is very particular, you know, about accuracy,' she said, with a conciliatory smile. Nevertheless, he felt reproved; she saw the momentary stiffening take his neck, and the ready colour mount in his cheeks. There were no safe topics; there never would be with Yuri.

'And Milo—how is it with his classes now? Has he learned to conform?'

She heard the note of anger and hate in his voice, though she was sure that he could not hear it, and would have been sick with horror and disbelief if he had been told that it was there. He would never stop holding it against Miloslav that he had continued to sustain the weight he himself had sloughed, and had, without hesitation or reproach, helped his friend to an escape he rejected for himself. Love him as he did, grateful as he was to him, he could never forgive Miloslav for that.

'Milo isn't at the Faculty any longer,' she said gently. 'He stood out from several decisions of his class, and in the end he was dismissed as an obstructive type. He'd seen it coming from the time that you left, he told me that himself. He lasted until the spring term, and since then he's been working in the Unitas publishing house. Until this month—of course he'll be in the army now.'

'So he didn't stand out against that,' said Yuri with a brief and rather cruel smile.

'He didn't want to stand out against it. Oh,
237

he doesn't like it, of course, but he says that since he's lived under the Germans once, and since his country, unlike mine, doesn't possess any colonies to be held down by force, he can't honestly object to military training. He isn't enjoying it, but who does? And, since I last wrote to you, Wanda and Petr Kasel have become engaged.'

'They are well matched, those two,' said Yuri, his impetuous lips curling. 'I am sorry, Emmy, I am not nice about your friends, but how can I speak about such people without being angry? He is one of the pets of the Party, so he gets office, the manager's job, that's for him! And she—how is it that someone like Wanda, someone so intelligent, so good, can lose her heart to Communism? How is this possible? I do not understand it! Why can she not see that it is all evil? Really, I do not understand!'

'She has seen other evils,' said Emmy. 'No doubt she made a conscientious judgment between them.' But to argue with him, even to the extent of suggesting that there could be arguments opposed to his, offered only a prospect of dismay. She was glad that they were already turning into the quiet street sloping gently upward from the Embankment, and she could deflect his attention to the house where he was to live until he had found his feet. 'Look, this is home. There's a garden inside that wall, a lawn and a vine. It's like a country house dropped into the city. You'll find London has quite a number of rustic corners like that.'

She drove through into the little courtyard where the vista of the surprising garden opened between the branches of two old chestnut trees. Yuri had forgotten the Ivanescu family now; they were only a shadow behind his hungry eyes, in which delight had begun to shine pathetically, as though he had been afraid to believe in the home which was opening to him until he had the very stones of the doorstep under his feet. Following her into the rear hall, bag in hand, he stood gazing up the stairs.

'It's very nice here, Emmy! Do you live here, close to the garden?'

'No, we go up one flight.' She took the brief-case from him, and drew his arm through hers as they climbed the staircase. 'The woman who has the flat opposite to mine across the first landing is away in Scotland until the end of November. She left her keys with me, and let me make up one of the rooms for you until she comes back to town. I thought it would be convenient, because I can cook for you as often as we're both in, and of course you can still be out whenever you want to, and have your own key.'

He said again, and suddenly with startling tenderness: 'Emmy, you are so good to me!'

'You mustn't say that, Yuri! I indulge myself by making a pleasant fuss of you, you shouldn't praise me for it. Look, this is for you!' She unlocked the front door of Mrs Rice's flat, and led him into his bedroom, showed him the bathroom and the kitchen which he could use if he liked. Why was she so anxious to fend him off from too much gratitude, not to let him be too fond? If she allowed him to pour himself out now upon her he might want his substance back some day, and blame her for his inability to be whole again. But it seemed to her that the fear she felt was more immediate than that, and simpler. If his reserve gave way too soon it would also give way too completely, and he would be washed away in the flood of his own emotion, broken to pieces in a disruption she shrank from witnessing. Even when she touched him, he shook as though his body might break apart.

'There, all this is yours. Come across the landing when you're ready. Look, I'll leave my door open for you. I'm going to cook breakfast.'

When he tapped at her half-open door and came in to join her he looked brushed and refreshed, and had shed the unbecoming duffle coat, and changed into some light shoes. She frowned at his thinness, which caused even his old, well-made suit to hang loosely upon him.

'You need food, and plenty of it, I can see. Food, and regular hours, and peace of mind.'

'Who has that?' he said, with a wry smile.

'At least we can begin with the food.' She

poured coffee for him, and brought all the components of an English breakfast, which made him open his eyes wide in surprise, and look for a moment young and light-hearted again, as though the world had become normal, and he was merely on a first novel visit to friends in England, and intended in a few weeks to go home full of the small, absorbing details of his discoveries. 'Now tell me something about yourself. When did you leave the camp? I suppose everything is much the same there?'

'It does not change much. I left quite early yesterday morning. You see, it took me just one day and one night to come to you. It was too quick, I have not caught up with my body yet. How can people bear to go anywhere by air? One has no time to experience anything, no time to make adjustments. Even now I feel a little sick in my mind.'

For the first time his tongue was loosening, and the English phrases came more easily.

'Until you've slept here,' she said, 'and slept well, things will feel uncomfortably alien. After that you'll have made the first little impression of your personality in the stuff of this country, and everything will come more easily. Don't worry about it.'

'Your blankets, Emmy—I hope you don't mind, I sold them to help with my fare. It was easier than carrying them, and I was very short of money after I bought these shoes and one or

241

two other small things.'

'You were very wise, of course. We must get a new overcoat for you, too, now that you're here.'

'Oh, but you must not say anything bad about the duffle coat, it kept me warm in some of the worst nights. It was one more blanket for my bed, that is why it is a little shabby now. And I had also some of your tins left, so I gave them to one of the poorest families. You cannot imagine what a treasure a tin of corned beef can be, Emmy, when you have four children, and all hungry.'

'I'm glad you had some things left to give,' she said, smiling at the kindling colour of pleasure in his cheeks, and the relaxing warmth of the coffee softening the too strained brilliance of his eyes.

'It was a part of the feeling of beginning something new. But I had so little to bring that I shall have to buy some clothes as soon as I can. No one will want to employ me if I am not neat. This suit is the only one I have—do you think it would pass for two or three months, until I have earned something to buy another one?'

'We'll go shopping this afternoon, and buy whatever you need. You'll let me be your purse until you're settled, won't you?' She saw him open his lips to protest, and the jealous shadow came down again anxiously upon his brow, but she went on calmly: 'Only as a loan until you're ready to pay it off. But you must make a good impression, as you said. If you like the idea of working in the offices of a small shipping firm here in London, there's a job waiting for you with a man who used to be a great friend of my father's. He wants you because of your languages, and you'd have a great deal to do with his Latin American connections. The line has a wide trade there. I told him you could offer fluent Spanish and German, good English, and a little Russian as well. Those are real assets here, you know—we're not a nation of linguists.'

It was necessary to continue talking until his inevitable impulse to resent the gifts for which he was so helplessly grateful had passed; but necessary also to be silent at the right moment, so that she might not seem to be aware of the tensions between them. Walking the high wire, she thought, is a far less considerable achievement than looking at ease while you do it.

'Does it sound attractive to you? If you preferred something else, I'm sure you wouldn't have much difficulty in finding it, but I thought it would be necessary for you to have somewhere to start.'

'It sounds wonderful,' he said in a whisper, and sat gazing at her across the table with dark eyes dilated and softened by sudden tears. 'Please—you must forgive me if I am a little nervous and difficult. It is such a sudden change—I am in a free country, I can work with hardly any restrictions, I can write and say whatever I like. It is too much for me, all at once like this. And you—I owe it all to you, and now I am here with you, and I do not know how to repay you, except perhaps by asking still more, by asking and asking—'

'You would be giving me something I want very much,' she said, with careful gentleness, 'if you would ask me for anything you need.'

A tremor passed over his face, and for a moment, while the quivering smile lasted, he regained something of the beauty she remembered from the days of victory, when both he and his country were newly at liberty. She knew that it would not last, that the vivid pride would dwindle again into petulance, and the candour into a defensive reserve; all the same, she was painfully moved by it.

'There will be things you'll need,' she said.

'Yes—'

'And you will ask me?'

'I will ask you.' The shining regard of his eyes hung upon her like a weight bearing down her spirit. She felt the terrible oppression of obligation which giving lays upon the giver. His load of indebtedness was light by comparison, a little anger could slough it in a moment, he could walk away and leave the shards of it lying. But she had no recourse to anger with the deprived child she had admitted to her life, and by no word or action of hers could she ever again be rid of him or withdraw from him the silent forbearance of her love.

*   *   *

They went together to the offices of Maxwell and Fremantle the next day, and talked over the job with old Michael Fremantle. The interview was a success. Yuri was immaculate in a new suit, probably the first ready-to-wear one he had ever put on in his life, but it looked well on him. The stimulus of shopping in a city where everything was new and intriguing had revived to some extent the pure pride in himself which he had seemed in danger of losing. He exerted himself to be liked, and he was liked; and of his qualifications for handling foreign correspondence there was no question. So Yuri had a job waiting for him to step into it on the following Monday morning, and her responsibility for him, except as a friend who could provide him with the opportunity of other friendships, was already virtually over. Yet she could not feel that the weight he cast upon her heart had lightened.

As they were taking their leave, the old man asked mildly: 'By the way, Emmy, have you heard anything about your visa yet? It's time something was happening, isn't it?'

She cast one quick glance at Yuri's suddenly alert face, and shook her head. 'No, nothing yet. I wrote again, but they say the Embassy here is no longer responsible for granting entry, it has to go to the Ministry at home. I suppose that's bound to mean a certain amount of delay.'

'But it must be five, six weeks now since you applied. Letters could have gone back and forth a couple of times since then.'

'Ministries don't hurry. At any rate, I haven't been refused yet,' she said, with a faint smile.

'Well, I hope you'll have good news about it soon. Good-bye, my dear! Good-bye until Monday, Mr Dushek; I hope you're going to be happy with us.'

They walked in silence to the Underground station, and as they went down the concrete steps Yuri drew close to her and took her arm. She felt him shaking with some emotion for which she could find no reason which was not disquieting.

'Why didn't you tell me you'd asked for a visa?' he asked very levelly.

'I don't know,' she owned, frowning. 'Because there was nothing more to tell you yet, I suppose. I'm still waiting to hear their answer. I think I've grown a little superstitious about talking about it.'

'Emmy, why do you deceive yourself? Why do you pretend to yourself that they'll ever let you in again? Why do you go on behaving as though my country still belonged to the civilised world? It's gone, gone, gone!' he said

246

violently, digging his fingers into her arm. 'Can you never face the truth?'

'You are only saying the things people here said to me when I asked for a visa last year,' said Emmy, feeding sixpences into a ticket machine. 'I knew then that they might be true, I knew they might not. I knew I had no right to blame them for not giving me a visa until at least I'd asked for one. The position hasn't changed since then,' she said. 'You were wrong then, you may be wrong now.'

'You are simply stubborn,' he said furiously. 'Last year was the twilight, now it is full darkness. You only hurt yourself more than you need by shutting your eyes to the truth.' He followed her through the barrier and on to the escalator, incandescent with a burning distress which was not for her, but all for himself. Perhaps he no longer saw anything clearly for the emanations of himself in between.

'I enjoyed the twilight,' said Emmy. 'No doubt I shall find something nice about the night.' But she looked at him with concern, for his clenched fingers hurt her arm, and his face was grey and pinched with protest at her levity. 'Why are you so angry about it? If I don't get a visa, you are so much nearer being justified. If I do, I can reassure you as well as myself that our friends are safe and well. But why should you resent it that I even try to go back? Am I to give up my friends as easily as that?'

She felt him flinch before the sentence ended,

247

and knew that he had anticipated another and more cruel ending. But she could not take back without worse damage the insinuation she had never made. In whatever she might say there would always be something to scarify a creature so determined to suffer.

He sat beside her in the train, taut and still, trying to contain himself utterly, to hide his feverish resentment from the eyes of the people who moved indifferently around them. Occasionally he persuaded his voice to a calm which permitted speech, and asked her, in an undertone flat and precarious, as though it might shatter at any moment: 'They wanted to know everything about you, didn't they? More questions than ever before? And they asked you, I'm sure, why you wanted to go there?'

'Yes, naturally.'

'And what did you tell them was your object? To study the social services?' he asked with an indescribably inimical smile.

'I told them I wanted to re-visit all my friends there, and take a holiday. What else could I say? That's all I wanted.'

'It wasn't the way to get it. You should have said you wanted to study our new, free, people's democratic life, and our cultural releases, the new energy we're giving to living. You should have said you wanted to be able to breathe again after stifling here in this uncongenial air!'

'The things you've so often heard said to the

248

American occupation forces in Germany, in fact,' she said, with a patient smile, 'only in reverse. I don't do business like that.'

'You should, if you want your visa. But in any case I don't think you'll ever get it. You are too much an artist, you talk in terms of friends, and private affections, and personal honour. They have abolished the word friend. In a generation you will be able to say it to the young people there, and they will look at you blankly, honestly not understanding what you mean.'

'I don't think so. I have found them very tenacious of values like friendship. More than that, I've found that even official contacts with them refuse to remain on an official footing. They have more warmth—or at any rate a more readily bestowed warmth—than most people have here, Yuri,' she said very seriously, 'as you may easily find when you begin to meet the English for yourself.'

'You should not denigrate your own country,' he said unwarily, writhing in his private nightmare of inexplicable pain. She felt the reality of his suffering, and suppressed even the gentle shadow of her brief smile, to avoid twisting the barb in him a second time. 'You wish me to forget, in all these words, that before I even came here you had made your plans to go away from me.'

'You are talking nonsense, Yuri. I have always intended to go back, and you must always have known it. When I applied for a visa I didn't know how long we might have to wait for your permit to come here. If I'd been lucky enough to get what I wanted, I should have left everything ready for you, and my brother would have met you at the station. And I should have come back,' she said, with a rueful smile; 'you could have been quite sure of that.'

He made no reply, because he had drawn perilously near to the final bitter complaint against her, and even to him, in his extremity of jealous pain, it was clear that he must stop short of accusing her here, in a Circle Line train full of strangers. She felt the effort of his silence, and for a moment almost guessed at the words he had managed to contain; but she could not believe in her own intuition, and put it away from her resolutely. Certainly he was sick. Certainly he had transferred the hatred he had felt of his country's new government, and his sense of his own wrongs at its hands, to the country itself. That was why he could not bear that she should still feel able to go back there in friendship. It made her a traitress to his implacable cause; and that in turn offended and confused him, because she had offered him help and he had accepted it. As Yuri saw her, she was running with the hare and hunting with the hounds. He talked arrogantly of personal friendships and private affections, but in reality he, too, had abandoned all such complications; there were only allies and opponents in the world, and she was trying to be both. She surmised that he felt himself already compromised, almost soiled, by contact with her neutrality.

'The next station is ours,' she said, putting off the end of the argument, and led him out from the teeming train and the warm, windy subways into the cold mist of the evening, and down towards the Embankment, where all the waking lights were dimmed and mellowed by the emanations of the river. They let themselves into the house by the garden door, and in the autumn twilight the trees were dropping, with tiny sounds like the recollections of sighs, the first of their tenacious leaves. Grey-green in quiet, the enfolded space of grass and shrubs slept within its high red wall, that fended off the distant noises of the city and kept with infallible detachment its private peace.

'It's going to be foggy,' said Emmy, switching on the landing light. 'I'm rather glad we begged off going to Ralph's tonight. You go in and light the gas-fire, Yuri, I'm going to make some tea. I'll be with you in ten minutes.'

When she brought in the tray and set it on a low coffee table at the hearth, he was sitting in a long chair, drawn rigidly back within the shelter of the wings, with his face in shadow. She was aware of his eyes following her movements intently, and knew that none of the

251

tensions had resolved themselves for him. Since it was necessary for someone to take up the discussion where it had foundered, she relieved him of the effort.

'Yuri, I remember when you wrote me your first letter from Germany, you said that you knew I didn't feel about things as you did, but you hoped we could be friends in spite of that. So you mustn't hold it against me, you know, that I want to go back. I know you feel very strongly about what's happened in your country, and I can understand that from your point of view it seems shocking that I should continue to consider it my second home. But I don't share your opinions, I've never pretended to. You think everything there is evil; but I haven't found it so. You think we ought all to sever relations with your country; I think we ought to do everything we possibly can to prevent even one channel of communication from closing. It's no use arguing about opinions. All we can demand of each other is that we shall respect each other's views. If it seems to you an act of treason that I should go back, what you have to remember is that it seems to me a duty. As well as a joy, of course!' she added candidly, and lifted her thoughtful grey eyes to smile at him.

Silent over his cup, frowning down into the glow of the fire, he had accepted the duty without an inflection of his lips, or the contraction of one nerve in his delicately

252

shadowed cheek; but at the apparition of the joy he made a tiny, abrupt movement, drawing his head back, turning his face away. She heard the cup chatter for an instant in the saucer before he could command his hands into stillness and steadiness, and reaching out stiffly, set it down upon the table.

'If you feel so strongly about it that you can't go on thinking of me as a friend, you mustn't be afraid to tell me, Yuri, I shall understand, and I shan't make things harder for you. What you mustn't do is keep any such thoughts to yourself and worry about them. We know each other well enough to speak freely. But if we *are* still friends—and I hope we are—then you know as well as I do that there's no question of indebtedness between us. Whatever I can offer you is already yours, just as you have always made me free of your life over there. So don't begin to think you're taking favours from the enemy, Yuri, my dear. You mustn't start finding bribery and corruption in my tea and scones. I won't expect you even to moderate your language in argument on account of them.'

He did not turn his head towards her, so she could not see if he smiled, as she had meant him to do. But his fingers did not relax their nervous grip upon the arm of the chair, and when he spoke at last it was to say only, with a sigh of despair: 'You don't understand!'

'No, probably I don't. So explain to me,

child. I want to understand, but let's not pretend it's always easy, even between friends. What really matters is that we should be able to tell each other what it's necessary to know. Tell me!'

'What is the use? You have your own priorities,' he said with bitterness, 'and of course you must act in accordance with them. *I* understand now, at any rate, I understand very well! I never counted for anything at all with you, it was just that I was from *there*! Even when I'd been forced to run from it, my nationality, that I'd be glad to change, was still the only claim I had on you. Either that, or I got into your grace, just over the doorstep of your grace, at one remove more, because you thought of me as a dependant of Milo's family. I don't know which you loved best, them or their country. But I know it wasn't me—never me! You never loved me at all!' he cried, suddenly springing round upon her so that the light of the lamp and the glow of the fire burned abruptly over the beautiful desperation of his face, convulsed with pain. 'You don't love me!'

He made it the most terrible of accusations, as it was the most astonishing. It came from his lips in an agonised gasp, and wrenched after it a burst of tears from his eyes, as unexpected to him as to her, for they flowed down cheeks fixed in anger rather than shaken by the tremors of grief. He put up a startled hand and dashed them fiercely from his cheekbones,

254

where their moisture had made high, glittering points of light. Gathering on his lashes, they troubled his vision of her, and he closed his eyelids tightly for an instant, and tossed them indignantly away, as though some other person had inflicted them upon him against his will, to hamper him in the conflict he invited with her. He leaned forward over the table, his dark eyes flaring, the channels of the tears gleaming to his chin.

Emmy, motionless in her chair, holding his gaze with a face amazed and pale, said very slowly and gently: 'Yuri, did I ever, in any letter I wrote you, tell you that I loved you?'

'Do you write those things in so many words? Is no one ever to find love expressed without the need of the word love? I thought I had proof enough,' he cried, trembling. 'I thought what you did for me was done for love. You wrote every week, sometimes oftener, letters so kind and so loving—I thought, so loving—that they could not come from someone who did not love me. You sent me gifts, you understood about being cold, and hungry, and lonely. I thought so much of a person could not be given freely for anything but love. I lived on your letters all the summer, Emmy—on those, and on the hope of coming to England where I could see you and speak to you. All the summer I followed on maps where you went, and tried to find news of you in the papers. When you were in Salzburg, look, I cut

255

out these pictures from a German magazine. Look, how the critic also praises you!'

He had pulled out his wallet now, and with stumbling fingers was unfolding some carefully kept cuttings, which he suddenly leaned and laid upon her knees, himself plunging to the rug at her feet. 'If you knew how often I unfolded this and re-read it, and how proud it made me, and how happy! You see?—"pure, elegant and musicianly singing"—I know it all by heart! See, I kept also this little notice about Edinburgh, because you were there. I loved you so much, and I was sure it must be so with you, too.'

He folded his agitated hands upon her knee, and raised his stained face to her and to the light without shame. 'I was ready to wait, and to make a footing here for myself before I made any demand upon you. But I was sure it was with you as with me. And all the time I was deceived! You felt nothing for me but pity. No, not even pity! You felt *nothing for me*! Simply, here is a poor little piece of wreckage, not worth pulling ashore, except that he is from *there*, and so he has a claim on me. Only a poor, pathetic casualty of the cold war, but Miloslav is fond of him, so I must feed and clothe and welcome him, find him a job, and a place to sleep—'

He hid his face suddenly in her lap, clutching together the folds of her skirt to cover him. She let her hand pass with tenderness about his bowed shoulders, and was glad he could not know how near to the truth he had come.

'Yuri, is there only one way of loving? We've known each other for three years. I am very fond of you.'

He said in a muted cry, without looking up: 'It isn't enough! Yes, there is only one way that matters to me, and I need you that way. Oh, Emmy, love me! Emmy—love me!'

'I never meant to mislead you. I said nothing to make you believe I was in love with you.'

She felt at once exhausted and fulfilled, as though she had come to a point of decision which some part of her mind had foreseen ever since she had embraced him on the platform at Liverpool Street, and felt his thin body quake at her touch. She made her caressing hands very quiet and calm now, promising nothing more than the affection she had always given him; but she understood, in some fashion which had nothing to do with his outpourings, the magnitude of the illusion of love he had built up about her. Unless she gave him everything he asked of her he must begin from the last ebb of bankruptcy all over again, by the ladder of some other passion, perhaps equally fictitious. He had left behind, as she had once warned him, more of himself than he knew; in one country he had shed his roots, his background, his friends, his sense of belonging, and in another his illusions about himself. Yuri knew, none better, how far he

257

was fallen from his conception of the brave, the just, the proud young hero, too brave, too proud, to endure any encroachment upon his integrity. He had accepted perforce his own diminution, but somewhere in him the deprived spirit grieved night and day after what was gone. Who had more need than he of a consuming love, a kind, durable, comforting, fulfilling body in which he could rock his spirit to sleep and forget to listen to the jangling sounds of his own disintegration? He might even be healed, he might recover himself, if he could find something better than hate to hold his damaged being together.

'Yuri,' she pleaded, 'be content for a little while, live, and work, and get used to being here. You're young enough to wait, you have time for love.'

He stirred protestingly, and winding his thin arms about her body, raised himself against her, his mouth reaching upward into the hollow of her breast.

'I have time, but no hope! I want only you, and you won't love me. Emmy, love me, or I shall die!' Whispering, kissing, his lips had reached the little cup at the base of her neck; she felt their heat upon her skin, and shivered, drawing back her head from him.

'—I shall die!' He had felt her resistance, and by its gentleness he knew how to assess its firmness. His voice shattered in a sob of pain, and he tightened his arms about her

258

despairingly, but she braced her hands against his shoulders, and thrust herself up from the chair, breaking his hold, which had never had any confidence of keeping her. Drawing herself away from him she walked into the bedroom and closed the door behind her; and there she sat trembling upon the bed for a long time, until the unbearable pathos of his touch had passed out of her flesh.

When at last she gathered her tired senses and went out to look for him, the living-room was empty, the news-cuttings lay forgotten upon the rug where he had left them. The door of the flat across the landing opened readily when she tried it, but within all was dark, and Yuri was not there.

*   *   *

It was nearly midnight when he came home. She had put out the lights in her flat and was sitting by the gas-fire in her dressing-gown, listening to every sound that echoed upward from the well of the stairs. The outer door, propped ajar, let in all the last infinitesimal noises of the night, the faint, cold contractions of wood, the soft dripping of the trees outside, the fumbling of a hand along the panelling after a light-switch, the moist, sad passage of a car going down to the Embankment. Emmy listened, and did not move. She was waiting for the stealthy turning of his key in the lock downstairs, then the slow, cautious shuffling of his feet across the dark hall, and the pause while his hand felt for the newel-post at the foot of the stairs. He would not switch on the light. All his will would be dedicated to reaching his room without giving her warning of his return. All, except perhaps the minute dissident cell which would be giving all its energies to ensure that the attempt at a silent and undetected entry should not succeed. Something of Ilonna's uncynical shrewdness must have infected her mind if she could entertain such a thought without feeling any contempt or superiority towards him. She had no fear that he would not come back. There was nothing else for him to do. His few possessions were here, he had very little money on him, and no other friends to whom he could go. Moreover, he had not yet finished playing his hand.

And he had played it well. Desperation had taught him this trick of delaying the end, of leaving her time to think, and silence in which her own mind would take up the brief he had let fall. He might almost have known already how nearly she was convinced that the long-delayed visa would never come. 'Lubov,' she thought, caressing the image of his sadly tranquil face within her closed eyelids, 'God knows if I shall ever see you again, or touch anything you've touched, or have any creature of yours to care for, except Yuri. Lubov, how good must I be to him? There must be a limit somewhere.'

She heard the tiny, metallic note of the key, and the faint indefinable sound of the house door opening, no complaint of latch or hinge, only as it were a shifting of the dark, a rearrangement of warm and cold air. Yuri came up the stairs very delicately, light of foot, sidelong, breathing softly. Only on the dark landing his outstretched hand, feeling for the handle of his own door, struck the panels too sharply, and caused a wooden coat-hanger within to jangle indignantly against its hook. He muted it quickly, and there was silence again, so complete and aware that what she sensed in it was the intensity of his listening, just within the door he had not quite closed after him. She did not move, and presently she received out of the quietness the soft, reluctant sound of his footsteps passing on into the bedroom. But still he had not closed the door against her; nor did he come back to it afterwards and release the catch, though she waited a long while in the half-hope that he would lift the weight of decision from her.

She rose at last, put out the fire, and, crossing the landing, went in to him. There was a small reading-lamp burning in the bedroom, on a cabinet beside the bed, but with its shade so tilted that it wasted its light upon a segment of wall and the corner of a book-shelf, leaving the pillow in shadow. He must have pushed it away when he flung himself upon the bed. She had this in common with Yuri, at any rate, that neither of them really knew how to despair. Even when he had given up believing that she would come in to him, he had not fastened the door. And she, when a frontier had closed in her face with force and finality, would still be found searching along the barrier for a wicket gate, a legal loophole, a weak place in the wire, by which she might yet pass within. 'We are incurable,' she thought, looking at the motionless brown head buried in the pillow, and folded frantically within the hugging arms which made him deaf to her coming. 'Hope is a terrible disease.'

He had already undressed, and put on the new pyjamas he had bought the previous day in Regent Street. He was lying stretched and taut along the closed bed, and even now that he had thrown away all his care to be either beautiful or touching, he remained both. She felt no impatience any longer with the calculations of his flight or his return, the careful arrangement he had made of sound and silence moved her to an unprotesting pity. One must fight with what weapons one has, when the stake at least is real; and his need, if not his love, was a terrible reality.

She felt at the shoulders of his jacket, which he had flung down upon a chair by the door; the cloth was damp with mist. He had gone out without his coat, perhaps hardly realising at the time what he was doing, or perhaps realising with remarkable clarity. Like children in their unceasing war with the adult world, he had done everything to make his own state more piteous, and her self-reproaches more poignant.

She drew near, and he heard her. She saw him stiffen, the tight lines of the back of his neck tensed into higher relief, and his body, which had been quietly shivering, grew instantly still, but he did not lift his head. When she laid her hand upon his shoulder, and felt him cold as marble through the poplin, he shrank a little from her touch, but otherwise did not move. She was afraid for a moment that he had passed beyond believing in his own pretences, and could no longer be comforted even by achieving the symbolic prize on which his heart was set. If he had emerged at the other side of artifice he would certainly die of exposure.

She sat down beside him on the edge of the bed, and laid her arm about his shoulders. 'Yuri, why did you run away like that? Get into bed now, you'll make yourself ill.'

He turned his face more rigidly away from her, and besought her in a whisper: 'Emmy, please go away!'

'Don't be foolish! You're shivering with cold, and I feel responsible for you.' She could give him, if need be, the last gift he needed to make all the rest acceptable, but she would not lie to him. 'Yuri, I care for you very much, and I want you to be happy here. You are being unkind to yourself and to me. Please get into bed!' She took him gently by the arm, and made to raise him, but he pulled away from her with a wild gesture of pain.

'Don't, Emmy! I can't bear it!' He dragged himself up on one elbow, and lifted his face to her at last, grey with weariness about enormous distracted eyes. 'Don't you see that I must go away from here? Can't you understand that I can't go on taking anything from you? I came because I thought—because I believed—But how can I go on with it now? Don't hate me, Emmy, but I must pay everything back. I must ask you to give me a little time—'

He was not acting now; this was honest; it had escaped from his grip and slipped through all his conscious and unconscious snares, and all he could do was stumble after it as best he could. Events were out of his hands. All the more firmly she felt and accepted her own hold upon them. He was weeping, silently, from some deeper place than had ever before been tapped in him. She put her arms round him, drawing him gently into her breast, and some of her warmth passed into him, and gave him a moment of ease.

'Yuri, my dear, don't friends have any rights?'

'Oh yes! I'm ashamed, but, Emmy, I can't

help myself. If there was any balance in what we felt! If you loved me—or if I didn't love you—Do forgive me, but I must go away. Perhaps they'll give me a small advance on what I shall be earning. Oh, Emmy, don't hate me!'

The two years between them might have been a whole generation; she could not have felt more enlarged with tenderness if she had been holding her son in her arms. She rocked him calmly, feeling his trembling abate gradually, in long, diminishing sighs. In the end nothing would be wasted. There was no longer even any need to remonstrate with his implacable pride over the gifts or the giver. In her heart she had always known that it had passed out of her power to deny him anything that was hers, from the moment that she began giving.

'Hush, now, don't agitate yourself so, there's no need. Where did you go, alone?'

'I don't know. I walked a long way, but I don't know where.'

'How did you find your way back? Did you ask someone?' She rose, letting her arms cajole him to lift himself from the bed, and with a sweep of her hand turned back the covers.

'Yes, two or three times. They understood me well,' he said, looking up at her darkly out of a cloud of exhaustion, 'but I lost myself again trying to follow what they told me. Then I found the river, and it was this Embankment where I have been twice already with you. So I knew where I was.'

'You must get some sleep now. We can talk tomorrow. I promise you shall make whatever plans you think right.' She shook the pillow smooth, and he crept brokenly into the bed and lay still, only quivering now and again with retreating spasms of cold. From beneath the lofty, tired brow his dark eyes watched her cross the room away from him, and pass through the doorway without a word. She felt him taking leave of her, quite bereft now of all but the last spark of hope, grieved and abashed that she could go without so much as saying good-night.

She went to the outer door and quietly closed it, and then, without haste and still in silence, returned to him. His eyelids, which had closed upon his misery, rolled back abruptly. He watched her stretch out her hand to switch off the light, and only at the last gleam of its passing did the sudden incredulous flame of understanding kindle in his eyes. In the darkness he drew a gasping breath, and raised the covers to let her in.

He was afraid to speak at first, or to touch her. It was she who laid her arm over him and drew him to her, embracing him gently with hands and breasts and thighs, holding him to her heart until the shivering ebbed out of him, and the warmth of his triumph flowed in strongly and filled him with power. His hands folded her slowly, while he drew great, eased breaths that seemed to enlarge and recreate his body. She let him take, because it was much more to him taken than merely given as an act of grace, the peace and fulfilment and delight he needed. She lay quiet, more than consenting, cherishing and aiding him with sad, kind, resigned hands. There was nothing he could do to give her peace, nor to take away her peace from her.

Afterwards he fell asleep, one arm still lying over her body with heavy tenderness, the other hand curled in the warm hollow between her breast and his. His sleep was all that sleep should be, a dying to all doubts and questionings, to all that hurt, or humiliated, or frightened him, a withdrawal into innocence. She heard him drawing into his being, in soft, long breaths, food and drink and blood and life, and sighing out serenely into the cup of her shoulder the lingering, haunting fears that inhibited his maturity, the fear of losing face, the fear of having chosen badly, the fear of feeling ashamed, the fear of being pitied, the fear of not being loved. She lay still, pitying him, not loving him. It did not matter, he would not look beyond the ritual gestures.

She thought once, calculating the risks she could not choose but run: 'Supposing he should want me to marry him?' But the formulation of the question brought its own answer: 'But he won't! I'm safe from that.

When he's no longer hungry and ill, he'll let me go without too much regret. When Yuri marries it will be for a different reason, and a different kind of love. I've seen him in need, I've seen him cry, I've professed other gods than his, I'm stronger than he is—no, when he's whole again he'll have no use for me.'

She lay in the half-sleep of her weariness, and felt no doubts of the wisdom of what she had done. She had put her body at his disposal as inevitably as she would have given a bed to a lost child, or food to birds in a hard winter, or a little time and companionship to a man dying of loneliness. It was not the irrecoverable act that filled her with this quiet anguish; it was the touch of that thin, curled hand warm against her breast, the weight of the sleeping head numbing her shoulder, the rumpled hair crisp under her cheek, the soft breathing, so close that she felt its rhythm passing into her substance. She wept, silently, from eyes wide open in the darkness.

In the early hours of the morning he started suddenly out of his sleep and threw out his hand to feel for her, in a waking terror that after all he might find himself betrayed by a dream, and lying alone; but the swift reassurance of her voice charmed him back to sleep so readily that he did not notice she had called him by the wrong name, and she drew down his groping hand into her breast so quickly that he never afterwards remembered that the cheek he had touched was wet.

*   *   *

So after all there was no need for him to take up his fragile baggage of dignity, and move on yet again into some other and equally precarious refuge. He remained in Mrs Rice's flat until half-way through November, and then, with the luck of his own regained self-confidence, found for himself a small flat in a lofty and narrow old house in Kensington. The situation was ideal, discreetly distant from her and considerately near. He hugged her like a triumphant boy as he told her about it, radiant in the joy of feeling events bow to him, even in such little things. It was very small, certainly, but what need had he of more space, with his meagre possessions? If he outgrew it some day, he would leave it. And in any case, it was little more than a means of establishing respectable territorial rights; it did not have to contain the bed of his spirit.

    She kissed him, and approved his success. She had let him hunt and find unaided; it was what he needed to set him up securely in his own esteem. And indeed he was beginning to feel the ground of security growing solid under his feet by that time, and to grow sleek and relaxed in the relief of finding himself more than adequate. He was settling down well in his job, and Maxwell and Fremantle were pleased

269

with him. Her friends had opened their circle to embrace him without question, he was beginning to strike out from her side and make contacts of his own. He knew himself to be acceptable, since she accepted him. His hair had grown out of its harsh cut, and was recovering its spring and lustre, and coiling into classic grape-curls above his temples. He had put on a little flesh, too, and the sharp anxiety of his bones was softening into the old dramatic serenity, so that he had his beauty again, and soon would no longer need the particular stimulation of her approval. Plenty of other people were ready to testify to his attraction; Emmy had watched with detached pride the effect he had had upon her own family, and had seen him grow like a sun-warmed plant in the rays of their appreciation. When he had enough of it, and could feel secure that it would not betray him, he would be able to dispense with the first healing warmth he had won from her. She made no attempt to hurry the day, nor to postpone it; she was too sure of it to try to change the tempo.

In the Christmas gaiety at the border cottage she watched the children take possession of him. He was moved by their adoption, he had never been an unofficial uncle before, and he felt it as an accolade. She had never liked him quite so much as when she saw him through Christopher's eyes, the youngest, most athletic and charming of uncles, and the one most sensible of the honour of the connection.

Everyone liked Yuri, and everyone told her so. Even Malcolm, whose restrained jealousy extended to every other male of her acquaintance, did not fail to point out to her how widely Yuri's view of the state of his country differed from hers and how far more realistic was his judgment than hers. Probably he hoped that Yuri might at length prevail on her to give up her attachment to that lost land, and settle down to a single citizenship which would make her more amenable to his own tentative approaches. When Yuri had prised away the despairing grip of the Ivanescu from her heart, then it would be time to deal with Yuri's personal challenge. He was not to know that nothing remained to be contested, nothing to be achieved.

Others, however, also remarked upon the same discrepancy in their reports from the excommunicated country, for Yuri was more than willing to talk about his views. And after all he was a native, they said gently, he should know. Emmy smiled, and replied that the thirteen million people who still found it possible, in some cases even pleasant, to live in his country were also natives; that she knew some twenty of them reasonably well, and many more on terms of acquaintanceship, and none of them would have agreed entirely with Yuri's account. But she knew that they were not impressed; the argument of Yuri's birth remained unanswerable for them, and for his repudiation of his birth they made no allowance. After twenty years of exile he would still be an expert, and she, after twenty years of adoption, still without authority.

Once, when he had called for her after her lesson, and they were walking through St James's Park together in the first moist, smoky greenness of spring, he said abruptly, and with so much energy that she knew he must be expecting some reservations on her part: 'I've been asked to write some articles for the bulletin, Emmy. They want a series on the current situation over there, and then later they've offered to make room for a regular column on international affairs. There aren't so many of us here, you see,' he said proudly, 'who were actually journalists.'

Even his voice had gained confidence, had made itself and its alien turns of phrase at home in London. He had lost some of the tricks of literal translation which had moved her with so many memories at his first coming.

'"They" being the Democrats in Exile, I suppose,' she said. She knew the club, and the paper they ran, and knew that he had been frequenting their circle for more than a month. But the matter had never been discussed before.

'I've been going there sometimes on Friday evenings,' said Yuri. 'They think I could be

272

useful on the paper, and I think I ought to do whatever I can. I know you don't think as they do, but I do, and I'm going to write for them.'

'You must do what you think best,' said Emmy.

'Yes, I must. But I wish you could be with me,' he said, between sadness and exasperation.

'You know I can't. I think they are going the wrong way about it, and making nothing but mischief. But you must do whatever you feel to be right, and not worry about me. I haven't argued with you, have I?' she asked, looking up at him with a calm but unsmiling face.

'No, but you ought to be with me. You could be doing so much,' he said vexedly, 'and you are doing just nothing.'

'Don't ask me for any more than you have, Yuri. I can't join your friends because I think they are doing the wrong things, from the wrong motives, and in the wrong terms. They deal in sweeping generalisations without evidence, with a fact here and there to prop the whole thing up. It isn't my idea of truth or justice, much less of a useful approach to the problems of the world. But we needn't talk about it,' she said quite tranquilly. 'If we do, those are the things I shall have to say.'

'I do not understand you,' said Yuri, burning bright with the old baffled anger. 'You, who have been there, and know something of what is happening, how can you

273

hesitate?'

She said nothing, it would have been waste of breath, and if she tried to put her own viewpoint she must of necessity criticise his, and they would quarrel. The only reason that they never quarrelled was because at the brink of the danger zone she would always fall silent. He felt her silence none the less surely as a criticism and a reproof, its tenor was too serene and immovable to be acceptable to him. His cheeks mantled with a flush of annoyance which became him very well, his eyes burned to a shining red colour from their soft dark brown. People passing looked at him with interest, and young girls eyed Emmy with curiosity and envy. They would not have grudged her Lubov, could they have seen him, nor turned for a second look at him in the street. Of some kinds of excellence there is no visible record. Beauty, she thought, is amoral, it has also no dealings with either truth or justice.

What was notable was that Yuri no longer required to be reassured or comforted, or at least he was approaching that degree of self-sufficiency. The physical flattery of love can do much for the mind, as well as the body. He no longer felt doubt of his own course, only impatience with hers, and resentment that she would not align every particle of her life with his. She had only to wait, and his separation from her would take place as naturally as that of the child from the mother, and with much less grief. The only thing she had still to watch with care was that she should make no move to snatch herself away from him before he was ready. She could bear to be deserted; he could not. Whenever she thought of it in these terms, she knew that she was longing for her freedom, and she opened herself to him once again with terrible gentleness for fear of the premature gesture which might undo all his good. And in these moments, and sometimes when he came to her in the full triumphant conviction of his vindicated masculinity, at his most confident and his most vulnerable, she felt a desperate affection for him clouding her vision, and her heart failing with fondness.

'You are like so many artists,' said Yuri, relaxing suddenly into a half-unwilling smile, and taking her arm gently, 'you want to deny that there has to be a choice, you want not to see that you have to be for us or against us. And then, you are a woman, too, so you don't have any use for logic. I am sorry I was bad-tempered! We have a compact, like in the fairy stories. I don't try to look into your soul, and you don't try to look into mine, or perhaps we should fly apart for ever.'

He could not, she thought, have evolved this elucidation of their relationship a month ago without agonies of suspicion and distress, but he uttered it with ease now, even kindly.

The tensions were passing out of all his

dealings with her in the same way. When she had again asked for application forms for a visa, and deliberately filled them in in his presence, he had merely smiled and shaken his head regretfully at her inability to give up hope even of the hopeless. Now that he had her he was not afraid of rivals. What did he care how much love she spent on other people or other countries, as long as he came first with her? And the proof of his victory he exacted still with ardour, and repaid with startling tenderness, constantly confirmed in his sovereignty, and grown generous out of his new plenty. In any case, there was no need to agonise over her desire to go, since it would never be fulfilled. This attempt must end like the last, in an inconclusive and increasingly desultory exchange of letters, unprofitable and sterile. They had neither accepted nor refused her, only fended her off with soft, delaying politeness, until further persistence had seemed even to her a waste of the blood of her heart. Watching how she searched through the letters daily after some response to this new attempt, Yuri was sorry that she must still suffer. He could afford to feel distress on her account, now that he felt none on his own.

It was Saturday, and they were going to have lunch together at her flat and then go to a cinema. In the hall Yuri collected from her letter-box three letters which had come by the noon post, and, turning them unselfconsciously in his hands, recognised the meticulous spacing of the typed address. He looked up at her as they climbed the stairs side by side, and said in a tone nicely adjusted between pleasure that she should at least be receiving attention, and deprecation of too much eagerness in case she should find only disappointment within: 'Oh, you have a letter from *them*!'

It was nice of him, she thought, to suppress his absolute certainty that she could go on besieging that impervious door for a lifetime and gain nothing. He handed the envelope to her with a soft and expectant smile, but his eyes were far too calm for the eyes of a man awaiting news.

'So I have! That's only about twelve days' delay—they could only just get a reply in the time. Does that mean yes or no, do you think?' She owed it to him to contain her own terrors. Was that the secret of her calm, or was it rather that she stood already on the immovable rock, beneath expectation, beneath faith or despair, and could not fall now whether she gained or lost? Or was it that she had so orientated her spirit that 'no' meant nothing to her now but a delayed 'yes', the necessity for new approaches, a going about to circumvent an obstacle which must have limitations, if only her life proved long enough to discover them? Some things one gives up easily, others with effort and pain, but there are things which cannot be given up, even if a whole lifetime must be spent in clinging to the shadow they cast, and trying in vain to touch the substance. Then holding fast is no more a virtue or a vice or an absurdity than is the tree's downward thrust of its root, or the obstinate inhalation and exhalation of the body's breath. If she was never to see Lubov again, the remaining years of her life would be spent in exploring inexhaustibly the thousand ways of trying to reach him, and in remaining intact in spirit for the day when she did reach him.

'It's certainly very quick,' said Yuri, as he opened the door of the flat for her. 'Perhaps it isn't a definite answer yet, perhaps they just want to ask something more, something that wasn't very clear in your application.' He found it difficult to pretend that he felt any doubt of the contents of the envelope. She had refused to take the hint of evasion, and stop asking. What was there to be done with such a woman, except give her a blunt negative, and be done with her?

Emmy stood at the window, her back turned to him, while she opened the envelope. She heard him strike a match and light the gas-fire, and then go into the kitchen, as he usually did, to fill the kettle and put it on to boil. When she turned, holding the brief, impersonal note in her hands, he was standing in the open doorway, looking at her with dark, sympathetic, half-smiling eyes, pitying her, making her silent promises to outweigh the cruelty of stony-hearted official departments with the generosity of his affection. She looked back at him in silence, her face quite still, her lips parted, the grey lustre of her eyes limpid and empty as the sky.

Yuri moved across the room to her with a beautiful, fiery delicacy, and laid his arm about her shoulders, and his lips against her forehead. 'Darling, I'm sorry! You mustn't mind too much. You knew in your heart there was no chance at all, you've always known it. Don't be unhappy about it, Emmy, don't!'

She lifted to him a long, quiet look burning into intelligence slowly, first the rising gleam of light in the depths of the eyes, then the tightening of all the lines of her face, the intent contraction of her mouth.

'It isn't what you think, Yuri,' she said, with astonished quietness. 'It's yes. I can have my visa, they're letting me in.'

She had been so empty of expectation, either good or bad, that she did not wonder he had failed to read the answer in her face. She had understood the three bare lines of typing in an instant, she had even believed them, but she could not feel them. Only gradually did the sensations of relief, and triumph, and joy rise welling through her mind, and reach her eyes. For a moment she felt also something which was not joy, but a revulsion of hatred for Yuri, who had made away, however innocently, with

279

something which was Lubov's by right, something Lubov could after all have had if she had waited with more faith. She stared at him for one instant with a detestation he was too astonished to see, and then the mistaken fury was gone. What she had given away had been her own to give, Lubov would never question it or lay claim to it. She smiled at Yuri's amazed face, and put the note into his hand.

'See for yourself! They have authority to grant me a visa for a fortnight's stay, and I can collect it any day after ten-thirty. Nothing could be simpler.'

He read it, more than once, she thought, frowning over it in bewilderment, and already looking for a motive other than simple goodwill towards her. His curled lips and sceptical glance indicated an offended spirit, certainly, but the event was less of a blow to him than she had expected. Nothing nearly as large as that well-remembered fury of despair troubled his arrogant dignity now. It was no longer a kind of death to him that she should wish to leave him. What she saw in his face was no more than a confident man's pique at being proved wrong, even over something of comparatively little importance.

She thought, watching him: 'I must be careful not to pull away until he has really relaxed his hold. I shouldn't like to cut the ground from under him a second time.'

It would indeed be fatally easy to shrug off

the last touch of him before he was ready, with her life suddenly filled from margin to margin with Lubov. Yuri had become translucent, the strong light shone through him; she would have to remind herself constantly that he was there, and had to be considered.

'This *is* a surprise!' he said, in the light, wary voice of suspicion. 'I wonder *why*? What's in it for them? What did you offer them this time, Emmy, to let you in?'

'What have I got to offer them, more than before? I said I would like to go to the Musical Festival in April, and that I would undertake two concerts if they had room for me in the programme. And I wrote to Marvan to the same effect. But why should that make any difference, if I wasn't acceptable in the autumn?'

'At least it would be something they could understand. To go there to sing, if you are a singer—that's practical. Didn't you know they have no use now for anything that isn't practical? To want to visit a country just because you have many friends there and you long to see them—no, that's not practical at all. Anyone with such sentimental notions is suspect at once. Do you know, Emmy,' he said, flashing into a bright, ungentle smile, 'I think you are being paid a professional compliment? Emily Marryat had a very good summer last year, she made a definite success in Salzburg and Edinburgh, and in the winter she had some very fine notices at home. If she wants to come, her name might now be considered worth a headline. Emmy, I think you are prominent enough to be a propaganda success, or they would not want you.'

'I am not concerned with why they want me,' she said dryly. 'I am only devoutly grateful that they do.'

'Then I'm glad, too! Yes, really! Surely you know that I would like you to have what you want? Only don't ask me to believe it is out of goodness of heart that they invite you in. Just take what is to be had, but don't be too moved by it.'

In the kitchen, the kettle, neglected, boiled over with a hissing of steam. He turned and ran to rescue it, clutching at his curls, and in a moment came back smiling into the doorway. His face had kindled to an alert eagerness, as though he too had thought of a way of turning her obsession to account.

'Emmy, when do you go?'

'I haven't booked my air passage yet, of course, but I said I wanted to travel around the thirteenth of April. The festival opens officially on the fourteenth.' She had not moved from the spot where she had opened the letter; the shock of achievement had first numbed and now excited her. When she looked at him, with the brilliant flush of wonder mantling in her cheeks, the focus of her eyes was set far beyond him, as though she could look through his substance, and scarcely be inconvenienced by the obstruction.

'Emmy, will you take some messages for me? You sent word of me to Milo, you said you felt yourself free to keep friends in touch with one another. And you see what an opportunity this is! Who knows if we shall get another? Will you carry my letters to them, Emmy?'

He came and folded his arms about her, caressing her hair with his warm cheek, glowing with eagerness. She was moved by the remembrance of the affection the Ivanescu family had always felt for him, and melted to the conviction that he too had not forgotten it. The self-exiled must seem to hate what they have abandoned, in order to justify themselves, but old love is not so easily destroyed, after all. It wanted only the opportunity of touching them again, and Yuri was quivering with the vehemence of his longing, and planning warm letters that should knit him inextricably into their thoughts again.

She cupped his face in her hands, and drew him down to her, and kissed him. 'Of course I'll carry your letters! Yes, do write! Milo will be so happy to hear from you!'

'There might be rather a lot,' he said, his breathless laughter ruffling her hair. 'I have so many friends, and I don't even know where all of them will be. But Milo will find them—just take them all to Milo, he will see them delivered.' His arms hugged her excitedly. 'Oh,

Emmy, I didn't realise, I didn't understand, how much this could mean to me. I'm so glad about it! I'm almost as glad as you!'

*　　*　　*

He brought his letters to her some ten days later, when she was moving about her bedroom in the throes of packing, her bed strewn with tissue paper and dresses, the rug littered with shoes. She had left the piano open in the living-room; she heard his fingers pick out in passing the air of a mountain song, and reared her head in pleased surprise that his fancy should be flying home ahead of her. He had not been to see her for five nights; the belated admission of home thoughts, after so long of denying and shutting them out, had proved far more absorbing, it seemed, than his diminishing need of the reassurance of her body. 'He's almost cured of me,' she thought, picking up the falling minor air of the song, which was inexpressibly sad, like most mountain songs from east of the Tyrol, even the violent ones. She raised her voice and called him in. 'I'm here, Yuri! Come through!'

He came in, looking flushed and light-hearted from his walk along the Embankment, and knelt in the confusion beside her. The quick, light kiss brushing her cheek was little more than routine now, though he could balance a great weight of kindness upon it

284

when he chose.

'I can see by looking at you,' he said, smiling, 'that at heart you've already left England behind. Did you collect your visa?'

'Yes, yesterday. Now I believe in it!'

'And I, too! I have had my fingers crossed for you until this moment. And your air ticket, you have that also?'

'Yes, I have it. I'm almost ready.' There were seven days between her and departure, but what he said was that England already lay behind her. Its colours had begun to fade from the moment that she had posted her letter to Lubov. 'My dear Lubov, On the fourteenth of April I shall be with you—' The world present to her here had paled, like a candle contesting against the daylight.

'Look, I brought these—' He drew out from his pocket a bundle of several envelopes filled fatly with his close, passionate hand. 'You see why I have not been to see you for several days. At least I have something to show for it.' He placed the little bundle in her hand, and folded her fingers over it. She reached promptly for the convenient rear pocket of her smaller case, which lay open on the rug, but he laid a hand quickly upon her wrist. 'No, better not! I should keep these in your handbag, I think that they will not look there, if you are to be a distinguished guest artist of the republic. But cases are always likely to be opened.'

There was nothing new in the words to make
285

her look at him suddenly with such close and thoughtful attention. She had known already that she was undertaking to hide what she carried, innocent though it might be. Yet the rapidity of the movement with which he had checked her caused her to sit back on her heels, nursing the thick bundle of papers, and consider him in silence for a long moment. He maintained admirably the placidity of his countenance, and yet he was not entirely at ease; the long fingers which had just left her wrist quieted their intensity by producing and offering cigarettes, and a lighter. He admired their steadiness; she felt their nervous tension.

'Yes, of course!' She looked down at what she held. All the envelopes were unsealed, he was punctilious in such matters. The topmost one had Milo's name on it. 'Yuri—'

'Well?'

'Yuri, you understand that I can carry only purely personal letters? They've always been honest with me, and so must I with them. I won't carry anything that's damaging to them. It's true they might think it unfair of me to bring word from you at all, however personal, but I must use my own judgment as to what's fair dealing and what isn't, since it's the only judgment I have. But I won't knowingly do anything to harm them, or their conception of their country. You do understand that, don't you?'

He had reared his head haughtily at the

implied doubt, in a way she remembered well. 'Of course! Do you think I'm trying to make unfair use of you?'

'Not by your standards, no. But I think we might differ very seriously on the subject of what is fair and what is unfair use. You've written—rather voluminously.'

'I've written to several people, and groups of people. Some of them have no names on, by the way, or only a nickname, but Miloslav will know where they are to be delivered from those clues. You're thinking,' he said, watching her steadily, 'that I've used rather a lot of words to send my love to them? Well, they're all open. Read them! See for yourself what I've found to say at such length.'

Again there was nothing wrong with the voice or the words, nothing wrong at all except the conviction growing in her that he offered her the remedy with so much tranquillity only because he was sure she would not accept it. She wondered how much it cost so highly-strung a creature to maintain his calm under her thoughtful stare. Nothing betrayed him, except the very slight paling of his serene face. 'No one,' she thought, 'should bet on the ordinary conventions of life holding good in such a situation as this.'

'You mean that, Yuri? May I take you at your word?'

'Of course, if you don't trust me.' He was smiling, but he got up quickly and walked into

287

the lounge, easing himself for a moment of the burden of her eyes. When he reappeared in the doorway, carrying the heavy Venetian glass ash-tray, she had unfolded one of the letters in her lap, and was reading it. Even then he gave no sign of uneasiness.

'You'll find a lot of expressions of opinions which are not your opinions, but nothing damning, my darling Emmy.'

His voice was light, even teasing; he was still betting, she thought, that she was doing no more than making a show of scruples, that she either would not hurt herself by doubting him seriously, or, more probably, that she would find the labour of reading without a dictionary too arduous and unprofitable to persist in it.

'You should have opened Milo's—you know I'm far more likely to talk treason to him than to anyone else.'

He sat down upon the bed, carefully laying aside one of the dresses outspread there, and set the ash-tray on the floor between them. But he was feeling the strain; she had been quiet too long, and she was too still. When she looked up he was careful not to meet her eyes at once, but smoked steadily in an apparent dream, half smiling to himself. The pure profile was dark against the pane of the window, the straight nose exhaled smoke gently, the short, strongly-curled lips brooded in repose.

'You under-estimate my knowledge of your language, Yuri,' she said in a low voice. 'I read it much better than I speak it. And your handwriting doesn't offer enough difficulty to compensate.' She looked down at the papers in her lap, reading clearly: '"Our group has discussed this possibility of conciliation, along with many other suggestions made by the more timid spirits here, and we are of the opinion that nothing can now be accomplished without violence. It is necessary that we should embrace the possibilities of help offered us by the Americans, who, alone of our possible allies, seem to have understood the situation. We propose to avail ourselves of the financial help they may be willing to give us, and also to make some concessions to their ideas in return for that help. We must not shrink from the idea of putting active saboteurs across the borders wherever possible, nor even, if events demand it, from executing summary justice on certain individuals. We are fully prepared to resort to assassination, if necessary. If you have not yet managed to get together an internal group in your district, I urge you to begin work at once. We need your efforts very quickly, if we are to have any chance of creating a situation in which the present State can be overthrown. When we have some proof from you, and others like you, that a rising from within can be counted on, then we can make an approach to our potential friends here with every prospect of being received sympathetically. Of Britain I do not hold out much hope, but Britain will not count for very much in the issue."' She looked up. 'I'm glad you don't hold out much hope of our joining you in your crusade, Yuri, at any rate. That's a comfort.'

Yuri had not moved. The ash fell from his cigarette and disseminated in a grey fall in mid-air. He leaned down and ground out the unburned half of it in the Venetian mortar, his hand shaking with rage. Two hot discs of red burned vividly upon his cheekbones.

'No, you will do nothing, you English, except hope piously for a revolution to happen without you. You are too feeble to see when action is necessary, and too squeamish to understand when it becomes cowardly to keep your hands clean any longer. I am not sorry you know what I wrote, I am glad! You made it impossible for me to say it to you, you were dear to me, you must not be hurt, your silly illusions must not be upset. Oh, my God, what is it with you? Do you not understand that while you are bowing politely to the devil he slips a knife in your back?'

'You, at any rate,' she said with difficulty, her hands lying frozen upon the testament of his beliefs, 'seem to have made your plans to slip your knife in first. I suppose that reversal makes everything all right?'

'Is it we who began it? We have only learned the rules in order to save something out of the smash.'

'Of arguing who began it,' said Emmy,

'there's never likely to be any end. Personally, if I found myself trying to preserve something I considered to be clean, I should also be interested in keeping the incidental mud off it. But that's beside the point. Are they all like this? This is what you called personal matter, is it? You really want me to carry these across the frontier for you?'

'They are legitimate evidence,' he said bitterly; 'they have to do with truth, and I have a right to give words to the opinions I have formed.'

'Yes. Everyone has that right, within reason, I suppose.' She laid the packet of letters suddenly beside him upon the bed, and got up and crossed the room to her writing-desk in the corner. In a moment she came back with another packet of letters, gay with the striped borders of air-mail envelopes and tied up with a green cord.

'You recognise these? They are the letters you wrote me from Germany. You gave quite effective words to the opinions you had formed there, Yuri. You had every right to. Do you remember? "These are certainly not an élite. They steal even from one another." And here: "They are only sitting here waiting for the Americans to take back their forfeited lands and re-settle them there." And have you forgotten this bit? "There are people here among us who would like to go back if they could. They say that if they had known the

West could openly sponsor this hope of reconquest they would never have left home, for whatever is wrong there, it is still home, and they would still fight for it against the Nazis and all their allies." And they will, Yuri, you were perfectly right. Even the ones who grumble most will do that.'

He was on his feet, facing her, not understanding, but already dark-browed with anger. She smiled at him, shaking the slim letters together in her hands.

'You wish to have proper freedom to utter the opinions you've formed, and to give evidence fearlessly to those who ought to be made aware of their dangers and their responsibilities. Very well! Then you will wish me to take these letters, and hand them over for the use of the authorities in your country. They are legitimate evidence, they have to do with truth. As you said!'

The scarlet flame of anger engulfed his whole face, burning into his hair. 'It is a bad joke! You have no right to make use of my letters, and you know they were not written for such a purpose. You are trying to make fun of me.'

'Not at all. You can't have it both ways. You want to give publicity to your evidence, or you don't. Or are you saying now that you wish only to give a carefully selected evidence, weighted all on one side?'

'You will let us all be destroyed,' he said, raging, 'for the sake of your own self-esteem.

Your little finicking justice, do you think it will be any comfort to you or anyone else when the whole world has been swallowed up by the devil you want to be fair to? No, of course you shall not use any words of mine to feed your illusions. Give them to me!'

She did not immediately move to surrender them, but only stood looking at him steadily, with her wide grey eyes limpid as the early evening light. 'All the evidence—or none, Yuri. Make up your mind!'

'Give them to me! You have learned nothing, you think you can stand aside and keep your own white hands spotless while the rest of us wallow to preserve you, and then shudder at the mud you see on us. But you will find it cannot be handled so! You too will have to take one side or the other in the end.'

'I don't think so,' she said seriously. 'Yuri, I really don't think so. But if you do push me into having to take one side or the other, it's their side I shall take.'

'You are mad! You would choose the worst evil there has ever been, because you think you see some imperfections on the other side—'

'You thought you saw them, too, Yuri—remember? As for the worst evil, you must make your decision about that, I'll make mine. But I'd rather occupy myself with that possibility of reconciliation in which you don't believe, Yuri.'

She turned, and tossed the second bundle of

293

letters upon the bed beside the first. 'Take them away! If you burn them and forget you ever wrote them, I shan't forget. If you ever give a different account of what you found in Bavaria, you'll see me somewhere in the audience, and I shall not keep quiet.'

He stood looking at them where they lay, and then raised his bitter, burning face and looked hotly at her. 'You will not take my messages, then? You will not do me so much justice, you who love justice so much? You refuse to do anything to help them or me?'

He felt nothing but this sense of injury, he saw no one but himself. She felt her own anger mount suddenly, suffocatingly, filling her body with heat.

'So you feel yourself to be the misused one! You, no one else! I am the one who has treated *you* badly. Knowing my views, you still don't feel ashamed to try to deceive me into an action you know to be against my principles. You see nothing wrong, nothing underhanded in that. And when the trick fails to work, you see nothing wrong in trying to persuade me by using my personal feeling for you as a lever. And beyond everything you proposed to do to *me*, you see nothing wrong with asking me to put all this perilous material into Miloslav's hands, and leaving him to distribute it for you. Milo, I see, is expendable in the cause of your vanity. You don't feel any guilt at all in the matter! Well, I won't put one hair of Milo's

294

head in danger for you. No, I will not carry your letters, they're not material I could touch in honesty. Your country has dealt in good faith with me, and so will I with your country. If ever I reach the point of taking your side against them—but you can be quite sure it isn't even a possibility—I shall no longer cheat them by asking for a visa. So I'm never likely to be available as an agent for you, Yuri, you may as well make up your mind to that.'

He gave a harsh, exasperated cry of laughter. 'Oh, you are fantastic! You want to play according to the rules while they eat the world. Don't you understand that they don't acknowledge any rules at all? Deal honestly with them, and some day they'll show you how much they appreciate your chivalry by throwing you in the gutter and walking over you.'

'I am not concerned with how they behave to me—it's not in my control. I am concerned only with how I behave to them. So it hardly matters that once again I disagree with you.'

'I am always to be the scapegoat,' he shouted, trembling with rage. 'On everything I do you will always put the worst construction. You say I tricked you, lied to you—I tell you, what I am doing is vital, and I *will* trick and lie to make a success of it, but all the same it was not like that with you. I knew you could not feel, as I do, how much depends on getting word to our people over there. It's the future of the world, perhaps, but you would never believe it. I told you they were only personal letters because I wanted to protect you from feeling implicated—to keep you safe from even knowing what faces us.'

'I don't know,' she said, her eyes burning dark purple in the fading light, 'that I ever asked for your protection against anything. But above all I object to being protected from *knowing*!'

'Then if you are not looking for safety, take the letters! Read them, if you like, take them with your eyes open.' He took a step towards her, and stretched out his hand as though he would imprison hers, but she made no move to meet him, and he stopped short of touching her. 'Emmy, you have never really considered, you cannot have admitted to yourself what is happening, or you would know what you ought to do. You say you don't wish to be shielded, and yet you keep your eyes closed. Open them now! See things as I do, and join me in trying to change them. Emmy, you *can't* be against me!'

Her face did not change, was not moved at all. She stood looking up at him steadily, her hands empty at her sides.

'I am not with you,' she said calmly. 'Miloslav is not with you, either. I don't suppose he made any secret of his dissidence, that wouldn't be like Milo, so you can hardly help knowing where he stands, and it isn't with
296

you. But he has princely notions of the rights of his friends to make unholy fools of themselves in their own way. I suppose you were counting on that to make him undertake even the distribution of treasonable material. What might happen to him didn't, I take it, matter to you?'

From the bright, high colour of rage he blanched suddenly into a startling pallor, and put up a hand to clutch at his throat as if the flow of words had curdled there and was strangling him. In a moment he said in a suffocating voice: 'I understand you! You are accusing me of taking advantage of him to do the dangerous work, while I live comfortably and safely here in England!'

'*No!*' she cried vehemently, in alarm and indignation. 'I know you'd run your own neck into a rope just as wantonly if you had the chance. No, I'm not saying you care less for him than for yourself—I'm saying you ought to care *more*. You have a right to endanger yourself, but none to implicate Milo, or Matyas, or Lubov—'

And now she had put out her hand to him, her voice had warmed to him, and the warmth and the gesture came too late. He had indeed sensed the softening in her tone as she cried out, and flung out his own hand a little way, willing to be placated, but as his fingers touched hers, her voice shattered upon Lubov's name. Anger had melted, and left her

297

vulnerable. She said his name, and her throat filled, and no more sound came. Yuri heard the name like a soft sob of anguish, and stood there stricken, unable to advance the remaining inch and take hold of her wrist. It was as though he had put his hand into her heart, hoping to find a place for him there, and found every cranny of it filled and possessed by Lubov. He understood everything. He knew that it had always been like that, that she had written her calm, affectionate letters to him in Germany, had pestered Home Office officials on his behalf, had come with patience and gentleness into his bed, all with her heart filled to the brim with Lubov. He knew what she had meant him never to know, and all the weight of her terrible kindness fell upon him suddenly and crushed him. He could not endure the humiliation, he could not bear to be the recipient of such a monstrous burden of compassion without love.

She saw his face for an instant as a mask of marble, fixed and dreadful in classic horror. Then he turned and snatched up the letters from the bed, and ran from her, out of the bedroom, across the hall, and stumbling and leaping down the stairs. She opened her lips in realisation and despair to call him back, but after all she made no sound, for she could not call back the one unguarded moment, and what else was there she could do for Yuri now? She let him go.

298

When the last sound of his footsteps had faded and the front door slammed upon his flight, her knees quaked under her, and she sat down upon the bed in the silken folds of her concert dresses, and shut her face between cold palms, and closed her eyes. And after a while there seemed nothing left for her to do but resume the folding of her frocks, each carefully interleaved with tissue paper. She bent her head over them, stroking the folds into position with tired, languid fingers, that moved without any motion of her will.

*   *   *

She waited for him to come back, or make her some sign that they were still in the same world, and he neither came nor sent her word. She waited three days, and then she went to his flat, but either he was not there or he would not open the door to her. She tore out a leaf of her engagement book, wrote him a note to the effect that she had been there and missed him, and slipped it under his door before she walked home. Alone with her packed cases and the quietness of her own flat, which was by no means ungrateful to her, she wondered why she went to so much trouble, and humiliated herself—Yuri would see it in that light—so much, if she did not believe herself to be in the wrong. It might have been simply because she was still fond of him, or from a profound hatred of waste; but she thought rather that she was taking steps to make it impossible for him to be deterred by the fear of humiliation from re-establishing some sort of relationship with her, on terms however changed. If he could feel that it was she who stooped to make the moves towards conciliation, at least he need not suffer any further torments of injured self-love, he might even feel able to wrest out of the situation some reparation for his wrongs. As for her, she was not dependent on what he thought of her, and her dignity could endure the more abject part. Rather that, than that he should go away like this, and drag his only firm anchor before he had others capable of holding him.

But Yuri did not come, nor write, nor telephone. Then she wrote to him, still calmly but with more urgency, asking for what he apparently would not give unasked, some sign that their friendship, whatever its imperfections, had not been entirely wiped out of remembrance. But there was still no visit, and no message.

The taxi came for her in the early morning of Tuesday, and took her with her luggage to the air terminal. Malcolm was in Sheffield on business, and did not even know she had achieved a visa, so on this occasion she was spared his kindly but disapproving valedictions. Ralph had her keys, and Pryor would be at the terminal to see her off, but this

300

part of the journey she made alone, and was glad of her loneliness. She looked up into the dove-grey sky of the morning, not yet flushed with the light of a slow-emerging sun, and was suspended in a fatalistic calm, eased for the moment of all necessity of effort. It was too early yet to think consciously of Lubov, or of all the new difficulties there might be to hedge him from her, even when the sea and the continent were crossed. But he was there, she was filled with him, a shining quietness.

Pryor met her at the doorway of the air terminal, and superintended the removal of her cases and the surrender of her outward ticket with philosophical good-humour. It was eccentric of her, no doubt, to wish to spend her occasional holidays in such an outlandish way, but he could afford to allow her her eccentricities, and even to give up all idea of expecting a dividend from her wanderings. She had done very well for him during the past year, let her have her lapses.

They sat drinking coffee, with a quarter of an hour still to while away before her flight could expect to be called; and the loudspeaker system, crackling faintly, poured out occasional messages for stray passengers in a metallic and monotonous voice. It was Pryor who heard her name, and lifted a finger for silence to catch the repetition.

'A special-delivery letter for you at the desk! I'll get it.'

'For me?' she said with an unbelieving smile, Yuri already put away so far out of mind, but for the faint, bitter sadness he had left behind him, that she did not think of him now. But when she tore open the envelope Pryor put into her hands, it was Yuri's handwriting that stepped stiffly across the single sheet of notepaper within.

'My dear Emmy,
    In thanking you for all you have done for me in the past, I regret I must also beg you to understand that it has become necessary for me to make full repayment of my debts to you. I am compelled to ask you to allow me time to pay gradually, but as my prospects here are now good, I hope to have to ask for no more than a few months' grace. In the meantime, please accept this first earnest of the seriousness of my intentions.
                    Yours in duty,
                            Yuri Dushek.'

She sat gazing at the calculated phrases with a still and tranquil face. He must have been very determined that she should have no opportunity to reply, and that this cruel gesture should send her out of England smarting. He had meant it to be a death blow, and in a sense the cheque for twenty pounds, folded into the envelope with it, was nothing less.

She lit a corner of the cheque from her cigarette, and watched it curl slowly into blackness, dropping the last remnant into the ashtray. The note she crumbled into the bowl after it. What had survived of Yuri lay flaked into drifting black fragments, stirring vaguely in their own fading heat. She thought: 'So that's all! That's over!...'

PART THREE

THERE

Resolution:

'The early Christians believed that the material world would end in their lifetime: science has given to us a new reason for that belief ... To them the shortness of the time was a means of grace; so may it be to us. It deprives materialism of its profit and tyranny of its power. It is an amnesty to all the imprisonments of the mind; it empties out all the philosophies of disintegration. It is a reason to love and to be at peace.'

Charles Morgan, at the XXVIth
International Conference of P.E.N.,
Amsterdam, 21st June, 1954.

Lubov was on the apron of terrace in front of the restaurant, just where she had left him eighteen months ago, his hands spread on the rail as he watched her come in. She had recognised the tall, slender figure before the aircraft halted, and withdrew her eyes from it only with the most superstitious reluctance in order to gather her things together and prepare to alight, as though he might vanish if she released her hold of him. Small, distant and still, he waited to see her emerge and descend to the tarmac; and when she came out into the watery April sunlight, and stepped down among the shallow, shimmering pools left from the early rain, he straightened up at once, alert and tensed with eagerness, and waved a long arm. Her raised hand, flung up into the sun, caught the salutation like a white flower. Across the intervening spaces of air they joined hands again, she felt the very energy and passion of his touch filling her palm.

Then she was satisfied. Insistent change, frowning through the innocent sunlight, already troubled her vision, the new, drab brown and grey paint of the airport buildings, sterile as a battleship, loomed over Lubov like a threat of barrenness and frustration, the worn monotony of flags, monitory red, draped

307

the frontage of the reception hall, the whiteness which gives to flying-fields their only grace had become all neutral, hard and military, a khaki void. But he was there, and unchanged, and she was at peace. There was no other mutation which had power to dismay her, if he remained unshaken.

The air hostess, revolving upon the heel of a smart non-uniform shoe, waved them after her towards the reception hall, and in through the wide glass doors. The little waiting-room seemed to have grown still smaller and darker since Emmy's last visit. Its walls were closely covered with display boards, on which marched figures above life-size, miners, nurses, farmers, housewives, railwaymen, truck-drivers, all resolute, all smiling, all formidable, advancing upon some unstated goal. Their exuberance, their giant size, caused the room to shrink, and their monstrous reality, for they were all photographs assembled into one huge montage, made them look like some new race of humans, the heirs and destroyers of *homo sapiens*.

'If I believed in you,' she thought, gazing at them warily from the wooden bench in the centre of the room, 'I should never again be able to see a man walking without seeing an invisible procession streaming down the street with him. But evidently I have defective vision. I can never see a procession like yours without losing sight of it in one face at a time. It's probably the wrong attitude, but at least it keeps me from being too elated about you, or too afraid of you. One can't come to terms with a procession. It has too many mouths to be suckled, too many bodies to be embraced, too many needs to be satisfied, too many sorrows to be comforted, too many hearts to be loved. And I can't believe in you, because except on cardboard I've never found you. Not here, not anywhere!'

They looked at her with large and radiant indifference, striding by on their interminable pilgrimage, and she looked back at them with a sceptical smile, and waited for the bored young immigration officer behind the wire cage to open her passport and call her name. The feet of the marching Titans trod a frieze of little national flags. The three other passengers, two Belgians taken aboard at Brussels and a silent young woman on leave from the London embassy, walked ceaselessly up and down the short length of the room in two conflicting rhythms. Behind the immigration barrier the young man dreamed, turning a pencil slowly in his thick brown fingers.

Two other people had entered the room, and were standing just within the door which gave on to the ramp and the Customs Hall. They talked together in low voices, their eyes roving speculatively over the four passengers. The woman was young, perhaps twenty-two or three, short and handsome and plainly dressed, her straight dark-gold hair uncovered and shining; the man young, too, plump and colourless, with intelligent mild eyes enormous behind his strong glasses. Everyone here seemed to be young now, the elderly had faded out of sight. Not one of the cardboard giants looked more than thirty years old.

The young woman approached with confidence, her companion following her. 'Excuse me, aren't you Miss Marryat? I have come from the Ministry of Culture to welcome you. And this is Dr Horda, who is here to receive you on behalf of the Musicians' Union.' Smiling, in perfect command of any situation with any guest, she extended a small, square, competent hand. She did not see any reason to mention her own name; she was from the Ministry, that was all the guest needed to know.

Emmy rose, grasping the cool young hand, so astonished, so unprepared for them, that she could think of nothing to say, not even the trivialities of arrival and greeting. 'How very kind! Yes, I'm Emily Marryat.'

The young man gave her a well-padded handshake and a brisk little bow. 'We have followed all your successes at Salzburg and Edinburgh last summer, Miss Marryat. We are very happy to be able to include you in our festival.'

Very little, after all, was required of her, except to surrender herself to their lively ministrations. They were adept at this, they had everything well in hand. The young man relieved her of her music-case, the girl took her arm, only a gentle, guiding touch at her elbow, delicate and deferential but of immense confidence.

'You have not been through passport control yet? I think we need not wait here. Just a moment, I will speak to him.' And after a brief colloquy with the young officer, she said contentedly: 'We can go down into the Customs Hall. They will come to us there. You must be very tired after your journey, Miss Marryat, aren't you? I hope you will not be too tired to visit a theatre this evening, because there is a performance we very much want you to see. Perhaps after a rest it will not be too much for you.'

Emmy disclaimed weariness, not yet committing herself to the theatre, or to complacency, or to acquiescence in being escorted. If this was the ordinary machinery of reception, it had never closed on her before, and its kindness and efficiency were not yet weighed and assimilated. She went down with them into the Customs Hall, identified her cases, and made to open them, but Dr Horda said simply: 'Oh, you have only your own personal things, I suppose? It is all right, that won't be necessary.'

'We have taken a room for you,' said the young woman, chatting gaily while the

311

Customs officer filled in the currency certificate, 'at the Hotel Corvin. I hope you will be comfortable there, I have seen the room myself, and I think everything is satisfactory. It is a very good hotel, one of our best. You must tell me if there is anything you need, but I think you will like it there. Also they speak English— not, perhaps, the waiters, but there is always someone on the desk who speaks it.'

This was the time, if there was to be such a time, for her to say outright that she did not need a hotel room, that she had not desired any help of the kind, that she had taken it for granted she would be staying with her friends, as she had always done before. But the newness of this welcome silenced her. It seemed she was known here now in her public character more perfectly than ever before, but she was no longer known as a friend and an intimate of this land. The machinery of contact, enlarged and perfected, opened smoothly to take her in. She felt curiously helpless in this situation; resistance would be ill mannered, insistence upon her responsibility for herself a rebuff she had no intention of administering to anyone, and yet silent acceptance would be in itself a deception, and one she could neither tolerate nor afford. Above all, there was Lubov, waiting now so patiently in the entrance hall, counting the last unbearable minutes with his eyes fixed and constant upon the glass door. He must not be thrust upon their notice too suddenly, he ought not to be bound to her too emphatically, he never could or should be denied. In a world which was better than a quicksand there need have been none of these problems, and human relationships could have been stated clearly and openly; but now every step was taken upon tremulous ground.

She said warmly: 'I'm sure I shall be quite comfortable there, and find all your arrangements perfect. I'm not used to being taken care of like this, you know. Marvan used to leave me to look after myself—knowing, of course, that I have friends here, and know my way about the town.'

The girl's dark eyes, beautifully full and regular in their oval settings, opened wide in pure surprise. 'You know our town? You have been here before?' Emmy could see her mentally searching the records of previous Musical Festivals, and failing to find there the name of Emily Marryat.

'Yes, several times. I can find my way round quite well, though it's eighteen months now since I was here. Didn't Mr Marvan tell you?'

'Oh, I don't know Marvan myself. He is not at the Ministry now, you know. Your letter to him was passed on to the proper person, and of course we made the arrangements for your visit.'

'I didn't know that. What is Marvan doing now?' asked Emmy, stowing away the signed currency certificate in her bag, and watching the curiously revealing face of the girl, in whose confident calm the tiny inflections of bewilderment and curiosity made ripples as swift and disquieting as wind does over still water. Perhaps it was even mystifying that the guest should ask after Marvan, who after all was merely the representative of his organisation, not an individual. Perhaps it had been incorrect of him to grow into something like a personal friend.

'He is working in radio,' said Dr Horda. 'I have met him there. I think he is in charge of some of the foreign-language broadcasts. There, we are ready? I have my car here for you. Shall we go through?'

It did not seem to Emmy that she ever actually made a decision, or that she even considered a problem. She simply said what rose naturally to her lips. 'There's an old friend of mine waiting for me outside, I saw him as we came in. Dr Lubov Ivanescu—perhaps you know him? Will you have room for him as well?'

The young man's mild eyes beamed blankly at her through the thick glasses. She thought that but for that pebbly magnification she might have read in them the same alert wonder which shone in the girl's gaze. Certainly the two exchanged a significant glance. He said promptly and pleasantly:

'Oh, yes, of course, it's a four-seater. We can take the small case with us, and I will have the other one sent on. Yes, by all means we shall ask Dr Ivanescu to join us. I don't think I have met him before.'

'Dr Ivanescu is a musician, too?' The girl was examining Emmy's face with a lively but still curiosity as they moved towards the glass doors. 'You met him, perhaps, at the conference of progressive musicians that was held here two years ago?' She was seeking, it was clear, some approved basis for such an acquaintance. The mere word friend, unsupported by all the recognised data of sponsored time, and place, and activity, disturbed her sense of order. Whatever could not be accounted for in terms socially acceptable was suspect.

'No, he's a lecturer at the university. I wasn't at the conference, but I met several of the Union members when I sang here a few months afterwards. I gave one recital at the club,' said Emmy, producing the more respectable of her credentials, and forbearing to discuss Lubov further, 'and a concert at the Mozarteum.'

Was she committed to explaining Lubov to these people? Nothing she said or did must be allowed to call attention to his already noticeable nonconformity, nor, perhaps, to her own, which would illuminate his by reflection just as surely. But too recognisable a perception that explanations were necessary must be as compromising as too bland a denial or too defensive a lie, and to be too voluble was

315

as damning as to be too reticent. So she offered nothing more, but passed through the door Dr Horda held open for her, and looked round the hall for Lubov.

He was standing between the bright glass show-cases of enamels and leather goods and textiles, his hands in his pockets, his eyes fixed steadily upon the doorway in which she would appear; and as soon as she came into view his whole face blazed up into an indescribable radiance of happiness. Nothing like it had ever happened to her before. She thought it justified her life triumphantly, even if she never accomplished anything else at all, to have been the cause of that illumination. Then he saw the girl from the Ministry moving with assured proprietorial pride at her elbow, the man from the Union following benevolently with her music-case, and it was as if he withdrew his brightness in an instant behind a veil of reserve. Was it the danger of shining so unguardedly before witnesses, or the indignity, that made him recoil? He did it with something of the lofty air of a very young man interrupted in a moment of emotion. Miloslav might have backed into his tower and closed the door with the same haughty finality, though not so quietly.

Confronted now with the problem of how to greet him, she waited for him to take the initiative, moving towards him meanwhile with the wary smile and extended hand which could be interpreted however he chose. But in a world of such profuse and painful subtleties this proved almost simple still. The lesser smile, loving and gentle and blessed by habit, came readily to his face, he sprang forward with the old eager stride, snatching off his hat, and she saw and delighted in the plunge of his head sidelong to meet his hand, so that the neatness of his hair should not be disarranged. This minute, fastidious gesture, less a vanity than a tribute to order itself, was all the reassurance she needed. Everything became clear; not easy, not satisfying, but prescribed and understood.

He kissed her above their clasped hands; the coolness of his lips in that demure family salute filled her with all the confidence of custom. He shut his arms round her for a moment, his cheek was against her cheek, his smooth, cold, thin cheek faintly scented still from its recent shave, growing suddenly warm with the touch of hers, and the vehement surge of his blood. She whispered soundlessly into his ear: 'Lubov!' and was unaware that she had said anything at all, though in the one word she claimed him, exulted in him, presented herself to him. Then they stood apart, and looked at each other, and felt upon their trembling but calm flesh the interested eyes of the two witnesses.

'How are you, Emmy? Did you have a pleasant flight?'

'Yes, thanks, we did. Calm and steady all the

way. How is everybody?'

'Oh, very well, of course, and looking forward so much to seeing you.'

She turned him towards her companions, letting her hand lie gently upon his sleeve.

'May I introduce Dr Ivanescu?'

The girl from the Ministry supplied, with a smile and a mannish little bow, 'Kraskova!' and extended her hand.

'And Dr Horda, of the Musicians' Union. I must say it's very nice to be met by so many people. Miss Kraskova is from the Ministry of Culture, and is very kindly taking care of all my affairs here. I'm being thoroughly spoiled,' she said, smiling at Lubov deliberately. 'I haven't even to look for a hotel for myself, everything's already done.'

Lubov said: 'Oh, we look after our guests, you know!' and returned the smile with perfect understanding.

'I've got a car outside,' said Dr Horda. 'You'll drive back to town with us, won't you?'

'Thank you, if you've room for me I'll be very glad to.'

They went out to the tarmac before the airport buildings, where the April greenness of the plateau opened suddenly before them in a limpid afternoon light, the sun-warmed road steaming gently after the morning's rain.

Even walking across the oval space of the car park beside Lubov was an inexpressibly tormenting pleasure. She had scarcely had time

318

to look at him yet, but she thought that his overcoat, the same one he had been wearing eighteen months ago, hung upon him more amply than before, and that his cheeks had grown by a marked shade more deeply hollowed, his eyes a little larger in their settings. His smile, in all the sweetness of its grave gaiety, had not changed at all; and the look he gave her, as he opened the rear door of the car for her, and their eyes met, was full of lively and undismayed tenderness. His fingers cupped her arm as she got in, leaving a magical warmth, an invulnerable spot.

Miss Kraskova followed her in and settled beside her with a flash of nylon-clad ankles. Lubov got into the front seat beside Dr Horda, gazing ahead along the shining steel-blue roadway as the car slid forward. The drab buildings, superstructure of a ship which never sailed, drew quietly back from them, regrouping in squat solidity beyond acres of green turf. They accomplished the wheeling turn on to the straight white road and began the long drive into the city, between the blank, rolling upland fields, corrugated with late ploughing and vivid with the viridian of young corn.

'You have known each other some time?' asked Miss Kraskova, studying alertly Lubov's profile, the set of the coat upon his spare shoulders, the trim cut of the brown hair tapering into the nape of his neck.

'Oh, yes, several years. I have quite a lot of friends here,' said Emmy, instinctively seeking to hide Lubov in a crowd of anonymous others. 'This is my fifth visit here since the end of the war, you see, and naturally I've made more acquaintances every time.'

'I can imagine that you would,' agreed the girl from the Ministry, with her vivacious and curious smile. 'I did not realise that you already knew so much about us. But you have not, I think, sung in the Music Festival before?'

'No, I never gave any professional concerts here until my last two visits. I'd sung occasionally at little private parties before, and on visits to schools, and that sort of thing, but not in public.'

'It's very interesting!' The word in its amiable brightness had almost a sinister quality. 'Then you have probably more experience of our hotels than I have, and perhaps I have chosen quite the wrong one for you. You have a favourite one? I could transfer the booking, if you wish it.'

No doubt Emmy should have come straight out with the fact, the no longer quite innocent and reasonable fact, that she had never yet spent a single night in any of the city's hotels, but was very well acquainted with the facilities of a family flat on the Lucerna. But she merely said: 'Oh, of course the Hotel Corvin is excellent. I shall be quite happy there. Do you often have to meet English visitors and look after them, like this?'

'Not so often as I would like, not many guests come to us from your country now. I also meet French groups, though—French is my second foreign language—and there are more of them.' The girl was enthusiast enough to allow herself to be diverted into this fascinating byway with goodwill. She talked animatedly about her distinguished guests, writers, trades unionists, artists, scientists, she had known them all. What a training for a girl of twenty, Emmy thought, how fulfilling, and how narrowing! No wonder she is worried now by somebody as unprecedented as Lubov. He doesn't belong to any of the organisations that ought to be meeting a progressive musician from the West. He's as indecent as if he were naked; indeed, without a group to sanction him, he is naked.

Out of the new, fresh green of lesser hills the hill of the battle surged on their right hand, abrupt to its forested crest, casting its long and bitter shadow athwart the sunlit afternoon. The chilling breath of tragedy, uncompensated yet, unredeemed, blew across the suave modern highway. In this one place time had not moved since the day of the disaster, though the long shadow which had darkened half Europe drew in now on the ebb to the foot of the mountain.

Miss Kraskova pointed, forsaking the French suddenly. 'Look, this hill is a piece of

321

history. Do you know what happened there? It's more than three centuries ago.'

Emmy's natural truthfulness had learned to temper its candour by this time, but the predisposition to openness was still powerful. Her look was enough. 'You *do* know!' said the girl, astonished.

Lubov turned his chin upon his shoulder with a laugh. 'I should have warned you! There is nothing on this journey with which you can surprise Emmy. She knows every inch of the way. Let her point out the sights to you, and you can take a rest.'

'I should be ashamed if I hadn't learned a little,' said Emmy, 'after four visits. But I don't know as much as Lubov is making out.'

'We shall try!' The dark eyes, vivid with intelligence, searched the way ahead. They were just coming to the last crest of the plateau, before the long, gradual descent into the suburbs, and on their left the sudden cleft of the ravine slit open for an instant, its rocks terracotta red in the sunshine. 'There, tell me about that valley! After whom is it named, what happened there?'

Emmy recounted, smiling, the story of the Women's War. 'It's no credit to me. I've had good tutors. I was never allowed just to take pleasure in the sights, I had to pass examinations. I'm afraid I'm not a very satisfactory guest for you.'

Miss Kraskova, however, continued to

question her as they drove through the villages of the city fringe, and passed the first looped endings of the tram routes. What was this building, that statue, the dome on the skyline, the hill across the river? Towers, whose individual shapes made them unmistakable one for another, were identified gravely. The bastions of the Citadel were named. Not disappointment, but the first wild warmth of an entirely personal delight, quickened in the girl's face. She no longer looked a competent official, but an intelligent and pleased child, won into unguarded joy by the discerning admiration of her most prized possessions.

'But it's true, you know everything! This is wonderful! Dr Ivanescu, were you the tutor?'

'One of several. But the truth is we could never answer her questions fast enough,' said Lubov.

'What is your subject? Miss Marryat has told us that you have a lectureship at the university.' She made a serious face at the reply. 'Oh, it would be asking a lot to want Miss Marryat to follow you into our language and literature. I thought perhaps you taught history.'

'She can read and speak the language a little, too,' said Lubov with his reserved smile, 'but no thanks to me.'

'But it is so interesting, this! Even to think it worth the trouble of learning a little,' said Miss Kraskova, glowing, 'you must have liked us very much. More than you would feel about some place where you had just enjoyed a pleasant holiday. More than just in the ordinary way of friendliness.'

The terms of friendship no longer sounded strange in her mouth, nor seemed to excite in her any bewilderment or disquiet. The official framework, after all, was malleable, could take on all manner of original shapes. The only thing that could not be done with it was to dispense with it altogether. Had Lubov been placed to their satisfaction, she wondered, by this time? She doubted it; every added warmth in herself, though welcomed with pleasure, added also to the irregularity of the attachment.

The filigree spires of the cathedral, revolving slowly as the road curved, transfixed a sky like a pearl, washed clean of blue, and iridescent with late sunlight. They came down to the bridge, and the river, high and pale with the icy colouring of the mountain thaw, throbbed underneath them against its caissons, tugging with silent, quivering power. Not into the square this time, but to the right along the embankment for a little way, and then, left again between the bright modern shops and the pavements surging with people, to the wide glass front of the Hotel Corvin, just off the main avenue. The slope of the Lucerna, visible beyond the distant bridge of Captain Evian, was a mound of snowy blossom, all its cherries and plum trees foaming into full flower.

'You have seen it like this before?' Miss Kraskova's voice had a new ease about it, as though she spoke now to an overseas cousin rather than a stranger. 'You should drive out one day along the road to the east, under the Citadel Hill and the Watchtower Hill. The blossom there is incredible. Perhaps we can find time for it. But I confess I have planned a very full programme for you—you must tell me if it is too much.'

They went in through the glass doors to a quiet and shadowy foyer and a reception desk retreating discreetly into a deep alcove.

'I will ask for the key of your room, if you will just come and sign in. There will be a form to fill in, too, but we can do that upstairs. I'm sure you will be ready for a rest. And then we can go through the programme I have suggested for you, and you can make any alterations you would like. There may be something you would particularly like to do—especially as I did not know how much you know about our city already.'

Dr Horda set down Emmy's smaller case beside one of the tables near the window and suggested briskly: 'Let us have a drink first, to celebrate your safe arrival, and then I shall go myself and fetch the other case from the terminal. Dr Ivanescu, you'll join us?'

Lubov shook his head. 'No, if you'll excuse me I'll leave you now. You'll want to talk over business, and then I'm sure you have arrangements for this evening.'

'Won't you just stay and drink some beer with us?' But he was relieved, in reality, that Lubov felt so delicate a conviction of being, for the moment, a little in the way.

'No, thanks, not now. I have to run a couple of errands for my mother,' he said, smiling at Emmy, 'before the shops close. But I'll call you, if I may, some time tomorrow, Emmy. You'll have an idea by then of what your commitments are.'

'Yes, do, Lubov! Ring me in the morning, and if by any chance you miss me, I'll call you as soon as I'm free.' She gave him her hand, and trembled at the close clasp of his thin fingers about it. It was not as she had planned, this homecoming, but it was all she could have at this moment; and at least she touched him, his palm pressed her own, his face and body filled her vision, his voice was in her ears. She felt, as something apart from her own longing, and the completion of it, the intense hunger he had to close his arms round her and hug her to his heart. She was aware how his flesh ached towards her, and with what an effort he withdrew his hand thus quietly and calmly from hers. She knew, too, that his reticence had nothing to do with fear of compromising either himself or her. He took this formal farewell, without a kiss, without an embrace, because it was not fitting that these people who acquiesced, however innocently, in a mutilated world should be the witnesses of such a reunion.

*　　*　　*

Miss Kraskova expounded her programme with pride over a hotel dinner which was certainly good, but lacked the more personal charms of Ilonna's cooking. The dining-room at the Hotel Corvin was vast, but well planned to dissimulate its size, and corners of it could look intimate almost to cosiness.

'I shall be at your disposal as often as I can, but for some of the evenings I will find for you another escort. There are so many things we feel that you really should not miss. We have so much to show now! Since the new revolution things are changing so quickly, so wonderfully, it is intoxicating. Look, I have written down for you what I propose.'

She spread the typed paper upon the table between their coffee-cups, and traced the items one by one with a pink-varnished fingernail.

'Tonight I have tickets for something very special. It is the second song and dance recital of a new regional group of folk-artists. You know that we have many of these groups now, small ones of part-time artistes in the villages and towns, and now these regional ones, made up of people who intend to give up their lives to this work. They not only perform, but collect and arrange, and even reconstruct almost lost dances and songs from the fragments they can trace. And they compose new songs and ballets, too. One day we shall have a national group, the best of all the smaller parties will be welded into one great company. But now this group belongs to the capital city, and is the most advanced point we have reached yet. They have their own orchestra, their own director, choreographers, conductor, costumiers, everything.'

'It sounds the sort of thing that can only be done when it's no longer necessary to show a profit,' said Emmy, looking up with interest.

'It is very necessary to show a profit, but not a material one, that is the difference. It will be maintained as a national pride, and you will see what kind of asset it will be.' Her smile was brilliant and confident. 'And tomorrow I would like to take you, if you agree, to a new Gothic gallery we have opened—painting, sculpture, crafts, everything Gothic is there— and afterwards, perhaps in the afternoon, you would not mind a small press conference? About the festival, of course, but they might also ask you some questions about conditions in England. We have heard,' she said sympathetically, 'how difficult life is becoming there. For the evening I planned only a short recital at the Musicians' Club. The concerts will be later, you will have plenty of time for getting acclimatised, but this will be just an informal evening, and if you would like an early night, then your part of the programme could be arranged first.'

Thinking of the ease with which she could walk from the Musicians' Club to the Lucerna, Emmy said at once: 'Yes, I think it would be a good idea, if you could do that. Could I be free by about half-past eight? It isn't a party?'

'Oh, that could be arranged easily. I will see that they know your wishes. Tomorrow night,' she said apologetically, 'I regret I cannot be with you, but I will see you to the Club before I leave you, and someone will escort you back to the hotel.'

'Oh, that won't be necessary. It's very close, and I know the way quite well.' The world had narrowed indeed if she could seize so hungrily upon the prospect of even a few hours with the Ivanescu, as though she must hoard every crumb in case of future starvation. And indeed by the time they had scanned the rest of the programme she was beginning to think that she would have to fight for so much as a glimpse of her family. Miss Kraskova had crammed the days full of crèches, factories, schools, discussions, meetings, musical museums, manuscript libraries, operas, castles, recording sessions at the broadcasting studios. 'Lubov, my darling,' thought Emmy ruefully, 'it looks as if I've come through the fence and across the continent just to touch the tips of your fingers and lose you again.'

'It is a little too much?' asked Miss Kraskova, watching her face with benevolent anxiety.

'I should be glad of some more free time, if I can have it without disappointing anyone. Of course, you couldn't know that I had been here before, and had so many people to look up. And you must be quite glad to have some free time now and again—you seem to work very long hours.'

'Oh, we have no fixed hours, we work as we are needed. We are very proud of our job, you see. But of course we shall delete some of these engagements.' She began to go through the list with goodwill, offering to cancel several of the evening dates she had proposed. It was as easy as that. One made a tentative movement, and the severely closed door opened willingly. Emmy recoiled ashamed from her own too subtle procedures; it was impossible not to be affected by the attitudes of the world, not to expect suspicion in small things where there was such a weight of suspicion in great things, but it seemed that this distrust, at any rate, was an injustice. The organisation of her days, the provision of constant companionship, was all the result of enthusiastic kindness and an unrelenting sense of duty. Its object was not to keep her under surveillance and always in the right hands, but to ensure that she should see

330

everything, be hedged about from loneliness and boredom, and know herself appreciated. Or was this, in its turn, a misleading simplification?

'Is that better? See, it will give you five, six evenings free, and we shall examine the position again. And now,' she said with undiminished cheerfulness, neither astonished nor hurt at having her planning mutilated, 'if you are ready, we can go along to the theatre. Our car will be here by now, I think.'

For the guest of the Ministry, however mistakenly adopted, there were to be no noisy dashes about the city by tram, no crowded jostlings about the streets on foot at theatre-time. They were carried to the Capitol in a Ministry limousine, and installed, not in two cheap seats anxiously snapped up at the last moment or on returns, but in a centre box on the circle level, its painted ceiling sustained by white and gilt caryatids, its royal blue curtains looped back within silken cords as thick as Emmy's wrist. The surroundings deserved diamonds, but received no more considerable compliment than Emmy's afternoon frock, for Miss Kraskova was still wearing her neat black suit and white tailored blouse. The theatre was full to the last seat; she remembered that every theatre here invariably was—'except for some propaganda piece, perhaps,' as Ilonna had once said.

'This company,' said Miss Kraskova

excitedly in Emmy's ear, as the cricket-like chirpings and warblings of the orchestra tuning up began to rise like vapour, 'is already so famous, I should never have been able to come tonight if it had not been for you. They keep always a small block of tickets available for foreign guests, you see, and therefore I benefit, too, because I must accompany you as interpreter. I shall not explain,' she said, with a sudden flashing smile, already far out of her official personality and every moment blossoming more brightly, 'that you do not really need an interpreter.'

'I'll be careful not to give you away,' said Emmy, laughing.

'But tonight I think I am really necessary, to explain to you where all the different songs and dances come from, and the stories that belong to them, because some of them are ballads in dance. Look, the lights are going down!'

Emmy had kept a corner of scepticism in her mind, defensive against this new entertainment which might, in its own way, be a kind of a propaganda piece. But the first abrupt shout of the orchestra, that quivering outcry of strings and horns, shattered it like a smitten glass. She had heard folk-music played in several countries, in several styles, with every artifice of artlessness, every resource of sentiment, but never before like this, with the intense pride and absolute authority of great art, freed from every self-consciousness, every lingering

332

quaintness. The tempestuous tunes, welling up and enlarging like flowers upon the air, lamenting, exulting, dancing, mounted in a flood of glittering cadences. The impetus of its onward surge took the breath away, lifted the hair on the head. Emmy found herself gasping and laughing, catching up threads of the songs she knew, being swept along upon the tide of those which were new to her. Nothing of the archaic remained in this music, it was as alive and expressive now as in its childhood, as applicable to the human predicaments of the present as to the stresses of the past. It was all this because a tremendous talent was performing it, and still more because something of genius had gone into the arranging of it. If she had doubted the quality of the group, she was already answered.

When the orchestral introduction ended, the lights were raised for a moment, and she saw the ripple of relaxation after great excitement pass through the auditorium, in a swelling sigh of pleasure, a rosiness of flushed cheeks, a sparkle of eyes.

'But you know some of those songs!' exclaimed Miss Kraskova, staring at Emmy with a glittering smile. 'I saw how you were following them.'

'I got interested in them years ago—naturally, how could I not be interested when I heard them? And they are quite easy to sing if one is prepared to learn.'

'You sing them, too? You will be using them in your programmes here?'

'Yes, a small group in each concert. I always feel that the audience could do it better, but they seem to like to hear me try.'

'In our own language, or in English?'

'Oh, the original! I have made a few translations into English, to use at home, but I prefer the original. It's almost always impossible to reproduce the sound values properly in translation.'

The lights were beginning to fade again, very gradually, but they shone wonderfully for a moment in Miss Kraskova's delighted eyes; and it was on impulse that Emmy remarked, seizing the moment as it passed: 'You know, you've never told me your name.'

Astonished, she repeated blankly: 'My name? Kraskova.' And then, her eyes softening into an altogether warmer and gentler intelligence: 'Slava!'

The curtains parted, and the choir of the group stood demurely drawn up in a semi-circle, the girls in front, the men at the back, perhaps forty people in all, brilliant as birds-of-paradise in snowy laces and vivid embroideries, with rainbow ribbons spilling from their sleeves, and necks, and waists, and the tail-feathers of cocks swaying from the men's hats and sweeping erect in the wind of the curtains' passing. They sang with the same intense conviction and precision with which their orchestra played, songs from all over the republic, and in many moods. They produced with equal certainty the restrained and tuneful choral singing of the west, and the high, hard but miraculously pure and true head voice of the eastern mountains, that could throw a chain of sound clean across the alluvial valleys.

So if this was the new voice they had found for their new civilisation, she thought, astonished, how was it possible to disbelieve in their justification? Technically competent music can be produced anywhere, music mechanically more perfect, perhaps, than this; but a voice of so much conviction and joy, so superbly surging forward, so innocent of any nostalgic glance behind, could not possibly emerge out of a fundamentally repressive or negative society. Find as many flaws as you like, she thought, clumsiness, over-exuberance, cruelty, anything so long as it is positive and energetic could be true of the country that sings like this; but nothing narrow, nothing sterile, nothing unfruitful, could give voice to such a music.

The dancers followed, performing a set of wedding dances, a bandits' dance from the mountains, a mimed fairy story, a courting dance from the east, in which the men, long and slender and unbelievably elegant in clothes designed still further to accentuate their slimness, cut out from the brilliant babble of girls each his chosen partner, against the efforts of all the others to baffle and confound him. It was easy to see that they made free use of ballet training without being limited by the conventions of ballet. They moved with the same superb conviction of their own excellence, the same ardour to communicate, the same assurance of needing no interpreter, which made their singers and musicians wonderful; and they startled and excited in the same way. Their colours rang like chords, and their sounds scintillated like colours. The men achieved prodigies of elevation, and laughed with delight in their own splendour. They hurled themselves into the air with supreme confidence that it would subdue itself to their movements, and it approved their faith, and bore them up as lightly as birds. The girls, their wide, bright skirts revolving like humming-tops, rapped out with their little booted feet a rhythm as intense and complicated as the chatter of castanets, and spread their ribbons and laces upon the air like elaborate wings. They were a shout of joy and achievement straight out of an optimistic heart; and no manner of sophistry could account for them in any other way.

At the end of the courting dance the last couple were left dancing alone, their companions forming a lightly swaying ring as backcloth to their duet. The girl was tall, but very slight and small-boned, with raven-black hair in a long plait, and great glittering black eyes of rapture that caught the light as she span, and seemed to send forth beams of light in return. Her head was thrown back, the spotlight vivid on her pale face and her slender milky arms, that floated upon the air in long, suave curves after her turns. She was smiling fiercely, incandescent with her own radiance. Her boot-heels made long drum-rolls, rapid as a woodpecker's drumming, then snapped off the sound into silence, so that for a moment the audience suffered a real illusion that she had danced herself off the ground, and floated weightlessly on the tremulous air. She had an electrifying beauty, something much more than physical; the beauty of a creature absolutely fulfilled, absolutely vindicated, absolutely happy.

Emmy had caught the first glimpse of her face as the spotlight fingered its gentle way downward and lit upon her brilliance of ivory and black. She recognised her then, but could not conceive that she was right, and she watched with wonder and uncertainty until the dance ended, and for the first time the entranced creature stood still. Then she knew that she had made no mistake. The dress with its voluminous petticoats changed her appearance but not her gait, the long plait of black hair must have been put on with her make-up, but the face, so marvellously changed, so reassuringly the same, was Wanda's face. Wanda's face, with all the hunger satisfied, all the discontent assuaged, all the frustration disseminated in this violent and radiant explosion of creative energy. Wanda's face as it had always been meant to be, eased, fulfilled, at peace.

*   *   *

Wanda was sitting in front of the mirror in a small dressing-room, the lofty, quivering head-dress of a bride reared upon her black hair, her embroidered skirts spread over the low back of her chair. They had sent her no warning, Slava led the way in with only a light rap at the door, and three enquiring faces turned calmly upon the strangers, but Wanda did not look round. Emmy saw her face in reflection, subtly changed as mirror images often are from the truth of their subjects, oval and pure and serious in beauty, the wired flowers of her head-dress shining above a brow as clear as snow. The enormous eyes, peaceful and still, shone night-black, examining calmly their own radiance. Upon these eyes Emmy fixed her own, and in a moment their focus shifted to meet her gaze.

The lovely face blazed into astonished joy. She pushed back the chair, disentangling her multitudinous skirts violently, and sprang across the room with outstretched arms.

'Emmy! Emmy, darling! But how wonderful! As if I had planned it!' They embraced in a tangle of rainbow ribbons. If the three girls with whom she shared the room felt any curiosity, Wanda did not care, and took no pains to allay it. She claimed her friend with a shout of triumph. 'Lubov *told* me you were going to a theatre tonight, but he couldn't have known it would be *this* one. But it's perfect! I wanted you to see me just like this, without any warning. He was going to try and get tickets for the whole family, for the programme we give next week. You see, by the time I was ready to write and tell you about the change, he had your letter to say you were coming, so I waited, and didn't write to you after all. I wanted exactly *this*! Oh, darling, it's been so long! Did you like us? Did you like *me*?'

But she needed no reassurance from Emmy or any other. She knew that what she had done was right; she was afire with her certainty.

'You know quite well that you were wonderful. The whole show takes my breath away. I've never seen or heard anything like it. And *you*! What it's done to *you*! You shine!'

'I am happy,' said Wanda, unlinking her arms and standing back to look smilingly at her friend. Her voice, like her face, had perfected itself, rang round and clear. She kept Emmy's hand warmly between her own as she recounted in one joyful breath the whole of her recent history. 'I began to dance with them a few months ago, when they planned the group, and it seems I was good at it, although I'd

339

hardly ever tried before. So I gave up everything else, and began to study seriously, and here I am.'

'You didn't tell me a word of this. Why ever not?'

'I didn't know for some time whether it was going to be a success, and if I was going to have to give it up, after all, I knew it would be too painful to talk about. So I waited. And then, when I was sure, you see, you were already almost on your way to us. I kept it all as a surprise for you.'

Emmy had glanced round belatedly for Slava, but she was in eager conversation with the other three girls, spreading out in her inquisitive hands one of the embroidered aprons, to admire the exactness of the detail. They were left free to devote themselves to each other for the remaining minutes of the interval.

'Lubov explained about the hotel, and everything? It was unavoidable, as things turned out. I hadn't bargained for it, but I couldn't get out of it.'

'Oh yes, we all understood. But you will come, won't you, as soon as you can? We're all longing for you to come. At any hour of the day or night, it doesn't matter.'

'You know I'll come! You know it's why I'm here. I hope I shall be able to reach you tomorrow evening, but it may be as late as nine. I must fall in with the plans they've made for me, but I'll try to keep as much time free as I can.'

'Yes, do! We want you so much. But this was wonderful, to see you tonight, when I didn't expect it.'

The warning bell was ringing for the end of the interval. Slava was already moving towards the door, and the three young dancers had begun to flutter like butterflies before the mirror.

'And for me, too. And above all, to see you in an apotheosis like this!' she added, relinquishing regretfully the hand which left hers with equal reluctance.

'It really seems like that to you, too?' Wanda drew her back for a moment, and held her close. Her voice was soft and rueful as she said seriously: 'Isn't it strange how things work out? Why should this perfectly incorruptible thing, to which slogans won't even stick, be dropped in *my* lap? Lubov has to fight for his purity every hour of the day. And here am I, the only one who didn't object to compromise, who didn't demand perfection—I'm allowed to be active, and approved, and immaculate, too. There's no justice in it!'

*   *   *

In the sweet-scented middle evening she left the Musicians' Club, and walked down through the central avenues of the New Town towards the river. All the city was drowned in the

341

perfume of flowering trees, so vivid and all-pervading now in the twilight that the ordinary smells of the streets, petrol, and cooking food, and acrid city dust, and the powerful, cold green smell of the river in its spring spate, could not survive against it. The chestnuts of the main avenues were alight with pink and white candles, and snowed florets upon her head as she walked beneath them. The hills beyond the river, planted everywhere with fruit trees, poured down upon the air a delirious sweetness. In the middle of the bridge Captain Evian's plaque bore a chaplet of anemones, blood-red and royal purple and mourning mauve in the dusk. Along the embankment the flowering almonds made the fading air flush like dawn, and all up the staircases of the Lucerna, between the crumbling sgraffito and the baroque stone vases, the heady boughs of the false acacia, vivid green and virgin white, leaned down faint with fragrance over the heads of lovers.

Within this embowered beauty the day stretched and slept, the early-rising and early-resting city grew quiet, and the distracting bustle of the day's traffic no longer interposed itself between her eyes and the silent aspects of truth. At the end of the bridge she stopped to buy cigarettes at a kiosk which was not yet closed, and the girl behind the window, perceiving her foreignness, gave her a long, cold stare, unsmiling; and when she had passed

342

she was aware of eyes following her, and glanced back to see both the girl and an elderly man standing upon the pavement, watching her out of sight. On the pathways of the Lucerna two lovers straightened and detached themselves from each other as she came by, and they too saw that she was from the forbidden places, and kept a superstitious silence, their eyes wondering and wary, until she had turned the next corner and vanished from their world. And when she reached the short street in which the Ivanescu lived, there was a hopelessly drunken man reeling along the pavement in front of her, silent but for the slur and shuffle of his dragging feet. He was the third drunken man she had seen that day, each one solitary, each one submerged in the darkness of a private and impenetrable misery.

She turned gladly into the dark hall of Number Seventeen, and put out her hand to feel for the minute-light; and already, as soon as she was within the house, a sense of ease and familiarity closed round her like warm air after a long walk in the frost.

The rickety cage of the lift clanked its slow and temperamental way up to the fourth floor, and she closed its doors carefully after her and sent it down again with a ponderous lurch. Before the door of the rear flat she kicked straight the frayed mat, which was always askew, and rang the bell.

The door was whipped open almost at once,

a stampede of quick light feet racing for the handle inside, a flurry of laughter and a struggle determining the winner. Wanda opened doors as one would expect her to open them, largely, full to the wall, stepping back with a gesture which presented to the visitor the flat and all that was in it. She was glowing with a beneficent smile, expectant and eager, and Lubov was at her shoulder, smiling, too. It was as if the first frustrating glimpse of him, and that journey into town in the same car yet still a world away from him, had been a kind of dream, not even recent, not even well remembered except for the moment of his kiss, the recollection of which quickened in her body now like a child stirring.

'Emmy, darling, it *is* you! I knew the ring; no one else touches the bell so discreetly. Mummy, come quickly. Emmy's here!' Wanda kissed and hugged her, laughing with pleasure. Lubov did not exclaim. He stood waiting for her, not smiling now; and when she detached herself from Wanda he took her in his arms without a word, and held her for a long minute against his body in a taut stillness, breast and hip and thigh pressed together as though they willed to pass into each other and become indivisible, and had no way of achieving it but this. And indeed they had none, she was already aware of that; the times had hardened, not softened, since they had acknowledged their only half-understood helplessness.

344

He kissed her on the mouth. Wanda had shut the door and banished the world, Ilonna was hurrying from the kitchen and Matyas in his slippers and shirt-sleeves from the living-room, and Emmy had to be surrendered to them in turn, to be embraced and exclaimed over. With reluctant gentleness Lubov gave her up; it was, after all, no more than passing her from his left hand to his right. What mattered was that she was there, within the fortress; he could touch her merely by reaching out his hand.

'Now if only Miloslav were here,' said Ilonna, furiously patting cushions into order upon the couch before installing Emmy there in triumph, 'the family would be complete again. Oh, Emmy, my dear, this is very fine. Sit down there, and tell us all about yourself. I am going to make some coffee, and you must try the cakes I have baked this afternoon. There in England I'm sure no one gives you poppy-seed fillings, or plums with cream cheese, and I know how you like them. There, sit! Matyas, give Emmy a cigarette. I shall be only a moment.'

'Where is Miloslav now?' asked Emmy, drawing Wanda into the cushions beside her.

'Oh, he is up in the north, they are only recently back at their depot from the winter exercises. It is such a pity, he has been selected for some course or other, and it means he will have no leave at all for six weeks, until the course ends. At any other time he would have asked for a week-end pass and come home to see you. But now it's impossible!'

Lubov confirmed regretfully: 'I telephoned him this morning and told him you were here. But it seems we've chosen the worst possible time.'

'I'm sorry; I was hoping very much to get a glimpse of him. But at least he's all right? And he doesn't mind the life too much?'

'I don't think he's ever been quite so fit in his life. I won't say he's *enjoying* it—what sane man could?—but in a way he's having rather a good time. He likes being a one-man resistance movement. And he has plenty of good friends among his mob. Don't worry about Milo— he's all right.'

'That's the main thing, at any rate. I did hope to see him, but I was afraid it might be out of the question. There are so many things I want to ask you, I don't know where to begin. There are such a lot of things that can't be said in letters.'

'A great many!' said Matyas with a wry smile. He drew up a chair and sat down near to her. She thought that his face was more lined than she remembered it, and his hair a little more thickly sprinkled with grey, but his mouth still folded into the old characteristic expression of slightly sardonic amusement, and his eyes were as bright and shrewd as ever. 'Especially letters to England.'

346

'Tell me now, then, tell me everything. What about the factory? How are things going there? Do you find the set-up much changed?'

'Materially, not very much, and largely for the better,' said Matyas with his immovable fairness. 'I've been able to draw on capital I never had myself. We've got a paved road up to the shops now, and a lot of small alterations I suggested have been adopted. I get less money out of the job now though it was never a gold-mine, exactly—but if anything rather more free time. I bring paperwork home with me several nights a week, and I'm at it sometimes pretty late. But then, so I was when the place was mine.'

'I see a little more of him, these days,' confirmed Ilonna, coming in with the coffee. 'But he worries more than he used to. And he has not the same satisfactions.'

Remembering the sceptical reporter who had raised the same doubt, Emmy asked with a smile: 'And you did get the compensation money? I couldn't induce my countrymen to believe that you would.'

'What do they think we are, swindlers? Oh no, we indulge in a little sharpish practice now and again, but we pay what we've agreed to pay. They beat me down a little, but I still got more than I expected.'

'But unless you're going to draw on that nest-egg, it means you've less money to keep house on. And it does seem to me that prices are up rather a lot since last time I was here.'

Ilonna sat down and began to pour coffee, without manifesting any loss of serenity over her straitened circumstances. 'Yes, the money is a little tight,' she said cheerfully, handing Emmy's cup, and proffering after it a plate piled with little golden buns. 'One can live very well until one needs to buy something more expensive for the house, replacements for curtains, or a chair, or a radio set. Then there is just nothing with which to buy it, because we have no reserves. It costs our living simply to live. You see that Wanda lives now most of the time with her company—did she tell you they have their own house in Ledva?—and so she has nothing to spare for our expenses here. If she offered it I would not take it, because I know she needs it for her own things. So we keep house without any margin, and when we need something extra we must make our plans to do without something we usually have, or to make do with less of something. It seems there is always something one can do with less of. Most people have fewer new clothes than they used to have. Have you noticed again the skirts made from coats, the dresses made in two materials from the good parts of two old dresses? No, perhaps everyone is still wearing a coat, it is not warm enough to put them off yet. But you will see it in the summer—not quite so much a mended and re-made wardrobe as when you first came here after the war, but

348

something a little like it. But as it is not so urgent, we can give more thought to it, and do the work more elegantly.'

She made this report with the same disinterested simplicity with which she would have discussed her fortunes had they been in the ascendant. Complaint was not part of her purpose.

'In England,' said Emmy, smiling, 'you would certainly be criticised for betraying the working classes by voluntarily adjusting yourself to bad conditions, instead of fighting for better ones.'

'I think that would be silly,' said Ilonna, her face dimpling into mischief. 'I think my attitude is most sensible, because my family would be able to put up a really good fight for better conditions if they had meantime the best possible food on which to fight, and the warmest clothes to fight in. And I should see that they had. To be adaptable is not necessarily to be complacent. Perhaps I shall have to adapt myself much more radically, if Lubov does lose his job.'

Emmy looked up sharply over her cup, from Ilonna's face to Lubov's. 'Is there any suggestion that you may be going to lose your job? You didn't tell me.'

'I haven't had time to tell you anything yet, have I? And, in any case, this is no more than one of those possibilities that's always with us. I've become a little tedious,' he said, with an unabashed smile, 'in my interventions for unpopular causes. I'm not the only one, but perhaps I've been the biggest nuisance. And certainly I've had longer rope than most. Mother's just arguing by the law of averages that I can't go on much longer without coming to the end of it. There's nothing actually threatened so far. But we like to be ready. Surprise,' he said, his smile deepening, 'can be so embarrassing.'

'If he loses his job,' said Ilonna placidly, 'I shall have to take some part-time work myself, perhaps in one of the shops. I could easily handle the flat and the cooking in half the day, with a little planning. And I should be quite good at serving people. Most of them are very nice, if you are nice to them. I believe I should rather enjoy it.'

It would have been easy to believe, had this been anyone else speaking, that she was whistling to keep up her courage; but Ilonna's blue eyes were already brightly speculative upon a future in which enlarged human contacts, novel experiences, unexpected interests awaited her. That the contacts might be difficult and the experiences often disappointing did not discourage her. Besides a practical mind, which could always take pleasure in surmounting circumstances, she had the endless blessing of human curiosity. All the same, for all her warmth their world had grown colder, and for all her capacious spirit the boundaries of their freedom had drawn more closely in upon them. Even Wanda did not deny it, though Wanda would hold it to be a form of justice; and if others hitherto landless had established rights on that marginal land, who was to say that Wanda's contention was unjustified? But somewhere along the quiet streets, solitary and silent, reeling aimlessly through his self-created darkness, the drunken man, soiled, unshaven, in working clothes, wandered from pavement to pavement of the unmistakable territory of despair, still dispossessed of all other lands. It was too complex, too full of irreconcilable extremes, to be comprehensible; her head ached with the effort to see it whole, but it was like trying to create a single harmony out of the multitudinous grandeur and goodness and stupidity and baseness of an individual human life, something only God was qualified to do.

'You find,' said Matyas, watching her troubled face with sympathy, 'that things are more changed than you expected?'

'More changed, and changed in so many conflicting directions. It makes no sense,' she said, her voice sharp with protest.

'What have you seen today? What have you made of what you've seen? Tell us! We're talking far too much, and you far too little.'

She looked down into her linked hands, and the procession of events began to re-shape itself there before her eyes, suspicions, misgivings, reassurances, triumphs jostling one another with malicious inconsequence. She began to recount everything that had happened since her arrival, the constraint and insecurity of the drive from the airport, the rapid thawing of Slava's official ice, the revelation of the theatre, the taxi-driver who had discussed Dostoevsky, the waiter who had begged her for a letter some day from England, as for a glimpse of the Grail, the people who had watched her passage along the street with cold, suspicious eyes, the shock of the drunken men, the joy and beauty and hopefulness of the children, the exuberant confidence of the adolescents, nothing consistent, nothing final.

'This morning we were at the new Gothic Gallery. Do you know it? Then you know how fine it is, how imaginative, what a work of art in itself. I think it's as perfect as Wanda's group, in its different way, and as single-hearted. You know what I mean by that—it isn't fine with an eye on propaganda, or national prestige, or any of the impure ends; it's fine because those who created it were devoted to the idea of perfection, and knew no other way to proceed. The director showed us round. He's one of the new young men, there's no mistaking that. A child of that age, in charge of such a place, would be unthinkable with us, and would have been with you, I think, three years ago.' At the very thought of him her face was brightened by a dazzled, amused and delighted smile. 'You should make that pilgrimage with him! You should hear him talk about Gothic art!'

'I have heard him,' said Lubov, laughing in reflection of her pleasure. 'He lights up like a pharos, and the statues come to life and follow him.'

'Like children after the Pied Piper! It's hardly an exaggeration, because he brings everything to life, a whole society comes out of the walls before your eyes. If ever I saw an absolutely happy and fruitful and productive man, he is one. I had the same sense of radiant artistic release that Wanda and her friends gave me last night. And there are more of these marvels, one can feel them in the air. If this is not a major virtue in a society, I don't know what is. And yet the old woman begged from me in the street,' she said, her face paling at the recollection. 'It was terrible, because I didn't even realise what she wanted, it was so nearly an impossibility. In some countries one expects it, but not here. And then, she came up so furtively, and slipped her hand in front of me with so much fear of being seen, that I really didn't understand, and all I felt was embarrassment. I thought she might be a little senile, but I know now that she wasn't. And she didn't say anything, and when I spoke to her I suppose I was too open, for she shuffled away very quickly, and it was too late then for me to do anything.'

'But really there's no need whatever for

anyone to beg,' said Wanda with a frown of anxiety, and a mild tone which belonged to her new happiness. 'She may have been a little simple.'

'I can't believe that would make her beg, because it's something I've never seen here in all the time I've been coming to you. It could not be a habit lingering after its cause is gone, and why should she develop it now without cause? All I know is that I saw it, and it was something I've never seen before in this country. And three times today I've seen what also I never saw here before—drunken men alone, unsociable, turning away from people, not towards them. If I've seen the extreme of happiness—and I think I have—I've seen its opposite, too.'

There was a brief silence, broken by Lubov's sigh. She looked up into his eyes, which were fixed in meditative tenderness upon her face. The pupils had widened and darkened to draw her in to the middle of his being, where his perceptions and hers moved with the same intensity, and spoke with the same voice.

'There was this. And there was the fact that everywhere people are reticent, unless they can voice what is easily recognised as the approved view. This is true now in some degree, I know, anywhere in the world, because nowhere in the world, as far as I can see, is nonconformity safe any longer. But the reserve is more marked here than in England. And there was, there is, the strangeness that surrounds me, myself. It seems there are no more foreigners, at least none from the West, except those who are clearly labelled, and come as guests of the government and representatives of something more than merely themselves. I don't mean that no one else is actually allowed in, but something much more baffling, that no one else *comes*. Probably it could happen; but because it no longer does, ever, I am as astonishing and as suspect in these streets, alone, as though I were a Martian. If people see me in a Ministry car, with Slava, then I am natural and ordinary. But when I walk over Captain Evian's bridge and up this hill, alone, people whisper and nudge one another, and wonder how I come to be here, and what I am doing without an escort. If I have any direct contact with them, they are kind, and pleased, and curious, but the universal thing is that first astonishment. It would be impossible now for me to go anywhere without being conspicuous. Wouldn't it?'

Matyas said gravely: 'Yes, Emmy, it would.'

'So now, Lubov, I realise what a heroic thing you did in coming to the airport to meet me, under official eyes. And I'm no longer sure that my association with you all, however resolutely honest, can do you no harm.'

She had said it, and at once the weight that had lain upon her heart all day was lightened, and the balancing burden of loss foreshadowed sank sickeningly in the scale. It should have surprised her, but for some reason it did not, to look round at all their attentive, affectionate faces, and to see every one smiling, almost laughing, so merrily, so unaffectedly, so gently that all the expectation of loss ebbed from her mind like vapour drawn upward and dispersed into the attraction of the sun.

'Isn't it true,' she persisted, 'that my merely coming here could make trouble for you all?'

It seemed to her that they took counsel with one another, silently and confidently, without removing their shining eyes from her face. Nor had they ever seemed to her to have drawn so closely and formidably together in pursuing their independent ways, nor shown so marked a family resemblance in their diversity.

'Yes,' admitted Lubov very gently, 'it's true. It isn't a probability, but it could happen. Just as it might in London, if some Russian who had come over to sing at the Festival Hall began to turn up nightly on your doorstep. It isn't much good denying it anywhere, is it? Or discussing the difference of degree, or the relative efficiency of our security officers and MI5. But we are not going to change our natures because of a stupidity like that, and neither must you.' The others did not move nor speak, but their smiling eyes acquiesced, and when he leaned forward in his chair and took Emmy's hands firmly in his, and held them tightly, it was as though the Ivanescu family, a

356

resolute entity, had asserted its inalienable rights in her. 'Emmy, you must never make plans to protect us by going away and not coming near us again. We shall never allow it. That mutilation would be more than safety is worth.'

'We already know,' she said carefully, 'that it's much too easy now, anywhere, for people to suffer because they insist on knowing foreigners too well. Some have even died of it.'

'People die every day,' said Lubov, smiling, 'of crossing the street. I'm strongly in favour of staying alive as long as possible, but it would be silly to pay too much for extensions that in any case can't go on for ever. We take all reasonable precautions, and live our lives as much as possible in the open; and then we stop worrying.'

They gazed at her serenely still, with that affectionate gaiety, endlessly borrowed from one another and endlessly repaid. The voice belonged to all of them, and uttered their considered opinions with inspired simplicity.

'We are not going to be deformed by circumstances,' said Lubov, 'and we are not going to delude ourselves that we can save each other by forsaking each other. It would be better to die.'

* * *

The second time she came to the flat on the

Lucerna, she had the whole evening on her hands. She had divided her morning between the postponed press conference and a museum of native music, and spent the afternoon rehearsing at the Musicians' Club with an accompanist who, after all her promptings, was not Helena; but the evening she had kept untouched, an island of promise in her mind.

At half-past five she boarded the tram that crossed the Sentinel's Bridge and climbed laboriously to the plateau above the Lucerna. When she descended at the street island and walked along the pavement to the house, the evening was golden with a chill but radiant sunlight, and the south wind was bringing the scent of fruit-blossom in drowning waves from orchard-hills on the other side of the city, two miles away. The river had drawn to itself, and gathered tenderly about its nine bridges and manifold islands and embankments its special spring visitants, the black-headed gulls. From the North Sea, from the Baltic, the restless flocks flooded in to the heart of the land of Europe to mate and build and breed. In the south the vast, shadowy, limpid, shining fish-ponds, reed-rimmed, sky-shadowed and silvery between their silver-green meadows, would be shrill and vehement with birds, their crying the most disturbing music on earth, their demoniac flight the most possessed of all dances. Between her eyes and the towers of the Citadel their wings like stars blinked back the sunlight, making the air tremulous with sparks of exultation.

She walked up the stairs this time, because she had had no leisure yet to assemble her impressions of the day, and she would certainly be expected to give a coherent account of them. What, for instance, was to be said about that press conference, marked by as much ignorance and prejudice as the one Pryor had arranged for her in England, but conducted on the whole with better manners and more goodwill? She had found herself resisting partisan comment here as there, and equally here pressure had caused her to fly to the defence of the traduced country. Yes, England's health service did indeed embrace wives and families; yes, old people were entitled without exception to a pension at a certain age, even if it wasn't in fact by any means an adequate amount; yes, the British working man still had a standard of living which was the envy of many of his neighbours, even if it had begun to be threatened by rising prices and enterprises altogether too private.

Everywhere arises the endless question of what is truth, and how is it to be kept immaculate? If I had been facing reporters in an uncritically Anglophil country, she thought, wryly smiling, I should have found myself saying everything the other way round. 'Yes, there *is* an old age pension, but it isn't nearly high enough, and if our living standards

359

are relatively high, they're now in real danger of a decline.' And it would still have been truth.

Matyas let her into the flat, and hung up her coat in the hall wardrobe. When they came into the living-room Lubov was just bringing in the tureen of soup, and Wanda was setting the last chair in its place. The whole family was home early in her honour, the table had fresh flowers, and Ilonna had obviously spent the entire afternoon over the kitchen stove, performing prodigies with flour and chocolate and vanilla sugar before she began work on the pork and cabbage, and the glistening salads. From this long labour she emerged looking as if she had been all day in the fresh air, her checks flushed with triumph, a bright green ribbon in her hair.

'There, who says our timing is not good? Emmy, I felt that you were coming up the stairs when I turned out the gas under the soup. It is quite perfect now, so come quickly, everyone sit down. Lubov, bring some rye bread, Emmy likes it. There! Good appetite!'

They had hardly drawn up their chairs when the door-bell rang. No one exclaimed or started, and yet the effect was, in its way, extraordinary. Frozen into a momentary stillness, they exchanged alert and thoughtful glances across the table, and the calm but perceptible tension, like a contracting cord, seemed to draw them still closer together. Fear was not an impossibility, but it was a factor with which they were learning to deal even

360

before it manifested itself. The last knock at the door, supposing that Western belief to have any foundation, would produce exactly this pause of reassessment and thought, before someone rose to open the door. And it would be done as quietly and briskly as Ilonna did it now.

They waited, listening to her light trotting steps in the hall and the click of the latch as she threw open the door; and then she gave a shriek of 'Milo!' and gasped and laughed as she was swept inward over the threshold, and they were all on their feet and pouring out into the hall after her. Miloslav's forage cap, flung at random over his shoulder, nestled in the ferny green of one of Ilonna's pot plants. His brief-case, dropped casually upon the floor, tripped Wanda as she rushed out of the living-room. Bare-headed, he was whirling his mother round in his arms, and the flying glimpses they had of his face as he circled were all a glitter of blue eyes and an incandescent grin. When he set Ilonna gently on her feet again, Wanda was waiting to engulf him. They passed him from hand to hand, questioning eagerly.

'How did you manage it? I thought you were supposed to be on a course?'

'You said it was hopeless. We'd given up expecting you. How did you get leave?'

'You should be so glad to see me,' he complained indignantly, 'that you wouldn't ask any questions about how. Emmy, darling

Emmy!' He flung his arms round her, and kissed her vehemently, rocking her delightedly against a chest which seemed to her to have widened out of knowledge in the eighteen months of her absence. 'Emmy, this is so good! I thought I was not going to see you, it was terrible, I was afraid I would have to wait another year. But we had great luck—I'll tell you everything presently. Tell me quickly, how are you? What is happening with you? And how long are you going to stay?'

'I should ask you that. How is it that you are here at all? I was warned that you couldn't possibly get here for six weeks, because of this course. I wasn't resigned to it,' she said, laughing at his mischievous face, 'but I was trying to get used to the idea. And suddenly you spring up on the doorstep. About twice as much of you,' she added admiringly, 'as there used to be! The army certainly hasn't done you any harm.'

Miloslav made himself as tall and large as he could for her benefit. He had put on an inch or more in height, and a considerable amount of muscle, and his face was tanned almost to the golden brown of high summer, probably from his winter manoeuvres recently completed. They had been in the mountains, she guessed, and out on skis a fair part of the day, and there must have been plenty of sunshine; that side of the life would certainly be no hardship to him. His fair hair was cropped unbecomingly short,

362

and the khaki tunic had not the fastidious fit of his civilian jackets. She wondered, looking at him appraisingly, if he would ever be able to wear those pre-service clothes again.

'You really have grown! But considerably, Milo! You look wonderfully fit.'

'Oh yes, I am fine. We were very lucky, because the winter camp was put off for a month, and so we got better weather, and even the best snow. We have been out of doors for over two months, we should look well. Only I am always hungry,' he confided, 'after so much fresh air. I am *very* hungry now.'

'Oh, the soup will be cold!' Ilonna, having retrieved his cap from its green nest and put it tidily away in the wardrobe, had time to remember the interrupted supper. 'Come and sit down, child, and eat, there is enough even for you. Wait only two minutes, I shall make the soup a little hotter.' She picked up his brief-case, too, from the couch where Wanda had dropped it, and took it away into the kitchen with her. Whatever else he needed to take back with him, when the time came, he would be sure to want a liberal supply of cakes and biscuits from her day's baking; so the most important packing was always done in the kitchen.

Miloslav made for the table with joyful eyes, and laid his own extra place, clattering happily about among the plates and glasses of Ilonna's cupboard.

'Oh, I see you have a stripe!' Emmy touched the white bar on his shoulder, and he slanted down at it a fleeting grin, and the expression came into his eyes, half-awe and half-devilment, which had always foreshadowed scandalous confidences.

'Oh yes—you know, it is funny about that. I got it in the early days, first of all our group, before I had time to show my true colours, and now several of the others have passed me long ago, and I am still like this, the next-to-lowest thing there is. I have done everything to lose it,' he said cheerfully, 'but it is still there.'

He sat down with zest to the soup Ilonna set before him. Across the table Emmy studied with a serious eye the young, lively face, and could find no double meanings in it. His disdain of promotion was the natural aversion of the positive mind for a negative profession, a profession by its very nature sterile and unproductive. When the Miloslavs of the world are driven to fighting, they fight simply and solely in order to restore a state of things in which they can as soon as possible cease to fight and get back to more useful occupations; for which very reason they do it infinitely more effectively than the professionals, who after all have accepted it as a sensible way of spending their lives, and have therefore no real quarrel with it. His army service was to Miloslav precisely what it was to most of the hapless eighteen-year-olds in Britain, two years of boredom and distaste through which he must pass before he could take up his real life and devote himself to his real interests. In the meantime, such relatively sensible labour and exercise as it involved would be more than welcome to him, and he would perform it with all his might. But to ask him to acquiesce in the hierarchy by competing for promotion was altogether too much.

'Well,' said Matyas, helping him to more soup, 'what did happen to this course of yours? If everything had gone according to plan you wouldn't be here. Didn't they select you, after all?'

'Oh yes, I have been there one whole day, but then there was a little trouble, and I was thrown out of the group. The lecturer,' he explained, not without a certain pleased astonishment, 'refused to have me in his class.'

His blue glance embraced them all serenely; he expected curiosity, but no censure, at least until they had made further enquiry. Wanda certainly frowned, but as much with anxiety for him as disapproval of his procedure.

'What had you done to him?' asked Matyas dryly. 'Did you drive him to it on purpose to get out of the course?'

'No, truly! But it would have been an idea,' admitted Miloslav. 'If I had thought of it I might have tried it, only then very likely it would not have been a success. No, this was quite unforeseen. I only contradicted him. He asked for comments after his lectures, but he did not like it at all when I disagreed with him. But I did, so how could I say anything else when he asked?'

'How, indeed?' agreed Lubov, raising resigned eyebrows. He rose and collected the soup-plates, smiling a little, though reluctantly; Miloslav was not bidding for anyone's admiration, but it was a family habit to suppress open approval of his eccentricities, as families often take care to do in the case of their intelligent and precocious youngest members. 'How is it you aren't in the cells?'

'Oh, be reasonable! I hadn't done anything except demonstrate my unsuitability for selection; they just threw me back to the depot and my old job. All armies are stupid,' said Miloslav simply, 'but ours is not as stupid as all that.'

'And they gave you leave, I suppose,' said Matyas, 'as a reward for getting thrown out?'

Miloslav bestowed upon the loaded plate his mother had just set before him a sedate but satisfied smile. 'I haven't got leave, I just slipped away for this one night. I must go back tomorrow. But even for one night it was worth it.'

He looked up with quick concern at the sharp sound of Emmy's knife and fork clashing upon her plate. She was gazing at him in consternation, which he hastened to allay. 'It's all right, really! You don't know the situation

366

with us. There are three of us who work together in one office, and at week-ends we are slack, so very often we arrange it between us that one of us can go home, while the other two cover for him. We take it in turns. I know it is not the week-end now, but they had another boy in my place, you see, because they expected me to be away until the course ended, so he will stay over until tomorrow, and they have the full complement.'

'But supposing you were picked up on the railway without a leave pass? After being slung out of a special course?'

'Ah, you don't understand armies! They don't know or care at the depot what happened on the course. Everything works in small, separate compartments. If I were picked up here in town, and they found I had gone absent without leave from the depot, well, that would be my crime, and nothing else. And besides,' he said cheerfully, 'I have got a leave pass. It's a perfectly good leave pass, I made it out myself.'

He smiled, suddenly the sweetest and most affectionate of all his many smiles, because her grey eyes had remained anxious for him in spite of this outrageous statement. 'No, really, Emmy, you must not worry about me at all. Everything will be all right. We have done this so many times, we know how it should be done. And you did not think, did you, that I would let you come and go away again, and make no effort to see you?'

'I didn't think you would find any opportunity,' she said, unwillingly returning his smile.

'Neither did I. You see, I told you we had great luck!'

His dual vision was, it seemed, as clear as ever, and the colours in his pictures of army life would never be falsified. He might heighten the high lights a little in order to be more entertaining, but that was the only violence he would do to the truth. And it appeared that Wanda, made free of the enlarged countryside of fulfilment, no longer even wished to circumscribe the perversities of others. She listened to Miloslav's tallest tales of his army medical, of his unit's ludicrous exploits in camp, of the follies of non-commissioned officers and the crazy logic of administration, with only a sceptical and untroubled smile, and, catching Emmy's thoughtful eye, said placidly:

'You would think him quite irreconcilable, wouldn't you? And yet don't you think he looks in very good condition?'

'He bears up well,' agreed Emmy gravely.

'Is it any use doing anything else?' Miloslav attacked one of his mother's most elaborate cakes, glazed with preserved fruit and festooned with cream. 'I don't like armies— who could, when there are so many sensible things waiting to be done, and no opportunity to get to them?—but in a way it's fun. The boys in our group are good company, and if you don't take anything *too* seriously it's a bearable sort of life.' He shrugged off the unwelcome interlude with a decisive gesture of his head and shoulders, and looked alertly at Emmy. 'We talked enough about me, you see I am fine. Tell me about Yuri! How is it with him?'

It seemed strange that she should not have foreseen this, yet it fell upon her with the suddenness of lightning, and something of the blinding shock. How was it possible that Yuri Dushek could have passed so quickly and so completely out of her mind? He had gone from the moment that she caught her first glimpse of the city itself, turning and turning slowly about the pivot of the airfield. Never once had his name or his face re-entered her mind, filled to overflowing with the delights of reaching home again. Yet there was no more inevitable question for Miloslav to produce, and she should have been prepared for it. Something of the urgency the subject might once have had was certainly eased, for she had written repeatedly that he was in London, that he was well, that he had a good job. Miloslav's soft-voiced 'How is it with him?' approached the matter on a deeper plane than this, and she found she did not know how to satisfy him. To the others she might, some day when he was not there, tell everything of that disastrous story except the extent of her own giving; but Miloslav had devoted some years of his young life to loving Yuri, and had staked more on him than even his family knew, and the whole truth about Yuri was something he must never be told.

'He's still working with his shipping firm,' she said, 'and doing very well, I'm told. He's made a lot of friends, quite apart from the people I know, through his work, and through a club he's joined. And he has a little flat of his own now, in Kensington.'

Sitting still there over the coffee-cups, under the full blue barrage of Miloslav's regard, was a position too vulnerable for her liking. She rose, and began to clear the table, carrying away the piles of plates into the kitchen, and replying to his continuing questions as she went back and forth. Wanda jumped up and tried to deprive her of the task, but in a moment she saw that her intervention was untimely. She sat down again, and was silent. How silent Wanda could be now, and how content!

'Does he like being in London? I thought he might have written,' said Miloslav mildly.

'He likes it very much. He did think of writing,' she said deprecatingly, 'but I was uneasy about bringing letters through the Customs. He sent his love.' Was that altogether a lie? Surely, surely he must have done that, daily, since he last walked out of this house and over the frontier.

Miloslav nodded understanding. 'Yes, of

course it's better not even to seem to be taking advantage of a visa, you were quite right. I'm awfully glad he's fallen on his feet there—I expect you saw to that. You'll give him my regards—and from all of us, for that matter—when you get back, won't you?'

'Yes, of course!' She could promise that, but she felt impelled to make it clear even to Miloslav that Yuri's path was likely to diverge pretty widely from hers in the future. 'I don't suppose I shall be seeing quite so much of him from now on. He has his own circle of friends, you see, by this time. And we don't always see eye to eye in England, any more than we did here.'

Miloslav laughed. 'I didn't always see eye to eye with him myself, for that matter, but I'm glad he's where he wanted to be, and very glad he's doing so well. Did he see you off at the airport when you left?'

He had risen, and was collecting coffee-cups so that he could follow her into the kitchen. Wanda, smiling resignedly at his eagerness, folded and put away the embroidered cloth. Ilonna, tired but satisfied after the success of her cooking, stretched out round white arms, smooth as milk, across the table.

'Emmy, leave them, my dear, the washing-up is not for you! We will have a little rest, and then I'll do them.'

'No, this is my job. It's the only one you let me do, I'm not giving it up. No, Milo, Yuri was

371

working when I left. When you've been only a few months in an office, you don't ask for a half-day holiday just to see somebody off on a fortnight's trip. But he sent a letter to the air terminal for me.'

She was bending over the sink, whisking soap powder into the hot water, and her face was sheltered from his too intelligent eyes, but the calm she felt at the memory of that arrogant gesture now was such that she did not think she had anything to fear even from Miloslav's percipience.

'I bet he'll meet you when you go back.' Miloslav was in the open doorway of the kitchen, swinging his weight lightly from one wrist upon the pivot of the latch, and resting his blue eyes upon her with a contented half-smile.

It was at that moment that the door-bell rang for the second time.

* * *

The alert silence fell like frost, sharp and cold, while all their intent eyes, accomplished in silent communion, took counsel together. Then Miloslav, reacting with candour, lunged out of his doorway, snatched up Emmy's handbag from her chair and his own khaki wool gloves from the couch, and retreated with soundless violence into the kitchen, closing the door quietly after him. By the time he turned to face Emmy's startled stare he was grinning, his eyes wide and bright in half-amusement, half-alarm. His brief-case was already here in the kitchen, his cap in the hall wardrobe, thanks to Ilonna's orderly mind. His army greatcoat was hanging in the passage outside the other door of the kitchen, but it was not in full view from the front door of the flat.

He made a quick motion of his fingers to his lips, and switched off the light. After an instant of apparent darkness the April twilight shone hyacinth-blue outside the window, glittering below with the lights of the city. Miloslav stepped across the room as softly as a cat, and laid his cheek against Emmy's, and his arm about her shoulders.

'If it *is* them, let's hope they'll both go into the room—there are always two.' His lips tickled her ear, because he was shaking with giggles, and could hardly whisper for the convulsions within. 'Then I'll slip out by the other door. If I have to run for it, kiss Mummy for me and tell her I'll write. And not to worry!'

Emmy slapped his quivering cheek lightly with a wet hand, and quaked with the infection of his excited laughter. 'Hush, idiot! Listen!'

In the shadowy dimness of the room they stood linked together, straining their ears after every sound from beyond the closed door. Someone had gone out into the hall and opened the door; Matyas, she thought, for the murmur of voices, indistinguishable at this distance, was all on one baritone level, unmistakably masculine. At first she could not be sure if there was one strange voice, or two. Miloslav had decided there were two, and his guess at the identity of their owners was half confirmed already; she could feel him tensed and still against her side, ready for evasive action at any moment, ready, too, to pay up if evasion proved impossible. It was not entirely serious, even now, but a kind of game of forfeits, in which he not only knew and respected the rules, but trusted his opponents to do the same. But he had stopped laughing, the better to listen. It would be bad play to take fright and slip out of the house before he was sure of the need.

He drew himself out of her arm, releasing her from his own embrace with a last reassuring pressure and a smile she saw gleam even in the dark, and stepped softly to the door, inclining his ear attentively against the panels. They were all coming into the living-room now, Matyas in the lead, someone lighter and younger walking briskly after him. Yes there were two of them, the rhythm of their steps crossed, producing a queer staccato, just before they stepped into the pile of the carpet.

Matyas said: 'Here is my son.'

Not Miloslav! Lubov! The boy stiffened in abrupt astonishment against the door, and turned upon her in consternation the large, light shining of his eyes.

A man's voice, low-pitched and equable, enquired:

'Dr Lubov Ivanescu?'

Lubov said: 'That is my name.'

'Dr Ivanescu, my colleague here and I are police officers. There is a matter we should like to discuss with you.'

'Certainly!' Lubov sounded polite but mystified. 'You want to speak to me alone?'

'No, no, there's no need for that, unless you prefer it. If you have no objection to your family being present, I'm sure we can have none. They may even be able to help us.'

Lubov said: 'Please sit down, gentlemen!' There were the grave deliberate sounds of chairs being moved, the slight hollow clash of the wooden cigarette-box being placed open upon the table, an ash-tray, heavy and of glass, laid beside it.

Miloslav stood pressed against the door, looking at Emmy. About the dilated blue eyes, wide and wild, all the lines of the young face had drawn into sharp relief, until it was the severe and responsible mask of a much older man that confronted her. At every sound from the outer room their fixed eyes compared, assessed, interpreted. She had never seen Miloslav look like that over his own crises.

'Dr Ivanescu, two days ago a certain packet was intercepted in the post, and opened. It was very natural that it should be. It was posted abroad, but the form of address was as we write it here—you'll agree a rather noticeable combination—and the packet, while it appeared to be nothing but a letter or letters, was of a bulk to call attention to itself rather readily. It was thought advisable to open it for examination, quite rightly—and very fortunately.'

There was a silence, prolonged beyond comfort. The two in the kitchen waited. Lubov waited, and when the waiting grew irksome prompted with politely controlled impatience: 'Well?'

'It was addressed to you, Dr Ivanescu.'

'To me?' Some echo of Miloslav's wide-eyed amusement had slipped into that exclamation. But louder than Lubov's voice, in Emmy's ears, was the stillness and silence of the others.

'To you.' A chair creaked, as though someone had leaned forward. Straining after every whisper of sound, they believed they heard something more, a tiny rustle of paper. 'This is the packet.' The voice this time was older, dryer, but no less level and detached. 'Examine it! Do you know this handwriting?'

Emmy knew it unseen, upon the instant, as though the police officer's hand had held it up in front of her eyes. She drew a deep, careful, soundless breath of disbelief, for surely no one could be such a fool as to send matter like that through the post. No, no one could possibly take such a risk out of recklessness. Something more was needed than folly, an unbelievable

376

malice of hate and despair. She laid her hand gently and urgently upon Miloslav's arm, and tried to persuade him away from the door, so that he should not hear; but he did not yield to the touch, but held his place, rigid with held breath and flaring eyes, his lips already parted with some apprehension of what was to come. And if he did not hear it now, he could not avoid hearing it before he escaped from this room.

Lubov said: 'Yes, I know it. But it doesn't make sense.'

Wanda, who must have been staring at the envelope with him, said blankly: 'Of course, we all know it. It's Yuri Dushek's writing!'

Miloslav drew breath very softly, taking an age to fill his lungs, and laboured at it as though he could not get enough air. He did not move. Whatever happened, he could not move; there was not enough movement in the living-room to cover any sound he might make here, and whatever Lubov's situation now, a young brother absent from his unit illegally could not improve it.

'Yes—the hand of Yuri Dushek. You remember the circumstances in which this young man left the country? You knew him well?'

'You have received letters from him before?' the older man supplemented gently. 'It's clear that you know his handwriting.'

'We've seldom had letters from him, never

except when he was on holiday, or something like that. There was normally no need for letters,' explained Lubov simply. 'He was always within reach. Yes, until he left the country we knew him quite well, he was often in and out of the house. As for his handwriting, at one time he was attending one of my classes, he did a lot of written work for me.'

'Were you expecting to continue hearing from him?'

'No.'

'We've had no communication with him since he left,' said Matyas.

'As far as you know. But I am asking Dr Ivanescu.'

'*I* have had no communication with him since he left,' said Lubov, 'and I was certainly not expecting any now.'

'However, you don't deny it is addressed to you?'

'Oh, it's certainly addressed to me. And in Yuri's hand; no doubt about it.'

Miloslav moved nothing but his eyes, searching Emmy's face helplessly through the obscuring shadows. Why? Why should Yuri do a thing like that? If you were uneasy about bringing letters through the Customs, and he agreed you were right about it—that's what you said, isn't it?—then for God's sake why should he take this far worse risk of sending them through the post? Why? Didn't he *know*—? She saw the more terrible thought come darkly into his mind: yes, he knew, yes, he foresaw all the possibilities. And now he had arrived at the point of understanding almost everything, by touch, by the silent communication of her hand, and his memories of Yuri's single-hearted frenzy. Shrewder than Lubov, he was already far ahead of the question or the answer, further ahead than Lubov would ever be until she led him by the hand.

'Dr Ivanescu, you won't deny, I think, that you gave a great deal of energy to defending Dushek after he was dismissed from the university. You fought hard to get him reinstated, and, failing that, to see that a good position was found for him.'

'I've done all that in several cases where I thought students were being harshly treated. I never thought that Yuri deserved to be dismissed from his class. I thought the university was injuring itself as well as him. But I didn't and don't think he was justified in leaving the country.'

'After a display of sympathy such as he had had from you, however, he might very well have thought that you would extend your help to—other activities?'

The deliberation of this man's speech made him easy for her to follow. With the other she had occasional difficulty; none the less she recognised without hesitation the quotation into which his probing voice now launched.

379

The portentous phrases of Yuri's treasonable letter, the same one which she had read aloud to its author in London, had a childish sound now in this sceptical mouth. Probably he was right to feel that these were the pretentious follies of an unimportant enemy, probably, too, it was helpful that he should interpret them so. Her more serious distaste for the hints about armed groups and assassination had been, no doubt, the fruit of inexperience.

'You recognise the tone? It's a passage from one of these letters.'

'I recognise it as something that's happening,' agreed Lubov with faint disgust, 'but I shouldn't have recognised it as Yuri's composition. It seems he's developed considerably since he left us. What do you mean by "one of these letters"? Are there several there?'

'There are eight. All of them very much like that. They are addressed to various people, apparently in various parts of the country. All the names are first names or abbreviations for them. It seems the recipient was expected to know where to distribute all these without any further clues.'

'In short,' said Lubov, 'he must be an initiate.'

'It is implied.'

'What are the names? May I hear them?'

His voice showed the first sign of strain, and Emmy, who alone knew why, alone felt rather than heard the slight tension of fear and pain. But in the list of names which the older man's voice recited evenly, Miloslav did not appear. And now perhaps Lubov understood as perfectly as Miloslav himself; for Yuri's one protective gesture made doubly clear his responsibility for all he had done. Miloslav pressed his burning forehead gently against the cold panel of the door, and closed his eyes, which were dazed with staring.

'I couldn't identify any of them by those names.'

The police officer said dryly: 'I should hardly expect you to be able to.'

'No, I realise that was a silly thing to say. Is there a covering letter for me, too?'

'There is a visiting card, engraved with Yuri Dushek's name, and written on the back of it the lines: "Lubov, Be so kind, and deliver these to their owners. We ask nothing more active of you, but this is urgent, and there is no one on whom I can rely but you. Yuri."'

In the middle of destruction Yuri must still word everything so that his own innocence might remain at least a possibility. Not a direct assertion that Lubov had promised help and sympathy, only these cautious, ambiguous appeals, leaving the issue of pre-arrangement open. For Lubov the same damnation, for Yuri the benefit of the doubt. It might, after all, have been just a desperate foolishness. He believed the letters were vital, he took an unforgivable but honest risk on getting them through, and trusted to luck that Lubov, once they were in his hands, would feel impelled to deliver them. Only Lubov had just said that he would not know where to lay his finger on any one of Yuri's familiars by those names, and Lubov, though he might lie at need, would never volunteer a lie where it was unnecessary. Yuri must have known how little the names would mean to him; therefore his object could not have been the delivery of the letters.

If she could thread this maze in one instant of silence, so could Miloslav, whose implacable honesty was itself far too subtle to be taken in by subtlety. He opened his eyes, and looked at her imploringly, and there was nothing in the world she could do for him.

'There is no implication there,' Matyas said vigorously, 'that my son knew anything whatever about these letters, or had had any traffic with Yuri since he ran away. We all know that he had not exchanged a word with him. He cannot be held responsible for the activities of another person.'

'Even if we accepted that view of the case,' said the younger officer, 'he must still be held responsible for opinions which obviously encouraged one young man to think him a possible ally in treasonable activities.'

'Are we all to be judged, then, by the estimates some ill-balanced acquaintance forms of us?'

'Where evidence of character is concerned,' conceded the older man reasonably, 'we are certainly interested in the testimony of more than one person. If they had all agreed with *this* version, the tone of this interview would have been somewhat different.'

'I have no complaint,' said Lubov. 'Am I to take it that you've already seen the Dean of the Faculty and the Rector?'

'Yes. The Rector will be calling a meeting of the Council, probably tomorrow. I should be prepared to attend at any hour, if I were you.'

'And in the meantime I am to hold myself at your disposal?'

'Don't leave the city. You would not get far if you did try. And let there be someone here who can tell us where to find you at any moment.'

'Very well, I'll stay within call. I have a class in the morning, and I shall take it as usual. As far as the meeting is concerned, unless they've called me before then, my lecture-room is the first place they'll look for me.'

Were they preparing to go? No one had yet risen, there had been none of the sounds of departure, only an indefinable tremor of ending, of breaking off, passed through the air and made Emmy and Miloslav tremble in their silent darkness. Their helplessness clung about them as the sticky cobwebs of suspicion climbed clinging about Lubov, impeding all action.

383

'There's nothing more you can tell us about these? Nothing more you wish to say?'

'I can only repeat that I have had nothing whatever to do with Yuri Dushek since he left the country, and that I knew nothing about these letters, or about any intention he had of writing such letters. I can't imagine why he addressed them to me. He knows me well enough to know that I would not deliver them to the addressees, even if I knew who they were. I can't believe that he was ever under any misapprehension about that.'

'And you can't account for his sending them to you at all?'

'No, I can't.'

'He can, of course,' said Wanda's voice, suddenly sharp with anger, 'only he won't. If he can't, I can, and if he won't, I will. I knew Yuri, too, better, probably, than Lubov ever did. Look at the contents of those letters! Look at the imposing package they make! Can you really believe that he thought, when he sent them, that they'd get through the post without catching someone's eye? And is it even possible he thought they would be examined and *still* delivered? Of course he never meant them to be delivered! He meant them to be opened. He meant this to happen—exactly what has happened. It is not a conspiracy against the State, it is a conspiracy against Lubov.'

'The man who did his best to help him when he was in trouble?' asked the older man mildly.

'You should know that that's a thing many people find hard to forgive. Lubov helped him and disapproved of him—can you think of anything more galling?'

'It argues a considerable degree of hate,' he said, but it was clear that the thought was not new to him, nor altogether negligible. Wanda had detected with eagerness that note of interested speculation in his tone, and was quick to take advantage of it.

'When he left here he was still trying to keep his balance. But once a man has run away, like that, what justification has he for his behaviour except the assumption that everything he has abandoned is evil? He has to convince himself of that in order to bear his own company. Worst of all, then, to him will seem the people like Lubov, who have denied him even the satisfaction of persecution.'

'I won't pretend,' said Lubov rather sternly, but gently, too, 'to know what goes on in Yuri's mind now. It's enough for me to be accountable for my own actions.'

'And you have nothing to repent of there?' It sounded as if the older man had allowed himself at least the shadow of a smile.

'No, I have nothing to withdraw.'

'You understand, however, that it's a matter of some gravity, and we must pursue it.' They were rising from their chairs now, the interview was over, and it seemed they had no intention at this minute of taking Lubov away.

'Naturally! You could hardly treat that sort of communication lightly.'

The general stir of movement in the living-room allowed the two listeners in the kitchen to move, carefully and slowly, making as yet no sound. They found themselves cold, as though the central heating had failed. Their tensed bodies moved with difficulty and pain. Emmy touched Miloslav's arm, and felt it shrink from her fingers.

The visitors were moving towards the hall, there was the sound of the door being opened. More distantly now, but still clearly, Lubov's voice said: 'I don't ask you to believe me, but I should like to say that whatever I have done has always been done in the daylight.'

There was a moment of silence, and then the older man replied, no less gravely: 'Speaking unofficially, as a man rather than a police officer, I believe you.'

They were gone; their footsteps crossed the hall, and for a moment were heard on the stone treads of the stairs, before the turn of the flight took them out of earshot. Then the outer door of the flat closed again, and everything was silent. Emmy caught at the handle of the kitchen door, but Miloslav interposed a long arm.

'Wait! They may not really go.' He was still whispering, and still listening, and he kept his hand over the light switch for a long minute, but there was no alarm of returning footsteps,

386

no creak and clang of the lift. They were gone. Miloslav withdrew his arm, and let his hands fall. His voice, for the first time raised from an undertone, sounded hoarse and unpractised, as though he had kept a monastic silence for a long time. 'Please! In a moment I'll come. Please, Emmy, go to them!'

*   *   *

She would never forget how they looked when she emerged into the living-room. She would never forget it, because on the face of it it was so little memorable. Matyas was just crossing the room to crush out his cigarette-end in the ashtray, his brows drawn together in a fierce frown of thought, his face tired in reaction. Ilonna was sitting at the table, her teeth clenched on the knuckle of her thumb in concentration, her blue eyes vague because they were focused somewhere outside this enclosed place, going over and over the dispositions to see where she could best apply her pressure to strengthen the defences. Framed in the doorway opposite, with the telephone receiver at her ear, a high colour in her cheeks and her black eyes brilliant, Wanda was calling up her legions.

'Petr, are you going to be in all the evening? Oh, good, I'm coming round, there's something I must see you about. Yes, it's very important. Of course, darling, I'll come at once—'

Lubov had come back into the room after seeing his visitors out, and was advancing purposefully upon the kitchen when Emmy emerged. She walked into his hands, and was held breast to breast with him, while he looked from the door, which had closed again hastily behind her, to her pale face, dazzled after the twilight she had left.

'You heard all that?' he asked with urgent quietness.

'Yes, every word. I nearly came out—it might have been better if I had. I could have told them—'

'And *he*, did he hear it, too?' Lubov rode over her revelation in the same violent undertone. She should have known that his deepest consciousness of need would not be for himself.

'Every word! It was impossible not to.' She cast a glance over her shoulder, as though she feared that Miloslav might hear even these rapid whispers hardly louder than silence.

'I must go to him,' said Lubov.

'No, leave him alone for a few minutes. He knows only part of it now, and I'm the only one who can tell him everything, I'm the only one who knows.' She drew Lubov away from the door, back to the table where the others had gathered, for Miloslav must learn no more of the truth in this oblique fashion. 'Lubov, I think I should go to the police. I know an

388

English friend in the case could be just one more suspicious circumstance, but no one else can tell them how the letters originated, and why they were sent through the post like that—if I don't appear, it never can be told. Lubov, surely there's more to gain than to lose, if I came forward?'

Without hesitation and quite peremptorily, Lubov said: 'No! I don't want you in this at all, I don't want it to touch you. What could you tell them? You mean you knew about those letters?'

'They're the ones he wrote in London when he heard that I had a visa. He asked me to bring them, and I said I would. I thought he meant only personal letters to Milo, and some of the other boys. He knew my position, I didn't think he would try to take advantage of me. But when he brought them to me I saw there was something wrong—I still don't know why, it was something about his manner—and I wouldn't have anything to do with them unless I knew what was in them. He told me I could read them—I suppose he was relying on it that I wouldn't, or that I didn't know enough to make sense of them. But I did! I refused to carry them, and we had a quarrel,' she said, feeling cold at the memory, 'that won't be patched up.' But she did not say why that quarrel was so final. 'I haven't seen him since. How could I guess he'd be such a fool—?' But there she stopped, because to her, at least, and

389

probably to Lubov too, it was so plain that the epithet was inappropriate. Whatever Yuri had been, it was not a fool.

'You never told me a word of this,' said Lubov, but without reproach, rather with indignant tenderness.

'Can you believe me, I'd forgotten it! I thought it was all over and done with, and until Milo mentioned Yuri, tonight, I hadn't even thought of him once since I touched down here. Never once!' For a moment she could still feel that in some way she had failed that unhappy creature even more disastrously than he had injured her.

'You could hardly imagine that he would turn on Lubov,' cried Wanda indignantly. 'Who does such things? What kind of person wants to destroy the people who were good to him? If it had even been me he attacked, one could have understood it better.' She had come in quietly from the hall, already in her hat and coat, clutching the folds of her scarf closely to her throat in a rage of purposeful energy. 'Look, Emmy, please forgive me if I leave now, but I am going to see Petr, and we shall contact some other people, too. We have to be ready with as many influential witnesses as we can get, to say that Lubov is absolutely reliable and honest. And you'll see that we shall have no trouble in finding them. Darling, I'll come back! You'll stay the night with me, won't you? Please, I do want you so much to stay!'

'If I'm not likely to be a further danger to Lubov or to you, of course I'll stay.'

Wanda waved away all such considerations with a contemptuous hand. 'No more will happen tonight. In perhaps two hours Petr and I will come back.' She laid her hand upon Lubov's arm in going, and the quick pressure of her fingers was more eloquent than poetry. She left the room and the flat in a gust of perfume, and the air trembled after the skirts of her blue coat as the door slammed.

Ilonna said, with approval: 'Petr is going to have to be very energetic to satisfy our Wanda. Lubov, you will have an army, or he will not get his wife.'

Matyas was watching the kitchen door from beneath anxious brows. 'Milo has not shown himself. This must be a terrible shock to him. He was very fond of Yuri.'

'In a moment I'm going back to him. When he knows it all, I hope he'll feel a little better about it. But, Lubov, surely if I repeated the story of the letters to the police, it would dispose of the only real evidence against you. No one but Yuri is going to assert that you ever knew anything about the things, or were willing to receive such a commission. And I can discredit Yuri's evidence. If I'm English, and suspect, he's a renegade, and damned. Surely my word is worth more than his.'

Matyas shook his head, with a slight and rueful smile. Lubov was smiling, too; he said very simply: 'You are English, and whatever your role in a case of this kind, you could only make one more confusion with which to hang me, my dear, and make it, in any event, quite impossible for you ever to come here again. Do you think I'm going to risk that? And as for Yuri, why should I wish to complete his damnation? No, I have conducted my campaigns in daylight, and I will not bring any evidence but my own openness, and the word of those people who choose to stand by me. I have as much ground for confidence in submitting myself to my country as men who fall under suspicion in England. I don't want your word to be measured against Yuri's. I don't want to find myself reduced to throwing stones back because stones are thrown at me. I shall deny what's untrue, I shall hope to be believed. And what I can't keep without grubbing in the mud for missiles, I'll part with without any tears.'

'But if nothing worse happens,' she said urgently, 'it means your job, Lubov.'

'My job's gone, Emmy. Don't even hope to salvage that. University staff have to be like Cæsar's wife, above suspicion. Go to Milo now and help him if you can. Emmy—' He drew her back by the hand for a moment to say softly: 'There was no letter for Milo, did you notice that? Was there one when you saw them in London?'

'Yes.' She saw that he understood all the implications of that omission. The hand which had abstracted that one letter had done nothing in recklessness.

'You see he still kept one soft spot for us.'

He had not asked why he himself should be hated so much, if Miloslav was spared. He merely advanced the one compunction, the single scruple, itself worth so much less than its apparent value, since whatever blow threatened one of them threatened all. By this sole ticket Lubov would keep Yuri within reach of grace while his own future was stripped from him.

She let herself softly into the kitchen, and closed the door after her. The window was a space of stars above and lamps below, in a velvet darkness between blue and black. Miloslav was sitting at the table with his arms spread out as a cradle for his head. There was no movement, and no sound; she found him only by the faint pallor of his cropped fair hair, and the gradual shaping of comparative light which gathered in the nape of his neck. There was not much, after all, she thought, advancing gently upon the dignified isolation of his grief, that had been spared Miloslav.

When she touched him he did not start, nor reject her, but lifted from the shelter of his arms a face quite fixed and calm with desperation. She drew a chair close to his and stretched her arm over his shoulders, and he turned voluntarily, with a great sigh that came up out of his heart with infinite labour, and laid his head in her breast. She felt the cold smoothness of his forehead against her neck, and trembled to the load of every deep, heavy breath he drew heaving into his body; and after a minute he stirred and wound his arms tightly about her waist, and began to shudder uncontrollably. There was nothing more for a while. He had no tears, he did not know how to break down, and until some of the tension found another means of passing out of him he had no voice, his throat and tongue were rigid. She laid her cheek against his head, trying to encircle him everywhere with her touch. She had more to tell him than she had told Lubov, though some day Lubov would know it, too. Life had become potentially too short for the indignity of embarrassment or the luxury of reticence. All that mattered was that whatever comfort there was to be had she should give him now, while there was time.

'Listen, Milo: Wanda has gone to see Petr. They'll collect every voice they can raise for him. Milo, I know—I know it's Yuri! I know, you find it hard to believe that he could do this awful thing. But when you know everything—'

He drew a breath that was torn down into the depths of his body like a gasp of pain. 'Oh, Emmy, to think I did this! I helped him to get away!' His voice was a dry whisper against her breast. 'But, Emmy, why? Why? How could he turn against us? I don't understand!'

'You shall understand, I'll tell you

everything. You won't have to hate him, only to be sorry for him. But he's gone, Milo, he's left us.' Her 'we', like Miloslav's, had not acquired any new meanings. 'He began to change before he ever came to England. I hope he would get over it when he had a sensible job and plenty of other interests. But it was exactly as Wanda said. Maybe it isn't always so with every exile, but it was with Yuri. There was only one way he could live with himself, and that was by being absolutely sure what he had left was bad, bad in every way, bad beyond saving. We couldn't talk about these things without quarrelling. We never mentioned them, we knew we were not together. And when he knew I was coming back to you, he asked me to bring in those letters—the same letters—'

'And you refused?' he asked, more firmly this time, and turning his cheek more easily into the hollow of her shoulder. 'Because it was too dangerous?'

'Because it was too dirty,' she said, 'though I didn't tell you that until I had to. I wouldn't carry them until I knew what was in them, and when I knew, of course I refused to touch them. You heard a little, I needn't explain myself to you. And then we did quarrel, Milo, once for all. Yuri will never come near me again. Like you, I'm damned! No, my case is worse, because Yuri depended on me.'

'So he sent the letters you wouldn't bring. He

knew,' said Miloslav, shivering, 'that they'd never get through. He can't have meant that they ever should.'

'I think as letters they'd ceased to matter to him. I think what mattered was that he should win the argument. When he posted them it was the most brutal and forcible way he could find of making his point. He accused me of wanting to be just to the devil. This was his way of showing me, at close quarters, what sort of devil it was I wanted to be just to.'

Miloslav lay very still against her shoulder. She felt his close, clairvoyant stare searching her face. 'Through the person you loved most,' he said. 'Through Lubov.'

Had he always known, or had the knowledge lain just outside his consciousness, until he needed it to understand the blow which had fallen on him and his? He had seen this, without her help, as more than an intellectual vengeance. He disengaged himself gently from her arms, and sat upright, drawing down her hands into his lap; and suddenly the tears ran out of her eyes and splashed upon their clasped fingers. 'He's ill, Milo. Nothing has any right proportion for him now. I don't suppose he ever fully realised he wanted Lubov to die. And it was my fault, too—there are right and wrong ways to help people—'

Miloslav freed her hands, and carefully and delicately put his arms round her. He had never touched her with any shyness before, but now

396

even her dear familiarity seemed to have drawn about itself a veil of segregated holiness. She had had no mystery for Miloslav until Lubov loved her, and Yuri sought sanctuary in her body; now his young hands folded her with respectful ceremony, with wonder. A new and earnest priest might have handled the goddess like that. And yet his own easy affection for her found no difficulty in getting its bearings within this new relationship. Besides, her weakness had released his tensions, which he himself had not known how to dispel. She felt his slender shoulder widen as she pressed her forehead into its shelter, and his breast enlarge to make a safe place for her.

'Dear Emmy, you mustn't try to take his actions away from him. Even people who are ill and unhappy have a choice—they do not have to lay everybody else's world waste as well. But I can see,' said Miloslav, picking his way fastidiously among words that had cutting edges like knives, 'that he must have been very unhappy, if—if he knew that Lubov would always be in his light—even in England—'

'Yes,' she said, in a very low voice, 'he knew that.'

'Emmy—did he love you? Or was he only looking for a place to hide?'

'I don't know, Milo. I thought I knew. I thought it was only that he had to be right, that he couldn't take help from me unless it was offered out of love. Friendship is enough for healthy people, but when you're sick you must matter to somebody more than the world, you have to come first, you have to stand alone. I thought what he felt for me was only an illusion, and when he had a new life of his own he wouldn't need me any longer. I shall never be quite sure now,' she said wearily, 'whether I was right or wrong. It all broke up too soon. He wasn't ready to do without me—and it only needed the two syllables of Lubov's name—'

'And he knew,' said Miloslav, with wondering gentleness, 'that he'd always been without you.'

It seemed to her that events always turned back and took a different course at the mention of Lubov's name. What had happened between her and Yuri had happened here again more beneficently, for it was she who poured out, no matter how inarticulately, difficult and painful confidences, Miloslav who received them and set them in proportion. And it was he who presently said, taking courage from her tired calm: 'We must go back to the others, Emmy, they will be worried about us.'

'Yes, we must go back.' Her eyes were quite dry, there had been no more tears. 'We must see what we can do for Lubov. When you are ready, Milo.'

'Do you want to look at your make-up first?' he asked hesitantly. 'Shall I put on the light?'

'Yes, please, Milo! And what did you do with my bag?'

They had never been less afraid of lights, their mutual calm was a single and surprising achievement. The sudden brilliance caused them to blink at each other like two nocturnal birds caught and caged in sunlight. The dark and glittering world outside the window dulled into an opaque blackness. They saw the unwashed dishes still waiting, piled in the cold suds in the sink.

'Emmy, do you remember the night before he left? He was here with me. We talked about the point at which it is legitimate to remove your allegiance from your country. He was sure that we had passed it. He had to go away in order to keep his purity. But, Emmy, if the people who are too pure for us only leave us to sell out to something much more stupid and unjust than the thing they're leaving, then what escape is there ever going to be for any of us? A lot of people here are not happy about the methods of our government. But if *these* are the methods of the only opposition,' said Miloslav bitterly, with a sweep of one indignant hand banishing Yuri Dushek from the pale of his mercy, 'where *are* we to look for a new beginning?'

*   *   *

The morning came like any other morning, and the family flew apart upon its diverse business, which not even Yuri had been able to bring to a halt. Matyas, the first to leave, went off alone towards the tram-stop at a quarter to six. Wanda, who had an early practice-call at the house in Ledva, and meant besides to continue her recruiting among some of her colleagues who were old students of Lubov's, left before seven, having kissed both her brothers, and exhorted the one to telephone her if anything happened, and the other to use a little discretion in getting back into barracks, issuing these admonitions in the severely maternal tone she might have used in instructing an eight-year-old to be careful how he crossed the road on his way to school.

Lubov's lecture was at eight. At twenty-past seven he put on his hat and coat, and took the shabby brief-case he had carried since his own student days.

'Emmy, will you come up after your concert tonight, if you can?' He looked much as he always looked, perhaps a shade paler and more finely drawn than usual, but perfectly composed; even his class, unless the news broke before his lecture, would receive no indication that this was a farewell.

'You know I will! However late it is! I wish I could stay here today, and stand by for news, but it's better if I fulfil my programme.'

The first rule of the game, apart from any question of the tactical advantages of being a dutiful guest, was that life goes on, and no half-measures about it, either.

'Much better! But I shall look forward to seeing you towards midnight. If there are difficulties, telephone us.'

'I shall come,' she said.

'I should have something definite to tell you by then—good or bad.' He smiled, quite without bitterness; there was nothing whatever to be done but go forward consistently through an ordeal which, after all, was not entirely unexpected, and which had fallen at last in a form which allowed him, most gratefully, to feel at peace with his judges.

He kissed her, kissed his mother, paused for a moment to drop a hand upon Miloslav's shoulder as he sat at the breakfast-table, and give him a reassuring shake.

'Be good! If I'm still at large I'll write to you in a few days, when there's something to say. Don't worry about us, and don't get up to any rescue acts. We shall manage. You watch your own step!'

Miloslav clapped a hand over Lubov's, and pressed it fiercely for a moment. But all he said, round a mouthful of buttered roll, and with the most determined casualness, was: 'See you in jail!' At least it made Lubov laugh as he let himself out and ran down the stairs.

Emmy and Miloslav went down into the city together half an hour later, he to catch his train back to his unit, she to be ready and waiting in the foyer of the Hotel Corvin when Slava came to call for her at nine. Foreign guests were not expected to keep the early hours of the townspeople, unless beginning a journey.

They went down by the Lucerna stairways, in the radiant morning sunlight of a beautiful day. Miloslav's brief-case was filled with cakes and biscuits from his mother's cupboard, not because he could seriously feel his usual amiable greed after these trifles, or she take her normal pleasure in keeping him lavishly supplied with them, but because the traditional gesture was a part of a routine of living which nothing must be allowed to threaten. On his cropped fair hair the forage cap rode at an impudent angle, but the wide forehead beneath it was scored with anxious lines, and he walked with his eyes downcast, the full lids looking heavy and tired, as though he had slept badly. Where the stone steps were worn he gave Emmy his hand, and this little gesture had still a flourish about it; so had the smart salute he brought up from his hip when they unexpectedly encountered an officer at a turn of the path. Looking up after this performance, he caught Emmy's sympathetic eye, and gave her a quick, flashing grin.

'In town we pop very quickly into a side-street, but here one would have to climb over the wall to avoid it. But it was good, wasn't it?'

'It was most impressive!' It was strange to see at the same instant the affectionate, teasing curve of his lips and the grimace that wrinkled his nose, and the quietly frantic anxiety of his eyes, and to be satisfied of the authenticity of all these expressions of feeling. She slipped her arm through his now, before they reached the streets where such an intimacy would be inadvisable, and drew him close to her, so that they had to match their steps in order to walk in comfort. She lengthened her stride, he curbed his; to a slower and more even rhythm they continued the descent.

'Milo, whenever I suggest caution you all laugh at me, but I'm not quite convinced. You really don't mind being seen with me? Not even in the town where we're sure to meet a lot of soldiers? You aren't afraid? And don't be insulted by the word, for you know what I mean by it.'

'Oh, I would not be insulted, of course. It is very practical to be afraid sometimes, and always sensible to be discreet. I am often afraid in the way you mean—that is, I don't go looking for trouble and insisting on it. But you know, if I were to carry discretion to the point of not being seen with you, going a different way to places to meet you, filling up my life with endless shifts to keep you a secret—or anyone who mattered to me half as much as you do—then I would think that kind of life really not worth all the trouble. It's all a question of the value you put on various things,' said Miloslav sagely. 'You can pay a fair price for things, but you should respect yourself, and not pay too much. And there are things which can be regarded as part of the game, and things which cannot. You saw that when I thought two military policemen were coming to try and catch me absent without leave, I naturally was willing to hide in the kitchen and try to get out unseen. But if they came to me and said: "Is it true that you keep up a correspondence with a lady in England?" I should say: "Yes, certainly, what of it?"'

'Then I think,' said Emmy gently, 'that, in the way I was thinking of, you are never afraid. And, believe me, some people would find it very strange that you could live here now and not be.'

'Oh, there are reasons for being afraid anywhere in the world, what is the use of selecting one place? And everywhere there is the same reason for *not* being afraid. It is a modern necessity,' said Miloslav, selecting English words with an audacity he possessed only when very much in earnest, 'because it is so humiliating to be afraid that if you live like that for long you have dwindled so small you do not really care for yourself any more. We found it out, you see, when the Nazis were here. In the little way we were afraid, we went secretly, and we took precautions, and all that, but in the big way we had to find out how not to be afraid. It was necessary, how could we bear to live with ourselves if we did not manage it? And do you know, when it was urgent, like that, we found that all the ingredients for not being afraid were there in us ready to hand. I am not a bit brave, but it was made easier for me because I was too young to understand what a very peculiar and revolutionary thing we were doing in simply deciding to live without fear. I felt how it was with the others, and it became the same with me.'

'And you can still do it?'

'For anything that matters enough yes, I think so.'

She thought so, too. He had not said, but she understood it perfectly in what he had said, that it would have been monstrous to fear his own countrymen, an injury to them as well as to himself. Not that they could not inflict ruin and punishment and ignominy unjustly, like any other human group, but that in some way it would nevertheless have been unworthy on his part to submit to a relationship of fear with them. He seemed to her more clearly Lubov's brother with every minute that she passed in his company.

'If only I could stay here,' he said longingly, 'to be with my parents now, and perhaps do something to help Lubov. Emmy, it's terrible to have to go away and leave them in this trouble.'

They had reached the embankment, and walked along a pavement already thronging with people, watching the pale blue April sky reflect upon the water of the river an unaccustomed silvery brightness.

'I know, Milo, but supposing you were picked up as a deserter, or at best for being absent without leave? You could only make far worse trouble for them by staying. And what could you do, to balance that? You know Wanda and your parents will do everything to organise a defence for Lubov. And we don't know yet that they'll even make any charge. You heard that man last night say that he believed Lubov was telling the truth. So you see that they haven't made up their minds to think him guilty.'

'Oh, I know, I know! It would only be selfish to stay here, and do no good and a lot of harm. I know it's true. Only I feel so terrible, Emmy, at going away and leaving him.'

She went with him to the station, and waited with him until his train came in. Along the cool arcades of the many platforms the shadows were a soft blue, and the gay colours of summer clothes were subdued to monotones, to flower extravagantly as they stepped into the sunlight. Miloslav sat down decorously upon one of the concrete seats, and nursed his brief-case rather forlornly upon his knees, looking a little like a schoolboy going back unwillingly for the beginning of term. He had fallen silent now, it was the worst time of all. She sat beside him, and felt his heart eaten with desperate pain for Lubov. When the tall train came sliding backwards into the bay it was easier. He put his arms round her, and kissed her briskly, and

406

drew a breath of relief at being about to go, since go he must.

'If I can get a forty-eight before you leave, you know I will. Legally, this time! Emmy, take care of Mummy as much as you can. She doesn't say much, but she's so terribly fond of Lubov. If anything should happen to him—'

He shook off his shadows, hugging her impulsively. 'Emmy, you see, the trouble with not being afraid is that it only works for yourself. You can never stop being afraid for other people.'

He released her quickly and, seizing the rail of the third-class coach, swung himself up into the corridor, and, halting in the doorway, saluted her again with the most creditable grin he could manage.

'Good-bye, Emmy!'

'Good-bye, Milo, my dear!'

'Look after Lubov,' he said, leaning from the window, 'for me, too!'

Steam broke upward and gushed between her face and his, hiding the reluctant sadness and resolute gaiety of his eyes. The train slowly began to move.

*   *   *

When Lubov came out into the cloisters, the afternoon shadows of the Renaissance arches on the library side of the court were already long and angular. The Council had been debating his case for over three hours; he could hardly say he had not received a fair hearing. His throat felt dry and rigid, whether with much talking or with the longing for tears he could not tell. His body ached as though he had been beaten, he supposed because he had been tensing his nerves for so long that relaxation, when it became possible, was less relief than agony. It was all over now. They had made the only possible decision; the only thing he could not understand was why they should have taken so long about it. Perhaps he ought to be grateful for that as, in its way, a testimonial.

He blamed himself for the worst moments he had had. It had been clear from the beginning that only one course of action was open to him, and therefore he had let himself slip into the assumption that the ordeal itself partook of the same simplicity. He had thought himself prepared, merely because there was no way out of it; and instead he had found himself being hurt by every word of censure and moved by every word of faith and sympathy to an extent which had almost made it impossible, at first, for him to speak at all. No one ever went into such a tribunal less prepared. The imagination, it seems, leaves disastrous gaps unless it is very carefully schooled, and even the expected has an appalling power to startle and dismay. If he had been a little more frightened at the beginning, he might have felt the blows less.

It was over, and he had lost his chair; what

else could they have done but deprive him of it, at least until the charge against him was either dropped, or tried and dismissed? Compromised people may continue useful in all manner of ways, but they may not teach. All countries think and feel alike about that, though some are more hypersensitive to suspicion than others. In America, he supposed, he would have lost his vocation long ago, without the need of this last shadow. Even in England a hovering treason charge would certainly be enough to get him removed post-haste from the vicinity of the impressionable young. And in any country and any language it would hurt as much as this, and open through the composed and dignified defences these identical wounds.

If he could have reviled Yuri Dushek properly, with the right ferocity, they might have been satisfied, perhaps, with suspension; it was Lubov himself who had made dismissal certain. Question and answer would not stop repeating themselves in his brain; he felt his cheeks burn at every remembered inflection of the interrogating voice:

'You still are not satisfied, then, that Dushek is and potentially always was a simple traitor?'

'I am not satisfied that there is anything simple about being a traitor, nor that the whole cause of such a change of heart as he has apparently suffered is within the man himself.'

'You think, perhaps, that this body treated

409

him unjustly, and has been partially responsible for his later attitudes?'

'I think we treated him, if not unjustly, without much mercy. To that extent we have something to answer for as regards his reactions. But I don't suggest anyone can ever unload his actions, in the last resort, on to other shoulders.'

'You do, then, consider him a traitor?'

'I think he has allowed himself to drift into acts which are certainly treasonable. But I am not happy about labels. He had weaknesses which made him a relatively easy victim for world pressures, once he had taken the disastrous step of abandoning his country. But the immediate cause of his wrong decision was a decision of ours which I also feel to have been wrong.'

'You are telling us, Dr Ivanescu, that we cannot escape our share of the responsibility?'

'I am sure we cannot. Nor he his.'

That was not the way to appease anyone, in these days of the ache for certainty, for committal, for a cradle in which to be rocked, and a blanket to cover us. But he could not, when it came to the point he really could not, command his tongue to any other language. And now he was here on the doorstep, thrown out not until his case was tried in open court, but indefinitely, and probably for ever. And he had better leave this place as briskly and resolutely as he could, and let his former

410

colleagues emerge decorously and go home, without the embarrassment of encountering him like a spectre in the doorway. That was probably why they were lingering and talking so long, to give him time to get away. Better to avoid the necessity for either giving him a word in passing, which might itself be regarded as a defiant gesture, or cutting him dead, which, to do them all justice, would be painful on both sides.

He stepped out from the graceful, arched shadows into the sun and received its warmth with gratitude. The edict would not be official knowledge yet outside the Council, he could at least go over to the library and surrender his keys without causing the janitor or the library assistant embarrassment. Perhaps he could even call at the Dean's office, if no one else was there, and return the book he had borrowed nearly a month ago. In the solemnity and circumstance of the tribunal the old man had looked unbelievably frail and tired, and kept his face lowered into the shadow of an almost translucent hand. It would be reassuring to have a word with him in private, Lubov thought, before they separated for good. On the other hand, it would be the nadir of bad taste to wait here for him, and force him to walk across the cloisters with a disgraced lecturer who had just been thrown out of his Faculty.

The stones of the library wall, five hundred

years old and mellowed to Indian red, scarred with many minor wounds of time, moved him unbearably. He put out his hand as he walked beside them, and touched their sun-warmed substance, which did not reject him. The tiny plot of enclosed ground under the chestnut tree by the public footpath was covered with fresh flowers, and a little laurel wreath, tied with a red and white ribbon, hung upon the tree, above the faded photograph of student Ivan Cerny, dead on the field of honour in 1939, here on this spot. The bullet that had killed him had scarred the tree after leaving his body, and left in the sap of the wounded chestnut a few magic drops of patriot blood. Aged eighteen, and one of the first to die. Of course, today must be the anniversary. Across the court the Gothic cloisters, noble and wide, preserved their dark recesses from the sun, and thrust upward with immortal aspiration their powerful and delicate lily-vaulting beneath every arch. Now that he was leaving, or at least relinquishing his peculiar rights in all these things, he saw them with a new and jealous poignancy, as receding colours freshen, and withdrawing faces grow more beautiful.

He handed in his keys, and the question he had dreaded was not asked. Then he walked over to the Philosophical Faculty and, hiding himself with some relief in the dim corners of the Old Building, made his way to the Dean's room. In the little ante-room he could wait

412

unobtrusively until the old man came through, and at least take a kinder farewell of him than that adverse vote in session. The thin white hand had been lifted only a few inches, as though the weight of the world lay upon it, and the ravaged face had remained averted as he gave his voice that Dr Lubov Ivanescu should be dismissed from his post. Who did he think he was fooling, Lubov wondered? Certainly not the victim, who felt no resentment of the condemnation in this case because he could feel no reality in it. And certainly not the zealots, who had only to look at him to know which way his heart went while he strained his strength to elevate his hand. To be accommodating is one thing, to be convincing quite another.

He sat down in a retired corner, and waited. If the Dean brought others back with him, he would go away and refrain from troubling him. But when the old man came in at last, dragging his feet along the corridor with a suggestion of terrible weariness, he was alone. Lubov stood up and revealed himself; and for fear it should be thought that he had come to beg for sympathy, he said at once:

'I came to return your Cicero, sir. I've kept it a disgracefully long time, I'm afraid.' He had the book in his hand as proof of good faith; it was the *Letters to Atticus* in an old translation, not to be had easily even in the libraries.

The Dean, confronted thus suddenly with

413

the face whose image was already being carried within his eyes inescapably, stood for a moment silently before him, in an attitude of quiet and resigned despair. He was half a head shorter than Lubov, and fragile, his grey hair was long, and lay in soft, thin wisps upon his neck, like a baby's, because he always forgot to get it cut, or could find no time for the operation even if he remembered the necessity. But he trimmed his own beard, which was immaculately pointed, and retained a dual strand of its original black. His face, which was square and strongly shaped, seemed now to have lost some of its definition, as though a slow process of disintegration had set in. Age can have that effect, but if he was old, he was not so very old. There was, moreover, in this dissolution, a marked expression of grief which does not belong to the deterioration of age.

He looked up at Lubov from under heavy, weary eyelids veined like marble, and said with a sigh: 'Ah, it's you! Well, come in for a few minutes, now that you're here. I'm glad you didn't hurry away without seeing me.'

'You're sure I shan't be disturbing you?' The special sensibilities of the outcast, Lubov found, are very rapid in development. Everything he did or said now, in every encounter—except, of course, with his own formidable family—must be so arranged as to allow the other party to escape if he wished to do so. The initiative must always be presented to him, as unobtrusively as possible, but unmistakably. And there must be no resentment or sense of injury if he availed himself of the opportunity of detachment.

The Dean, however, went so far as to take him by the arm and urge him towards the door of the private room. 'No, no, we shall have the place to ourselves. I put off all other business for today. What heart should I have had for it, after that? Come and sit down, Lubov!'

The office was darkly comfortable, panelled and cushioned in russet brown, and shrouded from the sun in the heart of the oldest building of the university. Lubov went to the bookcase which filled up the whole of one wall, and restored the Cicero to its place. The Dean took brandy and glasses from a cabinet beside his desk, and poured with a deliberation which was spoiled by the slight chatter of the bottle against the rims of the glasses.

'You'll still drink with me?' The liquid quivered in the extended glass. When Lubov took it from him it steadied, and lay still. He was glad to find his hands under control.

'Of course; why not?'

'Sit down, won't you. There ought to be a toast for this occasion,' said the Dean, wryly, 'if we could only think of it. Absent friends, perhaps!'

'I'm more concerned just now,' said Lubov, leaning back in his chair with a deep sigh, 'with present ones.'

The thin hand came up and shielded the trembling face. 'You think I ought to have saved you.'

'No! I'm sure you couldn't have saved me, and I don't even think you should have tried. You weren't trying a case, you were deciding whether a man with a serious charge hanging over him is fit to be teaching in a university. Looking at the question properly—not a very easy thing for me to do, perhaps—I should say you probably gave the right answer.'

'You know I gave the only answer I dared. You know I agreed with much that you said, you know I believed your denial of the specific guilt which is being charged against you. Of course we were trying a case! I was convinced of your innocence, and I voted you probably guilty. Lubov, don't talk to me of a right answer! I'm an old man, and I've lost my virtue.'

'If you'd voted the other way you would have achieved just nothing. I should still have been thrown out, and you would have damaged yourself. If you are valuable where you are, and I'm sure you are, then to risk your position for a sufficient stake may be good, but to throw it away on a hopeless case would be bad. It all turned out much as I'd expected. Only more painful,' he added honestly, revolving the brandy-glass slowly between his palms.

'If I had still had the courage, I should have

416

spoken for you, and if necessary followed you out. But I've left it too late, Lubov, the nature's gone out of me. And when the case comes to trial, how can you expect any better of me now?' The weary old hand was shaking so much that it seemed he would drop the glass, and Lubov leaned forward and took it gently from him, and, moved by the tremulous and insubstantial touch of the flesh of old age, kept the hand warmly enclosed in his own, as though he hoped to pour back again the lost nature the Dean lamented.

'You mustn't mind so much. I won't pretend I enjoyed it, but consider the evidence, and then tell me if from the viewpoint of any impartial person I've been wronged! As a man you've a right to take my word that I've had no traffic with Yuri and his fellow-exiles, but as the Dean of this Faculty you've no such right. On the facts of the case, how can I have any complaint? Stop worrying about whether you could have done anything for me. Think of the best of the work you're doing here, think of the boys and girls you're reaching for the first time, and tell me this isn't worth the loss of me!'

'This is the most gracious absurdity,' said the Dean, almost steadily, almost with a smile, 'that *you* should be comforting *me*. And I've nothing to give you in return, my dear child, not even my blessing. When I raised my hand over you it wasn't to bless you.'

'I didn't come to ask you for anything—

except, perhaps, the brandy, I certainly feel better for that.'

'You'll take a little more?' The old man reached eagerly for the bottle, but Lubov restrained him with a smile,

'No, thanks, I've had what I needed.'

'What will you do now? You already know, I take it, that they've decided on your arrest?'

'I was taking it for granted. They can hardly ignore a thing like that. Do you know—have they dropped any hint of when it's likely to happen? I should like to feel ready.' Remembering how little his preparations had effectively prepared him for today's pains, he added soberly: 'As ready as possible!'

'Very soon, I gathered. I should expect it tomorrow.' The Dean suddenly drew hard upon the hand which cradled his own, and leaned forward until his face was close to Lubov's. In his lean and discouraged cheek a nerve twitched agitatedly. 'Lubov, perhaps there is something I can give you, after all. Something I'd have used myself a year ago if I hadn't been faced with the problem of moving a whole family. It's a small thing, no carriage at all—simply an address in the Old Quarter. If I were you, I'd make use of it.'

Lubov had drawn back a little, and was sitting very still, his eyes wide and dark in doubt, and very attentive.

'At least you can rely on this gift being serviceable, I promise you that. I've known it to be used successfully twice before. You'd need a fair amount of money, but you need not worry about that, if you haven't enough, I have. But you would have to go tonight. Do you understand me?'

Lubov said: 'No.' He felt that it had already ceased to be altogether true, but it was simpler than trying to express the confusion of doubts and suppositions that flooded his mind.

'Go where I send you, Lubov, and they'll get you out of the country. You could be over the Austrian frontier by tomorrow morning. They have a route as perfectly worked out as you're likely to find anywhere, and it can be operated at short notice. I know, I've already seen it in action. Well, will you go?'

Lubov drew his hand away. The thumping of his heart shook his tired body with sudden violence; he had been through too much indigestible experience all in one day, it was surging back through his consciousness in a wave of distressed excitement, filling his eyes with a suffusion of tears.

'Are you sure you want me to answer? Haven't we been pitched into this conversation because somebody else took that way out, or one like it? Would you like me to follow him?'

'I know you too well to have any fear that you will follow him too far.'

'Some of us said that about Yuri, too.' He got up clumsily in his pain, and crossed the room to the casement windows that looked out

419

upon the court. The sun was now declining so low that it reached only the steep roofs of the Old Building. The tiles, rounded like fish-scales, had every one a sharply etched rim of shadow. Beneath the eaves lay a great well of indigo shade. He stood with his hand clenched against the glass, gazing down.

'Yes or no, Lubov? I can't offer you security from anything, I can only open a door for you. The way you conduct yourself on the other side of it is your own problem. At least you could begin in freedom.'

'Could I? Are you sure you know what freedom is? And where it is? I don't! And I have a family, too.'

'They would be innocent of any complicity in your escape, and their innocence would, I think, be obvious. You can be reasonably sure they would not suffer for your going—you know that.'

'I was thinking in terms of their disapproval rather than of their punishment.' He laid his forehead against the coolness of the glass and closed his eyes. He saw England again, he saw himself walking in London again with Emmy by his side. He saw a future in which the impossible happiness of loving her could emerge into true flower, and his whole body ached with longing. But he knew it was only the most cruel of illusions; when he tried to touch it, it shrivelled, leaving only a diminished travesty of a marriage, haunted by the robust and splendid thing it had intended to be. He for ever trying to atone for offering her an emasculated parody of the creature she had loved, she possessed by hatred of herself for reducing him to this—what would face them but a lifetime of trying to recapture the truth of love after its death and burial? Not to have and yet to have, or to have and still lack, which was the more destroying pain? But calm was coming back into his mind like a returning tide, strong and sure, not to be hurried, not to be deflected.

'Is it yes or no, Lubov?' the old man asked gently.

Lubov turned with a tired sigh, and moved along the shelves of the bookcase, his fingers tracing the lettering of gilded spines. It was here, his hand drew it half from its place, and caressed it, and slid it lovingly back again. Another old scholar had known what to reply to the same question, centuries before modern man thought he had discovered a new problem of behaviour. Lubov smiled into the Dean's illusionless eyes, and began softly:

'"—it seemed better to the Athenians to condemn me to death, and it therefore seemed better to me to sit here, and more just to abide the penalty they appoint for me—for, had I thought otherwise, my bones and sinews would long since have found their way to Megara or Boeotia."'

*   *   *

Emmy closed the enormous door behind her;
in the silence of midnight the house held its
breath as she climbed the stairs. Looking
upward, she could see the glow from the
Ivanescu flat before she reached it, for Lubov
had left the outer door open and the light
burning in the hall. He had been quite sure of
her.

She went in with her long skirts gathered
closely in her hands, because they took up so
much room, and seemed to her to make so
much noise in the vast silence. No one stirred
within the living-room, no one threw open a
door and rushed to meet her. She closed the
outer door after her, releasing the catch very
quietly, and in the obstinate stillness she was
seized for a moment by an appalling sense of
dread. Had they been here and taken him while
Wanda was at the concert? Was he gone
already? And where were Ilonna and Matyas,
if Lubov was taken? The flat felt empty,
without breath or life, a place deserted.

Then, from the bedroom where the parents
slept, she heard the faintest labouring sigh out
of someone's shallow and anxious sleep, and
the sense of horror left her. If they were in bed,
then Lubov was still here. She let herself softly
into the living-room. The bowl lights in the
centre of the ceiling were out, but the little
reading-lamp on Miloslav's desk was still
422

burning, casting a circle of light just as far as the edge of the table and leaving all beyond in a subdued twilight.

He was there, just outside the scalloped rim of the light, stretched out upon the cushions of the couch which had not yet taken on its nocturnal character of a bed, though it embraced the sleeper none the less kindly. He was already in striped poplin pyjamas and a dark green woollen dressing-gown. He had taken sensible steps, it seemed, to waste no moment of the last night, by doing all the tedious necessary things before she came, so that they might have an extra quarter of an hour together, at least. Then he had thrown himself down here to wait for her in comfort, and his own weariness, and perhaps the relaxation of the bath with which he still glowed and from which the hair round his temples was still damp, had betrayed him into sleep.

She went nearer to him, but she was afraid to go too near, for fear her presence should communicate itself through all the circles of his slumber. She stood looking down at him, and the tidal well of her fondness came flooding upward through her heart, filled her throat, stood like sudden dew in her eyes. There was not a line or a feature in him that had not the power to turn her body to agony, and fire the agony through and through with the extreme of joy. So ordinary, and so unique, was the thin, self-contained face, with its wide uncompromising forehead, and its large eyelids slightly swollen and pale with weariness, and the sudden grace of the mouth, young, unintimidated, delicately grave but with a generosity of line which was never far from a smile. A mysterious face, keeping its own inscrutable dignity. The heat of the bath and the unwisdom of this sleep after it had raised an unwonted colour to his cheeks, making them look less hollow, and the relaxation of his parted lips had given him, considering his situation, a decidedly frivolous look. There was something impressive, too, in the way he had gone peacefully to sleep, leaving all the doors open upon his helplessness, for friend or foe to come in.

She had only to look at him, and every part of her mind was moved into marvellous subtleties of experience. With the maternal part of love she thought: 'He ought not to sleep uncovered like this after a hot bath, he'll catch cold!' and with a partner's pride: 'To be able to sleep like this with his world coming to bits is the mark of a man who carries his own peace.' And with the heavy, sweet, silent, receptive expectancy of love itself: 'He will be like this in my arms. When I awake I shall see him like this. And if it is possible to love him more than I do now, I shall love him more then.'

She took off her coat, and with the impulse of caution which was always with her now, put it away in the hall wardrobe, and shut even her scarf and gloves out of sight, moving quickly and quietly. Then she gathered her bell of rustling blue-grey skirts up in her arms, and went into Wanda's bedroom, and there undressed, borrowing nightdress and dressing-gown and slippers from Wanda's possessions. When she had washed, and stole back into the living-room, Lubov was still asleep. This time she went close, but even the tremor of her movements did not disturb his rest. Only when she bent her head and kissed him on the mouth, with the symbolic deliberation of some attempted disenchantment in a fairy story, did he open his eyes, large, dark-brown, unfocused, and stare up wonderingly into her face.

Recognition grew out of his bewilderment gradually, like an opening flower, expanding to embrace with the beauty of its contentment first the eyes, then the whole face. The curve of the lips which was almost a smile became fully a smile, though it seemed scarcely to move or change.

'Emmy!' It was hardly loud enough even to be called a whisper, but the delight in it seemed to fill the room. He put up his arm, slid his hand round her shoulders, and drew her down to him. His lifted mouth felt for hers delicately, touching tenderly first, and cold to the touch, then fastening and clinging, and burning into a sweet and startling heat. He held her upon his

425

heart for a moment, and then withdrew his hands gently, letting them pass with pleasure down her arms until she pressed her palms against his, and their hands locked and clung. 'Emmy, it *is* you!' His dreaming gaze, still half bemused by sleep, wandered over her ruffled hair and Wanda's blue dressing-gown. 'You've been here some time? Why didn't you wake me?'

'Not ten minutes! And I made good use of the time. Wanda fetched me from the hall in Petr's car. She's sleeping in Ledva tonight, because she wants to get hold of her director in the morning.'

'For me, of course!' said Lubov, with a dazed and sleepy smile.

'For you, of course! She told me what happened at the Council meeting. Lubov, my darling, I'm sorry!' She was baffled by the inadequacy of words, and to become articulate she had to employ once more the eloquence of her body, the momentary caress of her cheek against his.

'It was only as I expected,' he said gently. 'Did she tell you there's more to come? It can't stop there, Emmy, they'll have to go through with the business now. We've got to be ready for that, too.'

'Yes, she told me. She said you'd been warned to expect it tomorrow.'

He sat up, digging the heel of his hand childishly into his eyes, and yawning. 'We must keep our voices down, because I hope my parents are asleep. I made them go to bed, they were both so worn out, and he has to get up early and go to work whether I am in jail or not.'

The deliberation with which he used the words caused her to stiffen with disapproval for a moment, and he saw the tightening of her hands and the slight shock of her recoil, and protested reproachfully: 'Oh no, you mustn't think I said it to hurt you! It's to myself I'm saying these things. I have to get used to the idea. And I had a lesson today against thinking it can be done easily just because it has to be done.'

'Was it bad?' she asked. It did not matter, after all, what words she used; what he heard was the utterance of her heart.

'Bad enough! It was exactly as I'd thought it would be, really, Emmy. What I hadn't realised was how much it could hurt. It's myself I didn't know enough about.' He was more awake now, his voice, even in the subdued whisper he kept to guard his parents' sleep had regained its fullness and form, and his smile was contemplative and interested, ready to find rueful but salutary amusement even in his own alarms and stresses.

'Do you want to talk about it? I don't ask, but I should like to know.'

'Yes, I want to talk about it to you. To no one else, but of course to you.' He reached out and drew her down beside him, and told her everything that had happened. The silence, post-midnight now, and instantly invested with a deeper and more august quality, was hardly disturbed by his soft monotone, which disciplined even his most unforeseen pain into a civilised serenity. Nevertheless, after his fashion, apologetically, with the greatest reluctance to upset anyone by admitting to wounds, he communicated something more than he said; no stains showed, but she felt him bleed. As much to comfort herself as to caress him, she slid her arm beneath his and encircled his body closely. His old dressing-gown had worn thin, and she could feel his bones beneath the flesh, slight, shapely, too meagrely covered. She listened, and his voice was so complete in its calm that it seemed he needed nothing from her or anyone; but she touched him, and his flesh had all the vulnerable tensions of humanity, pathetic and lonely.

'Emmy, there is something else I must tell you. Afterwards I saw the Dean. Emmy—he offered me a way of leaving the country.'

After a moment of silence she said: 'And you refused?'

'And I refused.'

This time she was silent for so long that he began to tremble a little. 'Emmy, was I wrong? Do you reproach me? Will you believe that, although I could not go, it was far worse than I had ever dreamed, to be offered a way of going towards you, and not to take it?'

She was shocked by the tremor she had occasioned in him, and tightened her arm and folded him more closely in protesting tenderness. 'You would have found yourself going away from me, my darling, not towards me. Of course you were right! Haven't we agreed that for us that was not even a possibility? Were you afraid that I should have changed my mind?'

'I love you,' he said. 'It is easy to know that a thing is right, and still not easy to do it when it seems to separate us for ever.'

'If you had accepted that way out, you know as well as I do that it would only have seemed to unite us,' she said. 'I love you, too, I love you like my own life, but I love you as you are, and I don't want to have to try to make do with anything less. And besides,' she said, venturing deeply into the stream, 'I think that if you retreated a step from the person you are, it would not only be to betray yourself and me, but the world as well.' She took his free hand solemnly in hers, and drew it into the hollow under her breast. 'Lubov, we've felt sometimes that being still and silent was not much of a contribution towards saving the world. But now I'm not sure. Sometimes it seems to me that just by remaining erect we may be doing everything a man can do. It even seems to me that it may be enough.'

'At least,' he said, in a great sigh of gratitude,

'we have to keep certain things in our own hands. My country can ruin, imprison, even kill me, but it cannot change me. Only I could do that. If I had loved you even a little less, I might have agreed to go. How crazy it seems, Emmy, to be trying to tell you that I love you too much to marry you!'

'That would not have been a marriage by our standards,' she said. 'Ours will be.'

'Ah!—our marriage! Emmy, when will it be?' He was smiling, though his smile had that clear, illusionless sadness which only he knew how to keep sweet. And if he had waited she would have told him then, but he had still a certain wonderful weight upon his mind, and she kept silence instinctively until he could lay it in her breast.

'You know, Emmy, when it came to the point of making a choice, whether to go or stay, I found there was even more involved than I had realised. Whoever runs from a charge here, and takes refuge abroad, is himself making a charge. The act of flight is an accusation. It points back, and says: "Look, my country! I have left it because justice is not to be had there." Emmy, there may be people here in my land who have the right to make such a charge, but I have no such right. Nothing unlawful has been done to me. Someone has lied about me, but it is not my country. There is false evidence, but it is not my country's. There has been an injustice, but it is not the fault of my country. The procedure against me is justified by the evidence, and I have no complaint to make against the good faith of my accusers. Shall I charge *them* with what *Yuri* did? Therefore I could not run away, even if I wanted to. I have found out something so very simple, Emmy, that it dazzles me every time I look at it. I have found out that to be wronged oneself confers no right to wrong others.'

He sighed and smiled, having safely delivered the prophetic child which had burdened him, and turning her face towards him in the hollow of his hand, kissed the middle of her forehead. 'You can easily see that I have spent part of the day in the Philosophical Faculty!'

She said no word, only gazing at him in the dimness above the rim of the circle of light, her eyes large and luminous with tenderness.

'So we shall see it out here,' he said. 'In spite of some miscalculations on my part about how easy it is to bear things for which one is prepared, the general thesis was sound. When you know the only possible thing you can do about a situation, it may still be difficult, but at least it can be done.'

'Yes,' she agreed, 'it can be done. So this is our last night, Lubov. Certainly the last for some time, perhaps the last of all. I am only wondering,' she said with astonished calm, 'why we have wasted so much time.'

It seemed to her that he understood then, but if he did he was not willing to take advantage of a moment with which he considered only his misfortune had presented him. Deliberately he said, drawing gently away from her: 'It's very late, and I am very selfish to keep you talking so long when you also are terribly tired. And I did not ask you, even, how the concert went! You had a success?'

'They seemed to think so.' Her eyes held him in their confident shining, and would not be evaded.

'We must sleep, Emmy. You have things to do tomorrow, and I should like to be in condition to make a good showing. We shall be up early, because of my father, so there will be still a little time to be together, before you must leave me.' He swung his feet to the floor, and rose a little stiffly, withdrawing himself from her touch with a quiet resolution which did not conceal his pain. 'Did Wanda leave you everything you want?'

'Everything!' she said, with a wild smile, and, rising, watched him retreat a few steps from her. She wondered how far he would fly if she pursued, and was moved to see his desire and distress when only her voice and her eyes followed him, and the mysterious duality of words which had become eloquent of themselves when they were no longer needed.

'I must make up my bed,' he said, his face firmly turned away from her; and he bent, and

432

made to lift the cushions to open the box-base. 'You won't need it, Lubov.'

He turned then, looking at her in desperation, his cheeks flushing. 'Emmy, I am not begging for anything. I did not intend—'

'Why should you beg? There is nothing here which is not yours already. I know you did not intend to make any claim, but I have rights, too, Lubov.' She moved towards him slowly, and now he did not turn away from her, but stood and waited, and his hands, which had fallen to his sides, advanced a little to meet her of their own will, the long fingers tensed, so that her heart ached and she held her breath with awareness of their anguish. 'Lubov, we have been waiting for someone else or something else to give us what was already ours. If you are not my husband to the very heart, tell me so now, and I'll go away and leave you alone. And if you think I am not your wife for as long as I live, whether I ever see you again or no, tell me that, too. Our citizenship isn't legitimate in the world's eyes, why should our marriage have to be?'

He said in a frantic whisper: 'If you knew how much I want you, you would not torment me. Emmy, if you have any doubts at all, I beg you to go away quickly, and do not say any more. Have you not seen that I dare hardly look at you?'

'I have no doubts at all,' she said, 'and I won't be sent away.'

433

Her lifted hands touched his cheeks. He jerked his head away with a gesture of distress, but where her finger-tips had rested the blood burned vividly.

'Emmy, Emmy!' he groaned between exasperation and longing, 'do you know what you're inviting? You said yourself this was our last night. Can you imagine what it will be like afterwards if it should be the only night?'

'Yes, I can imagine a future of nothing but regret that we wasted what was offered us.' Her hands persisted, clinging to his shoulders, passing with fierce gentleness about his neck, drawing his head down to her, folding him cheek to cheek with her, and heart to heart. 'Or a lifetime of thanking God that we had everything, even if we had it for only one night.'

Lubov's rigidity melted suddenly in a passion of trembling. He uttered a tiny, exultant, agonised sound, muted against her cheek, and, winding his arms about her, snatched her into his heart, tightening his clasp as though he would fuse her into himself, and be completed indissolubly for ever. The repeated cycle of their meetings and separations proceeded even through this moment, but there was no conflict between the two they remained and the one they became. Their translated bodies, embracing in torment and delight, quivered together about a great matched heart-beat, filling the darkness with invisible light, separation with possession, ruin with achievement, ending with beginning.

*   *   *

He waited all the morning, in spite of his long forethought and his memories of the night, which were more radiant and calming than he could have believed possible, too nervous to sit still. It was not a simple matter of what was to happen to him, it was the much more hurtful question of how he was to bear himself that devoured his mind; and when the doorbell rang at last, early in the afternoon, he found with relief that he was glad, and went to answer it briskly, almost as if he had been waiting with eagerness for this visit. Two uniformed police officers stood on the landing. He looked at them with an almost welcoming smile, and stood back for them to enter the flat. Ilonna, her hands white with flour, came out from the kitchen, the little agonised frown upright between her fair brows, her blue ribbon slipping out of its bow.

'You want me? I am Lubov Ivanescu.'

They said yes, stepping over the door-sill with slight constraint because their boots were dirty. It had been raining softly all the morning, and they had not yet left all the mud of the street behind in the hall and the lift. The first was a young fellow, hardly older than Miloslav, pink and fresh and blithe, the second

435

older, perhaps fifty, with a well-trained face, noncommittal as carved wood, but the expression in which his sealed features had set from long experiment with difficult duties remained a coolly tolerant placidity.

'We have orders to take you to Security Headquarters, Dr Ivanescu. Will you get ready, please? We have a car waiting outside.'

'I was expecting you,' said Lubov. 'Would it be in order for me to ask you whether I am being charged, and what the charge is?'

The older man shook his head. 'Our orders are simply to bring you. We've no warranty to discuss your case, and no information. I'm sorry!'

Ilonna had wiped the flour from her hands, and, trotting across to the wardrobe, brought out Lubov's overcoat and hat. The haze which dilated her blue eyes was no more than a dew from the tension of anxiety which would never slacken until he came home again. Assuming that he would, some day, come home again. Those tears were never going to fall. They did not impede her vision as she brought out the cashmere scarf he had already discarded for the warmer weather. Tears served no purpose, but the scarf might. Cells seemed likely to be cold places, though she had no first-hand information about them.

'Have I to take anything with me?' Lubov asked. 'I'm afraid I don't know the ropes.'

'Whatever you need will be provided.' The

young fellow's tone was seriously reassuring, entirely without irony.

Ilonna, stretching up her round arms, as pink and white as the blossom on the hills, put Lubov into his coat, settled the shoulders with gently smoothing hands, and frowned at the loose way it hung on his too lean body. She approached him with the scarf neatly folded. Lubov's instinctive protest melted into an indulgent smile. To her he was her small son in trouble, quite incapable of taking proper care of himself while he had such a load on his mind. He bent his head meekly, and let her settle the scarf tidily inside the neck of his coat, and fasten the buttons securely over it.

'Are you sure you oughtn't to take your raincoat, darling? It was coming down quite heavily when I came in from the butcher's.'

'Oh, Mummy, it's only a matter of stepping across the pavement and into the car. I don't need a raincoat.'

He put his arms round her and hugged her, and gave her the customary kiss she always expected on his departure. His mouth was firm and casual, and his movements almost buoyant. This was so much better and easier than waiting, and an ordeal which had proved to have at least a genuine beginning might, some day, have an equally definite end.

'Good-bye, Mummy! Kiss Father for me, and don't worry too much.' He settled his hat before the mirror with his usual quick care, not out of bravado, but because it was a part of the natural procedure which emerged of itself from his hands, and as soon as the gesture was released he saw and was grateful for its virtue. The wheels of the days had to go on turning.

'I'm ready. You don't have to—there needn't be any—' He looked down with a significant frown at his hands. 'I assure you I have no intention of giving you any trouble. I'm as keen to get this over with as you are.'

The bright-faced boy looked shocked, and cast one frowning glance in Ilonna's direction, as though Lubov had committed a social error. The older man, unmoved, said dryly: 'You can put your mind at rest. We have all the authority we need.'

'I'm ready, then. Shall we go?'

Ilonna ran out to the landing after them to stuff two new packets of cigarettes and a clean handkerchief into Lubov's pocket. 'There! You'll be able to smoke, won't you? Are you sure you've got your lighter?'

He cupped her chin in his hand and kissed her again, smiling. 'When she rings up, give her my love. And tell her I believe everything will be all right.'

He went down the stairs between the two policemen, walking so vigorously that it might have been thought it was he, and not they, who had reason to look forward to arrival as something accomplished.

The days dwindled, slipping through her fingers like sand, the precious few days which alone linked her to the possibility of seeing Lubov again. Every day, twice, three times a day, as often as she could safely immure herself in a call-box without being observed, she telephoned to the flat, always asking for news, seldom receiving any. Between these living moments, when she had communion in one Ivanescu with them all, even the absent ones, she found out how to die, and still go on dutifully walking round galleries, factories, churches, making the appropriate remarks, being grateful for the delight Slava took in showing her beauty, and the growing kindness even she, in her half-death, felt between them.

On the first day, when Ilonna delivered Lubov's message to her, she experienced the same release of tension which had eased his heart. The thing had at last begun, therefore they were a step nearer the end of it. She questioned with passion, and received the sad and negative answers with firmness, refusing to be discouraged.

'You don't know where they have taken him? Do you think they'll let you see him? There's been nothing else? They haven't questioned you? Or any of the others?' But there was nothing. Lubov with his escort had walked out of the house and into the car, and been carried away, no one yet knew where, no one knew for how long, no one knew to what fate.

'Isn't there anything we can do? Anything at all?'

'Only wait, Emmy, that's all.'

'Ilonna, I wish I could come to you! I can't get away, I have to go on doing the things I'm supposed to do. Darling, are you alone?'

'Now I am; but the woman from the flat below was here with me. Emmy, people can be so good! She happened to be on the stairs and she saw them go down. She came straight to me. She laughed, Emmy! She says it's ridiculous, not a soul will ever believe it of Lubov, and she says her husband will speak for him—he is a good Party man, you know, from before the war; his word carries weight. Don't worry about me, Emmy, Matyas will soon be home now. Don't worry at all!'

That night she went with Dr Horda to the opera. It made matters singularly easy, because she could keep silence, and even let the tears rise to her eyes if she would, since no one could tell by their shape or heaviness that they were for Lubov and not for Tatiana; but she would not accept that indulgence because there would be other nights with no such easy veil for her face.

The next day was bad. She dialled the number of the flat twice during the morning, and a third time in the afternoon, and could get no answer; and when she tried once more after dinner, before going with Slava to an amateur concert somewhere on the outskirts of the town, she was answered by a voice she did not know, a man's voice so level and flat that in almost any language it would have identified itself as belonging to a policeman or a civil servant. With what presence of mind she could salvage from the shock of astonishment and disquiet, she asked for Wanda, thanking God that she had not rushed headlong into English as soon as the connection was made. An unknown girl ringing up the daughter of the house would surely pass as normal enough, and whatever reserve had entered her tone could scarcely surprise a man who must know his own voice would be unexpected from that household.

'I'm sorry, Miss Ivanescu is not here just now.'

'You don't know when she'll be in?'

'I'm sorry!'

'Oh, never mind!' she said. 'I shall see her at rehearsal tomorrow, I expect.' There were more than sixty girls in the ballet and choir of the folk-group, she was surely safe enough in submerging herself among such numbers. She hung up the receiver with a trembling hand. It wouldn't do to try that again without a complete verbal line of retreat all prepared.

So the police were in the flat. It shouldn't have surprised her; they had a duty to go very thoroughly into Lubov's correspondence and since they would find nothing incriminating, their thoroughness was Lubov's strength, not his weakness. But she could not follow the logic of her own reasoning, and feel glad of the impersonal hands turning over his papers. Miloslav had been right, she could not stop being afraid for Lubov. Her cell, perhaps, was a colder and straiter place than his.

Now she dared not attempt to telephone again until they had had ample time to finish their examination of the flat, nor could she possibly go there until she had contacted some member of the family, and been reassured that the way was clear. Until tomorrow at least she was helpless, without comfort, without news, tormented by endless questions which could not be answered. What infuriated her more than anything was the helpless sensation of having to conceal even the most innocent of connections as though some guilt attached to them; it was a distortion for which the world could not be forgiven. It wronged everyone, and it did indeed impart to her own actions some compromising strain of guilt; but she had no alternative. He had wanted her to stay out of the affair, and she must do as he wished.

On the morning of the third day she dialled their number again, the careful sentences ready in her mouth in case the wrong voice should reply; but this time Ilonna's voice, unmistakable in its light, rising tone, answered her at once, and she felt her knees go limp with the relief of hearing it.

'Thank God! It's Emmy here! Where were you all yesterday? I couldn't get anyone until evening, and even then—Is there any news?'

'Oh, Emmy, I am so glad to hear your voice! But there's not much to tell you. I was sent for yesterday to the police to answer questions. I was there all day, and they met Matyas when he came home, and brought him in, too. We didn't get back until about eleven o'clock at night. But we didn't mind it, because they have been into everything we could possibly tell them about Lubov, and you know, my dear, that there is nothing but good to tell.'

'I know it,' she said quickly, 'but do they believe it? Were they all right with you? Did they seem well disposed?'

'How can you tell? They went on questioning and questioning, all about him from a little boy. They did not try to say anything bad about him, they only asked. I think they really wanted to *know*, and if they want that, it is good.'

'Ilonna—they didn't let you see him?'

'No,' said Ilonna sadly. 'I asked, but they wouldn't let me.'

'Or tell you where he is?'

'No. Matyas thinks he is still there at headquarters, but we don't know. And, Emmy, today they have sent for Wanda.'

Emmy imagined that beautiful, fiery

443

creature launched like an arrow in Lubov's defence, glowing with absolute faith in him, believing in the integrity of her country, expecting justice so confidently that surely no one could deny it to her.

'If I can get away this evening, can I come round? Do you think Wanda will be back?'

'Yes, do come! I will send a message to Petr, in case Wanda goes straight there for some reason when they have finished with her. But I think she will come first to us. Yes, Emmy, come! It will do us good just to see you.'

'About nine, then, I hope. We are going to a recital at the Record Theatre, but it will be only a short programme.'

The memory of this conversation, the promise of the meeting in the evening, made this day easier to bear; and when she climbed the stairs at last, and walked into Wanda's impetuous arms on the threshold of the flat, she could almost have believed that the whole affair had been no more than a bad dream, and that Lubov would come striding out of the living-room to perfect the welcome with his kiss. All the remaining Ivanescu were at home this time; they could sit down together over coffee and discuss the case soberly, counting with reserve the small gains Wanda insisted on thrusting before them.

'I was there until nearly six, and I know they are interviewing dozens of other people who can give evidence about Lubov's attitude. I did all I could to discredit the suggestion that Yuri and he could possibly have had any understanding about working together, because the only evidence for it comes from Yuri, and who is going to take his word for anything? Of all the witnesses they could have, here is the one who should least be trusted. Do you think they do not know that, too? They are going through all the records they have of Yuri's associates here, to see if they can trace the people to whom the letters were written. There's no doubt, from what you told us, that they're all real people. I would believe he made them all up to ruin Lubov, but it seems the letters were all written while he still expected you to be his postman, so they cannot have been just imaginary people. But the letters have no proper names, just nicknames or Christian names, and no addresses except whatever internal evidence there may be in the text. I don't think they will get very far with them though it seems it was a matter of indifference to Yuri whether they were traced or not.'

Emmy said: 'Everyone here has become expendable to Yuri.'

'And Yuri and his friends are expendable to me! I wish he would put himself just once within my reach, it would be enough. I would wish that all his friends may be traced and charged, if I could be sure they would not lie and drag Lubov down with them. But you see that if they resemble Yuri they would certainly

445

do that.'

'Don't be too ready to wish them harm,' said Matyas dryly. 'There's another possibility that doesn't seem to have occurred to you, but fortunately I rather think it has to the police. If Yuri's moved into a fantasy world in which he expects every one of us to be desperate and unbalanced enough to be ready for recruitment into his secret army, it seems to me he wouldn't wait for much invitation from his old acquaintances before drafting them in. I dare say if those letters had ever reached their addressees, some of them would have been every bit as astonished as Lubov was—and just about as likely to welcome their assignments.'

'You think they aren't taking Yuri's underground movement as seriously as we feared?' asked Emmy. 'That first night, if you remember, they didn't seem as much impressed as they might have been. I hope you're right! That would be the best thing that could happen, for the charge to be dropped for lack of evidence.'

'At any rate,' said Wanda firmly, 'they'll check every letter of Lubov's that can be found, and talk to everyone who knows him. And that's our strength, that the more they investigate Lubov, the more they find out about him, the more people they ask, the more surely they must see that he is innocent. The more closely you look at what is white, the more surely you will see that it is not black.'

'You used to be afraid,' Emmy reminded her, 'that he had compromised himself by defending other people too warmly, and too often.'

'Yes, openly, in broad daylight. That can be shown to be unwise, unpatriotic, what you like. It cannot be shown to be treasonable. It can lose a man his career, but not his freedom, not his life. Treason is something done in the dark, or under another face. Lubov has only one face, and he shows it to everyone without any concealment. They must come to the conclusion that he is honest, because he *is* honest.'

'Do you think he'll ever be allowed to teach again, even if he's released?'

'No, and neither does he. That's over. But it is of no use worrying now about what work he will do when he is free; let us first make sure that he *will* be free.'

Upon this task she had certainly spent her day, and in the possibility of success she undoubtedly believed.

'You still don't know where he is? Won't they let anyone see him? I couldn't ask for myself, naturally,' said Emmy, feeling the alarming sting of tears within her lowered eyelids, 'but I thought perhaps his mother—'

'He'll probably be kept isolated,' said Matyas gently, 'until they decide whether to charge him or drop the case.'

'Do you believe, honestly, that there's a

447

chance they'll drop it, and release him?'

Matyas thought that over for a long minute of silence before he said with solemnity: 'Yes. God knows I'm not able to guess at the odds, but I believe there's a chance. Lubov has this great strength, that he's never asked any favours, never pleaded for any good opinions, never trimmed his sails to catch the public breath. There isn't a soul who knows him but knows he's made whatever criticisms he had to make openly. It isn't the Lubovs who have only to be blown upon to be overturned—it's those who were too anxious to run with the wind. And it isn't the Lubovs who are most despised and distrusted by their opponents—it's the ones who come rushing with armfuls of flattery and flowers, and keep their criticisms for whispering in corners. No government on earth, Emmy, my dear, is ever going to love Lubov—but I believe ours is sufficiently honest to respect him.'

*   *   *

On the fourth day—for her calendar now was regulated by the date of Lubov's arrest—she asked Slava over coffee, her face carefully tranquil: 'Could I get my visa extended for another fortnight, do you think? I should like to stay a little longer, now I am here.'

Slava looked up with the bright, blank face of surprise which always saluted the moments

448

when her charge became suddenly not quite comprehensible; daunting moments for her, since this particular foreign guest had been found in large measure so congenial. The flower of politeness, Slava dissembled her disquiet as often as communication failed; but her face had always that superlative smoothness which is not necessary to peace.

'You would have to ask at the office. I don't know if they would grant it, but you could try. You would have to tell them why you want to stay longer.'

Yes, of course! Love is understandable but not practical. Love is not something you can give as a reason for wanting to stay. And, after all, it was not easy, when she had asked in advance for a fortnight's permit to visit a musical festival and contribute two concerts to it, to begin alleging a sudden consuming desire to plan other concerts. She had had time to think of such practical matters before, and ask for a month if she wanted a month. Emmy began to see that she was inaugurating something which was not simple at all, and to anticipate that everywhere her proposal would be met with the same puzzled and guarded politeness.

'I should like to have more time to add to my repertoire of folk-songs, for one thing. I want to see more of the work your new groups are doing, and to learn some of the songs they've collected.'

449

'Oh, there is a book,' said Slava, brightening, 'a new collection already published. We shall get it for you, to take back with you.'

'And then, of course, I just like being here.'

Slava smiled with the proud eagerness with which she responded to every compliment of affection paid to her country. She could well understand that as a reason for wanting to stay, but not for staying. The truth was that everyone here had so much to do, and was devoting himself so rigorously to the right distribution of his time, that the sudden misappropriation of a whole fortnight seemed an unthinkable act of sabotage, impossible from a responsible person. Slava could believe and be grateful that Emmy should feel tempted, but could not credit that she would succumb.

'Well, if you really want to apply, we can go along to the office and ask for forms. I can help you to fill them up, we need not wait there.'

So they stopped the car that afternoon at a tall building on one of the main streets, and went up to the fifth floor, to a bare, light office where a young man with the closed and guarded face endemic among the protectors of frontiers looked up at them over a desk piled with papers, and by a slight elevation of geometrically level eyebrows indicated his willingness to listen to whatever they might have to say. Slava talked volubly, too fast for

450

Emmy to follow all that passed, but she knew that the plea of her desire to study the newly collected folk-music would be put forward faithfully. It came better from Slava than from herself, already with the half-blessing of one Ministry; but the other Ministry remained unimpressed. The young face, schooled to a stony dispassion, turned towards the unaccountable stranger. His eyes, living and wary in their impassive settings, looked her over coldly, yet with perceptible reactions of curiosity, wonder and suspicion.

'You wish to stay here for another two weeks?'

'I should like to.' Her voice was calm; it would not do to care very much. Too great eagerness would be in itself a suspicious circumstance.

'You did not suggest, when you requested a visa, that you might require it for a longer time.'

'It hadn't occurred to me that I should. But travel being the greatest expense involved, I find I should like to put in a little more time here, and a little more work, without the necessity of paying another fare.'

'Your present visa is good for almost another week. Perhaps the ground could be covered if you would outline to Miss Kraskova exactly what you require in the way of facilities.' His voice was pleasant and friendly, but his eyes watched her with distrust. As often

451

as she approached the gateway he guarded, his hand would be ready on the bolt.

'Miss Kraskova has been very good, in every way. But you must realise that the folk-groups I have found here are something quite new to me, about which I had heard nothing in England. I could not know how important they would be.'

He was pleased by that tribute, she saw the quick brightness come and go in his eyes, though the austere face remained motionless. He could not altogether trust that warmth; many people had pretended friendship who had gone home to proclaim enmity the following week. She felt herself, for a moment, to be functioning within two minds, her own and his, and the one was scarcely more strange to her than the other. It was then that she began to feel, deep within her, and as yet without acknowledgment, that she was attempting the impossible.

'Miss Kraskova and her colleagues,' he said carefully, 'have all their time mapped out in advance. I am sure she is expecting more foreign visitors, probably on the very day that you leave for home. It is not easy to make rearrangements in a time-table as full as hers. I doubt if she *could* be at your disposal for the extra time.'

Emmy did not say that she needed no escort. It was the obvious thing to say, but she contained it. Too many people already knew that she was independent, that she could find her way round the city almost like a native, and speak enough of the language to ask for information where she wanted it. It was as well that this jealous young watchman on a threatened border, watching the West with dutiful eyes, should neither learn nor wonder too much about her. She was only just beginning to appreciate the virtues of being inconspicuous.

'At any rate,' said Slava, 'we could fill in the forms, if Miss Marryat wishes, and see what can be done.'

'It isn't as urgent as all that,' said Emmy, withdrawing with great gentleness, so that even her retreat might not be too narrowly remarked. 'I don't want to upset your plans at all, and no doubt I can get quite a lot of material to take back with me. What do you think? Shall we take the forms with us, and I can think what I'd better do.'

The calm, the lessening interest with which she had accepted his polite obstruction, took shape in her voice, and it seemed that he was disarmed, and had lost a little of his fierce defensive interest in her. After all, she would never ask for that extension. Too many questions had to be answered, too many motives examined in black and white. To insist would draw too many devoted, protective eyes upon her, and deflect their fiery gaze too surely upon all her friends here. She would gain

453

nothing, certainly not the respite she was pleading for; and lose much, perhaps her chance of ever being admitted again. No, all must be done in order. You come when you have agreed to come, and go when you have stated you mean to go.

The young man gave her three forms, double sheets covered with questions to be answered. She knew they would never be filled in, but she put them in her handbag, thanking him with a casual smile. The wariness of his manner had eased a little, something which was almost a smile answered her. Her last glimpse of him, as they closed the door upon his polite bow, showed her a sentry relaxing for an instant astride his guarded frontier, watching the passing of a slight shadow which was not, after all, cast by an enemy. It saddened her to think of his unremitting warfare, and yet she understood him, and felt an affection for him.

Accept the inevitable, then, she told herself, as they went down the stairs; get ready to go. You have five days left. There may never be any more. Oh, Lubov, shall I ever see you again?

* * *

She stood under the shadow of the gold-fringed curtains, and watched the orchestra rise to the conductor's imperious summons, in the lake of light under the great Mozarteum

454

chandeliers. The autocratic hand which had driven them like a marvellous machine through the Haydn symphony could not make them move together now. They disembarrassed themselves casually of their instruments, eased them familiarly on to one arm, or parked them like bowler hats beside their chairs, and rose lazily to their feet, some not even bothering to straighten up completely, gazing out into the vast gilded cave under the starry blue ceiling with good-humoured grins of contentment. They did not take their ovation too seriously, nor dedicate themselves to oneness for a second after their communal miracle was over. The entity fell apart with aplomb into some fifty assorted individuals, amazingly various, reassuringly unique every one. Emmy watched them nod their offhand acknowledgments, and smiled in the bronze brocade shadow, grateful for their diversity.

She had dressed for her last concert with unusual care; what is final must be made memorable. She wore the new deep yellow Grecian dress, with ear-rings made of antique gold coins in her ears, and a yellow ribbon in her paler hair. Among so much soft and fluent gold her grey eyes became changeable in smoky colours, tints of iris and violet and olive-green moving in them with the variations of the light. Three thousand people had taken pleasure in her, and would shortly do so again

455

when she emerged to sing her last group of songs; but of all the three thousand there was only one who mattered to her.

Somewhere at the very back of the stalls, in the dimness where face could not be distinguished from face, one of the Ivanescu sat waiting for her last appearance. She did not know which one it would be: Wanda, Matyas or Ilonna, it made no difference. Wanda had said only, when she telephoned that morning, that she had managed to get one seat, after haunting the agency all the week for possible returns, and that someone would be there, and would wait for Emmy outside the artists' door afterwards. There would be at least one more night in the Lucerna flat, one more family reunion, though lacking both sons, one more assertion of belief that the opaque darkness which hung before them contained and would disclose at last a credible future.

And was there no news yet of Lubov? The answer was always the same, and tormented both the questioner and the one who replied, but she could not keep from asking it. No, still no news. And when she extricated herself from the brief social exchanges and the flurries of congratulation tonight, and slipped out to link arms with Wanda, or Ilonna, or Matyas in the side-street, she would expose the same nerve all over again: Is there any news? The disease and the justification of the twentieth century, the inability to despair, matched inexhaustible powers of recovery in her blood against unrelenting crises of pain. She stood in the shadow of the golden curtains, herself all golden, with a face like an Athene, aloof and calm, and she would have felt herself to be near the end of her tether, if she had not already found out by long experimental convulsions that in fact there was no end to her tether.

The conductor made his final bow, and came striding through the curtains, mopping his forehead as soon as he was out of sight of the audience. He was an old man, but moved like a boy, his high shoulders thrusting an aggressive passage through the air. He passed close to her and, turning, smiled in some astonishment, caught by her stillness in the bronze-gold shadow. The members of the orchestra, with much tramping of feet and displacement of chairs, streamed after him at leisure and made off to some relaxed place where they could smoke and stretch their legs for twenty minutes, while the English soprano sang.

When it came to the point, after all that preparation, she was not ready. It had become an ordeal to simulate the giving of a whole personality, when only half of herself was here at all, and at the last moment there was the tremor of her body, the reluctance to go forward. The cavern of dusky gilt and many-breasted whiteness expanded before her eyes for the third time that evening, receding into lofty shadow, starry overhead with the gilded systems of heaven, starry on all sides with the pale faces tier on tier, fluttering and reverberating with hands. She bent her head to the happy applause. They had accepted with generosity everything she had offered, but it was for this they had come, for the omen of the stranger singing their own native songs. To Dowland they had listened with startled delight, in absolute stillness, possessed instantly by music they were ideally equipped to understand and appreciate, and it had not mattered that the accompanist's affinity with that classic and poignant perfection had been less complete than theirs. Purcell and Arne had proved, perhaps, less accessible, but they had been pleased with those, too; and her second group, from their own modern songs, had moved them to a different kind of delight, but left them still able to be critical. Now, in the folk-songs, they would listen to her with hearts disarmed, conquered before she began the assault.

It had never before seemed to her that she was doing an unworthy thing in offering them too readily what she wanted to give and they longed to receive. Now she had one dubious moment of wondering if she had not been in some way suborning them with a trick, buying her way into their grace with easy gifts which acquired an exaggerated virtue only because of their scarcity. Was she indeed too tired and too desperate to love them any more? Had they never been anything but reflections of Lubov?

But it was quite different when she began to sing. She lifted her fair head, and uttered the first long, poised, exclamatory notes of a song from the eastern mountains, that hung like a hawk for two long lines, and then descended in swooping flight, voice and accompaniment quivering together in quickening cries of loneliness and expectation; and the organic silence, the silence that grew, welled quite suddenly out of the dimness, and like an intensely drawn breath filled every stronghold of the light, until the cavern of listening people dilated and ached with it. The great stillness of unity held them all suspended together, as its own tension holds a tear. She was not in doubt now, she had not lied to them. Nor had they lowered their standards, after all, for gratitude or any other impure motive. They were moved by her gift not for its partisan fervour only, but for its own intact virtue. She had her honesty still. Better, she still had her legitimate part in this land and these people. Singing, she was delivered from her burial in Lubov, which had threatened to violate both herself and him.

How had it been possible, even in this suspense, to fear that Lubov could separate her from the love of other people? He united her with all his kind, whether they used him well or ill; his function of reconciliation was not vulnerable to change.

She sang a dance-tune from the western

459

borders, with a bouncing pipe-rhythm, and after it one of the sad old conscript songs of sons taken from their mothers and clapped into imperial uniforms to fight for causes they hated. It had lost none of its force for being a hundred and fifty years old, it was something that was still happening all over the world. Then one of the gay and optimistic love-songs from the fat farming villages, with a charming wild waltz air, and some difficult intervals which made it rewarding to sing; and finally, because someone had remembered it from last year and sent in a shy request for it, the tragic song of the dividing river.

The living stillness enfolded them all, the devoted silence of the will made them a unity, taking up with her the threnody of love.

"'Oh quiet stream, flowing down to Danube's shore
Lost is my love, my love returns no more—'"

She had approached it with too much confidence, too little awareness of the sheer power of moving sounds, the full, plaintive, aching Slav syllables that were bitter and beautiful on the lips, like summer fruit gilded but not yet matured. The constriction took her throat with terrifying suddenness on the upward cadence of the third line, and she fought for the possession of her own voice, the muscles of her neck and face tensed, her tone hardening with effort; and then she had passed clean through the moment of disintegration, and stood on the far side of emotion, and there was nothing she could not sing. The tears might break out from her eyes and flow like rain, but her face would keep its magnificent dignity, and her voice its heroic tranquillity. It had never happened to her before. She escaped from caution, from all the limitations of the senses, from the fear of failure, from not being complete; and this prodigy had come about not because she had somehow found a miraculous way of walking the waves of that quiet stream, without getting so much as the sole of her foot wet, but because she had plunged into it and let it pass over her head.

'"Last night I dreamed a dream that he was near,
That he, my dear, my dearest entered here.
He laid his cheek against my cheek as I slept,
And with gentle chiding asked me why I wept."'

The rippling descent of the last line, regaining its balanced level at the end and wonderfully maintaining it, flowed onward into the sweet impersonal passage of the river, the aloof accompaniment which never began or ended, but only entered the senses and left them again, out-distancing thought. She was filled with the

461

memory of Lubov's stillness in the night, of his unpractised hands that touched so devoutly, of the long, trance-like lingering between waking and dreaming, rocked in the dark happiness of achievement, reluctant to depart even into sleep. Her voice soared, celebrating the joy she would never have again.

'"Barren, oh God, oh my love, this life must be!
Still my head aches with longing after thee,
And my lost heart with its sorrow sure must break
Ere it can forget thee, darling, or forsake."'

The river flowed away, bearing the last long echo of love on its indifferent waters, out of hearing, out of sight. Her hands, which she had folded together under her breast in the intensity of her remembering, relinquished the exquisite illusion of Lubov's hands, and fell empty to her sides. All the haze of faces had become one dazzling watery star.

*   *   *

Round the side door, where the Titans shouldered up the heavy stone lintel and the flight of worn steps went down from the light into the dark, a few cars waited, and a few enthusiasts had gathered to see the celebrities leave. The English soprano was the first to
462

come, her long yellow skirts, soft as muslin, gathered up a little in one hand, her grey eyes lambent as opals for a moment in the flame of the lamps, then lowered as she descended the steps. Their eyes, quietly grateful, undemandingly affectionate, followed her passage with smiling contentment. She did not wait for a car, but drew her coat about her against the cold, clear air of the April night, and walked away slowly towards the distant brightness of the square. The street, narrowing, closed in upon her and veiled her in its own obscurity, on either hand a palace, its deep windows barred in behind wrought-iron grilles, its sgraffito walls corrugating the darkness with deeper shadows.

'Walk up towards the square as though you were going back to the hotel,' Wanda had said, 'and before you reach it you shall have company.'

Even Wanda, it seemed, had reached the point of acknowledging that they must avoid too assertive a statement of connections which might be misinterpreted. The pressure of the world's fear had become as deforming as that. Friendship was something that must never be denied, but should not be flung with too challenging a candour in the face of convention. It took a cold war to produce in Wanda the slightest respect for discretion. Even now it had not gone so far as to change her radically. She had been pleased to hear that

463

Slava had seized the chance of an evening with her own family, since the Mozarteum was no more than two hundred yards from the Hotel Corvin, and even a foreigner of less experience than Emmy might have been allowed to venture such a modest journey alone; but all the Slavas in the world would not have prevented her from claiming her friend had the luck fallen in another way.

Emmy walked slowly, waiting and listening for the expected footfall behind her, the swift, confident clash of Wanda's high heels on the cobbles. She was almost sure it would be Wanda. It surprised her, therefore, when the step her ear finally distinguished from the more distant sounds of the street turned out to be longer and softer than the impetuous ring of heels she had expected. Not Wanda, then, after all. It must be Matyas. He was overhauling her now, in a matter of seconds his hand would slip through her arm and draw her close. She could feel the approach of his body, a warmth, an impression of height. Yet, listening, she marvelled that Matyas should walk so lightly, with such an elastic spring from every step. She had begun to strain her ears after discrepancies, her body tense with concentration. In the darkest passage of the street, where the great sunken doorway of the palace retired a yard and a half into blackness and the cobbles swerved inward to the hidden courtyard, she drew aside suddenly, and flattened her shoulders against the vast carved doors, and looked up at the man who came out of the night on her heels.

At the last instant it had flashed into her mind that this might not be the friend for whom she had taken him, and in the second before she saw him distinctly the full possibilities crowded in upon her consciousness. Had she said or done anything to arouse worse suspicion than her nationality in any case invited? Had things reached the point where it was expedient to keep her under constant observation? Was this some agent whose job it was to follow her? For whoever he was, he was not Matyas. Or was he merely some innocent concert-goer making for home, and she nothing to him but a friendly voice remembered with pleasure, and having no present body?

She was aware of excitement, but not of fear. Fear, as Miloslav in his considerable wisdom had instructed her, is a violation of the personality to be avoided at all costs, and the heart, left any option in the matter, rejects it instinctively. She watched the tall figure loom up out of the dark, and turn in and pause before her, and for a moment she assessed without dismay, but without recognition, its character and weight and proportion, as a shape imposed upon her senses and challenging her intellect. Then, in a breath, all was changed. The set of the shoulders, the inclination of the head, the long slenderness of the figure all assumed in one instant the deeper meaning which translates a pattern into an identity. His face, faintly luminous in the dark, glimmered out of the deeper shadow, and became the face she had only failed to know because it was impossible that it should be there at all. He was smiling. He held out his hands, not touching her.

'Emmy—did I startle you?'

She whispered: 'Lubov!' and hung for a moment clinging to the rough detail of the door, because her body had dissolved into water and her knees were failing under her. Then she was in his arms, her cheek against his, her eyes closed, and her lips were gasping out broken phrases that gushed like arterial blood: 'Lubov, my darling—it *is* you? I can't believe it! I'm not dreaming? It's really you? Oh Lubov, my dearest—' Her tears welled over, bursting through the closed lids, dewing his cheek and hers, a blessed, a restoring rain.

Shaken to the heart by the sudden and immoderate storm of her silent weeping, he folded himself about her tenderly, reassuring her with long, caressing pressures of body and arm and head, stroking her with hands grown clumsy because of their sympathetic trembling. 'Oh hush! Darling, don't cry! It isn't a dream, I promise you! I'm real—feel me! I'm here holding you, I'm free—'

She wound her arms about his body,

drawing him closer to her heart, flattening her hands jealously against his back beneath the sharp shoulder-blades, to touch with every nerve and taste with every sense the miracle of his true presence. 'Oh Lubov, oh Lubov, I thought I should never see you again!'

'But I'm here, I'm free, it's all over! Oh darling, don't cry now! All the time I've been away, they told me, you never cried, and now you drown us both in tears!'

'I can't help it!' she said. 'Don't pay any attention to me. It's nothing! It's only joy—joy doesn't hurt people!'

Footsteps and voices advanced along the narrow street. He drew her into the embrasure of the palace doors, and with arms wound protectively about her shoulders and head stooped to the long, motionless, silent kiss that habits in dark doorways, shielded her from the curiosity of the world. The darkness covered her betraying finery, and they became the most ordinary and the most touching of the night's creatures, the city lovers embracing in the glades of the stone forest, their only solitude the generosity of the passersby. Aware of them, the two homing people turned their heads for a moment, then, knowing them, passed serenely, talking in placid tones that left their island unviolated, safe in another dimension.

'Lubov, how did it happen? I expected Wanda—I didn't know! Why didn't she tell me?'

'She couldn't tell you, darling, she didn't know. It happened only this evening, all in a moment. They suddenly sent for me, and told me I could go. It was six o'clock when I got home, and Wanda was dressing for the concert, but she gave me the ticket instead, and sent me here to you. There was no way of letting you know.'

'You were there at the concert? Oh Lubov, if you knew how deep down I was tonight, and all the time you were so near!' Her tears had ceased to flow, she stood with her cheek against his shoulder, her palms warm with his warmth, her arms circling him gently.

'I wanted to send a message in to you,' he said, trembling, 'but I was afraid. It was the last moment, I couldn't risk upsetting you. I wanted you to be so wonderful! And you were, Emmy, you were! And I loved you so,' he said huskily, his lips moving against her cheek, 'my heart was bursting.' They stirred and drew apart a little to look at each other, their eyes large, solemn and calm now in the darkness.

'Lubov, are you really free? Is it over? They couldn't change their minds and snatch you back again?'

'They won't do that. I'm really free. When they sent for me, I thought it was for one more interrogation, but this time it was to tell me that no charge was being preferred against me, and I could go home. They gave me back all my belongings, and my outdoor clothes, and turned me out. They won't change their minds now.'

'So in the end,' she said with wonder and joy, 'they trusted you. And, Lubov, they justified you!'

He took her hand and drew her arm through his, savouring with slow, happy movements the regained freedom of touching her, taking into his senses with astonished joy the tones of her voice, the texture of her hair, the coolness of the wrist on which he folded his embracing fingers.

'Shall we walk home over the bridge? Or would you like to take a car?'

'Let's walk! I shall be conspicuous in this get-up anywhere, but there won't be many people on the Lucerna at this hour. In the morning I can borrow a dress from Wanda, as I did last time.'

It was the same journey they had made together once before, and yet it was unlike anything that had ever happened to them. They walked with a third positive presence in them, like a child not yet conceived, a future being lying heavy and wonderful in their minds. Lubov had been believed. It was still possible, even in a world like this, for partisans to respect and trust one who was not a partisan. It must be even possible for opponents to respect and trust each other; it wanted only the solid ground on which trust could stand erect. Truth still had validity. Yuri had lost even the argument.

For a second time they went, linked like lovers, over the bridge of dead Captain Evian, past the plaque now hung with fresh lilac, fragrant in the cool of the night, down to the island which was not an island, and over the tiny bridge which spanned the river which was not a river. Violent and quiet in the night, the weir thundered and surged, the motionless mill-wheels on the backwater stirred their fingers of fern in the surface current of the stream. They began to climb, very slowly, exulting in every step, the staircases of the Lucerna.

'Lubov, what will happen now? Is there any possibility of your being taken back?' Her voice longed for it, but was not greatly troubled by hope.

'No. I've forfeited that. You mustn't think, because they've decided I'm not a traitor, that they think me a good citizen. There was plenty against me apart from Yuri's letters. It didn't make me a criminal, or even a—what's the phrase with your people?—a bad security risk. But it did and does make me a slight liability socially. I can expect to be treated with fairness, according to their views, but with reserve. I'm free but not rehabilitated. They'll allow me to be useful in some harmless job, and to earn my living like everybody else, but not, I think, ever to teach again.'

'Will you be allowed to choose your own

job? Or do they direct you into something?'

'Not exactly direct, though it will work out something like that. Most jobs are allocated through local offices of the Ministry; when I apply it will have to be there. So they can offer me what they think fit, and keep back those jobs for which I'm undesirable. There'll be a choice, but with that limitation upon it.' He looked down at her, and in the light from one of the bracket lamps upon the crumbling garden walls of the hill she saw him smile. 'There'll be something for me. Perhaps as a clerk, or a shop assistant, I can be an asset to the national economy yet.'

'Lubov—' She had hesitated to ask him to look back, but the smile had a firmness that filled her with calm. His face was pale, and looked a little dazed and drawn with the sudden release from strain, but its thoughtful sweetness had not been damaged. 'Lubov, how did they treat you? We didn't know even where you were. Every day someone asked, but they wouldn't say. It's difficult not to imagine the worst things possible.'

His hand pressed hers, folding her closer to his side. 'You shouldn't have worried, Emmy, I was all right. No one mishandled me. They did their job as decently as it can be done. I was two days in a cell at headquarters, and then they took me to the little prison at Dostalka. I had a cell to myself, but most days I was out of it for several hours, being questioned. That certainly

471

went on and on, but I can't complain, it was I who benefited in the end by all the hours we put in on it. I can't complain. The worst thing I had to bear,' he said in a low voice, his taut fingers quivering upon her wrist, 'was the thought that I might never see you again.'

'It might have gone on for another week,' she agreed, infected by the shiver which had passed through his body and invaded hers. 'I might have been gone. Even if they'd let you go at last, it might have been too late for us. I tried to get an extension, Lubov, but I saw that it would be hopeless. And I had only these few days, and no way of knowing whether I should ever get another visa. Oh, Lubov—'

'But I'm here! I touch you, I see you! We have three nights left! And more reason to believe in another meeting, my beloved darling, than we had a week ago! We haven't lost, we've gained!'

They had reached the top of the last staircase, and turned together to look back over the city, its quiet suburbs already faintly hazy in darkness, its heart a cobweb of chains of light. The floodlighting of the Citadel had severed it from the hill on which it stood and borne it aloft into a sky delicately dusted with stars. The spires of the cathedral, the bastions of the castle, floated in air like some enchanted castle of crystal out of a fairy story. The river, gathering to itself reflections of every terrestrial and heavenly light, lay faintly gleaming in its bed, coiled between the blossom-heavy hills, a luminous serpent, ringed with bracelets of darkness. Above this radiant and secret city they leaned together and kissed, embracing each other with grateful bodies and assuaged hands, with reverence, with rapture.

'I love you! I'm with you again! And we have three nights and three days left. Emmy, we're rich!'

*   *   *

In the tired, radiant, talkative evening, before they had yet grown used to their almost complete happiness, it was quite completed. Just before supper Miloslav erupted upon the doorstep, in boisterous spirits and without any warning. He had heard from Wanda by telephone that morning of Lubov's release, and had argued and persuaded his way into driving one of a convoy of lorries coming into town for stores during the afternoon. He had to return to one of the suburban depots for the night, and would be off again next morning, but he had three whole hours honestly at his disposal, and had saved at least twenty minutes of that precious time by hitching a lift in a van from the outskirts of the city instead of waiting for a tram.

He fell upon his delighted family with all the exuberance of his relief and joy, kissed his

473

mother and sister heartily, hugged his father breathless, and dragged Lubov into the kind of rough-and-tumble in which they had not indulged for years, discovering with charmed surprise that for the first time in his life he had the better of the tussle. The match ended abruptly when two of the fragile wine-glasses brought out especially for this evening of celebration were swept from the table and broken. Miloslav, chastened and contrite, gathered up the fragments and submitted himself guiltily to his mother, who first cuffed him, half-heartedly but as in duty bound, and then with better will kissed him. He could have made a clean sweep of her glass cabinet that night, and Ilonna would not have been able to care.

The supper-table was complete again. Miloslav sat down among them, eased of some of the ebullient energy which had been tormenting him, and ate a heroic meal. The passing of the greatest burden from his mind had taken a great many lesser ones away with it; Emmy doubted if during those few hours he gave a single thought to Yuri Dushek, until Matyas asked him over the last round of coffee:

'They didn't come asking you any questions, then, Milo? We rather thought they might.'

'So did I, but they didn't. I didn't know whether to hope for it or to be afraid of it. I didn't know whether I should be doing something useful or disastrous if I invited it. If I could have been sure—I thought about it all the time, but I was no nearer knowing what to do, so I waited. And nothing happened.'

'Just as well!' said Matyas, thinking of the list of names which had meant nothing to Lubov, but might have meant altogether too much to Miloslav.

'I know! I don't suppose, even if I'd gone and volunteered what I knew, that they'd have been satisfied Lubov had nothing to do with it. Sometimes I though they might let me clear him, other times I knew it would only make things worse for him as well. But I felt responsible—' The shadow of all his knowledge passed once over the brightness of his face, and cleared again like the passing of a cloud. Yuri, after all, in throwing and losing so great a stake, had enriched them with a quite unforeseen increase of faith.

Miloslav left at ten o'clock, his brief-case bulging with eatables. When he kissed Emmy at departing, on the landing above the dark well of the stairs, he whispered in her ear, on a quick impulsive breath: 'Don't worry! We'll take care of him for you!' and startled himself and her by instantly blushing crimson at his own indiscretion.

It seemed to her, considering the nature of the one who gave it, as good a pledge as she need have. 'This is the last I shall see of you on this visit,' she said, holding him for a moment longer when he would have broken away.

'You'll come back again,' he said buoyantly, and hugged her again willingly.

'I shall do my best.'

'You'll come,' he said with confidence. 'Walls a hundred miles high won't stop you. You'll always come back.'

He went off at a headlong run down the stairs, turning once in mid-flight to wave a hand to them all, and cast up out of the stone well a dazzlingly young and droll and durable smile; then he was gone with a last dancing staccato of light feet, and the silence of the night closed over him.

It was not easy to realise that in the middle of so much joy, in the very act of recovering Lubov, she had already begun to say a new good-bye to them all.

*　　*　　*

In the wide dark silence of the bed they lay side by side, watching the space of sky that filled the window put on its midnight jewelry of stars; encrustations of stars in a sky already velvet dark with the colouring of early summer. Along the orchard hills of the city the blossom of cherry and plum and pear was browning and falling, ripely, without reluctance. The season turned, the days ebbed; tomorrow Emmy, the next day April, would be gone.

Between their dreaming bodies, spent and

happy, their hands lay with linked fingers, stirring sometimes palm to palm with long, stroking caresses. She had forsaken her own pillow, and come to his, laying her cheek against his shoulder. The tendrils of her hair brushed his thin cheek, and the regular, soft coolness of her breath fanned his arm. They talked like old married people, contemplating from an inviolable strong-hold the burden of the day. It seemed to her, because she had had so little of it, and could look forward to revisiting this bliss so rarely in the future, the most wonderful and desirable luxury in life.

'It's a nice piece of irony,' Lubov said with sleepy tranquillity, 'that I should end up in the very export-import house in which we did our best to instal Yuri. Did I tell you it was the same one? The job we had ear-marked for him was somewhat more important than the one I've accepted, but I suppose if I live my past down I may be able to work my future up.'

He had begun work that day, accepting with equanimity the best of what was offered to him. It seemed to her a poor sort of use to make of his talents, to employ him as a packing clerk among books and prints destined for overseas sales.

'I suppose it might have been worse,' she said, sighing in the darkness. 'It might have been haberdashery instead of books. But, oh, Lubov, it grieves me to see you wasted.'

'Now you begin to talk like a real

reactionary wife. All it needs from me is some urgent reassessments, and I shall be able to take a proper pride in my job. Don't worry about me, Emmy; I shall do very well.'

'But it's going to make so much difference to the household, too. Ilonna told me today, Lubov, what she's done. Isn't it like her? As soon as circumstances close in on her, she clears another space to move into.'

For Ilonna had quite simply gone out, as soon as she was sure on what meager level the family income was liable to be lodged for some years to come, and got herself a job in the cutting-room of a big dress-shop in the New Town, and on the next Monday she would lock up the flat at half-past seven and trot off to the tram-stop after the rest of the Ivanescu. She had agreed to work from eight to two each day, and was placidly confident that she could handle the flat and cook an evening meal for her returning brood in the time remaining to her, without the slightest difficulty. When she talked about it, her pretty checks grew pink with excitement, and her blue eyes, so exactly like Miloslav's, were round and bright with interested anticipation.

'My mother is a formidable person,' said Lubov, and Emmy was aware of his smile by tiny, mysterious signs even in the darkness, the tender, light note of his voice, the slight tension of his cheek-muscles against her temple, the warm contraction of his hand. 'She will be a

478

Heroine of Labour some day for cutting out more and better dresses than anyone else in the province. She will have a little ribbon decoration to wear in her lapel on May Day, and we shall all boast about her.'

'But of course!' She was smiling, too, at an image which began by being absurd, but suddenly regarded from the opposite angle became heroic. 'You will become a thoroughly well-adjusted family, I can see it already. Wanda has no problem, except how to dance like an angel, and still have children between triumphs in the most practical and economical way. She will be a National Artist before she's thirty, have two boys and two girls, and live happily ever after.' She could not recite this happy ending, even in lightness of heart, without seeing that the success of Wanda's marriage had indeed become many times more probable now that she had also a successful career; and if that was a paradox, it was one other countries might well take note of. 'And Milo will emerge from the army with several stripes, in spite of himself, because he has really no capacity for doing things badly, even the things he never wanted to do. Matyas will raise production of lacquers to record heights, and be given a bonus for over-fulfilling his plan. The whole Ivanescu clan will be socially approved. Except you, my poor love!'

'Yes, I'm afraid they'll all have to blush for me. But not for long, Emmy.' She felt him quivering with soft, internal laughter, and suddenly he laid his arm over her body, and drew her close. 'Shall I tell you a true parable for the times? Tell it, when you go home, to your people in the West, tell it to Yuri if you ever see him again. They may be able to find a moral in it—I can't, though I'm perfectly certain there is one. Once upon a time, in this same university, Emmy, there was a very famous, middle-aged philosopher, who held a chair, and was very busy and celebrated, and lived on the most intimate correspondence terms with half the other famous philosophers in England, France and the United States. He was always going to write a great work on philosophy, and somehow it never grew beyond the first chapters, because he was too popular and busy to have the time to get on with it. But when the change came here he was thrown out of his chair as a stubborn Western liberal, and put to useful work on a building team, transporting bricks and other materials. And everybody said, what a waste! But he really was a philosopher, and he had a tidy mind, and couldn't bear to see things being done badly. So one day on the job he got a team of three together, and worked out a brand-new way of coordinating effort to load twice as many bricks in the same time. The method's called after him now, they use it all over the country. He got a prize for it, and now he works fewer hours than he ever has in his life before, lecturing on his method and thinking up new ways of saving effort, and on the strength of his new celebrity he's living a quiet, untroubled life of the spirit in his free time. His book was published in an enormous edition early this year, and now he's writing a second one which will probably have even bigger sales. I like to think about that story,' he said reflectively, 'because I can't imagine its implications ever being exhausted. I think it should be told to all the people in your country who want to over-simplify what's happening here. I think if they ever really began to grasp its complexity they might be quiet.'

She turned herself softly upon the pillow, and leaned and kissed him. 'I see that some day you will be a Hero of Labour for inventing a new way of packing and mailing books.'

'Well, if I do achieve such glory, the odd thing—or the logical thing, according to the way you look at it—is that my fall from favour in one sphere won't operate against my fame in another. If you look, Emmy, you see signs of grace in so many, such odd, such delightful places.'

The night sky darkened to black from its glossy cobalt, the stars dilated in the enormous quiet splendour of the small hours, and the room was filled with a faint dove-coloured light which grew out of every pale surface; from the sheets and the billowing quilted feather-bed, the middle-weight one for spring;

481

from their dreaming flesh, from her arms and shoulders, the pallor of her hair, his smiling face. In the next room Matyas and Ilonna were asleep long ago; in Ledva Wanda lay, beautiful and triumphant after a concert in the City Theatre, still smiling her joy into the pillow; but Emmy and Lubov did not want to sleep. Towards dawn they might drowse in the memory of happiness, and open their eyes from time to time to rediscover each the beloved face. They wanted no more of sleep than that.

'Lubov, what will become of Milo when he comes out of the army? What sort of life is there for him?'

'Oh, he'll do very well, degree or no degree. He's too valuable to be wasted, he's young, and clever, and we don't throw brilliance away, in spite of appearances. Don't worry about Milo.'

'No,' she agreed, remembering with pleasure the shrewd blue eyes balancing anxiety and amusement as he had explored the nature of the greater and the lesser fear. 'I think it would be taking a liberty to worry about Milo.'

She was surprised by a luxurious yawn, and hid it in his shoulder. The weight of his arm over her body was like the burden of her physical happiness, positive, heavy, dearly welcome, soon to be forgone.

'Emmy, you have to travel tomorrow—I think you should rest. Am I hurting you?'

482

'No, don't take your arm away. I do rest, Lubov, I rest in you. It will be a long time before I get such a rest again. I shall have plenty of time afterwards for sleeping.'

'Emmy,' he said, suddenly drawing her to his breast, 'when I was in Dostalka, and thought I might never see you again, I wrote you a letter. It tried to say everything I can never say like this. If I gave it to you to read now it would seem like a distortion, because it was never meant for a time when we could be together. But after you've left me—when you're in the plane and on your way home tomorrow night—will you read it for me then? I should like to think that you had it. I should like to think that you would keep it, because it will never be out of date at any time when we're apart, and if ever there comes a day when we find ourselves separated for ever, that will be the occasion for which it was really written.'

'I shall read it,' she said, 'and I shall keep it all my life. But there'll never be a day, while we're both alive, when I shall accept that we can be separated for ever. Give it to me in the morning, Lubov, before I go.'

'No, at night, at the last moment, you shall have it. I'm coming to the airport with you.'

'Do you think you should, Lubov? Slava will be there.'

'Why not?' he said tranquilly. 'We brought you together, we'll take you back together. I'm very lucky that there's a late flight as far as

Brussels—if you had to take the afternoon one I shouldn't be able to see you off. I couldn't ask for time off the day after starting at the warehouse, not even for a boss like mine.'

'I should think not! That would really stamp you as irreclaimable!' It was wonderful to discover how gently, with how much confidence, with how few explanations they could laugh together now, as though the relationship they had achieved made every load lighter. 'Did you meet the director of the corporation, Lubov, or are you judging him by someone else's account of him?'

'I met him. It seems he sees everyone who joins the staff, no matter how humble the spot they're going to occupy. But I'm judging partly by someone else's account, too. I made friends with the vanman in the canteen over lunch, and he told me a great deal about our director. It went with what I'd thought myself when I talked to him. He's another tract for the times, Emmy—do you want to hear it, or shall I kiss you and be quiet?'

'Kiss me, but then I want to hear it.'

'You are only trying to make up to me,' he said affectionately, 'for no longer having a class to lecture. You won't turn into one of those self-sacrificing wives, will you?' He kissed her, every soft, deliberate movement prolonged with love, and then, slipping down lower in the bed, lay with lips and eyelashes and sharp cheekbone pressed against the

484

warmth of her arm.

'The director of our corporation is a Communist. Not a nominal one, not a new one, not for safety, not for ambition. He is a Communist from before the war, from the time when it was worse than unfashionable even to be critical of the social system at all, so he must be one from conviction. He has good qualifications, a degree, plenty of experience, it couldn't be said that the assumption of power by his party has pitched him into a very profitable position for a man of his size. He took over the job, so the vanman tells me, early last winter, and the first thing he saw when he looked round his office was the monitoring system that enabled him to listen in to what was going on in all the departments of the building. Not a new installation, Emmy, I assure you. And the first thing he did was to have it dismantled and taken out. He drives no car, and they say that all the winter he never possessed an overcoat—two or three old ones with no particular owners are kept hanging in the lobby there for general use when running in and out to the warehouse or the stores, and when it was really cold he borrowed one of those. You know, there's reaction set in against too much comradeliness, and it isn't done to let your subordinates call you by your Christian name. Nothing personal, of course, but the hierarchies must be respected. Everyone calls him by his Christian name as soon as they've

485

been there long enough to get acclimatised. He isn't interested in listening to tales, unless any of his workmen wants to talk about his own troubles. When my vanman had something on his mind, he detected it and asked him straight out about it. It involved some quick attention to his home property, and building labour's hard to get, but he got it—at the firm's expense and in the firm's time. And it's leaked out by accident that this director of ours draws a salary which is less than his deputy gets, and hardly more than his heads of departments get. And why? Well, it isn't the salary they affixed to the job, it's all he'll take. He feels that a man has no claim to more money than he needs, simply because he's in charge. I think he feels that being in charge is something one can never sufficiently earn, rather than something one can never turn to sufficient account. It would be interesting, wouldn't it, to describe such a man to the people who use the term "Communist" as though it applied to a sinister sub-species. Tell them about him, Emmy, when you go back. And when they say cannily that if he exists he must be a prodigy here, ask them to look round at home, and then tell you if they know of any country where he wouldn't be a prodigy. And when they admit they don't, remind them that it's *we* who have at least one of him.'

Listening to the meditative undertone thus expounding, exploring, defining, she knew that he was already caught, that wherever he went and whatever he did he would find the material of curiosity and discovery. His field could be narrowed, his opportunities cramped, but as long as he had one human creature about him he would have the means to live, and an interest great enough to turn living into an art. After all, she thought, her heart expanding in a great sigh, how happy we are!

They were sinking together, without their will, but with a serenity against which they put up no fight, into the shadowy borders of sleep. They stretched their bodies into greater comfort, cradling each other solicitously, and still upon the one pillow they slept, still linked in the few glimpses of dreams that visited them, dream and waking never far apart, so that sleep lost its only disadvantage, the unawareness of happiness.

Towards dawn they awoke, so close still, and so conscious of the brevity of their time, that she had no sooner opened her eyes than he reached out for her with the quick, waking need that melted her heart into wild tenderness. She took him in her arms, murmuring blind, sweet endearments, and kissing him between the caressing sounds which were hardly words at all; and afterwards, in the lovely lassitude, they fell asleep together again, breast to breast, so readily and so peacefully that they never had time to reflect that this might be the last such measure of delight they would ever enjoy.

When they awoke for the second time the stars were already pallid in a sky growing greenly bright with the imminence of the dawn, and the day of departure had climbed the eastern hills, and was sending the first saffron rays of reflected light down towards the city.

PART FOUR

NOWHERE—EVERYWHERE

Tragic coda:

He is homeless who has two homes.

At the Customs barrier she said good-bye to them both. Slava Kraskova, having taken her hand in the firm, confident grip so well remembered from the day of arrival, suddenly blushed and hesitated, and, leaning forward with less than her usual competent grace, kissed the departing guest quickly on the mouth.

'Because of you,' she said, in a burst of impulsive words, 'I can never feel the same about England again. Whenever anyone mentions England to me now I shall always see Emmy, and I shall have to think kindly of Emmy's country.'

Lubov stood waiting with an indulgent smile until they disengaged, his hat in his hand. The familiar and beloved ritual, all he could well offer her in this populous place, was something she would not have forgone now for the most passionate of embraces. It gave stability to a broken and chaotic world, it made her believe in her return. When she turned towards him from Slava's hand-clasp, he took the two prescribed paces to meet her, and enfolded her hand in his with the old warm and candid pressure, and inclining his tall head, bent to give her the fine, firm, resolute kiss that belonged to the family, and bestowed on her

491

with all ceremony the family's collective blessing.

'Have a good journey, and come back soon!'

'Yes, do!' said Slava warmly. 'Come and see us again as soon as you can.'

'You may be sure I'll try. Thank you for everything you've done for me; you've been very kind.'

'Oh no, I loved it! I always like meeting guests from abroad, but you are special. Come back again next year, you could have a tour in some other parts of the country, and I could come with you. Don't forget!'

'I won't forget!'

She must go, the official was looking back for her through the door of the immigration office, and if the plane left on time, in twenty minutes she would be in the air.

'My love to everyone who remembers me,' said Lubov.

'I won't forget. Good-bye!'

'Good-bye!' they said, standing back a pace as though to release her from the tension which made it impossible for her to go. She moved to the open door with her chin still upon her shoulder, the pale smile, now growing wan with regret, still glimmering upon her face; and her eyes held Lubov's to the last instant when the door closed between them and took him from her sight. It was a silent, heavy door, automatically controlled, and closed itself with agonising slowness, so that as she looked back through the narrowing gap, so placing herself that Lubov should keep to the last her waning image, she had time to suffer the whole long descent into dismay and despair. An age passed while the brown eyes in the thin, proud, gay face clung unblinking to her eyes, devouring her, drinking her, translated strangely from composure to suffering as the space narrowed. She wondered if he saw in her so blinding an anguish, such an apparition of deprived love, and whether Slava could help being burned by its heat, when she stood so near him; but she thought that this must be in a sense an enchanted vision, not shared by those who stood on the same side of the door. She tried to smile at him, and could neither smile, nor move, nor breathe until the click of the door latching released her; only their eyes held fast to the final moment, surrendering nothing, still fiercely fixed long after the panels of blonde wood stood between them.

They would both wait to see her plane take off, and then Slava would offer him a lift back into the city in the Ministry car, and he would accept. She wondered, as she laid her currency certificate before the Customs officer, what they would talk about on that journey; but of course it presented no real difficulty: they would talk about her. Slava, perhaps, would do most of the talking, Lubov would listen, and reply, and remember. He might even be glad to hear her name so familiar on the lips of a girl who had not known her a month ago. It might enable him, as it helped her, to believe in another return.

She recovered her passport, and saw her luggage cleared. Not a quarter of an hour to wait, and a clear evening for flying. She found a seat in the forward lounge, close to the glass panels which looked on to the concrete plain of the airfield, and waited for her flight to be called. Half a dozen business-men, of an age and a type so international as to be unidentifiable, sat at the bar drinking brandy, and in the blindest corner, their backs turned indifferently upon the tarmac, two air-hostesses sat yawning over coffee. They had seen so many aeroplanes that it was more entertaining to gaze at the posters on the wall. Through the windows, far off across the plateau, two tiny house-lights gleamed through the deepening dusk. Emmy thought: 'Unless we take off on time I shan't be able to see him, it will soon be dark.'

The day had passed so smoothly and quickly that there had been no time to feel, but on final days nothing has any longer any proportion or accuracy. She had lunched with the members of the Musicians' Club, and the talk after lunch had gone on until four, thus relieving her of all that part of the day in which Lubov could have no hand. The remaining hours were for rest and packing, but her packing was already done. Lubov, who finished work at four, but

494

had a twenty-minute tram ride to reach home afterwards, had come to look for her in the café of the hotel soon after five o'clock, and since then he had remained beside her, while Wanda had rushed in for one brief hour before tearing herself away towards another concert in the suburbs.

Emmy's damaged senses, all tuned to departure, reminded her now how precious those evening hours had been, and tormented her with regrets that she had been able to realise and appreciate them so imperfectly. But afterwards, in the long months before she could hope to see him again, every moment would come back to her with its true value; and in the meantime his seal ring was on her finger, and his letter, the letter from the Dostalka prison, in her handbag.

From the outer door a stewardess called the flight number for Brussels. The six business-men downed their brandy and moved forward, reclaiming from tables and chairs their thick, prosperous brief-cases. Emmy joined them at the door, and answered to her name, and they were waved out briskly into the night. The darkness was deep blue, the ring of lights from the restaurant and the airport buildings silvery white, and the shape of the tower could still be seen as a faintly lighter pillar in the dark. Somewhere over there, on the apron of terrace jutting out into the concrete tableland, Lubov stood watching for her. But she would not see

495

him, though he might see her; the night was too far advanced already, only small black shapes, indistinguishable one from another, moved before the windows of the restaurant.

All the same, she raised her hand and waved in that direction as they set out after their guide across the tarmac, and kept her eyes fixed upon the little moving figures all the way to the foot of the ladder. She was glad that the men had outdistanced her by so far that they felt no obligation to wait for her to enter first, so that she had time to look back once more, and lift her hand in a final salute. And then she saw him, sharply silhouetted against the light, tall and slender, identifiable by his shape, and by the immediate response of his uplifted arm and blessing hand. By these, and by the surge and straining of her heart, that knew him without need of light.

That was all. She mounted the ladder and entered the plane, taking a seat upon the near side so that she might still look for him, but she could not be sure of him again among those little moving phantoms contorted by the peculiarities of the glass. Now he would be concentrated all upon the vibrating plane, as she upon the plot of earth that held him.

It seemed to her now that she was always departing or arriving, never at rest. In England, as here, she might speak of going home, but always in passage she felt that she was going away from home. A world at peace would not have been too wide a dwelling for her, but this world was not at peace. Even the migratory birds, she thought, who have two countries, either equally home, do not have to reconcile them in their hearts. Only man divides the world artificially into spheres of love and hate, and invents deforming barriers of passport and Customs and policy under the impression that he is keeping his own hearth pure. So I am a nomad, she thought, I am a stateless person condemned to go backwards and forwards for ever on a ferry between two inimical lands, neither of whom can ever fully accept me because I have loved the other. And this is for life. Or until so many of us are lost on this ghostly ferry that we acquire a new citizenship by the power of our numbers, and become the greatest community on earth. Until, in fact, we are so many that by natural right we inherit the earth. But when will that be?

She smiled sadly towards the glitter of lights, which was already beginning to wheel slowly away from her. The engines roared, gathering purpose. They began to move forward, leaning to the rushing air, moving up steadily to the far end of their runway. Now she could no longer see the restaurant, but only the wide, blank spaces of the field, the fixed lights along the runway, and the winking lights of the tower. There was a wait of several minutes with the engines ticking over steadily, and then the urgent mounting roar began, surged to its climax, steadied, and they raced forward into the wind. She felt the sigh of achievement, the levelled-out note, when they left the ground, and watched the lights drop away, gathering into their constellations, the pattern of the airfield condensing slowly into the pattern of the city. The lost city, the beloved city, the city where Lubov was.

She was going home. She had left her home. She had no home.

When the lights had become a milky nebula, far below and fast falling behind, she opened Lubov's letter.

'My beloved darling wife,

'I write this to you at a time when I do not know whether I shall ever see you again, or ever have another opportunity of sending a message to you. I hope, in the event of my being committed for trial, to get permission to have this sent, for I do not think there will be anything in it to which the authorities will be likely to take exception. It will naturally be read before it is sent, but I think you will not mind that when you have read it, and as for me, I have never uttered anything I would so gladly make audible to all the world.

'I do not find myself very coherent or very articulate when I am with you. I try, but what needs to be said seems pretentious

498

when spoken. Be kind to me if it even reads less well than I would like, but believe, I beg you, that I am now in a condition at least to know what I want to express, even if the expression itself falls short. I find myself in a situation differing only in degree from what our situation has always been. I may die soon and suddenly, without a chance to communicate with you again. I may be cut off from you, though alive, through years of imprisonment. Or I may be so happy as to be with you again in a matter of days. Emmy, how is all this different from the life we have lived during the last year, when every letter we wrote to each other might be the last letter to cross the barrier, and every day some failure of the nerves or slip of the hand somewhere in the world might have precipitated the war in which we should both die? Every separation is in a sense a final separation, everything that comes to an end may be ending for ever. I imagine people who write books feel themselves to be writing against time. We have good reason to live every moment as though it were the last.

'But where I am now I have a solitude in which to see more clearly the nature of these truths which are not new. More than anything in the world, Emmy, I want to say to you that I would not change anything I have done, or make a different choice at any

499

point in my life, or commit myself where I chose to be uncommitted, or extricate myself where I chose to accept committal. It seems to me that we dedicate ourselves in two different ways, by committal and by submission. My committal is to truth, as near as I can find it in whatever issue confronts me, and nothing less, not this country nor that creed nor all the kingdoms of the earth, will do. But my submission is to my country. Where I think it does wrong I cannot join in the doing, where it judges unjustly I can neither acquiesce nor be silent; but if occasions can arise when I must withhold myself from its actions, there never can be any when I will withhold myself from its experiences. Whoever stones my country stones me. I love it, and I won't separate myself from it.

'You know that when I speak of love of country I am not thinking in terms of a nation, with a political system, a government, all the trappings of modern civilisation. What I love is the land I've known since I was a child, the corn and the fruit that grows here, the people round me, the language they speak and the poetry they write in it, the music that came out of the life here, the songs I learned to know before I could walk properly. It seems to me that if I did not love these I could never be fit to love at all.

'So you see that I can make no complaint, even if I die, though I very much hope to live. We have talked about our position in a world broken in two, and I know that you, like me, find it impossible to surrender your judgment to any other keeping than your own. I know, too, that you understand, as I do, that no matter how absolutely we submit ourselves to our countries, and however irrevocably we recognise our membership in them, that refusal to abdicate our own will makes us exiles in another and deeper sense.

'The truth is, my dear love, that human personality is so heavy a load to carry that it must be heavenly ease to find some great maternal lap in which to lay it down, with all its intolerable burden of loneliness and uniqueness. Churches, States, parties, factions, offer such a secure, such an infantile repose. I think we are tempted sometimes to think there is something new about this corruption, but the more I reflect, the more I am sure that it has always been so, and in only two particulars has the situation changed in our time. In the first place, technical development has taken one of those disproportionate leaps forward that complicate history, shortened distances, accentuated dangers, frightened us all out of our wits, made us look round in more desperate anxiety than ever for somewhere to lay down the burden of ourselves. But in the second place, to this increased pressure we have learned how to oppose a greatly increased moral obstinacy, in order to continue to resist all attempts to take our godhead from us. In my time I too have lamented that the non-slanted man, the intact man, was being driven out of existence, but when I stop to consider more exactly, I know that he is not dying out: he increases and multiplies. I know there are not many of him; but I believe there are more than there ever were before.

'Emmy, be patient with me if I labour, I am a little tired, and I have been interrupted now and then. But you see how important it is for us that there should be others of our kind, and that we should know there are others, even when we have not the comfort of their companionship. It is so terribly easy to despair, for ours is the hardest of all lives to sustain in loneliness, especially as its very nature is loneliness; but when we meet some unexpected creature of our own kind, even if the contact is no more than a sceptical smile on some face still full of humour and optimism, or a word in defence of what it is not fashionable to defend, we must surely know that we are in possession of something better than all the empires in the world, and worth all the security.

'I believe in man. I believe he will overtake his disastrous technical dexterity in time; but even if he fails, I know he will leave somewhere a remnant capable of essaying the whole journey again.

'And I believe in God. I believe in Him because I have seen man, and seen in him sometimes something so marvellous that God was already implied.

'Emmy, my own darling, that's almost all. The rest I can say with so much more eloquence. I miss you terribly, I long for you, I am desolate without you, but because I have not always been without you I would not change places with any man on earth. I would rather have the remote hope of some day touching your hand again than the whole body and the heart's love of any other woman. I love you so much that you make everything clear to me, and everyone dear to me, and I think I shall love you a little more every day I live. I send you two kisses for your eyelids when you fall asleep, and one for your mouth when you wake. Every night receive these from me, and know that I am and shall always be

Your devoted husband
Lubov.'

Written beneath, in a different ink, was the postscript:

'I wrote this in the Dostalka, having asked the warder for paper on the understanding

503

that whatever I wrote would pass through official hands before delivery, whatever happened to me. I had just finished it on the day of my release, and had it in my hand, when I was sent for from my cell for the last time. It was a new officer who came to fetch me, and he was a little upset by the irregularity, and made me give up the letter, but when I explained the terms on which I had been given permission to write, he hesitated, not quite knowing what to do. It seems the warder had no right to make such a concession. He said he would have to read it, and I told him he was at liberty to do so; and when he had read it, which he did with careful attention, he gave it back to me, and said that if I came back into custody there he would see that it was posted, but if I was lucky enough to go free I could deliver it myself. And this is all the more remarkable because he must have known that officially I have no wife, and may well have known your name.

'This is only one of the encounters which give us light to see by. I thought you would like to know about it.

'For we do give light if we keep the most irreplaceable of all assets, our own equilibrium. The thing about darkness by day, the darkness of the world, is that it enables us to see how many among us carry their own illumination. So when you are

504

airborne, and look down upon the dwindling lights of my city, you may be reassured that even in the desert of after-midnight not all those lamps go out. And I, following to the last glimmer the plane that takes you away from me, and a little dismayed by the immensity of the night into which it vanishes, shall remember the shining of your spirit within it, and see it with changed eyes, no longer blundering without purpose or hope from darkness to darkness, but proceeding secure in the radiance of its own certainty, out of a light into a light.'

Very little in this book is imaginary: somewhat less than half the incidents, fewer still of the human situations, scarcely any of the background. The city is more than one city, and the country more than one country, though they naturally draw most strongly on the city and the country I know and love best. None of the characters is drawn from a living person, except the Communist director described by Lubov at the end, who is word for word as reported to me by someone who works under him, and for whose word I vouch absolutely.